T0365923

FICKLE

PETER MANUS

DIVERSIONBOOKS

Diversion Books
A Division of Diversion Publishing Corp.
443 Park Avenue South, Suite 1008
New York, New York 10016
www.DiversionBooks.com

Originally published in September 2008 by Virgin Books.

For more information, email info@diversionbooks.com

First Diversion Books edition January 2017.
Print ISBN: 978-1-62681-842-2
eBook ISBN: 978-1-62681-839-2

To DJM with AML

1

LIFE IS PULP

Noir the Night Away With L.G. Fickel

January 21 @ 11:48 pm
>I WITNESS A SUICIDE<

Strange end to a strange evening tonight—at around 8:30 a man committed suicide by dropping himself in front of the inbound at the Hynes T station.

GIVE IT TO ME STRAIGHT

marleybones @ January 22 12:05 am

You...want to run that by us again, fickel, with maybe a scosh more detail?

fickel @ January 22 12:12 am

I do. Earlier this evening I was standing on the Hynes subway platform (freezing my ass off) when a man bumped me on his way by—a tad peculiar because the platform was almost empty. Far more peculiar was the fact that he just kept going. Dropped over the edge right at my feet, putting me in the unfortunate position of witnessing everything. Train moshing—a thrill I'd never realized was missing from my life.

proudblacktrannie @ January 22 12:23 am

O my lawd spill AWL, gurl—u need 2.

fickel @ January 22 12:25 am

Here's how it went down. The guy pushes by me like he's propelling himself, does a half turn on the edge, then goes in backwards, maybe so he didn't have to see it. Train came on him fast—he didn't have time to get up or roll. The truth is he just lay on his back between the rails, like a man going to bed. Freaky all around.

Of course the train driver slammed on the brake, so there was this unearthly *SHREEEEEEEEH* of metal on metal. Almost saved him—I swear, the front of the train seemed to do no more than nudge the guy, and I remember thinking *"ohdeargodthatwassofuckingclose,"* but then the man's vest *burst* and this spray of tiny grey and white feathers spurted up. I remember the down floating around, puffing to and fro in the train fumes, and then, well, then there he was, down in the pit. He was like before, except rumpled, you might call it. Most of his head and shoulders were underneath the train, but his neck bone was kiltered to one side and exposed—I'd never thought about what color the inside of human bone was. Most horrid of all, of course, was his face, maybe because I didn't expect it. It had been pushed down onto his chest—I guess the front of his body had accordioned into itself, more or less, while the back lay where he'd positioned himself. So there his face lay, flat against his chest, eyes open with the sockets empty. The skin was dark with blood and decorated with a sprinkling of the down feathers that stuck to it here and there...little spots of white fluff...

I felt like I had to stand there looking at him, my feet stamped to the platform, or I might—I don't know—topple forward into the tracks or something. Everyone else scattered. It was like a stampede, started by one person with the others spooked into conformity. And then all there was was the muffled pandemonium from inside the train.

At some point someone—I believe a man who'd come down to investigate—pulled me back and aimed me at a bench. I sat there, quivering.

chinkigirl @ January 22 12:49 am

Please *please* tell us you are shitting us, fickel, and all this is an allusion to a Max Nosseck caper I'm not quite catching? Or are we group-writing our own noir again? Tell me that's it?

fickel @ January 22 12:51 am

Alas, fickel shits ye not, chinkigirl, and I'm definitely not launching one of our pulp fiction games. I should point out that the whole thing took place several hours ago. I waited around to give a statement to the police.

roadrage @ January 22 01:03 am

You have this experience and walk in your door and blog it—you are my **BLOGODDESS**.

36-D @ January 22 01:04 am

omg, so how horrible was it for you to talk about with the cops?

fickel @ January 22 01:05 am

Pretty effing horrible. I mean, blood and some amount of guts I can take in stride (I like to think), but the sight of a man's facial skin, fully intact like some rubber mask, pushed down off the front of his skull to lie against his exposed rib cage, is unlikely to leave my mind's eye for a long, long time, and attempting to act normal during my interview with the cop made it all the more...*gothic* might be the word I'm hunting for. Train jumping—NOT recommended for those interested in emitting a "cry for help."

36-D @ January 22 01:11 am

{{{{{*MAJOR Vicarious Shudder*}}}}} Nightmares, anyone?

webmaggot @ January 22 01:13 am

Wait—using the T to KILL YOURSELF? I mean, I could see doing a swan in front of the Acela, but the BOSTON GREEN LINE? It's light rail. Guy must have been an optimist.

i.went.to.harvard @ January 22 01:14 am

Optimistic for someone whose outlook was so bleak that he decided to end his life. One of those fatalistic optimistic types.

chinkigirl @ January 22 01:15 am

Actually, it's people who stick a gun against their forehead who most often fail to die. Flinch at the last second and miss the frontal lobe, end up a paraplegic, but very much alive.

webmaggot @ January 22 01:16 am

Life sucks so much you want to die, then you wake up shitting into a ziplock with no way to kill yourself because you can't move your arms or legs. Bummer, mon.

proudblacktrannie @ January 22 01:22 am

Serious question: u ok, fick?

fickel @ January 22 01:23 am

Serious answer: jury's out, but all I could think about walking home was the banter I could count on from my bloggies, so *please* do not get sanctimonious on my behalf. You know, it occurs to me that I now truly understand the meaning of the term "dumbstruck." It's like there's this aura of ****stupid**** around me that won't drift. Inside, maybe I'm a bit more, I don't know, waiting calmly for the signal to panic wildly, if that makes any sense? Of course, I'm also numb from having walked up the g.d. esplanade in the wind after giving my statement. There's this light hail blowing across the Charles—my face feels like I got a sandpaper facial. I'm actually sitting here in coat and gloves writing this. Maybe I just need to thaw.

hitman @ January 22 01:28 am

U 4 Real?

webmaggot @ January 22 01:29 am

So what was the guy like? Asian? I got it in my head somewhere that Asians are statistically the most likely to do a train dive. (No offense, chinkigirl, but check out *Jisatsu Sakuru*—kind of did it for you guys and train jumping—*and-a one, and-a two, and-a...*)

chinkigirl @ January 22 01:30 am

That's Japanese. I'm the other type of slit-eye. Why would I be offended, anyway?

webmaggot @ January 22 01:31 am

Sore de wa minasan, sayonara.

proudblacktrannie @ January 22 01:32 am

Hush, silly douche. So what was it like with the cops, fickel, luv? Are they all human fistfuks, or is it just vice?

fickel @ January 22 01:33 am

The cops were okay. Basically I spoke with a guy named Ty—a sergeant, I think. He wasn't wearing a uniform. He was, I want to say, 36? Meaty build—maybe burly is more what I mean. Rumbly voice, unadorned diction. And he was extremely patient, by which I mean he let a lot of silences go by between his questions and my answers. That probably sounds like very little but I appreciated it hugely.

36-D @ January 22 01:35 am

Wedding ring?

fickel @ January 22 01:36 am

On the cop? Umm, not that I chance to recall.

proudblacktrannie @ January 22 01:37 am

4th finger crease from removed wedding ring as he trolls for female witnesses?

fickel @ January 22 01:38 am

Can't say I noticed that either, proudblack.

proudblacktrannie @ January 22 01:39 am

I just ask because you make him sound so *utterly* dishy.

fickel @ January 22 01:40 am

I do? Well, well, maybe I do. Anyway, he just wanted me to go over the "sequence," as he put it. Guess I was the "star" witness, since the train conductor went into shock and had to be carried out on a stretcher—no surprise there.

roadrage @ January 22 01:42 am

Munchable female witness = lucky copper.

fickel @ January 22 01:44 am

I'm munchable? You can tell that from my blogging style?

roadrage @ January 22 01:45 am

Yer *smokin'*, fickel—do not screw with my J.O. image of U.

proudblacktrannie @ January 22 01:47 am

Of course she's hot. And she knew the cop was looking for some. But fickel's too classy a dame to offer her vag on the first suicide. Now nuff said about that.

webmaggot @ January 22 01:48 am

Hey, fickel, you ignored my question about the dead guy. Chinki?

fickel @ January 22 01:49 am

Sorry to blow your theory, webmaggot. He was white, probably American. Mid-40s is what I told the cop. Dark hair with a lot of silver threads, worn longish—he could have been an architect? Writer? One of those professions we all ogle in college but don't stick with. Carefully groomed 3-day stubble, and for clothes, I'm going to say a black ribby sweater, long maroon scarf tied Euro-style, down vest, pricy boots—you get the picture.

proudblacktrannie @ January 22 01:55 am

Woof! This is a man who KILLS HIMSELF?

fickel @ January 22 01:56 am

I have no idea how much of my description is accurate and how much is dead off—it was two seconds at best that I actually looked at him as he pushed by me on his way to...you know.

hitman @ January 22 01:57 am

HEY, U 4 REAL?

webmaggot @ January 22 01:59 am

The cop's name was Ty? That's probably short for Tyrone? Black dude?

fickel @ January 22 02:01 am

Hmm, you're rather "visual" tonight, webmaggot. The cop was white. The VERY white Detective Sgt. Ty*ler* Malloy. Short red-blond hair. Intense face—close-set eyes, deep forehead lines, and a crooked bottom lip that he moved around in a way that suggested he had a toothpick in his mouth (which I don't think he did). Body muscle-y but not in a health club way, and generally big enough that his sleeves were always going to be a little short. Clothes: army-navy mac, nondescript suit, green shirt, yucky tie. Think Southie-kid-makes-good, Bean-town locals.

proudblacktrannie @ January 22 02:02 am

Tyler? A cop is named Tyler? I'm rooooolling on the flooooooor!!!

fickel @ January 22 02:03 am

It wasn't like TV; I guess in real life people named Tyler go to cop school.

hitman @ January 22 02:06 am

HEY B'YOTCH WANNA ANSWER ME OR IS THIS SITE JUST FOR YER LITTLE CLICK OF BLOG PANSIES? R U 4 REAL OR IS ALL OF THIS A CROCK FOS THAT YOU BOOKWORM GEEKS INVENT FOR CIRCLE JERKING?

fickel @ January 22 02:07 am

E-gad, hitman, before you scream me blind: YES, I AM FOR REAL! Not always—perhaps not even often—but, sad to say, I am very much "for real" at the moment.

webmaggot @ January 22 02:09 am

And it's book and film geeks, dood. We're into cheap downer pulp entertainment from the forties, in whatever form. S'called noir.

hitman @ January 22 02:10 am

No kidding pole-diver. So fickel, if you're for real, how can you type with gloves on?

fickel @ January 22 02:11 am

They're my fingerless gloves, which I often keep on while I'm online because my apartment's heat sucks; it's either hot as hell's kitchen or cold as a witch's clit.

36-D @ January 22 02:12 am

Fingerless gloves—you are SOOO Dickensian, fickel.

fickel @ January 22 02:13 am

Actually, I'm sooo Tolstoyan: So many men, so many minds, so many hearts, so many kinds of love... But whatever.

proudblacktrannie @ January 22 02:17 am

U trollop, u! ;o

fickel @ January 22 02:18 am

Yes, but do you have to tell the world? G'night, blog.

2

GIVE IT TO ME STRAIGHT

chinkigirl @ January 22 06:09 am

Wake up, fickel. Something occurred to me last night (while I was getting laid by my honey—and I can't *believe* I just wrote that!) Anyway, you wrote that the suicide guy pushed by you, but the man you described would not shove by another person.

fickel @ January 22 06:11 am

You're right, early bird; he was definitely of the "civilized" variety, if you judge by looks. So?

chinkigirl @ January 22 06:12 am

Yet he pushed by you on a nearly empty platform...

marleybones @ January 22 06:38 am

Hi, I'm on. And I'm with you, chinkigirl: he wanted fickel's attention. An audience.

i.went.to.harvard @ January 22 06:52 am

Morning, all. Of course, when you're taking that last walk off the edge of your life, so to speak, you're not thinking "What would Miss Manners do?"

marleybones @ January 22 07:23 am

I don't know. Manners become instinct by the time we're adults. I'm thinking the man bumped fickel to make sure she'd witness it.

fickel @ January 22 07:24 am

Maybe he wanted to get my attention so that I'd stop him.

chinkigirl @ January 22 07:31 am

That occurred to me.

36-D @ January 22 07:49 am

I am not one to analyze (not before I get my face on, anywaze), but am I sensing some element of BLAMING YOURSELF? A man committed suicide, fickel—that is not your responsibility.

fickel @ January 22 08:00 am

I just wish I'd been quicker on my feet. I can still see the way his scarf rose on the train's draft, hovered there between us, quivering in the air like it was groping for me, asking me to grab it. And his eyes, also, I can't say for certain but I think they were...begging? You do hear about people who contemplate suicide for a long time, and then regret it only after they've swallowed the pills or stepped off the bridge.

roadrage @ January 22 08:02 am

As in *Golden Gate*. Seen that? Now there's some ballazz noir for you right there.

fickel @ January 22 08:12 am

Anyway, I simply stood there staring at him. I *know* that it was a couple of seconds and that it is completely understandable that I would freeze, but I just wish I hadn't.

hitman @ January 22 08:21 am

Hey, so aside from some metrosexual making steak tartare out of himself in front of you, what was so strange about your evening? Your post said "strange end to a strange evening."

fickel @ January 22 08:23 am

Well, well. For a guy just pausing to sneer as he passed through, you're back quick. But your question's fair enough. I went to a Stravinsky concert at the Berklee. Strange sound—prelude to a train wreck. Strange audience—lots of prematurely white-haired intellectuals in geometric glasses sipping stingers. Added up to a strange evening. Then I walked over to that retro music shop on Newbury and picked up a vinyl of the *Le Sacre du Printemps*. Also atypical for me but I thought that if I didn't do it then and there, the old-fashioned, over-the-counter way, the urge would fade fast and I'm trying to broaden my music taste (something to do at 25). Then I went to take the T over to Harvard Square to blog. Never quite got there.

roadrage @ January 22 08:24 am

You are sophisticated, in addition to having a stripper bod, fickel. God u make me **HOT**.

fickel @ January 22 08:25 am

Yes, well, lies are essential to humanity.

leo tolstoy @ January 22 08:33 am

For in the end what are we, who are convinced that suicide is obligatory and yet cannot resolve to commit it...

fickel @ January 22 8:38 am

Well I suppose that's something to suck on for the day. Thanks, stranger. For now, however, work beckons (an' dat ain't no lie).

3

LIFE IS PULP

The Noir Boudoir of L.G. Fickel

January 22 @ 11:17 pm

>ONE COP TWO COP RED COP BLUE COP<

So last night, as you know, I witnessed a train suicide while standing around minding my own business at the Hynes T station. Being an exemplary citizen, I waited and gave a statement to the cops. (Okay, I went paralyzed, but by hook or by crook I *became* an exemplary citizen by giving a statement.) The cop I met, as I mentioned last night, was sympathetic, and not unbeddable in a burly-bear-ish way. TODAY, however, I was at work, trolling through the raw log on this site, when Sergeant Burly-Bear shows up.

Here's him: rumpled mac (mach-OH), blah-de-blah suit, pale shirt with his wife-beater T showing through (giggle, giggle), tie from the color-blind rack (ouch—man got no woman at home).

Here's me: fitted white blouse with cuffs rolled to just below the elbow, midnight-blue cashmere cardigan (worn on my shoulders, sleeves tied loosely in front), black pinstripe skirt from vintage shop, semi-opaque stockings, suede J & D flats—i.e., my usual editor couture. He catches me gazing into my screen, playing the edge of my oversized tortoiseshell glasses against my teeth as my jaw-length china chop tickles my chin where it curls under just so—i.e., my usual editor's pose. I wait a beat, then swivel my chair around slowly and find my gaze resting directly across on the front of his pants. Fun fact? You can tell a lot about a man in gabardines. I blink at his *triomphe-masculin*, then raise my eyes to his face. His chin has a cleft that apparently presents some shaving difficulty.

He has another cop with him (middle-aged butterball—tight-rippled hair, moustache, pointy lapels), but that one hangs out in the stairway so I barely get a look at him. The office where I work—picture a big, once-elegant room with water-stained wall paneling, smelly heat, four oversized clunky desks, incongruously slick computers, clutter everywhere—anyway, the place is essentially deserted, so Burly-Bear and I are by ourselves out there in the open. We have the following conversation, him with his flat feet spread to shoulder width, me perched behind my desk with my crossed knees peeking over the rim:

Burly-Bear: So, uh, how you holding up, there? Able to sleep last night?

Me: I'm okay. And you?

Burly-Bear: Me? I'm good. Good. (Nodding like people don't usually worry about cops' emotional responses and he appreciates my compassion.) So we've been doing some checking on the guy's background.

Me: Uh-huh?

Burly-Bear: The jumper, I mean.

Me: Yes. (Like who the hell else?)

Burly-Bear: Yep. The department looks into all violent deaths, mattah-fact, which includes suicides. Most people don't know that. Think suicide's not a police matter.

Me: (grave in the face of this inside information) But it is.

Burly-Bear: Yeah, most people think that if a death's a suicide, it's just some psychiatric thing and therefore not something the cops are going to care about.

Me: But you do care.

Burly-Bear: Correct you are. (He snaps that out like a marine.)

Me: So you investigate.

Burly-Bear: Correct you are.

Me: (wondering how the guy ever manages to pick up anyone at this pace) I see.

Burly-Bear: So we have some information on our jumper and we'd like your help, again.

Me: (a little thrown) My help?

Burly-Bear: Correct. We'd like you to take a look at something, actually.

Me: Not the body. (Then, after a blush) Sorry.

Burly-Bear: No. Not the body.

Me: Well, then what?

Burly-Bear: We want you to take a look at the guy's apartment.

Me: (surprised) Why?

Burly-Bear: (cagey) Something interesting there we'd like to show you.

Me: (waiting for him to clarify. He waits, too, then finally gets that I have all day.)

Burly-Bear: Last night you said that you didn't know the deceased.

Me: I said that, yes.

Burly-Bear: Thing is, seems like maybe you did.

Me: I knew that man in the tracks?

Burly-Bear: That would appear to be the case. There's evidence to the effect in his apartment.

Me: (rather amazed) What kind of evidence?

Burly-Bear: (backing off a step and dipping his head) We thought you should see it.

Me: (the meaning behind all the pussyfooting dawning on me) You mean now?

Burly-Bear: If it wouldn't be too much trouble.

Me: (indicating the POS I was doing a text verification on) Umm, I'm at work?

Burly-Bear: (running a cool eye around the deserted office, then back at me) Y'know, I'm not so sure the boss man is going to miss you if you step out for a bit.

Me: (automatically) Boss lady.

Burly-Bear: (tipping his head) I stand corrected. I hope you'll excuse my presumption of male dominance (this delivered too solemnly to be anything but sarcasm).

Me: Excused (pushing my glasses up my nose). Besides, there are whispers that this particular boss lady stands over the bowl when she visits our unisex loo. Lord knows what's up her skirt.

Burly-Bear: (grim lip-spread, although he'll be repeating that one back at the precinct)

Me: Problem is there's an editors' meeting going on. (I tip my pencil at the ceiling.) Up there.

Burly-Bear: (scratching his head) Excuse me, but ain't you an editor?

Me: (cute-ing him right back with a wry face) I'm an editorial assistant. That means I'm the office peon who takes calls and entertains walk-ins at these heady moments when "decisions" are being made behind closed doors.

Burly-Bear: You can interrupt the big meeting for an emergency, I'm guessing? Maybe get the second-most lowly editor out here to babysit the big room?

Me: (hesitating—then realizing that I'm not being offered an option. I text Noah that I've got a "thing" that I'll tell him all about later. I stand and head toward the back to get my coat and check my hair. Just before disappearing, I turn around.) I'll just...? (I point over my shoulder, sensing the need to seek permission to go out of Burly-Bear's sight.)

Burly-Bear: (cocking his head)

Me: I'm very quick for a girl. All my guy friends tell me so.

Burly-Bear: (satisfied that I'm not going to cut and run down a fire escape) Absolutely.

We pick up Burly-Bear's partner on the way out, me twiddling my fingers at Noah and generally trying to act like I'm not being "asked to cooperate in a police investigation." Burly-Bear's partner turns out to be one of those dour career cop types—expressionless paunchy face with sad eyes under apologetic brows, a fat beauty mark on his cheek, feminine lips. He's wearing a double-breasted suit, tie bar, and a knockoff Armani trench. He's also Latino, so all he needs is a fedora to be a wiseguy out of *Touch of Evil*. He gives off the air of having a well-oiled gun strapped to some furry part of his anatomy. I never quite get his name ("Escroto" became his name in my head—you'll see why). He doesn't care for me—that I catch loud and clear—but I can't tell if it's personal or a thing he's got against all snotty white cunts.

Burly-Bear himself is cool enough. He drives a rust-trimmed seafoam-green Mustang, and he opens the door for me and even manages to check out my legs as I tuck myself in. I'm generally comfortable with silence, and I like that he doesn't try to make time with me on our way across the city. Traffic is its usual shitty self, and I spend the time watching the back of his neck, the way his hair bristles out where the skin rolls over his collar. This is a guy who shouldn't have a tie job. In spite of my surprise that his visit to my office hadn't been just to make a pass, I can tell he's planning to ask me out after I've seen whatever he wants me to see in Mr. Suicide's place. Don't ask me how I know.

Mr. Suicide lives—or lived—in the warehouse district off South Station. It had never occurred to me that there are residences there, but there it sits, three broad metal stairways up, a marvel of ballbreaker minimalism with its steel-on-rollers front door and its exposed beams. One far-off brick wall is completely covered in fifteen-foot-high white bookcases, stuffed. Someone had dropped in a Formica-style kitchen area in front of the factory windows—you get the drift. It's a night owl's space, SoHo chic, although maybe not as successful on a nondescript January morning, with last summer's bird dung shivering against the windows like dirty tear tracks.

I wander a little, noting the upside-down glasses by the sink, the on light on the music system, the pile of unshelved books—then turn to find the cops watching me.

Me: He didn't close shop. Isn't that peculiar for a suicide?

Burly-Bear: (shrugging) Place looks clean. Smell the lemony stuff?

Me: It's not tidied, though. Look at his workspace (I walk over); there's old coffee in this mug. (The guy was reading *A Confession*, I notice. How heady—unless, of course, he was just another affected lech who fanned his face with Russian lit in the neighborhood Peet's as a means of trolling for Emerson chicks.) This apartment is waiting for someone to come home.

Burly-Bear: (throwing a laugh at Escroto) What'd I tell you? (trying to give me the impression that he'd said something about my sensitivity to detail before they'd picked me up.) Check out the head, would you?

Flattered in spite of myself, I try a door just past the kitchen. The bathroom's tiny and smells of ammonia. I flick open the medicine cabinet and view a semiorderly clutter: prescription bottles, a bag of pink razors, some "designer" men's products. Nothing but the wrinkle cream hints at desperation. I emerge to find Burly-Bear scratching between his nostrils as he gazes out a window. Escroto is on his cell by the front door. Burly-Bear raises his brows at me.

Me: It's a man's bathroom. Clearly didn't care too much about where he did his three esses.

Burly-Bear: Three esses?

Me: Shit, shower, and shave? (I feel myself blush.) I thought all guys used that one.

Burly-Bear: (snorts—his sign of amusement) Catch the Lady Shicks?

Me: You wear them out and they're good for that stubbly look. So sez my brother.

Burly-Bear: So how about the bedroom.

Me: Look, I honestly don't get the point.

Burly-Bear: Humor me, huh?

Me: (never a fan of patronizing bullshit) Fine.

I cast about and see a set of metal stairs. Up them is a sort of suspended interior balcony with a barely-there pipe railing around its rim. The furnishings consist, basically, of an armoire and a queen-sized bed with a punched leather headboard. On the single wall, there's a giant framed poster of a sphinx body with a very female head—it's two pictures merged, actually, and it takes me a second to recognize it as that Clarence Sinclair Bull do-up of Greta Garbo. All in all, think pricey home furnishings catalog, but with the mess a little more authentic. The bed is unmade, the sheets and comforter a buttery knot. Next to the bed is a metal folding table, on it a little blood-colored leather-bound book. Over past the armoire are a bunch of good-looking shoes—apparently Mr. S did not dick around when it came to clothes. I look at Burly-Bear.

Me: I see the same thing as downstairs. The same man.

Burly-Bear: Lot less tidy, though.

Me: It's his bedroom. He let it go.

Burly-Bear: Or maybe he shared it.

Me: No signs of a mate, as far as I can see.

Burly-Bear: Check out the his 'n' her reading arrangement.

Me: (glancing at the twin reading lights clamped to the top of the headboard) I'm not saying the guy never got lucky. I'm just saying I don't see anything like makeup or women's clothes. I should have counted toothbrushes, but I've only been a detective for ten minutes.

Burly-Bear: Maybe she cleared her stuff out.

Me: Without a trace? If she was anything to him, she'd have made a mark on his place. Now that you've got me focused on it, I haven't seen one thing so far that smacks of a chick gift.

Burly-Bear: Chick gift?

Me: The little tchotchkes no man would buy for himself—the coffee table book, the platinum pen. Although that Garbo poster looks a little more obvious than the rest of his stuff. Cheaper, too. Could be a gift from a younger woman.

Burly-Bear: A girlfriend's going to buy him a poster of a woman?

Me: (patiently) We don't *completely* resent one another's very existence, Sergeant.

Burly-Bear: (carefully not responding, as if life has taught him differently) There's these. (He opens the top drawer of the dresser and displays a plastic baggie in which are some panties—some flirty little floral 'n' lace $150 bikini silks, to be exact.)

Me: Well, they're definitely for a female.

Burly-Bear: So there was a girl in his life.

Me: (facetiously) Unless he wore them himself.

Burly-Bear: (dead straight) The elastic's not stretched out. Maybe he cleaned his girlfriend's stuff out after she left, like "good riddance" (glancing at the baggie) except for a memento.

Me: Sure, why not? Although there hasn't been a real clean-up here recently. Look at the bunnies. (I point a toe at the base of the armoire, where gossamer dust balls shiver.)

Burly-Bear: (slowly, as if thinking aloud) Okay, so maybe she broke up with him some time back, and he lived with it, not forgetting (he bounces the plastic bag with the panties in his hand).

Me: (helpfully) He brooded.

Burly-Bear: Yeah. He brooded. Let the place go. Then finally he contacted her, wanted to meet up, see if they hadn't made a big mistake, breaking up. Maybe she met up with him only to make it clear to him that she'd moved on.

Me: So he killed himself over a woman. Is that the theory?

Escroto: (from behind me) And maybe that woman's you.

Me: (turning, startled that such a prize hog had crept up the metal treads so quietly) Tidy, except for the fact that I didn't know him.

Escroto: You sure? Because you didn't seem all that surprised when we showed up at your office. (His accent is pure Staten Island, now that he's finally offered a sample.)

Me: (definitely feeling intimidated, although I don't tend to show emotion that much) I thought (I hesitate) I assumed Sergeant Malloy was just checking up on me.

I glance at Burly-Bear and catch him watching me like back in my office. It strikes me just how much of a cop he is. It's not the obvious physical strength or the at-ease, ready-to-spring way he stands. It's more the... call it cynicism. He sees every scrap of deception that passes before him trying to put itself over as the stuff of natural life. This whole train of thought lasts less than a second—I don't really articulate it to myself until later. All I experience right then is the realization of how utterly alone I am in that apartment.

Burly-Bear: (snapping into role) Correct you are. I was checking in on you, just like you say.

Me: (staring at him for a long moment) Look, what's the evidence that you referred to back at my office, the whatever-it-is that got you thinking that the man knew me? Because it sure as hell isn't that slutty lingerie.

Burly-Bear: (throwing a thumb over his shoulder) Computer down there?

Me: (I walk to where I can look down. The desk is made of two stubby wooden file cabinets and a slab of black-tinted glass.) I see it.

Burly-Bear: You're in it.

Me: What does that mean?

Burly-Bear: Guy had what's called a flickr page. You're pictured. Got you at Silvertone. Also at the Roxy, bunch of places. Talking maybe twenty shots over an eight-month period. Mostly candids, many close up. Got you smiling into the camera at Fenway.

Me: (after staring at him for many seconds) It's some other girl.

Burly-Bear: Looks like you. In a couple of them the hair's kind of (he makes a bumpy motion next to his head).

Me: (involuntarily smoothing my hair) I was trying something. (Then, a tiny bit of shrill entering my voice as it dawns on me) I went to that ballgame with a client, ages ago.

Burly-Bear: Remember who was playing?

Me: (shaking my head) It's the only time I've been to Fenway. It was cold. They lost.

Escroto: (flatly) So maybe you do remember the dead guy, now you think about it, huh?

Me: (keeping my attention on Burly-Bear) I did not know him. I don't care if I'm in his flickr. People put whatever they want in their flickrs. If that's your evidence of some connection between me and this...unfortunate man...I'd like to go.

Escroto: See that right there? (gesturing with his head at the red-leather book by the bed)

Me: (looking at it, then at Burly-Bear)

Escroto: Guy's diary. Believe it? By his bed and everything?

Me: People write in them at the end of the day, so that would be the handy place.

Burly-Bear: Oh? You keep one?

Me: (wondering for the first time if this blog is a diary and, if so, whether it's anyone's business that I keep it) I had one that locked when I was ten. It had a shiny plastic cover with pink flowers all over. I wore the key (I draw a finger across my throat) around my neck.

Burly-Bear: (I score a snort) So I find this thing, I'm thinking: a diary, how gay is that?

Me: Men call them journals.

Burly-Bear: Still...

Me: (shrugging—why do guys care so much about whether one another is straight or gay?) You've read it; you should know.

Burly-Bear: I've leafed through it, true.

Me: And?

Burly-Bear: Handwriting's feminine.

Me: Handwriting serves as far less of a gender marker than people tend to think.

Burly-Bear: Oh?

Me: I work with writers, so I've picked up the occasional tidbit on writing styles, handwriting, that sort of thing.

Burly-Bear: Anyway, the thing's all about a lover he calls "E."

Escroto: You know, like your name starts with.

Me: (ignoring him) He never uses a full name?

Burly-Bear: Not a once.

Me: Could it have been a man he's writing about, just to play out your gay theory?

Burly-Bear: Calls her "she."

Me: A man might use female pronouns to refer to a male lover. It's common.

Burly-Bear: That so? And you know that how?

Me: We've published some gay lit. I got to proof it. Lots of what we call "pronoun liberties."

Burly-Bear: If it's a he, that puts a couple of passages in a whole new light, let's just say.

Me: Sounds like a good read. His estate should submit it, once this thing is cleared up. Look, why am I here? You could have told me about the flickr account and this so-called diary somewhere else. What's supposed to happen—am I supposed to do something that reveals to you that I've been here before?

Escroto: (stepping up off the top step, which puts him too close to me for my taste—he chews those old-fashioned violet tablets, from the smell) You mean like the fact that you didn't have to ask about where the bathroom and bedroom was?

Me: (coldly) It's a loft. Any half-wit could have figured out the layout in about five seconds. Wonder how long it took you. (My delivery's totally straight but I score a snort from Burly-Bear and a nasty eye flutter from Escroto.) Look, what does it matter whether or not I knew the man? I didn't, but so what if I had?

Burly-Bear: Well, then we'd need to know why you'd say otherwise at the death scene.

Me: (suddenly irritated almost beyond words at his dogged cop-think) Well, that's crystal clear. (I walk right at him and he steps back—not like he's afraid but more like he gets how to handle women and you do it by letting them think they have some ability to intimidate. Anyway, I go by him and pick up the little diary from the bedside table. I squeeze it, then slap it back down on the table top.) Fingerprints, just for you. Can I leave now?

Burly-Bear: Hey, no one's accusing anyone of anything here.

Me: I'm just paranoid—that it?

Escroto: (leaning against the stair rail and checking his nails) Thanks for the set, miss, but, uh, we ain't got no prints to check those against.

Me: (blinking at Escroto, then back at Burly-Bear) I have no idea what that's supposed to mean.

Escroto: (talking slow, like I'm playing dumb and we all know it) Lemme try again: no prints but a few of our dead friend's in the entire apartment. You know, like as if someone rubbed the place down: handles, knobs (he reaches over and runs a finger along the edge of the Garbo frame)—all your basic surfaces that might hold a print. Like as if someone came over here late last night and went over the place, someone who didn't want anyone knowing about her ever having been here. (He stares me down and I try to meet his eye but falter—why shouldn't I be intimidated? Then he goes on.) Must have been a very cool broad to be able to erase all her prints and leave his on stuff like the dresser drawers. Of course, DNA's tougher to erase. That bed's seen a couple of good rolls lately. A DNA sample's what would really do the trick in eliminating your presence here. So how's about it?

Me: In your dreams. (I walk forward. Unlike Burly-Bear, Escroto doesn't move and I'm forced to step over his crossed-at-the-ankle two-toned wingtips to head down the stairs.)

Burly-Bear: (coming after me down the stairs) I'll drive you back to your office.

Me: (heading out the door without looking back) Don't concern yourself, Sergeant. (Then, softening a tiny bit in spite of myself, I half turn.) I could use the walk.

Burly-Bear: (stopping at Mr. Suicide's doorway) I hear you.

I don't start to cry until I'm two blocks from the place, walking fast.

So: *what the HELL is going on?*

GIVE IT TO ME STRAIGHT

roadrage @ January 23 12:44 am

I may have done too much blotter at some point to be really solid in my alphabetics, but in what dictionary is L the same letter as E?

fickel @ January 23 12:46 am

Not following—oh, I getcha. My name starts with E. I go by a nickname that starts with L.

roadrage @ January 23 12:47 am

I still don't get it.

36-D @ January 23 12:48 am

Like Liz for Elizabeth. Don't be dumb, hun-bun.

roadrage @ January 23 12:49 am

Excuse my continuing stupidity, but if a chick's name is Elizabeth and she goes by Liz, wouldn't the guy she's sleeping with refer to her as "L" in his diary? I mean, he'd be on nickname terms with her, wouldn't he?

i.went.to.harvard @ January 23 12:52 am

Maybe he'd assert his special place in her life by being the only one who doesn't use the nickname. Kind of a reverse pet name thing.

roadrage @ January 23 12:54 am

Oh, like when you go by Skeet but your mother insists on calling you Norman *in public*?

chinkigirl @ January 23 12:56 am

Take heart, roadrage; my mom's nickname for me was Pussy. After the willow.

roadrage @ January 23 12:57 am

I am humbled.

webmaggot @ January 23 12:59 am

My theory on what's going on: the cop is jerking your chain.

fickel @ January 23 01:00 am

uhh, come again?

webmaggot @ January 23 01:03 am

Burly-Bear wants your happy box, babe, and all this is foreplay. Staged foreplay.

marleybones @ January 23 01:05 am

That theory's a bit fantastic, don't you think?

webmaggot @ January 23 01:06 am

Take it from the male of the species. There's a lot of strategy in getting a chick into the sack, and you gotta use what resources you got. Cops is no different than the rest of us dogs.

marleybones @ January 23 01:08 am

Wow. So how far do we take this? Are we saying that fickel is not in the dead guy's flickr? Are we saying the little book by the bed isn't a diary that describes the mysterious E? Heck, was the whole thing an invention some cop came up with on the strength of a handy bit of luck that a train jumper took himself out in front of an attractive witness?

hitman @ January 23 01:09 am

So, like, maybe the loft is actually *Burly-Bear's* love nest. Maybe Escroto is not even a cop, but is just some buddy who's pimping for Burly-Bear. Maybe this is not a murder investigation at all; instead it's just, like, the scuzziest pick-up job of all time.

36-D @ January 23 01:10 am

fickel, sweetie, what do you think: could this possibly be some elaborate set-up for scoring?

fickel @ January 23 01:12 am

DIIK. But the one thing I can swear to is that Burly-Bear was disappointed when I rejected his ride back to my office, and, even at the time, it flashed through my head that *that's when he'd been planning on asking me out.* But the idea that the whole thing was cooked up as some elaborate pick-up scheme is as much of a stretch as any of the pulps we've come up with.

wazzup! @ January 23 01:16 am

HALLO American pals. Am writing from the glorious Netherlands where nothing ever happens!!! I have been lurking for weeks now—love love love the group stories especially. Still a smidgen confused however; is this suicide real or yet another excellent long and winding tale???

I would like to add with every due modestness that I have some pertinent knowledge of "polar" art as well: did you know that many of the finest examples have their basis in *factual story*, thus lending a sense of truth and verisimilitude to otherwise fantastical and seemingly far-fetched plots? Such as, let us take for example, *Double Indemnity*, the plot based on an actual serial killing nurse. Did any of you know this?

fickel @ January 23 01:17 am

How-di-do, Hollander. Interesting. However, this "excellent tale" happens to be real.

wazzup! @ January 23 01:20 am

Amazing! Was ready to vote that your cop is Dix Handley from John Huston's *Asphalt Jungle*.

fickel @ January 23 01:22 am

I see what you mean. He does have that expressionless, “rolling something around in his mouth” thing going on when he thinks.

proudblacktrannie @ January 23 01:32 am

fickel, my luv, please listen to me and take my advice: cops are scum do not f*** this one no matter what he looks like. JMO but believe me!

hitman @ January 23 02:34 am

...and a hush fell over the weblog...

4

FULL FRONTAL

EXISTENTIALISM ENGORGED

01.23 @ 03:44 AM:
I SEE DEATH AND GUESS WHAT—SHE'S DOABLE

A fraction of a second of time that I spent on the T last Sunday night:

I'm plugged into my earbuds and e-balling a VMan over some sweaty lad's shoulder (Russian Topless Tennis Tramps—great concept and a damn great shoot) when the driver slams the emergency and everyone goes flyin.

I'm already holding onto a pole because I'm just bending forward to grab a look at the station as we come into it—don't ask me why but I get off on the visual of coming into a train station—so I have a pretty good shot of the approaching platform. I see this girl standing on the edge, way, way down at the far end. She is one of those all-in-black chicks, not goth, not dyke, more like...feminist poet, I'm going to guess—dark coat and skirt, tall boots, chalk-white face and fingerless gloves—and she's looking straight down into the tracks, which, in that split second I'm focusing on her, clicks as weird because most people look at the train when it's coming in, especially if they're standing right on the edge of the platform. This chick never moves a muscle.

Next fraction of a second:

The train is jamming to a halt—brakes so loud I can actually feel the metal-on-metal scream in my nads. I get the beginning whiff of something like burning oil, and my feet catch the first tremors of the whole train car trying to buck like it wants off the track. Everyone's falling all over each other and screaming their brains out. Humankind is so pathetic.

Next fraction:

The train has stopped moving—passengers shriek and flail. Some smelly homeless creep is practically dragging my pants down as he goes. The driver—middle-aged black lady—her hands are kind of palpitating in front of her giant titties as she gets set to belt out the loudest, longest freak-out bellow you're going to hear north of a New Orleans funeral. Past her knee is the bottom of the train car's windshield, and just above that comes this little puff of goose feathers. Just a couple of them. Poof—then they disappear.

Next fraction:

I look back at the platform—I'm close to the chick now, maybe fifteen feet with just the train window between us—and she's a piece of work: nose like a blade, art deco hair sliced across at the forehead and jaw, hands boney and strong with short nails, and some sort of fifty-foot-long scarf in a bunch of murky colors—one of those dippy chicks who is somehow hot, and at that moment, the very moment that I shift my attention to her she raises her long thin eyebrows and tightens her lips, kind of bunches them with the corners pointing down like she's swallowing a mouthful of hot buttered cum-yum. She looks right at me without seeing me, lets a breath out, and catches the tip of her tongue between her teeth.

WHAT I'M SAYING IS—and squirt it up my nose if I'm wrong but I am not wrong—THE CHICK LOOKS SATISFIED. Swear to giddy God, she is GROOVING on the fact of some dude getting mulched by the T at her feet. And at that moment, I know—I know—I KNOW that she either shoved the guy or AT THE VERY LEAST was pushing him off her when he fell. Either way, she did it, and she's feeling pretty damn good about it—no remorse, I mean this:

Not. One. Drop. Of. Remorse.

It's monster freak-zoids like this make the world a safer place for all womankind. I salute thee, brave, cold-blooded killer chick!

Then I'm knocked to the floor by the homeless dude, get my head sat on by an old Bible thumper, roll away and end up with my face squashed between the mams of a four-hundred-pound opera singer in polka dots who holds me there until I suffocate while a passing poodle dry-humps me from behind.

End of moment. Everyone in the train shares a cigarette.

tALK. NIHILIST DOGS

eddielizard @ 01.23 03:59 am

Righteous post, man. See the killer chick after?

fullfrontal @ 01.23 04:11 am

talking with a cop. plays it meek and trembly, now that she's done killing for the day. then she walks to central square. chick glides through this ice storm like she's a farking vampire. lives in a dump. scored some doobie on her street, tho.

losmuertos @ 01.23 04:38 am

you followed her?

fullfrontal @ 01.23 04:44 am

how else am I going to know where she lives, brainiac?

boytoucher @ 01.23 05:16 am

she smokes weed?

fullfrontal @ 01.23 05:32 am

What d'yak you talking about? Oh—no, doof, *I* scored on her street. She just gives the niggah this little wave and shakes her head, like she knows him and considers it out of politeness that he offers it to her when he knows by now that she doesn't smoke. Like Mary Sunshine in the Hell Zone or some such shyzzle. Only now she's killed a guy so she's earned her stripes.

bonitoestoria @ 01.23 05:39 am

what you want with her, hansum?

fullfrontal @ 01.23 06:16 am

Lemme see, I want to figure out a way to meet her, try to get to know her, and see if she's the type of woo-man I could talk into whispering "chugga-chugga-choo-chooooooo" with her tongue in my ear while I do her.

WHAt DER YUH tHINK I WANtS WID HER?

5

LIFE IS PULP

Feed the Beast With L.G. Fickel

January 23 @ 02:17 pm
>BURLY-BEAR IS SQUARE?<

**UPDATE!—UPDATE!—UPDATE!—
UPDATE!—UPDATE!—UPDATE!**

Burly-Bear just showed at my desk (does it occur to him that every steely squint, every shred of his threads, every loose-limbed swing of his heavy arms shrieks that he is a **COP**, and that a wee small white-shoe-wanna-be Boston publishing shoppe might be chock-full of nosy parkers who would be both fascinated and repelled by anyone amongst them who finds herself involved in a police matter?)

So while inquiring eyes bulged forth from inquiring skulls, the B-Bear passed me a fat yellow envelope containing "som'n' for me to read." At first I thought the guy had dug a novel out of his bottom drawer—*Memoirs of a Flatfoot* or some such goodie. I went to put it aside but Burly-Bear stood there, waiting to see my reaction, so I took a peek. It was a copy of Mr. Suicide's diary, fresh from Kinko's. Yipes!!!

When I asked what I was supposed to do with it, he said that he'd found my observances insightful back at Mr. Suicide's place and hoped I would do him the favor of assisting him in the investigatory matter by offering my consideration of its content. Double Yipes!!!

I said I'd do what I could. Burly-Bear kind of circled his hand a couple of times like he was gearing up to say something, then thought better of it and said he'd be in touch. All this happened just this second, and I am immediately blogging it, mostly so as to be exceedingly busy so that Noah will remain hovering at a distance while I figure out what to tell him.

GIVE IT TO ME STRAIGHT

36-D @ January 23 02:20 pm

LOL! Roadrage was right: the cop wants your happy box!

webmaggot @ January 23 02:28 pm

Ahem...all due respect, ma'am, if you review last night's postings, you'll see that I was the one who came up with the happy box hypothesis.

36-D @ January 23 02:31 pm

I stand corrected, hun-bun. *You* have the sleaziest mind on the blog.

fickel @ January 23 02:32 pm

Regardless of that: *what do I do*? I admit my hands were *shaking* when I took the package from him—still are, as I type this.

marleybones @ January 23 05:35 pm

All his words?—"observances," "insightful," "favor"???

fickel @ January 23 06:26 pm

Would I use "observances?" Is that even a word?

chinkigirl @ January 23 09:38 pm

Was his breath minty fresh? Tie tight and straight?

fickel @ January 23 09:40 pm

Umm, his breath was minty with a powerful undercurrent of fresh cigarette. Hair aggressively en brosse. Tie loose—top button undone. Very "sexy cop calendar," overall.

36-D @ January 23 09:44 pm

He smokes and tries to cover it. OMG—I am in need of smelling salts.

proudblacktrannie @ January 23 09:55 pm

personally I have just died and gone to gay cop heaven. (In my heaven he's gay if that's okay with everyone else?)

hitman @ January 23 09:56 pm

Let's talk: copper wants yer clam and are you going to give it? That's where we're at, right?

fickel @ January 23 09:57 pm

No comment from everyone's favorite odalisque.

hitman @ January 23 09:58 pm

translation: you're a slut

marleybones @ January 23 09:59 pm

Out of bounds, and not the 1st time. I propose that hitman be banned. Anyone care to weigh in?

36-D @ January 23 10:03 pm

I vote yes. Go drag your knuckles back to the cave, creepy male person.

hitman @ January 23 10:14 pm

Hey, no offense, ladies, but women who sleep with guys they just met are what's known as "sluts," and please do not give me that crap about how when men sleep with someone they hardly know they're studs but when women do it they're sluts because it's been said a zillion times in a zillion folk songs written by a zillion lesbians each and every one of who thinks she's saying something totally new. If you're a chick who sleeps around, fickel, just accept it: you are what's called a slut.

fickel @ January 23 10:58 pm

I think you're trying to say, in your own twisted way: what's wrong with being a slut?

hitman @ January 23 11:02 pm

Finally, a woman confronts the gorilla in the corner. Medal of honor for bravery.

marleybones @ January 23 11:14 pm

With enlightened guys like you around, who needs rape laws?

hitman @ January 23 11:16 pm

Rape is a protectionist creation of postmodern radical feminism. Most cultures didn't even recognize the concept before the 1600s.

36-D @ January 23 11:18 pm

Lemme guess, you're posting from some fed pen?

webmaggot @ January 23 11:20 pm

Kewl, we really got all types on the blog now. Everyone grooving the diversity? I am!

fickel @ January 24 12:05 am

That's actually a question that's occurred to me, hitman. Where *did* you suddenly appear from, now that it seems that you plan to dwell a while?

hitman @ January 24 12:06 am

ah-ah-ah, bad form, fickie: no askie for personal data on the bloggie, remember?:

Hi, I guess this the big "first entry," where I give a shout-out to the anonymous world of blog trolls and pray like hell that I attract the right ones to mine. I have spent enough time putting this damned thing up, so let's hope the effort pans out. This blog is for lovers of noir, both roman and film, and both classic and neo. If you read and reread James Ellroy, Ian Rankin, Derek Raymond, Leigh Brackett...and if you watch and rewatch Rififi, Stray Dog, Drunken Angel, M, Night and the City, *etc., etc., this is the site for you. If you don't know any of the authors or titles I've mentioned, press on, seeker.*

Rules (INPO): (1) No real names or otherwise pushing your ID on me—I'm in Boston and you may be, too, but I'm not looking for lunch or bed mates. It's a blog—deal. (2) Do not make up cutesie "noirish" names: if Coffin Ed or Cissy Chandler shows up, you're outta here. (3) Not really a rule, but just a corollary to Rule 2: I am very open to "grown up" noir games—working out a plot as a group, critiquing favorite stories or films, etc. I have done this on my own, and could totally get into a collaboration.

Okay, end of rules. So who am I? Let me intro myself by identifying a favorite noir, and maybe others will ante up with that as well. So, favorite noir...tough call, but I'm a tough doll. I'll go with Jean-Patrick Manchette's The Prone Gunman. *Not what I'd call mainstream noir, but so what? Anyway, Manchette's world is utterly black and truly lit'ry, and for my penny the mix of grim and comic and realistic and stylized and bleak and not-quite-heroic is, well, quintessentially noir. Plus who the HELL can write like JPM? So, anyone out there want to dance?*

Well, I'm out here, Fick-Elle, and I'm into noir and that's all you require for membership. Signature noir? I'll throw in Jack Kelly just for snickers and howzabout *Line of Sight* as a nice tight read, which no one else ID'ed, as far as I can see.

So, uh, can I be in the club now, fickie? Can I, can I, can I?

fickel @ January 24 01:09 am

Fair enough, my newbie Punchinello, no more personal questions from me. Just answer me this, hitman, and seriously for once: Last night you said that Burly-Bear was investigating a murder. What did you mean by that? What murder?

hitman @ January 24 01:29 am

RBTL, fick.

fickel @ January 24 01:35 am

Read between the lines? That's all you're going to give me?

hitman @ January 24 01:38 am

Chew on it awhile; you're a smart girl, ain'tcha?

fickel @ January 24 01:40 am

Duly chewing. G'night, blog.

leo tolstoy @ January 24 03:24 am

who are you people who make such song and dance of your banalities...?

fickel @ January 24 06:02 am

Ummm, do I *know* you?

6

GIVE IT TO ME STRAIGHT

36-D @ January 24 07:08 am

GAWD I cannot believe I am blogging before my morning ciggie-butt. Well, fickel, you're an incurable insomniac so we *know* you've read it. What's in the diary?

fickel @ January 24 08:33 am

Hi. Just got to work and am pretending to check email before drilling through the S-load of text checking that was on last Friday's EOD. In other words, I'm going to have to go with "no comment," at least for now, on posting about the diary.

Plus, to be quite honest, there's not much to it but what's there is, well, not to speak ill of the dead but there's a whiny "why does life suck for me" quality to it that's a tad soporific.

Bottom line: I don't know how I feel about discussing a dead guy's personal slam book online.

36-D @ January 24 09:02 am

Ohhhhhhhhhh (pout) but we discuss everything! Some of which is a LOT more personal than some unnamed, dead stranger's midnight kvetchings.

fickel @ January 24 09:19 am

I know, I know. And normally I feel pretty safe and anonymous out here in the cacophony of the internet. But that's with my own dirt. Somehow this is different.

hitman @ January 24 11:12 am

Wow a slut with principles.

fickel @ January 24 11:57 am

I think of myself in just those terms. You probably think I'm kidding, too.

7

LIFE IS PULP

The Noir Boudoir of L.G. Fickel

January 24 @ 6:42 pm
>NEVER TRUST A COP<

Well, it's happened. I just learned that I am an "unofficial figure of interest" in connection with the possible murder of Mr. Suicide. This is *not* a joke, and I think the idea that Burly-Bear is pulling a hoax to explore the lining of my pantyhose is pretty much out of the realm of possibility. It's Burly-Bear, in fact, who has offered me the friendly advice—*completely* against protocol—to consult with a lawyer. I am, however, prone to be quite suspicious of that particular amphibious subspecies.

Any advice much, much, much, much, much appreciated.

GIVE IT TO ME STRAIGHT

i.went.to.harvard @ January 24 06:54 pm

The cops think *what*?

webmaggot @ January 24 06:56 pm

They think she pushed the guy. Thought you were supposed to be the mensa member, harvard.

i.went.to.harvard @ January 24 06:59 pm

Well, I'm either very stupid or smart enough to be DUMBFOUNDED.

36-D @ January 24 07:00 pm

fickel, I work for a lawyer who is an absolute ROTTWEILER—do you want him to contact you? I can make it happen NOW, if you give me your celly in a private message he will call you IMMEDIATELY. My lawyer is tough and he has gotten scum out of jail—let's just say we're based in Providence and leave it at that. By which I mean is no one is better at crim defense and he is up in Boston a LOT.

fickel @ January 24 07:03 pm

Just a sec. I don't think the cops are at the point where they truly suspect anything. 36-D, thank you for the lawyer offer, but I am seeing a man tonight who also has a high-power attorney, and I think that he will probably insist that I talk with him. Anyway, I'll let you know.

proudblacktrannie @ January 24 07:11 pm

Just leaving for work—and not to belittle the seriousness of your situation, fickel, m'luv—but are you "seeing someone?" Quote from your comment: "*I am seeing a man later tonight*"???????? Dahling, why not a *peep* about this before?

roadrage @ January 24 07:12 pm

OMG fickel you are shagging some dood who is not me when I am PANTING for you, even knowing that you are a hard-bitten moxie who's a suspect in a subway kill.

fickel @ January 24 07:14 pm

Have no fears, I am high and dry as ever. The man I am getting together with tonight is old (77, although quite attractive in a rugged way) and very married (trophy wife younger than his own kids—meaning she's 50). I met him through work. My boss put together one of those programs at Harvard's Mem Hall—that grisly Romanesque structure just past the Yard—designed to showcase our classy little indie publishing op. The program: *What Ever Happened to Baby Jane?: The Cultural Significance of Late Period Noir* (drew a MEGA-HUGE audience, btw), and since it was my brainchild, I got to root around for some local talent to do the readings and came up with the Colonel. Not that he's actually a colonel—I just call him that in my head because of the military bearing.

Anyway, the Colonel was a bit actor for about ten years, back in his twenties. Played the punk in *The Big Sleep* (not quite a noir to purists, but come on), then had a string of parts as the kid soldier who dies in a bunch of war dramas. Then he went on to publish twenty novels.

That's TWEN. TEE. NOVELS. In short, he's one of those highly accomplished, colorful, successful figures that no one's quite heard of, living large just off Route 128.

So he was incredibly flattered to have been unearthed, and did readings from his books—all hard-boiled police procedural stuff—that went over *very* well. Apparently the experience got him juiced up to dust off a memoir, one of those "character actors who brushed shoulders with the greats" pieces. I've been helping him edit and collect permissions from all the household names we'd like to include. It's a long-term project (a lot of these household names we're chasing down could have been the "waxworks" crew from *Sunset Blvd.* so we are operating through their estates, a slooooooooow process). Anyway, as a result I see a lot of the Colonel. He has a high-priced attorney I've laid eyes on in passing at the Colonel's manor (giant Spanish-style stucco villa situated betwixt a bunch of other stately manors on some undulating country route way off in Concord country).

In any event, I am sure that the Colonel will insist I consult with his attorney once I unload my problems on him tonight.

proudblacktrannie @ January 24 07:19 pm

Good to hear that this is just a sweet old sugar daddy, fickel, because do be assured that by now your personal cop Burly-Bear is ON THIS BLOG lurking and the last thing he wants to read about is some other man getting all up inside you since he is the reason you even know anything about the cops and their dirty thoughts.

Okay nuff said I gotta new rumba numbah t'night everyone wish me luck kiss kiss all around.

marleybones @ January 24 07:22 pm

About the idea of Burly-Bear monitoring the blog, I actually know the tiniest bit about tracing sites on the internet (this is my S.O's area, so I'm just parroting here) but it would not be easy to do by simply knowing fickel's name and trolling around to see if she authors a blog. I'm sure the cops know how to monitor internet traffic better than most of us (particularly the feds), and they have de-encryption software but there's still a limit on what they can and can't fingerprint online. Bottom line: If Burly-Bear is on this site it is more than likely because someone gave him the web address, and if no one did that then it is more than likely that he is not lurking, at least not yet. Just understand that anything we write may *at some point* be read by the BPD, if this case stays interesting for some unforeseeable reason. If that's okay with you, fickel, then blog away.

fickel @ January 24 07:25 pm

Thanks, marleybones. I honestly do feel relatively safe out here in all the hubbub. I'm registered anonymously, my address is encrypted, and I don't broadcast the fact of my blog anywhere but in this great electronic void. Burly-Bear would have to break into the computer I'm on now, or at least my station at work, before he could know we're chatting. It's a lot safer than either landline or cell phone communicating—that's for certain.

chinkigirl @ January 24 07:27 pm

You are actually editing a ms? That's excellent news, fickel. Some "glorified gopher"—you are a full-fledged editor. Plus the man's a pulp legend. What a coup. Chin chucks to you.

fickel @ January 24 07:29 pm

Thanks, but the glorified gopher image is actually accurate. The manuscript is still in fairly rough form, and the Colonel's agent (who is, in fact, the above-mentioned lawyer) has not submitted it anywhere yet, so I'm doing a lot more fact-checking and copyright-permission-seeking than actual editing. It's all freelance, just between me and the Colonel (and at $25/hour, kind of like babysitting money). Oh, and his novels, while good, are, like I said, all police procedurals set in the late fifties and sixties—they all merge together in your head after you've read a couple. The "noir connection" was slim, I have to admit. But what a voice, and he reads like a dream—Robert Mitchum, if you close your eyes.

i.went.to.harvard @ January 24 07:41 pm

Hey, folks, could we get back to topic? Much as fickel is trying to be cool with this, it sounds bleeping serious to me. fickel, can you try to tell us how you handled it when the Burly Man told you that at least some of the cops suspect you of *killing a guy*?

36-D @ January 24 07:43 pm

OMG could you please NOT put it that way? fickel is not a "suspect." A couple of cops just haven't concluded that the death was a suicide for reasons that involve fickel.

webmaggot @ January 24 07:44 pm

Hate to bust it to you, lady, but you didn't make it sound much better.

fickel @ January 24 07:46 pm

I don't care how it's phrased, and, to answer your question, i.went.to.harvard, I am alternatively scared silly and damned angry about it. And yes, it was Burly-Bear who tipped me off, which was somewhat risky for him.

proudblacktrannie @ January 24 07:47 pm

oh BLOODY HELL, I am still ON I am going to be SO SO LATE FOR WORK. Details of aforementioned conversation with Mr. Cop-Cop, fickel, and *quickly*, if you please????

fickel @ January 24 07:48 pm

Well, my heart's not in it, but here goes:

Setting: pebbled stoop of shabby walk-up, off-off Harvard Square (i.e., my place)

Time: early evening. Dark, though, and temperature doing that 6:00 drop-off from damp and chilly to damned cold.

Me: Just home from fetching dinner on Mass Ave (pancit skinny noodles: **yummy**) and attempting to collect mail. I'm wearing sweatpants (and no, not designer sweats, which would have been *really* embarrassing), hopelessly tattered sneakers (baby toe—clad in Wicked-Witch-of-the-East-red-and-white-striped socks—actually peeking through the canvas), and an old fisherman's knit sweater that has so gone to pills that it basically looks like a wool explosion, freeze-framed in early boom.

Him: TRÈS off-duty: dingy shirt with tails dangling out below red-to-pink frayed sweatshirt, big jeans, shit-kickers, mac—somehow none of this disguises the fact that he's in animal-solid shape. Must have cruised up while I was telling the mailbox how to ream itself. I turn and there he is, his trusty Mustang idling at the hydrant. (*Side bitch*: why do cops always let their vehicles sit there idling for hours? Are they trying to lure environmentalists in for a gratuitous rubber hosing?) I notice he's decided to start growing some gingery facial hair. Is that for *me*, I wonder with a faint stirring inside?

Burly-Bear: Oh, hell, sorry, did I scare you?

Me: (recovering with a breathy laugh) Actually, I was hoping you were my landlord, in which case I'd have been the scary one.

Burly-Bear: Help you with any of that?

Me: (hipping my mailbox closed). I'm good. Is something going on with...the guy? (I actually hesitate to consider whether it would be improper to call him Mr. Suicide.)

Burly-Bear: Actually, there is something going on, to tell you the truth.

Me: (staring at him for a long second) Well?

Burly-Bear: Look, this is kind of touchy. Think you might want to be sitting.

Me: (knowing enough to take him seriously, but damned if he'd be infiltrating my apartment...yet. I sink down on the top step of my stoop, my eyes on his) I'm sitting.

Burly-Bear: (hesitating, then sitting on the stoop, too) Take this in stride, okay?

Me: I'll see what I can do.

Burly-Bear: Couple guys in homicide are convinced that it wasn't a suicide. Got a witness who's pretty insistent. Plus there's the vic's profile: lifestyle, finances, lack of note or anything. That and your name starting with "E" and all (shrug, hand circling in the air)... adds up.

Me: I don't get it. Adds up to what?

Burly-Bear: Witness says the guy was arguing with a girl on the platform. Says it got physical just as the train was coming in.

Me: So what happened? (Then getting it) They think *I* was arguing with him? (The second penny drops) They think I *pushed* him? But why? (Then, finally able to think, I snap a finger and point at him.) But why would I *stay*? If I'd pushed him, wouldn't I have run? I mean, everyone else did. It was like a bloody fifty-yard dash out of there, stairs and all.

Burly-Bear: (nodding sympathetically, but it registers somewhere deep in my head that he's watching me in his coppish way) Couple-a guys think maybe you went into temporary shock. Like you realized what you'd done and went paralyzed. It's happened in other cases.

Me: (staring at him) You sound like you're one of those "couple-a guys."

Burly-Bear: (flushing) What the hell you think I'm doin' here?

Me: (realizing that he might be very much on duty, stretching his good-cop act to the max, but what good would it do me to let on that I might be thinking that?) Sorry. Really. I can't help being angry, though. Next time I'm tempted to act like a decent citizen and lift a finger to help the police, let alone act like a decent human being and be a little impacted by a stranger's death, remind me not to, would you? Oh, and next time one of your fellow dicks is bellyaching about how no one wants to "get involved," remind him of me.

Burly-Bear: Lookit, I'm with you. Way I see it, anyone shoved that guy would have been history. Even if they'd done it half by accident and went into shock, a pusher would have recovered enough to stumble along with the crowd. You staying put—in my book, that's proof of your innocence. (Getting out a pack of Marlboros, he knocks one free and offers it.)

Me: (shaking my head vaguely as he lights up for himself) Why would other cops think differently, though? I mean, how could they think something so totally *off*?

Burly-Bear: (blowing smoke before answering) Mostly it's the coincidences. You on the platform, you in the guy's flickr.

Me: But there must be hundreds of pictures in his flickr. Hundreds of anonymous people who live in Boston.

Burly-Bear: (his tone not quite spontaneous as he taps some ash) How would you know that?

Me: (disgusted) Everyone who has a flickr account loads a thousand snaps in the first month. Thing's addicting.

Burly-Bear: You got an account yourself?

Me: You don't need an account to get the gist of it. Everyone ID's their "friends" and then they look at one another's photos and go, "Nice shots, dude, you're a real artist." Just tool around on it for fifteen minutes and you'll see exactly what I'm talking about.

Burly-Bear: I'll do that. You, uh, read the guy's diary?

Me: I read some of it, and the picture it painted for me was of depression, if you'll excuse my lack of compassion. I could easily accept that the man who wrote those "entries," if you want to call them that, could live out his natural life and function like a normal person by all outward appearances. Heck, I could even accept that the guy who wrote that thing *was* a normal person. But, at the same time, the emotional state of the man who wrote that diary is not at all inconsistent with jumping in front of a train. (I pause, then go on less adamantly when Burly-Bear doesn't respond.) Besides, E couldn't possibly be me. Do I come across as some sexed-up femme fatale?

Burly-Bear: You got (hand gesture) your own thing going on. (I feel myself redden and try to ignore it.) Anyway, the diary's being analyzed by a shrink. In the meantime, ain't you found anything in it that could alibi you?

Me: In what way?

Burly-Bear: You know, some event he writes about that happened when you was in California visiting your grandmother.

Me: (shrugging helplessly) Until this little heart-to-heart, I didn't quite get that you—the police—were thinking about me as a black widow who kills her boyfriends with passing light rail trains. Besides, everything I've read in the diary is introspective—vignettes from a failed relationship. It's all so oneiric, you know?

Burly-Bear: Come again?

Me: A bunch of dream snippets.

Burly-Bear: (stubbing his cigarette butt) Well, take another crack at it, huh? Plus, I'm thinking you ought to sit yourself down with a lawyer.

Me: Got it. (I turn my head so he won't see my expression shifting from bravado to raw fear.)

Burly-Bear: Okay, then. (He stands up, then he reaches out and taps my knee) Lookit, better to be a little scared now and get this crud out of your life, right?

Me: (looking up, reasonably dry-eyed and under control) Damned straight.

Burly-Bear: 'Kay, then. Anyone asks, tell the truth about my being here tonight, right? Just, uh, see if you can avoid sayin' anything that makes someone ask. Got it?

Me: (nodding) Got it. I suppose I should thank you for...

Burly-Bear: (cutting me off) Not yet, huh? Later on you can, I don't know, buy me a beer.

Me: (pretending to smile) Hell, Sergeant, I'll buy you a bottle of Four Roses.

Burly-Bear: (pausing as he rounds his car to glance at me over its roof—maybe it surprises him that I even know what bourbon is) I'll, uh, hold you to it.

He leaves. I go inside, dump my food, pour a scotch, and blog. Cut. Wrap. End of scene.

proudblacktrannie @ January 24 08:14 pm

At work and in the boss's office! Swee-pea, I think that Burly-Bear is the real deal. Are you *sure* he's a cop because I have yet to encounter an exception to that old saying "never trust a cop."

roadrage @ January 24 08:16 pm

Isn't it "never trust a *whore*?"

proudblacktrannie @ January 24 08:17 pm

My version's more reliable.

chinkigirl @ January 24 08:19 pm

So it sounds like the answer may be in the diary.

fickel @ January 24 08:22 pm

Sigh. God help me if it is. The thing is...well, I'll share a bit at some point. Right now I'm actually held up by some sense of punctiliousness over how one treats the recently deceased. Drat.

marleybones @ January 24 08:29 pm

Well, I guess that's understandable.

hitman @ January 24 08:31 pm

Drop the drawing room etiquette, fick. We live in an accelerated age of modern technology. There's a *new* etiquette.

fickel @ January 24 08:32 pm

Not quite sure about that (she said tentatively).

hitman @ January 24 08:33 pm

Opaque, as usual (he responded with jaded disgust).

fickel @ January 24 08:34 pm

Ah, yes, but then I'm nothing if not a portentous abstraction (she lobbed with sly wit).

hitman @ January 24 08:35 pm

You're a social whim (he flipped her off).

fickel @ January 24 08:36 pm

Quickly evolving into a moral axiom (she topped him with a crafty refinement of language that defied response). Oww, I just cracked my jaw yawning. That's only *supposed* to happen at work.

proudblacktrannie @ January 24 08:37 pm

Best perk up for your "date."

fickel @ January 24 08:38 pm

Oh-la-la—I'm fashionably late! Lights out, chil'ns: * click *

8

FULL FRONTAL

EXISTENTIALISM ENGORGED

01.25 @ 1:26 AM: TIME FOR ANOTHER EXCITING INSTALLMENT OF TEEE-TALEZZZ

Took the T to Killer Chick's place tonight. Quite a journey. Waiting for the train, some little negroid wanders round me, afraid to make eye contact but honing in like a fly circling horse tail. I check him out without making it obvious. Don't want to scare him off. He's this frail dude, hollow chested with these deep craters all over his cheeks, each one dark and round as a cigar burn, and this natty grey knitted cap that's sagging over one side of his head. Useful for sleeping on grates. Why these freakoids always want to get with me, I'll never understand.

He finally screws up the courage and starts like "'Scuse me, sir? 'Scuse me?" I give him a look and point to the buds in my ears. Instead of getting the message he nods and folds his hands at his waist, like to say he'll wait for me to finish what I'm listening to before he says his piece.

I figure what the hell and pop the buds. "Yeah?"

"It is an evening of great beauty, sir, is it not?"

"It's raining shit in my head," I say, just to jerk him.

He's flustered for fewer seconds than I'd have predicted. "I stand corrected," he says. He smiles and his teeth are black as charred wood, his gums a mix of brown and pink spots, like a dog's. "May I ask you a question, sir? I am attempting to survey the various gentlemen I meet in my perambulations to satisfy a particular curiosity of mine."

I reach into my shirt pocket and pull a couple of cigarettes out. "Smoke?"

The cigarettes look smooth and clean, and he's clearly tempted to grab them and go. But his blood-encrusted eyes waver past them. "I wonder, sir," he says, "Might I inquire if you would perchance be blond all over, or just where it shows?" He gestures with his hand from my head down to about the level of my crotch to indicate the various areas of hair he's curious about. Then he waits, his quivering head unsteady, his disfigured old face drawn up politely.

I admit, I'm stopped for a beat. Then I shake my head, tuck the cigarettes back in the pack and hand the whole thing over to him. Camel no filters. If twenty of those death-sticks don't kill him, nothing will.

He smiles again in a kind of weird-dreamy way—I think he proves something to himself just by gathering up the guts to ask. I walk away, putting my buds back in my ears. It's truly heartening, how resilient the desire to get laid remains in the most drug-addled, rotted-out, termite-infested walking corpse of a human being. The human race will survive the nuclear holocaust. It's just a fact, m'friends.

On the train things are clopping along fine and I'm looking forward to checking in on my favorite T freak, the lovely Killer Chick. Everything goes black heading into Arlington and then the train dies completely maybe thirty yards short of the station and we sit in the dark, listening to the sound of steam and smelling someone's b.o. This Poppy-Z type with brown lipstick and a tattoo necklace who I noticed sitting across from me just as the lights started blinking gets up and stumbles over to land heavily in the seat beside me.

"What you're smelling?" she says. Her voice is raspy. Guys are supposed to dig that but hers sounds like it's from screaming her fucking head off at someone. She points diagonally and even though it's pitch dark I'd already figured out who it was, which was so I could make sure not to brush against him on the way off the train. Most people don't know about second-hand b.o. but trust me, it's a real problem.

I don't answer but that doesn't bother her. "You have any Nicorette? I could use a tingle."

"No, I smoke," I tell her.

"Oh, got a cigarette?" she says optimistically.

"I gave them to a guy."

"How come?" she says, turning her head to see if I'm lying, which might be hard to detect by scrutinizing someone you've never met before in the dark.

"He was homeless."

"Oh," she rasps, considering that. She feels around in her stuff. "Here, want one of mine?"

"No."

"They're Parliaments," she says, nudging me. "What'd you think, Virginia Slims?" She sniggers to herself at that idea.

"I'm quitting." I take the offered cigarette and tuck it away.

"Oh, that sucks, I thought you were being charitable when you gave yours."

"Nope."

"So what do you do?" she asks, crossing her legs. She's wearing black shiny knee-high boots that catch what light there is when she swings her leg. The boots have thick soles and heels like rubber bricks. Also fishnet stockings, but you can only see those at around knee level, where one of them has a tear going on. "You work or anything?"

"I'm psychotic," I say. "It's a full-time thing."

"Tell me about it," she agrees. "What's your trigger?"

I try to see her face, but all I get is the glint of an eye and a lip stud. "What?"

"Hey, don't tell me if it's none of my business, but if it's being in a dark confined space I kind of think I have a right to know at the moment."

"Oh. It's not the dark."

"God, I used to be, like, so, so, so scared of the dark. When I was a kid I used to spend the summers with my aunt and she used to make me and my cousin take turns doing each other. That would be me and her own daughter. Can you believe how screwed up she must have been? Even I got it and I was four." She pauses to pick something off her tongue, which she scrutinizes, then flicks away. "And five. My mother went into detox two summers in a row. I don't know why always the summer, so don't ask. Just something weird she was into about the summer, maybe because that's when my father committed suicide."

"Sure, maybe. What happened to your aunt?"

She flounces a little, as if impatient. "What are you talking about?"

"You said she was screwed up, like it was in the past."

She snorts. "What, you think I'd be visiting that mess now?"

I pretend to consider. "Oh yeah, right, of course not."

She seems to find some gum that's already in her mouth and starts chewing. "So anyway, I was incredibly afraid of the dark after that."

"She used to make you and your cousin do it in the dark?"

"Of course not. How could she watch if it was dark?"

"Right," I say. "So how'd you get over being scared of the dark?"

She tilts her head. "You're not even psycho," she says.

"Count on it," I say assuringly.

"Say something psychotic, then. Something about us sitting here right now."

I think, then quote my favorite psycho: "The light of knowledge and life has caused an artificial erection to melt away."

She sniffs, apparently not totally dissatisfied. "You're the type who thinks you can get with any chick. I can tell. Don't bother lying about it, either."

I shrug. "Okay."

"Yeah, well, don't expect to be getting any from me."

"I'm already going somewhere."

She pokes me with her finger, hard. "Like you wouldn't blow it off to get some. I know men."

"I'm gay," I say.

That stops her for a beat. Then she spurts air from between her lips. "As if."

"I am," I insist. "I'm on my way to get it on with an old guy I met on the internet."

"Okay, what's Agucino?"

I consider. "A place in Italy?"

"Wrong," she says. She makes like to get up, but as she does she reaches over and manages to grab my entire sack in her fist and squeeze so hard that snot bursts out both my nostrils. "It's a shoe," she grinds out from between her teeth.

Sometimes I can't help thinking that God is smiling on me. I mean, who has my luck in meeting these squeaks?

So the Poppy-Z chick stumbles off down the train car in the dark. Since she never bothered to lower her voice during our conversation, people give her space. From the back, the silhouette of her rump is high and large in a way you'd never expect from the rest of her. Could be her meds. By the time the train lights up, I've managed to find an old receipt on the floor that I use to smear the mucus off my chin. The Poppy-Z chick doesn't look round when she gets off at Haymarket. From her body language, she's totally forgotten my existence. I like that quality in a freak who goes for your nads when she's annoyed.

From all of the above it seems like a promising night when I arrive at the crack den that Killer Chick calls home, and when she appears at her door only moments after I settle myself across the street I'm pretty heartened. She's got on one of those skinny suits women favor, black and white checks with this short jacket and a skirt that's basically pleats. Women go for these costumes because they display to all the other women their waistline which they've made twig-like from a careful regimen of starvation and vomiting. They forget to think about their boobs or buns because after examining themselves in the mirror every morning for several hours at every possible angle to gauge how other women will think their incredible shrinking torso looks, they don't have time to consider what men might think about their deflated tits and ass.

Anyway, she comes out of her trip-deck firetrap sniffing at her wrists, which is what chicks do when they've put on perfume and want to make sure they've achieved the exact level of cum-n-get-it cree cree they're going for. Apparently she's happy with her results and goes merrily tripping off down the driveway to whatever's waiting for her in the lot behind her place. A minute later up the driveway she bumps in some shitbox vehicle, side-swiping her building like it's maybe her second day behind the wheel. I already spotted the turd-mobile I plan to hot-wire so as to follow her and am heading that way when she gasses on past me without a glance. However, when she stops at the yield sign down the end of her block she starts playing with the rearview, like she's trying to see something behind her and thinks she's cleverly going to avoid turning her head. Fortunately I have the Poppy-Z chick's Parliament, so I busy myself firing that up and look pretty natural with my head ducked so the Killer Chick can't quite catch my face.

When I look up again, Killer Chick's driven off. I throw the cigarette away, just in case the Poppy-Z chick put something in it. Can't be too careful, man. Then I squeeze my "travel size" tube of vaseline along my slim jim and shove that ol' boy down the Crown Vic's window. Couple secs later I'm easing that baby up Storrow, right behind KC...

---

tALK. NIHILISt DOGS

chootah @ 01.25 01:49 am

you gunna knife this chick or something some day? If so, nice record you creating.

fullfrontal @ 01.25 01:50 am

How about I just walk up to her and blow on her and let her fall down dead from that?

boytoucher @ 01.25 01:56 am

Why, she don't like your breath?

fullfrontal @ 01.25 01:57 am

Yeah, it smells like dick, but that's just cause I'm double-jointed. What's your excuse?

garbo @ 01.25 02:00 am

you write like a maestro.

fullfrontal @ 01.25 02:01 am

what's that, sum kinda I-talian?

garbo @ 01.25 02:02 am

giggle giggle you're cute.

fullfrontal @ 01.25 02:03 am

Thank u kindly, strange new voice. Sup?

garbo @ 01.25 02: 04 am

Can't get you out of my head. Post a pic, so I can see what I've been imagining?

fullfrontal @ 01.25 02:05 am

Lemme guess: yer a dude.

garbo @ 01.25 02:06 am

What difference would that make? Would it make you gay to provide a pic for another guy?

chootah @ 01.25 02:07 am

She's a chick fer sher, mon.

fullfrontal @ 01.25 02:08 am

Amen t'that. Do you believe in first dates with happy endings?

garbo @ 01.25 02:09 am

We all do, gentle sir, when asked politely. Have you not figured that out yet?

fullfrontal @ 01.25 02:10 am

I am all of a sudden finding you interesting, strange person.

garbo @ 01.25 02:11 am

right back atcha, m'man

9

LIFE IS PULP

Noir the Night Away With L.G. Fickel

January 25 @ 2:22 am
>CURIOUZER & CURIOUZER<

Oh hi blog howz it goin? Home again, and lucky, too, after 3 cognacs with the Colonel. Please excuzzze typing errors plus any excessive cattiness as am trying to revive my buzz with very sticky bottle of Lillet left over from those 10 minutes when Lillet was *so* da bomb.

Sucked down some super-black coffee in that diner just by the ramp to 128 (vintage 1940) before attempting to navigate my way back to town but got nothing but the jitters out of that (plus I happened upon this eerily attractive guy there—some mysterious hottie who made me nervous for some reason I can't quite put my finger on, but that's a story for another blotto blog entry). Fortunately, no cops observed my wibbly-wobbly progress home, but, irony of ironies, I did observe upon alighting from my car back here at the shack that I am currently *under police observation*. There's someone parked behind my building, as I verified by leaving the lights off upon entering and then slithering across the linoleum over to the window to peek through the crack between shade and sash (*side note to self*: wash the floor, bitch). He is smoking out the window of his seafoam-green Mustang.

Better than some stranger, but, still, unsettling. I mean: is Sergeant Tyler Malloy of the Boston homicide squad monitoring my whereabouts to make sure I don't make a run for it???

I find myself wondering (in a room-rotate-y sort of way): was Burly-

Bear's appearance on my stoop yesterday evening just a ploy to see if I'd go racing back to Mr. Suicide's to, like, erase some more evidence as soon as I thought the cops had cleared out? Because he did make sure to mention that they were done over there. Or—okay, wait a minute while I run off to tinkle...ah, back now (*see* how fast I am?) where was I?...Oh, yes, something a teeny bit more consoling just occurred to me—maybe Burly-Bear is OFF duty right now and he's hanging around in my parking lot back there to make sure his creep partner Escroto doesn't sneak round to PLANT something incriminating HERE. That gotta be it, because if Burly-Bear was supposed to be watching me wouldn't he have needed to tail me out to Concord, just to make sure I wasn't trying to make a wild run for the Canadian border?

OMG!!!—I just had this amazing thought—maybe Burly-Bear DID follow me out to Concord and back *but I just never spotted him*!!!

Oh, wait a sec, but then he'd have needed to arrest me for DUI, wouldn't he? Except maybe when they're tailing you as a murder suspect they give you a pass on drunk driving, as long as you are the type who drives 25 mph when you've had too much. And, anyway, if he'd been good enough at shadowing to tail me all the way out to Concord and back without my spotting him, why was it so easy for me to spot him parked in my lot, where he definitely was already planted at the time I arrived home?

But...but...but...(I'll get it in a second) Ah, yes! But maybe he WANTS me to see him here, parked, watching my place.

Why, though? Why, I ask mine-self, why?

O * PERIOD * M * PERIOD * F * PERIOD * G!!!!!!!!!!!!

It's because he wants me to be *careful*. Because he's really a good cop, although not just in the playing-nice-trying-to-trick-a-confession-out-of-someone-way—he's *actually* on my side, and this is because in the very same instant that his partner Escroto fell deeply in hate with me, *Burly-Bear fell equally deeply in LOVE with me* (truly a far more plausible response to meeting me, if anyone's asking my HUMBLE opinion).

Okay, enuff fantacizing. I'm off to find a lime and a couple of ice chips, and then to my evening. No more Molly Bloom, I swear! YES YES YES—there it's out of my system.

GIVE IT TO ME STRAIGHT

proudblacktrannie @ January 25 02:44 am

u r trashed gurl and so am i (just in from one of those lovely frangelico evenings) but do know that Honey-Bear is sitting out there in his cop car w/ his cop computer open and he is lurking on our conversation. Luv u hon, even more so drunk than sober.

hitman @ January 25 02:48 am

Invite him in, fickel. Play him like he's playing you. Challenge him to say he knows nothing about this site.

fickel @ January 25 02:54 am

Just back, and realize now that I posted tonight's entry before I meant to. I was going to tell about my discussion with the Colonel but now I'm suddenly sick of being trashed and just want to chow down a few migraine tabs and sleep it off. Yes, by the way, proudblacktrannie, I am frightened as hell I don't mind saying because I do not know if I can come up with any "alibi witnesses"—or whatever Burly-Bear wants me to produce for various nights when Mr. Suicide's diary talks about his evenings with (or often without) "E."

Anyway, who remembers what they were doing at a moment six months ago when some middle-aged whiner stashed away over in some Fort Point loft happens to be scribbling away about how some freeloader drove him from one orgasm to the next before sneaking off to swap fluids with someone her own age?

So, hitman, what am I supposed to accomplish by going outside and inviting Burly-Bear in? What *is* this "playing him," may I ask?

fickel @ January 25 03:02 am

Ummm, hellooooo? No answer, hitman? Forgot to think that part through? Yes, well, I'd guessed as much. G'night, blog. Luv u, lurkers and all.

10

LIFE IS PULP

Feed the Beast With L.G. Fickel

January 25 @ 10:38 pm
>LET ME CALL YOU SCHWEETHEART<

Sooooo, about last night. If my bloggies could politely ignore my post, I will be eternally grateful. Drunken blogging is apparently not part of my repertoire. Shall we see how I do at blogging with a massive hangover?

I'm composing this, btw, in the circa-1948 truck stop diner just off 128 and about four miles down the rural route from the Manor—to my amazement this place has wifi. The Colonel, father-figure that he be, had me up to Concord *again* tonight, this time to meet his mouthpiece. I've stopped here (as usual) for coffee, mostly because I didn't want to make the drive home in the storm that hit, full force, just as I was jouncing along the last half mile or so toward the highway. Unfortunately, the rain's only gotten harder in the twenty minutes I've been huddled here—sheets of it are shaking the plate-glass window right next to me as I type—and, for those who need mood, there's even the occasional skitter of lightening, followed a half minute or so later by long, languid belches of thunder. And me, sitting here against this backdrop in my dove-grey fringed tweed Albert Nipon knockoff! Talking *major* mise-en-scène.

Any-ho, I give you the Colonel's lawyer: late thirties, well-constructed with a piston-and-steel quality to his movements, shiny black hair sleeked back from his forehead (I'd say damp from the rain but I *smelled* the pomade)—lovely olive-green suit (Caraceni, anyone?). Overall, he created an impression of being quite handsome in a F. Scott Fitzgerald-y sort of way, and so I assumed he was until at some point I finally happened to look directly at his face, at which point I was surprised to find that the man is actually rather ugly, his eyes flat and empty, nostrils like black holes, lips thin and blood red, facial bone structure somehow cruel and off-kilter. Let me anticipate your view of this lawyer by dubbing him Mr. Groin. The man was nothing if not a complete dick, as you will see.

So Mr. Groin strolls into the Colonel's sun room unannounced, rapping a couple of knuckles against the door in passing, which was plenty familiar, you ask me, as a way for a lawyer to enter a client's home at 9:30 pm on a school night. The Colonel doesn't bat a reptilian eyelid—but then he's gracious by nature. Our three-way conversation is short and not altogether sweet. Goes sort of like:

Colonel: (in that gruff patrician way of his) Ah, Groin, perfect timing. This is the young lady I was telling you about. Helping me sort out my magnum opus. She's witnessed a suicide in the subway, and now a couple of detectives are asking her questions about whether she chanced to know the fellow. The police seem to be harboring some half-formulated suspicion that the man was helped along in his determination to end it all. Preposterous, any way you look at it, but frankly the girl's a bit unglued by the whole thing and I thought you might help out.

Me: (hoping to cut through the damsel-in-distress crap) Actually, I half think that one of the cops is on the make...

Mr. Groin: (cutting me off) Just tell him you're represented. That'll get him off your back. (He smiles briefly after saying this—his teeth are so straight and white that I find myself immediately scanning his hairline for plugs.)

Me: But I'm not represented.

Mr. Groin: Oh, I'll handle it. Professional courtesy. If we need to sue at some point, we'll talk about fees; until then I'll consider you (here he drops an eye down my body, then flashes another of those lupine smiles at me) pro bono. (Somehow I'm meant to pick up that he's just made a funny about my inauspicious assets. He feels in his breast pocket, and I'd have sworn he's about to come out with one of those sterling silver cigarette cases—available on e-Bay for the fop in every smoker. Instead he flicks me a business card—off-white, fancy stock.) Next time anyone from the police contacts you, you give him my number. Apologize all you want, but stick to your guns. Believe me, they're used to it.

Me: (taking his card mostly to show the Colonel that I'm grateful he set up this little "meeting") But what if I'm not completely uninterested in cooperating with the police?

Mr. Groin: (offhandedly) So cooperate. Just cooperate through counsel.

Me: (needing to prod at his generous offer, for some reason) It's just that, I have to admit that the police are not without reason to be, well, puzzled about a few of the facts. You see—

Mr. Groin: (putting a finger to his lips and shaking his head, as if I'm a child. To my own amazement, it works—I actually shut up on command.) We're all puzzled about a lot of things that happen, Miss...(here he seemed to be groping momentarily for my name. It surprises me, as he comes across as one of those steel-trap-mind types who never forgets a name, no matter how insignificant its owner—or her tits—may be.)

At this moment, however, we catch the spatter of high heels out on the stairs, along with the jangle of car keys and a cheery: "Fuck me, look at the time! Don't wait up, sweetie, because I'm crashing at Monica's." It's Mrs. Colonel—a nip-tuck, nouveau-and-loving-it fifty-something who's gone mano a mano with Father Time and actually seems to have won this round quite handily. She favors flowy silk pantsuits designed to accentuate her always-erect nipples, has the audacity to do her hair in a soft, white-blond pageboy that half covers one aqua-bright eye, and attempts to draw attention from the approaching-but-not-quite-realized wattle under her neck with these major—I could safely say breathtaking—blue diamonds that lie scattered across her clavicle bones, webbed together in a coruscating constellation of white gold that's pure art. The omnipresent winking weave of blue-white stones, as you can predict, has led me to dub her "the Peacock" in my catty little bad-girl head. This evening she remains unseen but apparently very much appreciated, as the chuffed look Mr. Groin flicks in the direction of his own crotch reveals altogether too clearly. The Colonel chuckles indulgently as we hear the staccato punch of the Peacock's heels and then the thwump of the front door closing behind her.

Mr. Groin: So, let me take a very few seconds here to explain how the brain of a cop works in a suicide-slash-possible homicide in the T. PR-wise, they're looking for the fast fix. They don't care if it's accurate or whether it sticks. They want the public's attention span to be short and sweet, and that happens when the BPD comes off as homing in on a solve while the story's still above the fold. Sooooo, what could the cops make out of *you* to feed the good citizens of greater Boston? Let's see: waspish literary editor by day, dominatrix by night, kills her ex-lover out of some mix of sadism, guilt, and rage.

Me: How utterly theatrical.

Mr. Groin: (I score an eyelid flutter as he discerns that he hasn't frightened my panties into a twist.) Let me sum it up: you say you're concerned about the cops being puzzled? They're not puzzled. They're looking for a scapegoat, and maybe they've got one in you—*that's* what they're mulling over. Later maybe you prove you're innocent? They're cool with that, sweetheart, because no one will care.

Me: (impressed at his so readily recognizing me as the sweetheart that I am, but otherwise not wowed) Okay, but putting aside the predatory nature of the BPD, if you're going to be my lawyer, don't you need to know everything I know?

Mr. Groin: Not a good idea. What I need to know, I'll ask and you'll tell. Capisce?

Me: It's a plan, I suppose.

So I'm "represented." Hoo-freaking-ray. Let's hope Burly-Bear remembers that he's the one who suggested it.

OMG, UPDATE!!!UPDATE!!!UPDATE!!!
are things worse than i thought...
OR WHAT!?!

So I am sitting here in the diner, blogging away with a self-amused smirk on my mug, and I just glanced round to give the nod to the coffee lady when who (okay, whom) should I spot but:

THE {{{{{MYSTERIOUS HOTTIE}}}}}

This is the second time in the same number of days that I've seen this guy here—those of you who pore over every word I blog will verify that I mentioned him in passing last night but forgot to get back to discussing him. In any event, he is presently parked at the counter. I can see his face through the mirror and it is the guy. I mean, who could forget that long, sinewy rumpus masculinus?

Here is what he looks like: dark blond hair, bed-heady in that authentic way. Face scruffy and stubbly, *GORGEOUS* gray-blue eyes...you get the feeling he smokes in the shower. Bod: a titch over average height and I want to say "lithe" for some reason. Hands large, with big dirt-rimmed thumbs tapping on the rim of his coffee cup. Clothes scrumptiously beat: ancient jacket-coat in a ratty brown corduroy, couple of layers of dark shirts hanging out under the jacket's bottom, dusty-looking grey jeans below, and some sort of crusty leather boots on his feet. You just know you'd get a big slap in the face of sweat odor if he ever yanked off his T-shirt in your presence—why this seems almost shudderingly attractive I can't quite articulate.

Is this coincidence, that I am here and he is here, two nights in a row? Is he a "regular," so that any time I drop by I might as soon spot him as not? *Are* there regulars at this diner?—it's a highway stop. The waitress just offered him a warm-up and she didn't smile or meet his eye, but that could mean she's used to him. Or maybe she doesn't dare meet his eye for fear that he'll detect how heavenly it is just to glance across the counter at him.

OR IS HE A COP, tailing me when I wander while Burly-Bear covers the home turf and works on "opening me up?" I'm keeping my eye on the mirror even as I type this, and will catch him if he glances up to check out my reflection. But even if he does that, what of it? I'm the only young woman in the place, so it would be natural for him to check me out.

What's he waiting for, tapping those massive thumbs of his...tap, tap, tappity, tap...?

GIVE IT TO ME STRAIGHT

36-D @ January 25 11:13 pm

Okay, so when do you get to do the naughty with him?

i.went.to.harvard @ January 25 11:15 pm

Why am I not surprised that this is where the conversation goes? fickel: you need a lawyer whether you like him or not, and if he's aggressive and self-assured, well, isn't that what you *want* in a lawyer? fickel?

fickel @ January 26 12:12 am

Okay, I'm back on. I'm home now, locked in my apartment, virginity intact—and running through your comments. I don't know what I think. I definitely was worried that Mysterious Hottie was a cop back at the diner. Now that the rain and that rather jarring meeting with Mr. Groin are behind me, I think he's just a guy who goes there to eat. Probably has a night job, a pregnant wife, and three lovely brats under the age of six back at the trailer park.

chinkigirl @ January 26 12:13 am

Young dads bring their dinner to work in a bag, and it's peanut butter and jelly on white, a box of apple juice and a couple of Ho-Hos. Trust me on this.

proudblacktrannie @ January 26 12:17 am

i am in my boss's office at work i cant stand not being ON!!! i have 1 simple fact to add to your evening, fickel my deah one:

GIANT THUMBS = GIANT YOU KNOW WHAT.

When you think back on this night, remember those rock-hard thumbs tapping that coffee cup. nuff said gotta go.

hitman @ January 26 12:19 am

Glad to tune in and find the ladies in heat. But back to business: any contact from the actual cop (as opposed to the imagined one)?

fickel @ January 26 12:21 am

If Burly-Bear's out in my parking lot, he's done a better job hiding himself tonight.

36-D @ January 26 12:23 am

Does that make you nervous? I mean not knowing where he is or what he's thinking?

fickel @ January 26 12:24 am

A tad, now that you make me think about it.

hitman @ January 26 12:27 am

Lemme clarify, fick: you want the big cop hanging round, letting slip what the cops are thinking about you while he tries to peek up your skirt. But at the same time you're swooning over some dirtbag you spot in a diner who looks like his pits reek. What a tough spot you're in, fickel—whose vertical stick to hop???????

marleybones @ January 26 12:30 am

You *really* don't like women much, do you, hitman?

fickel @ January 26 12:34 am

Actually, in a big way hitman is right. Did Burly-Bear tip me off because I'm a woman? That's pretty likely. Am I letting him see that I notice that he's a male? You betcha. So as far as all that takes you, you're right, hitman: I'm "using sex" to get information. However, am I truly toying with him, playing it helpless, dropping hints that if he clears up the mess, he gets to bed me? 'Fraid not, hitman. So if simply being a female who notices a couple of men means being a tease or worse, well, guilty as charged.

hitman @ January 26 12:37 am

oh, you're guilty, fickel.

fickel @ January 26 12:38 am

Who are you channeling, anyway, Lawrence Tierney?

wazzup! @ January 26 12:39 am

Just tuning in on my way through my Favorites (you are climbing like a hit single to the Netherlands' number 1 noir site!). Excellent reference...*Born to Kill*...one of top ten noir on my famous all-stars list!!!!! Please google me up: www.dutchman!

hitman @ January 26 12:42 am

Gotta hand it to you, fick—you got cojones to be blogging away with this crap going on.

hitman @ January 26 01:16 am

fickel? You on?

hitman @ January 26 01:23 am

fickel, you don't take my junk seriously, do you?

fickel @ January 26 01:42 am

Look, why are you here? Why now? And don't give me that "noir fan" line—I don't buy it.

hitman @ January 26 01:44 am

I am a noir fan, big time. But seriously?

fickel @ January 26 01:50 am

Dead straight, if you're capable of it.

hitman @ January 26 01:56 am

Fact is I pushed someone once. In front of a train. And yeah, I get the shakes just writing this.

fickel @ January 26 01:57 am

Oh, I'm suitably skeptical. Is there a "why" you're gearing up to deliver?

hitman @ January 26 02:18 am

I needed to take charge of a situation. I'm wondering if you're involved in something similar.

fickel @ January 26 02:19 am

Take the psychobabble somewhere else.

hitman @ January 26 02:21 am

Look, sorry if I frightened you.

fickel @ January 26 02:22 am

Frightened me? Do I frighten that easily? Gosh I wasn't aware of it.

hitman @ January 26 02:25 am

Thought you wanted me to be straight with you.

fickel @ January 26 02:39 am

Look, hitman, I'm not cut out to be someone's online confessional. Good and evil haven't lined themselves up tidily in my life, and twenty years of spoon-fed Catholicism didn't clarify a thing. If it's absolution you're circling in on, I'm sorry, but you've got the wrong blog.

leo tolstoy @ January 26 02:42 am

The arbiter of good and evil is not what people say and do. It is your heart and yourself.

fickel @ January 26 02:45 am

Long sigh. I need a new url.

11

LIFE IS PULP

The Noir Boudoir of L.G. Fickel

January 26 @ 10:42 pm
>DIARY OF A SUICIDE-IN-TRAINING<

> *People have funny things swimming around inside of them. Don't you ever wonder about what they are?*
>
> –B. Stanwyck to the doofy guy in *Clash by Night*

Acting on hitman's "advice," I have decided to take charge of my life—the part of it that's beginning to make me a paranoid schizophrenic—by doing the cops' job for them and figuring out who Mr. Suicide was and why he clocked out in his particular way. I am not a psychologist, nor do I have much faith in that "science." HOWEVER, I have at this point read through the dead man's diary and also scanned his living space, and I believe I have as good a sense as the next armchair analyst as to what festers in people's noodles. And, of course, I saw his face, I mean, just before he did himself in. I guess that puts me in a unique position insofar as "knowing" this stranger. So here goes:

This diary only kinda-sorta traces the relationship between Mr. Suicide and this "lover" identified as E. It's not chronological, and more than one of the entries begins with "Just woke up from the most horrific dream." Mr. S never discusses E's profession, if she (he?) has one, or his/her age or his/her appearance in terms that allow me to truly picture him/her, and, unfortunately, just as my first skim-through of the thing made clear, my reread leads me to conclude that there is nothing readily apparent that differentiates me from E.

Soooo, now I've decided to change my tactic and try to use the diary as a vehicle for figuring out what made the S-Man tick—as well as what made him arrive at a conscious decision to stop ticking—if I'm going to build a circumstantial case in my defense to hand over to Burly-Bear and his buds in homicide.

This more careful review I have now begun, and as I seem to have lost, just lately and conveniently, my sensibilities about keeping Mr. Suicide's privacy private—I mean, it's not like he respected MY peace of mind—I have decided to post a representative excerpt from the diary here with the idea that maybe some of my favorite readers of metadiagetic malaise (noir, she means) could offer some thoughtful comments.

So read. Reread. Analyze to Death. (Oops—how inappropriately apropos.)

> *Just woke up and had one of those wild moments where you remember everything about your sleep world—the eerie way it hangs in its own space, your own unfiltered presence in that parallel universe. Guess what, E—I was dreaming about the moment I discovered you, here in Boston, a moment I haven't reflected on for quite a while.*
>
> *It was late spring, about midnight, and I was walking up Atlantic Ave., heading home, underwhelmed by a club that had been overhyped in* Bay Windows. *Strolling toward me was a couple, arms around one another, occasionally kissing. I love everything about casual public necking. I love the rush that comes from seeing two people enjoying the giddy adrenaline of infatuation. I love the visual—the way people look when they're draped all over each other, oblivious to the world. I love the voyeuristic tingle of watching a couple's in-your-face exhibitionism. You see public necking in Europe but hardly ever in the States.*
>
> *Anyway, it was just after midnight when I spotted this couple (in the dream, a kind of eclipse-y glow surrounded everything), and as we got near one another I had the urge to get a better look at you. Maybe it was fate, or something familiar in your walk, or the way your hair cheated me of a glimpse of your face. The man you were with wore one of those gaudy leather coats and had his arm cinched around your neck in a lazy, possessive way that blocked my view of you, and you, who were a bit shorter than he even in those Gestapo boots of yours, walked with your face tilted up as if to catch the kisses that might drip from his lips. I don't remember if I was fully*

conscious of what I was about to do, but when we passed I bumped arms with your companion. We hit harder than I intended—always tough to fake those little everyday moments—and I swiveled round, apologizing.

The two of you turned as a unit, arms around one another. The man you were with, who was very young (I remember this without recalling a single detail of his face) looked at me with hostility. You, however, just smiled, evidently still immersed in whatever he'd been murmuring. Your damp hair striped your forehead, and your eyes were a pair of greyed-over jewels, as if being with that other guy, inconsequential as he was, put you into some sort of scintillated trance (could have been dope, I realize now, but then—who knew). Your smile—that coyly chipped bicuspid and the nail-hole dimple in your chin—I knew everything in the space it took me to wave apologetically.

The tall guy turned the two of you and you strolled off. I did the same, but when I got to the next corner I reversed myself without hesitation. I headed directly to the all-night diner (where else could you have been wandering off to in that neighborhood at that hour?). I spotted you sitting in one of the tiny booths against a window. You were drinking coffee while the guy you were with spoke to the old Greek behind the counter, and when it was your turn to order you shook your head, as if whatever you were high on (coke? ludes? the after-buzz of a good screw?) had you completely satiated. I stood there on the sidewalk, my brain a tumble of rage and curiosity and... hope for what might happen, now that I'd found you. I'm sure you saw me, recognized me through the greasy screen. You didn't show it, though. You gave me a long, slow study, neither wary nor curious. You just drank me in, and then you half smiled and turned your head away. Was it something that your companion had said? Or was that smile for me—did you acknowledge what you would mean to me? Were you...apologizing—something you would never do again, of course—for the hell I've been through on your account?

Guyzzzzzzzzzzzzzzzz??????

GIVE IT TO ME STRAIGHT

chinkigirl @ January 26 11:12 pm

Gut reactions: romantic, writes relatively well with generally proper grammar, and, dreamy or not, the moment he recalls rings true. Also, Mr. Suicide sounds confident in spite of the self-deprecating tone—probably fairly successful as success is measured by outsiders.

marleybones @ January 26 11:15 pm

But inside the guy's just another middle-aged adolescent, fixated on young flesh: *classics professor*, anyone?

i.went.to.harvard @ January 26 11:17 pm

This reminds me, fickel: I'm not in the Boston area anymore myself, but have you been checking the papers every day for obits? I mean, a man kills himself in one of the most horrible and public ways imaginable, and in so doing shuts down the T for hours—wasn't it in *any* paper? And wouldn't that include information about who he was?

fickel @ January 26 11:18 pm

I've checked the *Globe*, the *Herald*, and Boston.com every day since he did it. Not a word. My understanding on obits is that if he's not a known figure his family could keep everything private and there would be no incentive for the papers to disregard that. While we're on this, I could add that it totally galls me that the cops (yes, Burly-Bear included) have been so careful to keep his name from me. And that includes removing his name from the buzzer at his apartment.

36-D @ January 26 11:19 pm

You're telling us your lawyer hasn't been able to get the name out of the cops?

fickel @ January 26 11:20 pm

And I've spoken with "my lawyer" when, exactly?

roadrage @ January 26 11:21 pm

My guess on the media blackout? The papers, in cooperation with the authorities, keep news of a jumper out of the public eye. The only way to stop desperate people from throwing themselves off the platform is to set up barriers which would slow down the entire train system, and the authorities don't want a bunch of copycats making that necessary.

marleybones @ January 26 11:28 pm

A conspiracy of silence.

36-D @ January 26 11:30 pm

I'm in Providence. Not a word in our papers either. Then I asked my mother's friend who works for the MBTA if she knows anything and she hasn't gotten back but she did say that the mayor's office could easily keep something like this quiet.

chinkigirl @ January 26 11:32 pm

fickel, about that reference to Mr. Suicide's name not being on his apartment's buzzer? I'm *sure* I'm reading into it, but have you by chance gone back to Mr. Suicide's apartment since the time the cops took you there?

fickel @ January 26 11:33 pm

Sigh. Would that be so crazy of me?

proudblacktrannie @ January 26 11:41 pm

Gurlz, gurlz, back to the diary—I don't suppose you recall anything like the moment Mr. S describes? Could you *possibly* have been spotted necking half drunk in the wee hours in the loft district with some forgettable himbo? Come to think of it, E could be *me*.

i.went.to.harvard @ January 26 11:43 pm

More to the point of differentiating yourself from E, fickel, do you have dimples and a chipped tooth? If no on both counts, then this entry is part of your evidence to give to the cops.

fickel @ January 26 11: 45 pm

I get dimples when I smile, a fact I've always kind of liked about myself until just now. I'm not sure I'd call my dimples "nail holes," but I don't see me getting off the BPD's subway pusher short list on that basis. On the other hand, my teeth are perfect, an absolute natural fluke, but, again, I don't see the BPD being much impressed. I do have Gestapo-style boots, but who doesn't? And no, proudblacktrannie, I don't remember the moment Mr. Suicide described because it never happened.

webmaggot @ January 27 12:02 am

Just in from a hot date—yes, sports fans, I-I-I-I...HAD-HAD-HAD-HAD...A-A-A-A...DATE-DATE-DATE-DATE!!!!!! (ten seconds of shocked silence followed by thunderous applause that deafens the world wide web for fifteen minutes) BTW, never point out on a first date that Naomi Watts has a perfect ass—just don't. However, smuggling Grey Goose into the theater definitely gets a girl rubbing up against yer...or at least feeling around for the bottle. Anywaze my brother used to live in the South End (he bites pillow) and *Bay Windows* is a gay rag. Since the dead guy read it, he's gay. E must be a gay guy. Mystery solved er wut?

36-D @ January 27 12:05 am

Uhh, Bay Windows is gay but I used to pick it up when I was up in Boston. They have it in the grocery store, for crissake. I used to like to go clubbing and you could read about what was going on where. Oh, and I'm not gay. Congrats on the date. Just a tip, though? If you get them really really drunk they get to wake up the next day and call it rape. :(

webmaggot @ January 27 12:18 am

Oh thanx, I'd ask her if she's really really drunk but she's busy blowing me as I type this so I'll ask later.

proudblacktrannie @ January 27 12:20 am

Bay Windows is for aging gays who live with their ADM's. And webmaggot is right, 36-D—there's a difference between a SATC type such as yourself doing the gay club scene and a middle-aged straight professional man doing same said clubs. The only straight men in those clubs are drug peddlers (bless them), undercover cops (homophobic creeps), and psychos sniffing around for a hate crime (who are deep inside the gayest of us all, AWAK).

roadrage @ January 27 12:21 am

ADM is...?

proudblacktrannie @ January 27 12:22 am

Almost Dead Mothers, luv.

chinkigirl @ January 27 12:23 am

Ummm, and SATC...?

proudblacktrannie January 27 12:24 am

Sex And The City. And before anyone asks, AWAK is "as we all know." Glory, am I talking to *myself* out here?

i.went.to.harvard @ January 27 12:26 am

Not to keep harping on the physical features, but Mr. S says that E's dimple is a *chin* dimple. fickel seems to be describing *cheek* dimples—the kind you get when you smile. I see this as a clear distinction. Also, he calls E's eyes "greyed-over jewels." Any chance your eyes are jet black or such a bright blue that they couldn't possibly be described as "greyed-over," fick?

fickel @ January 27 12:30 am

Dimples: none in chin but I do have a beauty mark that could be mistaken for one. My eyes are very dark brown—two damp spots of joe in the bottom of a couple of white coffee cups, you might say. But I think that Mr. Suicide's point is that E was stoned and so his/her eyes were foggy. So that could be anyone, including me on occasion in the semidistant past. All in all, there is nothing here that determinatively distinguishes me from E. The writing is all too internal, too arty-farty.

chinkigirl @ January 27 12:37 am

Although we *can* say that no physical description of E, at least none we've seen so far, may be pointed to as a real *match* with fickel. I find that heartening.

fickel @ January 27 12:39 am

sure, yeah, me too.

proudblacktrannie @ January 27 12:42 am

What I am hearing is that fickel needs to stay within kissing distance of the Burly one.

fickel @ January 27 12:44 am

Uhh, not to get all holy on you, but I don't like the intimation that I should be stringing the guy along to get me through this weird patch in my life.

proudblacktrannie @ January 27 12:46 am

Sorry luv.

fickel @ January 27 12:47 am

Look, now I've insulted you. Not intended, 'kay? :)

proudblacktrannie @ January 27 12:48 am

Nuff said, sweetie, u know I luv u regardless.

hitman @ January 27 12:57 am

I'm gagging here, you mind?

proudblacktrannie @ January 27 12:58 am

ES&D, sweetie-pie. And before I get a *million* queries, that's EAT S*** & DIE

fickel @ January 27 01:03 am

Actually, I'm glad you're on, hitman. POV on the diary?

hitman @ January 27 01:12 am

It's a fake.

i.went.to.harvard @ January 27 01:15 am

A fake diary?

hitman @ January 27 01:21 am

A fake dream, genius. He thinks E is reading the thing when he's out and wants to remind her of earlier days in the relationship and how, you know, deep he is into her and crap.

proudblacktrannie @ January 27 01:22 am

Lawdy. Your cynicism is so absolute that I actually picture you in grainy black and white, hitman. *Do* tell me you're unshaven and are sitting in a dark office building right now, swigging from a bottle you keep in your bottom drawer.

hitman @ January 27 01:24 am

That's me, shuggah. Now shaddup or I'll squash a grapefruit in yer face.

marleybones @ January 27 01:26 am

So let me follow this out. Mr. Suicide writes up this stuff as a cry for help to get E's attention. So when E isn't taken in—in fact, maybe is driven to move out on the man—it's all the more humiliating. So he pines, gets into self-loathing and recriminations, and eventually punishes himself (and E) with a lonely dive into the T tracks.

hitman @ January 27 01:30 am

Yeah, maybe my theory doesn't hold together too good unless he does the jump, like, right in front of E. That would tie it all together with a bow. Wouldn't it, fick?

fickel @ January 27 01:32 am

Mmm. In any event, now you all can see why this so-called diary is unlikely to present some sort of scheduling conflict I can just line up against my electronic calendar to "prove" my innocence.

chinkigirl @ January 27 01:33 am

In fact so far we've used it to "prove" the opposite. Ouch.

hitman @ January 27 01:36 am

Describe the handwriting.

fickel @ January 27 01:39 am

Fluid, generally artistic. Lots of fracture—places where he lifted the pen between groups of two or three letters. Some letters by the book, others his own formulations—sometimes even the same letter written two different ways, but the whole hangs together and appears reasonably consistent. Several errors corrected with impatient scratch-outs. In short, it's a nice, mature handwriting but it's also a three-in-the-morning-just-woke-up-after-too-many-scotches-scribble version of whatever his actual handwriting is probably like.

hitman @ January 27 01:46 am

You need to see the original.

fickel @ January 27 01:47 am

I...do?

hitman @ January 27 01:48 am

No substitute for the original. Go to the cop. Ask him.

12

FULL FRONTAL

EXISTENTIALISM ENGORGED

01.27 @ 3:06 AM: AN OPEN LETTER TO KILLER CHICK

Followed you tonight, killah. Wore a department store wig, thrift shop coat—just in case you really had spotted me in front of your place the other day. Kind of went too far—my oversized shades could have caught your eye as I carefully avoided staring at you from down the subway car. But I had nothing to worry about. You were inside yourself. Maybe you were reliving the experience of pushing the guy. Does it make a good memory for you? I bet it does.

We took the subway into the city. Most guys don't look twice at you, I notice—why the hell do I find you so hot, with your pinched face and your rubber-banded, tiny ponytail? You got up pretty abruptly to get off at Park Street, but I'd thought ahead and made sure to be standing near a door as soon as we got past Mass General. Good planning on my part because if I'd had to guess I'd have sworn you'd be heading to Hynes to check out the place where you actually pushed the dude. But that's not what was on your mind. Not tonight.

We walked from Park down through the shopping district and even though we were among the few people around I barely needed to worry about you spotting me, but then you headed into the financial district and I definitely needed to keep some distance between us. You never looked round as obviously you had no suspicion about being followed. You didn't walk fast but there was no doubt you were going somewhere,

I could tell. When we got to a street in the old Channel area where it was very dark and completely deserted, you did not slow down or check around you. You were confident—*self-possessed* is the word that's come to mind every time I've seen you, including right after you pushed the guy. It's a very cool quality you have.

When we got to a certain spot you looked up, studying a building. It was one of those old warehouses, made of grey stone and so a little different than the usual brick but not all that unusual. You stood there close to a minute, leaning back to see something. Then you faded back, crossing the wet, empty street without taking your eyes off the building. From the opposite sidewalk, you stared up at whatever the something was you were there to see.

I doubled back and trucked it like a son of a bitch around the block. This way I could come at you from the opposite direction and you'd have less reason to suspect that I'd been following you. I was worried that you wouldn't still be there, but when I got near I was happy to see that my gamble had paid off. You had your hands up to hold your collar together like you were cold. You had on your fingerless gloves.

God I want to bite down hard on those beautiful white fingers, one by one, eyeing your cold bloodless face to see how you handle the pain. Anything for you, Killer Chick.

I breathed down, which didn't take too long even though I'm out of shape compared to what I used to be, then I walked forward at what I hoped would come across as a normal pace. Walking by you was a risk, but I wanted to see what you were looking at.

When got about fifteen feet from you I glanced up at what you were so intent on watching, trying my hardest to come off as a guy who was just walking along, sees this girl looking up at a window, and then glances up himself out of curiosity. Problem was I couldn't quite put my finger on what it was we were looking at so I had to stop. The building was one of those converted warehouses, the type that are mixed use, some commercial and some residential—maybe with gang executions taking place down in the cellar even as dickweeds pay top dollar for the penthouse pads. It had a lot of big windows, the upper ones arched, some with fancy shades, some with what looked like sheets hanging over them. Up fairly high—maybe fourth or fifth floor—was one that caught my eye. There was some light coming from way back inside the place that made it less black than the other windows. I stopped and concentrated and, sure enough, the more I looked, the more I could tell that someone was moving around.

When I lowered my eyes, I was surprised to find you staring at me in a way that made it seem like you'd picked up that I wasn't just a passing stranger. Unfortunately I reacted by turning away and walking off quickly, which blew my whole thing of coming across as some passing dude. I'm sure I spooked you, and I'm sorry about that, but next time don't kill someone and expect to get away with it just because you're a hot chick.

Will you kill me eventually, Killer Chick? Lately I've been holding a blade up against my scrote whenever I jerk off. That's you in my head, Killer Chick. It's all you.

---

tALK. NIHILISt DOGS

garbo @ 01.27 04:34 am

You're sooooooooo hot.

garbo @ 01.27 04:38 am

I mean in a demented sort of way. I got a real soft spot for dumb guys.

garbo @ 01.27 04:44 am

Or do I mean creepy? Yeah that's it, you're a creepy, dim-witted sort of guy and all this makes me really hot for you. In any event, you can do me any time.

fullfrontal @ 01.27 04:53 am

you talk to yourself like this a lot, garbo? Cause I don't see no one answering.

garbo @ 01.27 05:04 am

A girl's got to amuse herself, does she not?

fullfrontal @ 01.27 05:05 am

Be my guest.

garbo @ 01.27 05:06 am

So how about that little get-together we've been putting off, sailor?

eddielizard @ 01.27 05:07 am

She is sum hoo-wah. Where you writin from chickie? Because I think I seein' you outside pokin at you cell right now. Look up at the man in the window little black hoo-wah with de titanic tits and the mountain of azz.

garbo @ 01.27 05:09 am

That's an actual whore you're trying to signal, loser. Better watch out or she'll take you up on it.

fullfrontal @ 01.27 05:10 am

Look you can blow me, OK? Mail me offsite. But if I show up and yer a dude it's off, got it?

garbo @ 01.27 06:14 am

Dudes do dudes better, dewd.

fullfrontal @ 01.27 06:16 am

I only swap with chicks. One of those primal things.

garbo @ 01.27 06:34 am

Chill, bruthah, I'm a chick. I can't help how you "read" me. And btw I swallow. We still on?

fullfrontal @ 01.27 07:03 am

bring a toothbrush.

13

LIFE IS PULP

Noir the Night Away With L.G. Fickel

January 27 @ 10:42 pm
>BIG BROTHER IS WA-A-ATCHING<

About all the hinting that Escroto is an azzzzz-hole: to some of you I may have been revealing some latent prejudices—am I anti-Hispanic? Nope: turns out the guy's simply an asshole. The warm smug feeling I'm nurturing at having got someone's number at first glance is some little solace, but all in all I'd rather not have lived through today. Here's why.

I decided to follow hitman's advice and so set up a "date" for myself this chillin' Saturday eve down at the police station, where I hoped to examine Mr. Suicide's diary—the original itself—in some sort of garbled attempt to gauge the handwriting, ink, mysterious smears, and anything else that might pop out at me when I opened it. I phoned ahead and the desk sergeant was as nice as pie. I don my wedge-heel lace-up boots and my faux-fur-trimmed coat, and thus I'm feeling kind of "kitted out," which my women readers know is a real confidence kickah. So I get to the cop shop around 4:45, that moment of dusk where night's kind of hovering overhead like a black cloth about to be dropped over the city's not-so-gilded cage. The station is "urban grim" in architecture, with a hell of a set of stone entry stairs jutting out, the obligatory twin ridged iron pedestals at either end of the stair's bottom step balancing their white orbs of light. Inside you've got your predictable study in oligarchical repression, the metal detector manned by drones with chubby holsters eyeing you to gauge whether you're a candidate for a strip search. I should have thought to leave my satchel at home—now the cops know that I'm reading an old print of *An Eye for an Eye*, wear Creed Santal, and carry o.b.'s for those on-the-road-time-of-the-month moments.

I ask for Burly-Bear, get sent up the medieval elevator, and step out into the checkerboard-floored corridor lined with pebble-glassed doors. I wander a bit and am just peeking over my shoulder at the elevator with some idea of backtracking when a door bangs open way down the hall and I see Escroto emerging from the restroom. He points a lazy finger at me as he saunters forward, then sticks his dry hand in mine.

Quickie side bitch to the guys out there—I get it that you consider ducking into the john just a "whip it, flick it, and zip it" affair—I'll even cop to being envious that you get to do it standing up—but wash your hands afterwards, for the rest of our sakes, huh? I don't relish the idea of shaking a hand that's recently been shaking a dick, and I think I speak for the rest of us non-pigs, both male and female, in saying so. Thanx! :)

Any-ho, I ask whether he might direct me to Burly-Bear, and he retorts that he will escort me in to see the man, all the while sizing me up with derision in his beady eyes. Like, what? Am I supposed to feel put down at the idea that I'm not trampy enough for his personal fuk fantasies?

Note to Escroto—the day you see the inside of my undies will be the day you identify me in the morgue.

So he leads me into a kind of desk corral and that's when Escroto does this stagey finger-snap and "recalls" that Burly-Bear is not available but is there anything that he may do for me?

I'm not exactly sure that he knows about Burly-Bear having given me a copy of Mr. Suicide's diary, and if he does not know then I sure don't want to be the one to spill it. So I just tell him that I might be able to assist them by taking a look at Mr. Suicide's diary. Naturally, if Escroto doesn't know that I already have a copy of the diary, my offer comes off as a flimsy attempt to lay my eyes on it, but I take solace in the fact that there isn't any real harm in his concluding that I'm just "some nosy clit."

I ask and he smirks and licks at his moustache—I think this is supposed to come across as "mulling." Fact is, it turns out, he has something else entirely on his brain, so, after deflecting the question of my seeing the diary, he gets to another topic. I'll do it in dialog so you can get a flavor for what a class act Escroto is:

Scene: cop corral—Escroto resting a haunch on the desk while I stand, my satchel tight on my shoulder like I've got leaving on the brain.

Escroto: Funny thing, you comin' here tonight.

Me: I aim to amuse.

Escroto: Something I want you to see. Surveillance shot from—waddayawannacallit—throwback music store you went into after the concert that evening. You know, before you hit the train station. (He reaches back, grabs a yellow envelope, and tosses it onto Burly-Bear's desk.)

Me: Why do I get the feeling you're trying to get my fingerprints all over whatever's in here?

Escroto: Dunno.

I extract a pile of overexposed black-and-white photo shots printed on shit-stock paper, apparently from a security surveillance camera. Each has a date and time stamp, digital monitor style. After a long moment, I catch on that the woman in the pictures is me. Black-and-white aerial is not my angle. My forehead and nose glare, my hair drapes my head like a shroud. My coat is shorter than I'd imagined, my skirt longer. I look thinner and less shapely than I like to think of myself. Overall, I come off as stand-off-ish.

Me: So what does this prove? I told you I was there before I went to the train station that night, and, lo and behold, there I am. What's the point?

Escroto: (studying me through his little spy cam eyes, no pretense at anything resembling friendliness now) Look a little harder, huh?

I leaf through the photos, come across a string of them in which a man is next to me, reaching for the same record I'm reaching for. We appear to glance at one another, maybe exchange a word. The sequence lasts about ten pictures, which seems to correspond to maybe fifteen seconds. It ends with the man leaving the camera range as I study the back of a record.

Me: Any clue about what I'm supposed to be seeing here, detective?

Escroto: (his turn at sarcasm) Aw, don't give up so easy. Give 'em another look, eh?

Me: (chilly sigh)

I look down at the photos, push them around so I can see several at once. The man's not very tall and is wearing dark clothes and a scarf that strikes me as a tiny bit fey. His face is mostly a glare, but I can make out what looks like a cleft chin, longish hair. Then I flash back on the subway station, the man's face dislodged from his skull, lying half-wrinkled against his chest with empty eyes. It's beyond memory—a reliving. The fact is I had no true recollection of what I'd witnessed in the subway station until there in the station, standing next to Escroto, viewing the surveillance photos and seeing Mr. Suicide, alive and smiling at me as we reached for the same record. Needing to steady myself, I place my fingers against Burly-Bear's desk and close my eyes, then immediately open them, afraid to be alone in my head with that image.

Escroto: Use a seat? (He nudges Burly-Bear's chair with his leg and it swivels an inch or two in my direction. I sit, more or less abruptly.) Waddah?

Me: (catching on) Oh. Water. No. Yes. Yes, actually. (I breathe consciously for a few moments, willing the death image back to the recesses of my brain, where it burrows itself, ready to spring out again in all its funhouse glory.)

Escroto: (resettling his haunch as he offers me the paper cup) You look a little shocked.

Me: I'd forgotten his face.

Escroto: Yeah, just, uh, take your time and let me know when you're ready to talk about it.

Me: Talk about what?

Escroto: (lazily scratching at his inner thigh) Howzabout the fact that you was shopping with a guy—a so-called stranger—maybe ten minutes before he got killed by a train directly at your feet. Guy you're supposed to not know, way you've been tellin' it.

Me: I wasn't shopping with him; I was browsing the vinyls next to him.

Escroto: You usually smile at guys you're browsing next to when they grab your ass?

Me: What?

Escroto: (leaning in, then dropping a finger on one photo. In it, it's true that it looks like the man is touching the back of my coat, his hand slightly cupped. Could be that he's either about to squeeze my butt or might be already doing it, if you *really* want to see it that way.)

Me: He never touched me.

Escroto: (jamming the finger against the picture) He's touching. And you're not surprised.

Me: We reached for the same record, smiled, and he walked off. There's nothing else.

Escroto: (sitting back). Pretty big coincidence, wouldn't you say? You and him checking out the records together, then you and him in the subway station together.

Me: (sensing I've won a point) The store is above the T. You see people with old records in that station all the time. Am I supposed to believe that you don't know that?

Escroto: What I know and what I can prove might be two different things. (He nods like there's a subtext going on between us, which there isn't.)

Me: (something dawning on me) This is the classical section.

Escroto: Howzat?

Me: I'm reaching for *Le Printemps du Spring*, the music I'd just been listening to at a concert hall near to there. So is—so is this man.

Escroto: Now he was at the concert with you? Kind of works against your "strangers in the night" story, wouldn't you say?

Me: I bet he was there—it fits.

Escroto: Fits?

Me: His place, his clothes, his diary, Stravinsky at the Berklee—all the same guy. So he must have walked over to buy a vinyl of what he'd just heard.

Escroto: (sarcastically) Oh, just like you did?

Me: Exactly. It makes total sense.

Escroto: (He thinks a little, and when he talks, I realize that we're actually in a conversation, at least for the moment.) You know what don't go with that, though?

Me: What?

Escroto: Guy buying a record after a concert, smiling at some girl. Don't go with suicide a couple of minutes later. Not to me.

Me: I agree. It barely seems possible.

I pick up one of the surveillance photos and study it. I recognize the perfunctory smile on my face. I'd have offered a flutter of eye movement in his direction, exactly enough to qualify as polite and no more. If you focus on just me, Mr. Suicide and I are strictly strangers, a pair of secret agents passing microfilm. *But, as I study the shots, I decide that Mr. Suicide isn't quite as cool and casual.* The way he heads directly for me, the sharp turn of his head to look at my face when we almost collide. He smiles big and his eyes are aimed at mine. In other words:

he'd bumped me on purpose in that store—only to go and bump me on purpose 15 minutes later, on his way off the platform!

I look up, excited to share this observation, and find Escroto staring at me with his dead eyes.

I think it's the outrageous unfairness of the game the cops are playing that makes me become very angry at that moment. Obviously they know a lot about Mr. Suicide by now. Obviously they must have concluded that he didn't commit suicide and that he was involved in some relationship that could have made someone crazy enough to shove him in front of a train—they must think this or they'd be off my back. And obviously they don't know all that much about that dangerous relationship or, again, they'd be off my back. What particularly galls and frustrates me, however, is that I'm sure that if the damned police would just let me know what they know, I'd actually be good at helping them solve their little bullshit mystery.

Me: I don't have anything else to say about these. I need to get somewhere.

Escroto: Thought you was looking to take a gander at the guy's diary. Wasn't that it?

Me: I don't have time to do that anymore. I'll do it another time.

Escroto: (pauses—I pause, too, as if seeking his permission to leave—which apparently satisfies him. I watch him gather the photo copies off

Burly-Bear's desk and slide them back into the envelope, then reach back behind himself to drop it back where it came from, which was sitting on top of an open copy of some book with the word "confession" in its title. *How to Extract a False Confession*, perhaps? *Confession of a Corrupt Cop*? At least he can read, which surprises me a little. Finally he speaks.) Suit yourself.

He watches me make my way out of there. I leave in a daze. I get home. I sit. I blog.

GIVE IT TO ME STRAIGHT

i.went.to.harvard @ January 27 11:37 pm

What happened to this lawyer of yours? Shouldn't you be deflecting characters like this Escroto by throwing Mr. Groin's name at him?

fickel @ January 27 11:42 pm

You try it when they're flashing pix at you and accusing you of canoodling with the dead guy.

i.went.to.harvard @ January 27 11:45 pm

Look, we know you were expecting the nice cop and the nasty one threw you, but you gotta keep that lawyer card in the back of your mind. Mr. Groin will find out Mr. Suicide's identity if you ask him to, regardless of whatever strategy the cops think they're playing out.

marleybones @ January 27 11:53 pm

But what to make of this weird record shop moment?

webmaggot @ January 27 11:54 pm

Do you remember anyone bumping your butt?

fickel @ January 27 11:56 pm

Now that I've seen the pictures it seems like it happened, since it must have. But he made no impression on me—he definitely did not do anything that seemed like a come-on. Oh, this is such a nightmare! It wasn't until today that I really minded what was going on, but now I'm feeling really close to this death. For the first time I get that I *do* have a connection to it.

chinkigirl @ January 28 12:23 am

fickel, you seem to be intimating that Mr. Suicide's casual encounter with you wasn't as casual as it would appear. I don't want to send you to a darker place, but do you think it's possible that in spite of your not knowing Mr. Suicide maybe the reverse was not true?

fickel @ January 28 12:37 am

You mean that he knew me.

chinkigirl @ January 28 12:38 am

Well, yes.

marleybones @ January 28 12:59 am

I believe that what chinkigirl is getting at, and what fickel is beginning to accept, is something that I think all the women on the blog have been wondering from the start: the possibility that Mr. Suicide may have been stalking her. That is, it's possible that Mr. S was following fickel around due to some obsession he'd developed over her. That's not a conclusion a woman is likely to draw all that easily or "sensibly;" hence my hesitation to bring it up earlier.

fickel @ January 28 01:03 am

Hold on a sec—I'm accepting *what*?

marleybones @ January 28 01:04 am

Look, I don't like the idea of putting words into someone else's mouth. chinkigirl?

chinkigirl @ January 28 01:05 am

Well, it's a theory that explains a couple of things. If Mr. Suicide somehow knew you, met you in passing and got—I don't know—obsessed with you, wouldn't that explain your presence in his flickr and his smiling at your face in a record shop and...well...

fickel @ January 28 01:08 am

You're suggesting that there was nothing random about his committing suicide in front of me—that it was something he meant for *me* to see?

chinkigirl @ January 28 01:14 am

All I'm saying is that people who are lonely and obsessive can get fixated on a stranger and maybe make them a significant figure in their lives, if they're that far gone.

fickel @ January 28 01:15 am

But why me?

webmaggot @ January 28 01:17 am

You look easy?

fickel @ January 28 01:18 am

But I *don't* look easy. Nothing promising whatsoever, from a "Dear *Penthouse* Forum" perspective, and certainly nothing to get obsessed over, if I may be so frank a critic of myself.

marleybones @ January 28 01:24 am

Well, maybe he thought you were attractive, even very attractive, yet cold. Maybe he fixated on you because he craved being rejected by you. I mean, we are talking about a guy who took a dive in front of the T as a means of escaping his problems.

fickel @ January 28 01:26 am

What you're saying is that maybe I'm walking around depressing lonely men whose eye I happen to catch because I come off so icy.

hitman @ January 28 01:27 am

Fatal without even trying. Spider-woman: deadlier than the male.

wazzup! @ January 28 01:31 am

Original title of *Born to Kill*!!!!!!! Another reference spotted! I live for this stuff!!!

hitman @ January 28 01:32 am

wtf?

wazzup! @ January 28 01:33 am

You gave homage to a NOIR CLASSIC—*Deadlier than the Male* was the book title and also original film title of one of the great noir flicks: *Born to Kill*. Female lead, anyone quickly?

36-D @ January 28 01:36 am

Well, it's way off topic but it was Claire Trevor. Back to the point: fickel's not cold or standoffish or any of that.

hitman @ January 28 01:38 am

You can tell that from the blog?

36-D @ January 28 01:39 am

Absolutely. I think I know something—a lot, even—about every one of the regulars on this blog I think we all do.

hitman @ January 28 01:41 am

Interesting, because what I get is that we are a bunch of people with not much in common except that we are into a *misanthropic* art style—who are using this anonymous form of interrelating as a substitute for socializing. I would say that the chances are pretty high that most if not all of us are not that friendly in our day-to-day lives.

chinkigirl @ January 28 01:44 am

Well, I'm actually pretty gregarious. I just find this blog utterly fun. And I love the connection with Boston, a city I'll always adore because it's where I met my husband and did my training, and got knocked up for the first time. fickel's site is just something I do after the rest of the household goes down; it's like my "me" hour. Sorry to blow your theory, hitman.

hitman @ January 28 01:47 am

Theory intact. You could be an exception, chinkigirl, or, of course, you could be scamming us. You could be some lonely, toothless old alcoholic.

proudblacktrannie @ January 28 01:49 am

Oh, get serious. I know I wouldn't be here, whatever my own situation, except that fickel is NOT cold or repelling. She is what attracted me to visit twice, then three times, and now nightly. It's her VOICE, people.

roadrage @ January 28 01:55 am

ditto, mon.

fickel @ January 28 01:57 am

Look, I love the idea that I've got this inviting web voice. But hitman is right, my persona could be completely different offline. I mean, I could be this person to whom Mr. Suicide could be attracted but unable to approach.

marleybones @ January 28 02:01 am

But you aren't.

fickel @ January 28 02:02 am

How do you know? How do I know, for that matter? It seems to me that those of us with just a touch of evil—the social drinker who causes an auto fatality, the parent with high standards who beats his child, the big man on campus who commits date rape, the judgmental woman who drives a man to desperation—would be the least likely to recognize the danger they are, the hell they visit upon their victims.

wazzup! @ January 28 02:04 am

Ah-ha, you f**k with our heads, clever one! Ha, ha, Claire Trevor!!!

fickel @ January 28 02:08 am

I'm not kidding. Maybe I'll be lucky enough to laugh later, when this thing plays out, but right now chinkigirl's theory that Mr. Suicide somehow drove himself to despair rings too true to just blow by. And it's chilling, truly chilling, to think that I might have caught someone's attention, I mean really hooked a man, and yet, all at the same time, that I might have come across as so full of foreboding and the promise of pain that a man might kill himself rather than risk approaching me.

chinkigirl @ January 28 02:10 am

Honestly, all I was focusing on was the depth of depression that someone might suffer that could make him fixate on some blameless woman. The woman could be anyone.

fickel @ January 28 02:12 am

Well, she was me. And, unfortunately, what you say reminds me of something from my past. So I'm not so sure that the woman who drives a man to suicide is so blameless just because she doesn't know him.

proudblacktrannie @ January 28 02:14 am

What from your past, luv?

fickel @ January 28 02:16 am

Not now. Let's just say someone harmed himself because of me.

hitman @ January 28 02:17 am

Jesus, fickel, get a grip.

proudblacktrannie @ January 28 02:18 am

yes, you really must. Go out back behind your building, knock on Burly-Bear's car window, and invite him in for a drink. u need to.

hitman @ January 28 02:25 am

fickel?

hitman @ January 28 02:45 am

Yo, fickel?

proudblacktrannie @ January 28 02:53 am

hopefully you took my advice, my lovely.

chinkigirl @ January 28 08:34 am

Somehow I don't think so, guys.

14

LIFE IS PULP

Feed the Beast With L.G. Fickel

January 28 @ 7:42 pm
>ME AND MY DEADLY JE NE SAIS QUOI<

Sorry to cut off so abruptly last night. I've spent the Sabbath attempting to get used to the realization that the explanation for this whole so-called mystery may be the one chinkigirl got us onto: a man with a tendency toward depression gets obsessed with me, follows me around for a year, and then kills himself out of despair over his unrequited love for me. Why that love would have been unrequited—he being a successful art-y type—is where the story makes no sense, of course. I mean, whatever made him presume that it was inevitable that he'd suffer so much unhappiness because of me that he was better off skipping all the middle stuff and ending it? It had to have been something he conjured up out of how I come across to strangers. And, obviously, on some level he considered it my fault that we would be unhappy together, because killing himself in front of me could only have been meant as a punishment of some sort. But the thing I cannot get past, is why he wouldn't at least *try* to approach me? I haven't been involved with anyone for a while, and if this guy was keeping tabs on me he'd know that. So what is it about me that made him so sure we were doomed before we even got started?

GIVE IT TO ME STRAIGHT

i.went.to.harvard @ January 28 08:02 pm

Maybe you got it right at the police station, fickel, and you just happened to be at the same concert as Mr. Suicide and then both of you just took the logical route to a record shop and the T on a night when he'd already decided to kill himself. Maybe the concert was his last, I don't know, celebration before he knocked himself off. Maybe at the record shop you just caught his eye and played the role of his "escort" to death's door.

marleybones @ January 28 08:14 pm

Folks who decide to commit suicide often spend their final days seeming pretty content. I've heard it a bunch of times, that a suicide's relatives were thinking that he was finally coping with his depression in the days just before the death, when he was actually planning his suicide.

fickel @ January 28 08:16 pm

But I was also in his flickr, remember?

hitman @ January 28 08:17 pm

Screw that—Boston's a small city with an even smaller nightlife. You're telling me you couldn't possibly have crossed paths with this guy ever before when he was out shooting pics? If you both like Stravinsky (pause to power puke) then you have some taste thing in common.

fickel @ January 28 08:19 pm

Huh. I'll have to think about this. Oh bloody hell someone's been leaning on my buzzer for the past ten minutes, and now he's playing a tune with it. Probably looking to buy some dope from upstairs. I better get rid of him.

LATER—LATER—LATER—LATER

Hi, blog. I see I never signed off. Just had dinner—well, if you want to call scallion rice and a finger of scotch "dinner"—with my brother, who is in the bedroom, sleeping off whatever he was on upon arrival.

webmaggot @ January 28 11:14 pm

Wait—your brother shows up and you put him in your bedroom?

36-D @ January 28 11:16 pm

Always count on webmaggot for that touch of grossness you thought you could live without. Obviously this is a younger—read SPOILED—brother.

wazzup! @ January 28 11:17 pm

Har-har-har, I am lurking at exactly the correct moment and have one word: *This World Then the Fireworks*! Score!!!!

webmaggot @ January 28 11:18 pm

Wouldn't that be 5 words?

roadrage @ January 28 11:19 pm

He's Dutch, give him a break.

fickel @ January 28 11:21 pm

Actually, my brother is technically younger, but just by one minute. And I put him in the bedroom because I like to blog out here. He snores like a fat cow, which is interesting because he is about the skinniest man ever. You can practically see his heart beating through his chest, or you used to be able to before the tattoos got solid. As you can guess, we're exactly alike. (That's sarcasm, although we are very much on a wavelength in certain ways.) Anyway, on the bedroom thing, I actually often sleep on the couch, which is this old daybed that I absolutely love to do everything on—eat, read, roost, even blog when I get utterly sick of my desk chair (old wooden swivel chair with plastic pad cushions—my *other* favorite piece of furniture). The bedroom, on the other hand, is dank and tiny and faces the street so I can never open the shades. And the radiator clanks. And the boys upstairs smoke dope directly above, like, 24/7. So I use it kind of like a storage room for my clothes. Plus the TV is in there, which my brother is into (sports—preferably of the "extreme" variety) and I am not like him in that way. Go Revolution. There—I've just exhausted my repertoire of sports talk.

proudblacktrannie @ January 28 11:34 pm

O my lord you have a twin—SO DO I. My twin and I are "identical"—not that you can tell anymore being as he is a straight-arrow power tool and I am...well, just about diviiiiiiiiiiine, lately. Ironically, he has a smaller wobbly than I do—mine is *such* an annoyance when I'm in something skimpy. And so annoying for my brother, all growing up—he's competitive about *everything*. In any event, twins are bonded no matter what—no wonder you and I are simpatico, fickel dahling. Is your brother like mine in being totally macho and ruled by the code of the sword—in other words the divining rod between his thighs?

fickel @ January 28 11:39 pm

Never thought of it quite like that, but I'm pretty sure he'd be comfortable with that description of his "picaresque" path through life. I don't know that's he's all that randy—it's more a matter of testosterone messing up his judgment We're very close, but I'm not sure that's a twin thing. We never had much family and it's been kind of tough, particularly when one of us got into trouble.

chinkigirl @ January 28 11:44 pm

What happened to your parents, if it's not out of line to ask?

fickel @ January 28 11:51 pm

Not to get into it too deeply, but my father left this world rather abruptly when my brother and I were about ten, and my mother put us in boarding school while she got her life back together, which has yet to happen. My brother would get in trouble in school—put it down to an "artistic temperament"—so we made our way through a few of your lesser-known private schools, by which I mean the kind that you go to when you get kicked out of another private school. Then I landed at McGill, even scored some money to get me through. My brother went to New York City and then suddenly moved in on my mother in rural—and it does get rural—Massachusetts. I don't ask what he does for cash. I don't ask why he shows up when he shows up. My role is to like him—that's what he needs me for and, frankly, it comes natural. That said, I'm actually a little nervous about him being here.

36-D @ January 28 11:56 pm

You're afraid of your own brother?

fickel @ January 28 11:58 pm

Not afraid *of* him. I think that he's on parole. You're not supposed to go wherever you want, and particularly not to places where there are "temptations."

i.went.to.harvard @ January 29 12:09 am

What temptations are there in Boston? Running the ten-minute red lights?

chinkigirl @ January 29 12:14 am

Try drugs. My own brother got busted scoring some ecstasy at MIT.

What a squid, but, as you like to say, i.went.to.harvard, that's another story for another day.

proudblacktrannie @ January 29 12:17 am

Ah, I feel like I know this boy. Welcome to the family, fickel's brother. I know you're not into real names on your blog, fickel—shall we refer to your male alter ego as fickel-bro?

roadrage @ January 29 12:19 am

limp. Hey what about dickel, as in fickel with a dick?

proudblacktrannie @ January 29 12:20 am

oh now that's *hot*

fickel @ January 29 12:22 am

Then dickel it is. In any event, I am more than comfortable having him here, but here's hoping that we're talking about a day or so and then back to wherever he's supposed to be. And I hope he doesn't get drunk and piss in my sink again. Do you KNOW how long it took for me to wash a dish after that?

leo tolstoy @ January 29 02:44 am

...as soon as I gave in to base desires I was praised and encouraged...

fickel @ January 29 07:25 am

Sigh. Hi, leo tolstoy whoever you be. Aren't you...lost in the ether yet? Hint, hint?

15

LIFE IS PULP

Noir the Night Away With L.G. Fickel

January 29 @ 8:42 pm
>I GO SHAMELESSLY SHAMUS<

Okay, finally I will answer chinkigirl's question from some nights ago. I've been going by Mr. Suicide's place. That's how I knew the cops had removed his name from his buzzer. And last night I discovered that someone in there has discovered that I am out here. So now what?

GIVE IT TO ME STRAIGHT

marleybones @ January 29 08:50 pm

Umm, can we back up a skosh? What is "going by Mr. Suicide's place" about?

fickel @ January 29 08:55 pm

Well, it's about...taking control...?

i.went.to.harvard @ January 29 08:59 pm

Not catching your drift, here.

fickel @ January 29 09:17 pm

Sigh. What I mean is that it just keeps echoing around in my head all day, while I'm trying to function, that I may have actually tortured some guy into killing himself.

i.went.to.harvard @ January 29 09:20 pm

So you go by his place? What do you do there, if we may know?

fickel @ January 29 09: 46 pm

I hang around. I watch the neighbors come and go, and wonder if any of them ever notices that the well-dressed guy from upstairs has disappeared. Sometimes I sit on the stoop across the street. I think. Strange, I guess?

hitman @ January 29 10:06 pm

We're talking once, twice, you've gone by the guy's place?

fickel @ January 29 10:09 pm

Let's call it several times. Late at night. The other night I noticed a light on inside Mr. Suicide's place, and so I stood there trying to will whoever it was to come to the window. Finally I rang the buzzer and no one answered, and then I walked back across the street to look up at the window, and I could see that there was someone up there, standing in the dark, looking down at me.

proudblacktrannie @ January 29 10:30 pm

What are you getting your sweet ass into, baby?

marleybones @ January 29 10:33 pm

This is getting a little morbid. Dwelling on the fact of someone's suicide is going down a twisted path.

hitman @ January 29 10:35 pm

Could we maybe just turn down the psychobabble a notch? So fickel, tell me this: what was it like, standing outside the dude's place and suddenly having it come to you that the dark-against-the-dark shape in the window above was someone staring down at you?

fickel @ January 29 10:36 pm

Well...it was noirish. ;)

hitman @ January 29 10:37 pm

CYA, bitch! Dig it! There's more, though. I get that sense?

fickel @ January 29 10:59 pm

There is more, in fact. Oh, fukk-a-dukk, be right back.

Okay, my main man is tucked in and snoring (why do I find comfort in that godawful noise?) No idea where he was until this ungodly hour, but of course I know not to ask. This, plus the fact that I've just thrown back a shot of something hard and cheap, has got me in the right mood for revealing.

So, after I did the shadow-to-shadow confrontation with whoever it was in Mr. Suicide's window and my brain finished tingling from the sensation of being a part of the naked city where no one sleeps, yada, yada, yada...I go for a walk. It's very quiet in Mr. Suicide's neighborhood on a Sunday eve, and I hear the sound of my heels echoing off the wet sidewalks. When I look up, there's the blue neon glow from a sign that reads:

ALL NIGHT (with a flickering "t").

The diner squatting below it is as grim as I've imagined it from Mr. Suicide's diary.

Let me give you a visual: tiny, narrow, almost otherworldly in its ugliness, presided over by an old geezer with a nose like a burnt potato under a radiator-rack forehead, sizzling hash and fried eggs that smell for all the world like flesh being cooked. There's a skin-and-bones calico crouched on the counter eating something off a plate, and an undernourished black man with scarred-up facial skin lurking way down where there might be some heat hovering in the air. The bum peeks out at me from behind some grey rasta stocking cap that hangs down the side of his head like a deflated condom. He's nervous—maybe the last woman he laid an eyeball on had him thrown in the can for even thinking in her direction.

I slip onto a stool, making the universal mime for coffee. The grill geezer flips his wiping cloth up onto his shoulder, then shuffles over and pours some black stuff into—I shyte ye not, gentle readers—a thick ceramic coffee cup with a faded navy stripe around its rim, along with the traces of some other woman's lipstick.

By now I'm, like, so Barbara Stanwyck it ain't funny. I shoot Grill Geezer a gruff "Thanks, Joe," and light myself a Lucky, shaking the match just so. Grill Geezer turns away to take a poke at the eggs, then slides a bothered look at me, like he's trying to place me but can't quite get there. Finally he tilts his chin my way.

Grill Geezer: Crim, you wanna? (Greek accent.)

Me: (I glance around and notice a couple of little metal creamers along the counter. The little bum's hoarding one, trying to shield it from my view with a quavering hand.) I'm good. (I sip.)

Grill Geezer: (transfers hash and eggs to a plate, goes down and skids it in front of the bum, then comes back to scrape around at the remnants. His curiosity about me is waning.)

Me: (pitching for casual) Hear about that suicide in the T?

Grill Geezer: (shrugs)

Me: Shame. Successful guy. Came in here a lot. You must miss him.

Grill Geezer: (scrapes a little more, then gives me an evil eyeball) Whaddayo wann?

Me: I'm just trying to understand. (I offer what I hope comes off as a jaded smile.)

Grill Geezer: So sure. Mistah Pale was in here some a time. He liked a work a night. What else you wanna ax?

Me: (encouraged) You know anyone he used to come in with? I'd like to talk to them.

Grill Geezer: Nah, I done know nuttin' like dat.

Me: I'm just trying to find his friends.

Grill Geezer: Yeah, that's good. You go fine em. Talk to um. (walks away)

I slip a buck under my saucer and leave. Mostly I'm psyched that I've gotten Mr. Suicide's name, or at least a lead on it. Since then, btw, I've poked around on the web and have found nary a Mr. Pale (or Payle or Palle, etc.) who could possibly be our Mr. S. But I'm sure that with a little persistence I'll shake out the right name.

So...thoughts?

i.went.to.harvard @ January 29 11:21 pm

You smoke? Somehow that doesn't jibe with my image of you.

fickel @ January 29 11:22 pm

What do you mean? Oh—that line about the Lucky Strike was just me casting myself as Stanwyck. The rest, however, is all gospel truth. TBH, like most twits of my generation, there was a time when I worked to cultivate a smoking habit. dickel and I used to steal cigarettes from my uncle and smoke them down behind the train station. dickel's habit stuck, mine didn't.

marleybones @ January 29 11:26 pm

My sisters and I used to pull the same stunt on my mom until she caught on and we got our asses handed to us. Your uncle never caught on to you?

fickel @ January 29 11:31 pm

Well, maybe he did and maybe he didn't. He wasn't the tattletale type.

marleybones @ January 29 11:36 pm

Ever think to ask him about it now?

fickel @ January 29 11:38 pm

That'd be tough. He lived with us for a short time a loooong time ago when I was, like, ten. I'm not even sure if he and I would recognize one another if we bumped shoulders on the street.

i.went.to.harvard @ January 29 11:42 pm

Hmmm, I smell a family feud.

fickel @ January 29 11:44 pm

Could have been. If so, I wasn't in on it.

marleybones @ January 29 11:47 pm

Ever think to ask your mom or dad about it? Family stuff's often very important when you're trying to figure out where you are in life.

fickel @ January 29 11:48 pm

My father's dead, remember?

marleybones @ January 29 11:50 pm

Of course. Sorry about that.

fickel @ January 29 11:51 pm

Don't be. Again, it was a looooooong time ago.

i.went.to.harvard @ January 29 11:52 pm

Mind my asking how he died? I ask because my both my parents died of alcoholism, and I've found myself wondering if you had a similar family history. Naturally, feel free to ignore the question if it's not something you care to blog about.

hitman @ January 30 12:55 am

Hmm, an hour later. Nice one, harvard man.

i.went.to.harvard @ January 30 01:04 am

Apologies. We children of alcoholics are always seeking kindred spirits.

marleybones @ January 30 01:05 am

My view is that i.went.to.harvard pitched his question about as well as it could be done. If fickel chooses not to answer him, that's cool, but there's no reason to jump on him.

36-D @ January 30 01:07 am

Hi, just on. Look, fickel's in kind of a tough place right now. Let's not scare up additional ghosts for her to contend with.

hitman @ January 30 01:08 am

WTF "additional ghosts?" Mr. Suicide's not from her past. He's from the other day...unless you're starting to think that fickel really did have a history with Mr. Suicide?

36-D @ January 30 01:09 am

I think *he* had one with *her*, in his head. That's what I think.

hitman @ January 30 01:10 am

Oh, the "stalker" theory.

marleybones @ January 30 01:14 am

Not stalker. Lurker.

hitman @ January 30 01:15 am

The difference?

marleybones @ January 30 01:16 am

Maybe Mr. Suicide was a lurker on this blog. Maybe he got to know fickel over this year through our conversations, and figured out who she was in real life. Maybe he took to following her in real life in addition to following her online.

36-D @ January 30 01:18 am

I just got goosebumps, literally.

marleybones @ January 30 01:19 am

I'm not trying to scare anyone, but this all starts to make sense when you look at it that way.

proudblacktrannie @ January 30 01:25 am

OMG—could fickel actually BE the "E" in Mr. Suicide's diary? I mean, let us face some facts: the cops know Mr. Suicide's identity, and they've without a doubt figured out who his friends and acquaintances are, meaning who his lovers might be...

i.went.to.harvard @ January 30 01:28 am

So if there was someone else who could fit the bill as E...

proudblacktrannie @ January 30 01:30 am

yes, yes *exactly*. In that case, they wouldn't continue to be hassling fickel.

marleybones @ January 30 01:31 am

But that doesn't make fickel "E."

hitman @ January 30 01:32 am

If I was a cop, I'd think it came close.

36-D @ January 30 01:34 am

Lemme get this straight—we think that E actually is fickel and that Mr. Suicide, like, fantasized the entire relationship, how it went sour, how she cheated on him, how he finally decided to kill himself because of her... Now THAT's out of a Cornell Woolrich.

i.went.to.harvard @ January 30 01:38 am

Ahh, one of the great dark minds of American pulp. Wasn't he a suicide, too?

marleybones @ January 30 01:39 am

Plus there was something about a diary in Woolrich's past. His wife's?

wazzup! @ January 30 01:40 am

Permit me, my dearest of friends! Woolrich was a closeted *homosexual* and eventually killed himself with much drink, and all of the sordid details of his gay experimentation were in a diary he left for the wife he had deserted, most probably to hurt her most terribly!!!!!! Anyone else seeing too many comparisons here for coincidence, as am I?????

36-D @ January 30 01:45 am

Wait, so now we're thinking that Mr. Suicide made up everything in his *diary*, including *E*?

proudblacktrannie @ January 30 01:48 am

It's a man's private book that he wrote in at night. Why shouldn't it be a fantasy? Nighttime is all about fantasy. Believe me, I make a good living off of that fact.

webmaggot @ January 30 01:49 am

Sup blog, just on—my luv life is suddenly keeping me BUSY (and naked!). So we're thinking that Mr. Suicide fantasized about fickel being a cold, slutty bitch who he obsessed over while she half lived with him and started boffing at least one other guy—am I pretty much caught up?

proudblacktrannie @ January 30 01:51 am

And the "relationship" got so painful that he killed himself...

marleybones @ January 30 01:52 am

...punishing fickel for her imaginary sins by offing himself in front of her...

i.went.to.harvard @ January 30 01:53 am

...which makes her real "sin" her simply being the fantasy.

36-D @ January 30 01:54 am

{{{{{{{ Group shuddah }}}}}}}

roadrage @ January 30 01:55 am

Sorry. Another freakin night shift—why do the stars insist on coming out at night? One thing I want to stick in—there *was* a real E—remember the silk panties in his bedroom?

36-D @ January 30 01:56 am

Uhh, don't some guys use those as a..."girlfriend?"

marleybones @ January 30 01:57 am

As in: maybe the panties were part of the fantasy.

proudblacktrannie @ January 30 01:58 am

I have more silks than I can count, and each one is its own fantasy, but then intimates are a professional thing with me.

fickel @ January 30 02:01 am

Hi. Sorry to have been AFC, but I had a thing to get straight with my brother, and when I finally got back it seemed best to just watch you night owls work collectively for a while.

Look, I have to confess something—deep breath—my father attempted suicide by lying down in front of a train. I think the cops know about it, and I think that it just adds to the list of coincidences that are keeping them interested in me in connection with Mr. Suicide's death.

proudblacktrannie @ January 30 02:06 am

Lawdy.

marleybones @ January 30 02:07 am

I admire your honesty, fickel. Must be extremely difficult to get into this.

fickel @ January 30 02:08 am

I'm not feeling very honest at the moment, after having kept that to myself for all this time.

roadrage @ January 30 02:10 am

Look, have you thought about bringing this up with Burly-Bear, since you're sure he already knows about it anyway? Sort of gauge his reaction to your coming clean?

i.went.to.harvard @ January 30 02:11 am

I strongly advise against approaching anyone but Mr. Groin with this. As a substitute, you might consider discussing it with the Colonel. No one else.

hitman @ January 30 02:12 am

Wait a sec. You said your father "attempted suicide," not that he committed it.

webmaggot @ January 30 02:13 am

Dood. With a train there ain't much difference.

fickel @ January 30 02:14 am

Sigh. Actually there is. My father lay down on a freight line. The train passed over him. Snagged him somehow, and broke his pelvis. Sliced his foot off, plus half of one hand, including the four fingers (the thumb remained intact). The engineer never saw a thing, but some people found him in the morning. So he survived. He was never himself again, and died a year later. Killed himself. Bottle of pills, this time. I was away at school when it happened. My mother didn't tell me for several months. She didn't want me and my brother coming home. She'd kind of had it with the lot of us by then. There. Now you know the worst.

hitman @ January 30 02:16 am

Yeah, brave girl and all. One question, though: WHY?

fickel @ January 30 02:17 am

Why wouldn't I blog about this readily? Guess, dipstick.

hitman @ January 30 02:18 am

No, WHY did the old man do it?

36-D @ January 30 02:19 am

Gawd. Learn some limits.

marleybones @ January 30 02:20 am

Well, you can give me a 1 a.m. verbal drubbing, too, 36-D (must be after 2 for you east-coasters!), but I think hitman's got a point. I think we need some brutal honesty here if we're going to do any good, and I think we *can* do some good. fickel's father's attempted train suicide is a frightening coincidence that the cops either are or will be all over. We bloggers—we're groping with only those senses we can translate into semilucid prose. If we're going to strategize on fickel's behalf we need whatever pertinent information we can get. If that's not going to be possible, well, back to fan fiction.

fickel @ January 30 02:27 am

I understand. I had a feeling it would get like this. So here goes.

My father was unstable from way back. Life was so unfair to him I can't even begin to describe it. He and my mother (and her brother) were their own little reenactment of the Quebec diaspora, and they settled in one of those sad "little Canada" communities. So they were poor, but only she was poor by nature, a Canuck my father fell for due to some heroic misperception that he could "save" her. I don't think she gave a shit about my father for a minute—okay, maybe before they were married, but she's the type who instantly loses respect for anyone who has low enough standards to associate themselves with her. Anyway, anyone else could see that my father had talents beyond the average man, sensitivities beyond what was good for him.

i.went.to.harvard @ January 30 02:34 am

You blame your mother for his death.

fickel @ January 30 02:36 am

I wouldn't go that far. I just don't have much use for her.

hitman @ January 30 02:37 am

You blame someone, though. Someone hurt him beyond what he could take?

chinkigirl @ January 30 02:38 am

Sorry to barge in, but my advice is that we refrain from jumping into analysis. Let's let fickel tell us what she needs to that may help us understand the current problem—the BPD's investigation of Mr. S's death—and leave it alone. Doesn't that seem the wisest way to go?

hitman @ January 30 02:40 am

Just reacting naturally. Cripes, you bitches are touchy tonight.

chinkigirl @ January 30 02:44 am

Yes, we are, and sorry to admonish—I'm merely suggesting that we react *less* than might come naturally if we want to maintain one another's trust and also our focus. We don't want anyone to develop regrets about something they've revealed here.

fickel @ January 30 02:45 am

I blame myself.

hitman @ January 30 02:46 am

What could you have done, as a kid, that would make a man lay himself down on a train track?

fickel @ January 30 02:49 am

I did...what I was told. I was the cooperative twin, remember? Not that my brother was completely intractable.

hitman @ January 30 02:50 am

Meaning? Spell it out.

i.went.to.harvard @ January 30 02:59 am

Meaning "good night," I'm gathering.

marleybones @ January 30 03:00 am

Brave girl. Sleep tight (all 4 hours you've got left!)

leo tolstoy @ January 30 04:15 am

...we are all created to be miserable, and...we all know it, and all invent means of deceiving each other. And when one sees the truth, what is one to do?

fickel @ January 30 10:44 am

Ah. Good morning to you, too, leo t. *Love* the encrypted identity. Makes you seem so...oh, I don't know...*undercover*?

16

FULL FRONTAL

EXISTENTIALISM ENGORGED

01.30 @ 12:06 PM: THE TWAT THICKENS...

Killer chick
Yer so slick
Who's the slacker?
Trick...or vic?

Was watching Killer Chick's place couple nights back, looking for some way in to her. Half expected to see the jarhead cop shuffle on up the stairs to dish up another steaming dog pile of "aw, shucks" foreplay. It don't happen, but something more in'erstin does when some skateboard weasel slides on up to the stoop and plays conga on her buzzah til she lets him in.

Let me give you the e-ball pat-down of this losah—maybe 5 foot 10 and weighin in at a buck fifty, all draped in grunge. Fatigue cargos, dirty jean jac over red-to-pink hoodie, army rucksack, hair razored to the skull—everything says "I swallow for drugs." I.E. typical slacker.

No kiss from K.C. but I could see she is both groovin on seeing him and totally comfortable in her sweaties, slipper socks and glasses in front of him. He's all "hey, wohman, whatchu whan outa me" with big bousheet hand motions like he thinks he's some sort of niggah, and she's all "yeah-sure-heard-your-bull-before" but she loves this weasel you can see it a mile away. Farkin little twerp must have ten inches in his jockeys cause he sher az hey-ell ain't showing much else he might offer to a class act such as our lover-ly murderous heroine.

They go in, then she comes out immediately, this time with her coat and black high top sneaks on (come to be thinkin, those would be *his* black high top sneaks she's wearing). I follow her out to Mass Ave, where she picks up a six of chilled Canadian piss for the little dude plus Kung Pao fried rice—I know this because I slip into the take-out hole and make like I'm filling out an order while she picks up. Close enough to hear her educated voice and her snooty snorty nerd girl giggle and to get an eyeload of her sweet ass-cheeks bumping around under her sweats.

So who is this slacker-dude prodigal? Almost seems like the Killer Chick's life is looking up now that she's done what she's done. Like the stars are on her side. Maybe the guy she tumbled had it coming, yeah, verily to wit, and God agrees she did us all a service.

Amen, b'yitch. Maybe I can't do you after all, cause I don't got the nads to argue with God.

I hang out, looking to maybe witness the slacker dude getting his bones tossed out of there if she goes to blow him and smells some fifteen-year-old clam on his skinny. Howevah, no such luck.

3 a.m. I get borrrrrrrrd n take off. Gots ta shave before work tamarrah.

---

tALK. NIHILISt DOGS

garbo @ 01.30 06:21 pm

You have something against underage girls, now?

fullfrontal @ 01.30 06:56 pm

Duh fark? Oh, I get you—you is j.b. Knew there was *somethin* funny goin on.

garbo @ 01.30 07:12 pm

well, I do *look* young, but you don't have anything to worry about.

fullfrontal @ 01.30 07:13 pm

you a virgin?

garbo @ 01.30 07:14 pm

Sure am...I mean besides what my daddy did to me. Do you think that counts?

fullfrontal @ 01.30 07:15 pm

Oh even beddah, a little princess scag spreading crabs through her teen years. Shouldn't you be talking some fat cigar-chewing sleezoid down the local muff shop into letting you pole-dance "just during the afternoon shift"?

chootah @ 01.30 08:11 pm

Hey man think you hurt her feelings.

fullfrontal @ 01.30 08:21 pm

Cry me a rivah.

17

LIFE IS PULP

The Noir Boudoir of L.G. Fickel

January 30 @ 10:24 pm
>COPS: DUMB...OR DUMBER???<

Well, again taking hitman's advice (note to new blog buddy—*stop giving advice*), I decided that Mr. Suicide's diary was still worth a first-hand gander, and so I got in touch with Burly-Bear and made an appointment, this time OFF cop turf and so free from the "chance" of getting thrown together with Escroto. My suggestion was that Burly-Bear and I run out to Concord to lay the diary in front of "my writer friend," aka the Colonel, who I assured le Burly had a whopping amount of sensitivity to diction and writing patterns from his half-century-plus in the novel-churning business, while also maintaining a brand of analytic detachment that only a true pukka sahib can sustain. Plus I'd be there, in all my wide-eyed vulnerability.

Who could resist such an offer? Burly-Bear slides up to the curb outside my office in his seafoam-green driving machine just as the grandfather clock in our waiting area strikes six in all of its harpsichordic splendor. I've been peeking out the window in anticipation, and with a flick of my mouse I'm out of there before my computer can say hibernate.

My second ride in Burly-Bear's car, I find, is a lot sweeter than the first. There's just something about sitting next to a big ol' plainclothes cop who handles the wheel with that two-finger panache while his massive thighs strain against the material of his gabardines that you gotta live through once. Makes a girl feel...I want to say "graceful" but there's more to it.

When you sit next to a guy who is really one with his vehicle, and he's driving you somewhere for your sake, and you know that on some level he's angling in on you, you feel under his control, but in the best way possible. I wouldn't say that the drive out of town that late afternoon was "sexual," but calling it "sexy" would not be off by much. Sitting there, I find myself hoping that he is getting a whiff of me, whatever scent my perfume gives off when it mixes with my natural odors. After all, it seems only fair that I add to the moment we're having.

Burly-Bear speaks little as we drain out of Boston with the rest of the drones, and it's not until we're coasting between the low rock walls of the ritzy New England community, the sunset-tinged fields and naked trees just merging into the winter evening, that he glances my way and gently grunts for directions. We draw up to the Colonel's graciously shabby villa and sit for a tic, like maybe one of us is about to say something, before Burly-Bear slings his arm over the back seat for the bag containing the original of the suicide diary. He moves suddenly and for some reason I flinch, which he notices but ignores. No idea what's going on there, on either of our parts. Probably best left unanalyzed, as chinkigirl would say.

We're greeted at the door by a powder-white domestic who can't possibly have enough life left in her to accomplish more than polishing one teaspoon a day between the occasional creeps down one or another of the long hallways to listen at a door or peep through a keyhole, her trusty back hump peering over her shoulder. She leaves us in the lounge (her word, not mine)—however, no secret passage to the conservatory is discernible.

Waiting for the Colonel, I wander with my hands clasped behind my pleats, admiring the gaudy oil paintings—one relatively new one that I pause in front of depicts the Peacock decked out in her signature ice—while the Burly-Bear stands more or less "at ease" on the pink oriental. They have some overfed goldfish swimming around in a massive glass bowl behind the sofa—it's all very bright and expensive and wonderfully nouveau, which for some reason gets me imagining what it would be like to have Burly-Bear push me down on the hearth rug and just take me. I give him a flirty glance or two over my cheekbone to see if he's thinking what I'm thinking. He pretends not to be, but we both know better.

Soon thereafter the Colonel marches in, full of self-effacing intellect and clearly impressed with Burly-Bear. Surprising myself but apparently not him, I flutter over and treat him to a light kiss on the cheek—something muddled going on in my mind about making sure that Burly-Bear sees that the Colonel and I are "intimate." The thunderclap handshake he and Burly-Bear give one another, however, dispels any idea that the Colonel will be prejudiced in my favor.

So we nix offers of coffee and sweets but nevertheless retire to the dining room to huddle around the sacred suicide text at the massive glass and iron table therein while the chandelier blazes down upon every neurotically inked nuance. At Burly's request, the Colonel and he stretch-roll semiopaque rubber gloves up over their hands—a quip about "hand condoms" pops into my little head but I wisely keep it to myself—and then, well, then the Colonel reads.

Here's the passage Burly-Bear selected for him, which he grinds out aloud in a flat, Bogart-style cadence:

I've been reminiscing again, E. You'd disapprove; "big effing whatever," you'd sigh with your usual eye roll. And you'd be right. Big effing whatever. But, nevertheless...tonight I was reminiscing about our introduction. Pimped, I could call it—our mock-serendipitous encounter was about as innocent of intention as a high-heeled girl in hotpants leaning over to peer past the rim of an idling car's descending window. Yes, we were "set up" by that most accommodating of lady friends, so famously mercenary herself, bedecked in her bedazzling bijoux that balmy spring evening, her warty toad in tow. Was she your friend or mine, or was she neither, but just a creature who plays with lives—that lazy lynx from Sleepy Hollow who called for iced cocktails between Beethoven and Béla Bartók???

Enough with the flipping alliteration, you would say. Have to admit, I agree, luv, as I've always agreed. Agreeing is my M.O., as you knew from the start. You the artist and I the mere clay. Mais certes.

In any event, I felt gratified and also flattered to find myself being set up with you by the rich pussy. After all, although both of you imagined yourselves to be using me for your separate reasons, I knew the truth, which was that you were being presented to me. You were to be my little toy to shred at will. And you certainly were yummy—I could have leaned forward and licked your coquettishly exposed chest right then and there, and, as it turned out, I had plenty more than a mouthful of you to gobble by midnight.

But aside from the weird feeling of being set up for sex, and aside from the giddiness of discovering ourselves to be the rutting creatures we'd never imagined ourselves—aside from all this, that "first" encounter was very much NOT the same experience for me that it was for you. Because, of course, I was already obsessed with you! Why, ever since I'd discovered you on the street where I live those months earlier and followed you back to that diner to get a better look, make sure you were you, I'd been living my life with your image in front of me!!! And so there is no describing the jolt of "meeting" you. You! I was being set up with YOU! My fantasy—my ONLY fantasy fuck since perhaps the age of fifteen when for about six months I suffered a craving for a certain 22-year-old junior varsity soccer coach who'd been energetic enough to suit up, work out, and—sigh—shower with the team (all platonic "bonding" between coach and athletes, or so it came off at the time). I was only the team manager, of course, but I had ways of scoring peeks into the shower room. That was my first encounter with a truly adult body—that odd merging of a civilized face and the creature living beneath its clothes. So, so forbidden, my first crush felt, and not solely because it was "gay." You were my second, all these years later. And oh you were to be exciting, I swore to myself.

Did our panderer know, when she brought us together? Does she know our secrets, now that you've tired of me? Do you whine to her good-naturedly, now that you are sick of me, sick of getting me together with your other "friend" and having us boys go at it so you may watch us sin?

But who cares what you tell the pussy. She's not to blame for our descent from the self-approbation of lust to the treachery of the "strained relationship." What is to blame, then? What would you claim it to be, if I were to lean over the rail and call out my question as you sit below me, pattering on that toy of yours? Would you pause to sigh and resume typing without a word? Would you smack the table with your palm, twist around to aim that glare of yours up at me, and have it out? Or would you slip soundlessly from where you sit at this moment and leave, only the click of the latch announcing that you are off? And if I were to throw on coat and boots and steal after you, would you go, again, to HIS place? The beautiful he-slut. From the fat to the fire—but I get ahead of myself. At least, you don't seem to have caught on to him yet. Me, I think you've pegged, at least subconsciously.

In any event, I won't upset you tonight. I sit, I write. Soon I will pretend to sleep. You will ascend only when you are sure that I am beyond waking and you will slip into bed, making sure not to touch me—shuddering at the prospect of our two skins touching. My E. You will pay penance until I say it's over. Anything else would offend your sense of...propriety, shall we call it? I've got you by your rectitude, one might say. The irony appeals to me very much.

When the Colonel finishes reading we all kind of blink, not quite meeting eyes. Even though I've read it, I need a moment to recover. When I do, I try to come up with some clever summation, just to break the ice, but nothing comes to me. Burly-Bear raises his head and trains his eye on the Colonel, immobile, a dog waiting for the kill command. The Colonel leafs around in the entry, reviewing what he's read, then lays it flat.

Colonel: Nasty little viper. But then that's intentional. The whole thing is very theatrical, as if he wanted E to find it.

Burly-Bear: (stirring thoughtfully, and giving off the vibe that he is going to strive to get but not give information—is that because *I'm* present?) Sounds genuinely angry, though, don't he, sir?

Colonel: Oh, it's not a healthy relationship these two have going on; that's for sure. There's some sort of showdown on the horizon. Whether it's suicide or...hell, if I'd written it in a novel there'd be a murder brewing. (He laughs—one short bark.) Why in the world can't people just accept when something's over? Why do we need our endings to be so cruel?

Burly-Bear: (shifting in tone) I been wondering, sir: how would you describe the writer here? I mean, as a writer yourself, could you make a list of his (he circles a hand).

Me: Salient characteristics? (I'm not even sure if I'm supposed to talk, this being a conversation in some form about whether the diary contains any indications that I could not have been Mr. Suicide's lover. But neither of them seem put off by my interjection.)

Burly-Bear: Correct you are.

Colonel: (raising his eyebrows, interested) The easiest place to begin is with direct descriptors, and I have to say that we're given very little of those to latch onto.

Burly-Bear: You think he did that on purpose?

Colonel: Seems more likely that the avoidance of detail is simply a product of the fact that the writer has no need to explain the obvious to himself.

Burly-Bear: (doggedly) So how do we get anywhere?

Colonel: We start with the premise, verified by some handwriting expert at your department's disposal, I presume, that this diary was written by our dead friend from the subway. So I ask myself: does it ring true as the ventings of a middle-aged man whose young lover is in the process of moving along? I'd say that's very possible. Middle-aged people can be damned needy, and that's one element here that comes through as real as real can be—the bitterly hurt references to the lover's roving eye, the desperate desire to return things to the way they were—that's all consistent with the lonely middle-aged lover, and all of that's very raw, in spite of the author's attempts at sarcasm. On the other hand, what do we do with these bits about how some female friend introduced the twosome?

Burly-Bear: The middle-aged man's got a female friend—a client, maybe, or the wife of a client. (He glances at me involuntarily—and, oh, you'd better believe that I latch right onto the fact that our Mr. Suicide was in some profession where he'd have *clients*.) So this rich woman friend sets him up with someone young she knows—personal trainer, hairdresser, dog walker—could be a hundred setups like that.

Colonel: But why was it *surprising* and *flattering* and even *remarkable* to our diarist that the young lover was being presented to him as a sex object? Wouldn't that be the usual way—the older male being the friend of this middle-aged lady, the young bit of flesh served up as a treat?

Burly-Bear: So what does that signify to you?

Colonel: (musingly) Must have been something special about the young thing. Something to offset the age difference.

Burly-Bear: Such as?

Colonel: (He sits up a bit straighter, if such a thing is possible.) Well, say the younger one is from an important family...an old Boston family...

Burly-Bear: Which could also explain why he only calls the girl "E" and writes the whole thing in a way that clouds her identity.

Colonel: Girl? (He barks a laugh.) Friend, I don't think there's a girl anywhere within a mile of this thing. Whole setup is queer as a three-dollar bill.

Burly-Bear: Sir, could you point me at some of the details that substantiate that?

Colonel: Hell, it permeates the thing. (He stabs a finger at a passage.) Here, here: he refers to the other one—this E fellow—running off to bed down with another man—a male slut, he calls him. And early on the writer makes a reference to having spotted E on the street with another man. All male, the way I count it up. Simple arithmetic.

Me: But E could, conceivably, be a woman who went off to bed down with this "other" male, yes? "Other" could be a reference to the "male slut" being some man other than the diary's writer. Similarly, it could have been a woman the writer saw on the street with "another man"—a man other than the writer, that is.

Colonel: (shutting me down with a condescending shake of his head) Man talks about watching a soccer coach in the shower, for crying out loud.

Me: But he presents that as a youthful aberration.

Burly-Bear: (utterly ignoring me) So it's a gay love affair gone sour, huh?

Me: (feeling pretty decisively dismissed) Unless, of course, he was bi.

(The two of them stare at me. I know that heterosexual men have difficulty believing there is any such thing as bisexuality, or at least *male* bisexuality. However, the way Burly-Bear is studying me makes me think that this isn't what's troubling him. I stir uneasily.)

Me: Well, he writes about the crush on his coach as if it's an anomaly. He puts the word "gay" in quotation marks. Why would he, if he actually considers himself gay? A lot of people's first crush is strange—same sex or even incestuous, the way I understand it.

Burly-Bear: But there's these mentions of some other man that both of them, the writer and E, have gotten together with for sex.

Me: Every heterosexual man I've met salivates over the idea of being with two women. If that makes sense, wouldn't it make equal sense that a bisexual male would want to bring together another man and a woman?

Colonel: (coloring as if he's discovering me to be a more distasteful young lady than he'd realized) Don't know about any of that multiple-partner shenanigans. One thing I do know, though. The reference to Bartók. I know when that concert took place. The wife and I have season tickets to the Berklee. I missed that program last spring. No Beethoven that evening, as I recall it, but perhaps they altered the program, or maybe that's just our writer's penchant for alliteration. Wife went without me. I believe our lawyer accompanied her...(here he pauses to chuckle) he's an officious fellow, quite useful in such situations. April 11, it was. Don't know if that's helpful, but I notice that this diary entry isn't dated. That would make this relationship with E falling apart about nine months ago.

Burly-Bear: (jotting a note) Could be very helpful. May I ask how you remember the date?

Colonel: (answering without hesitation) Red Sox home opener. I faked a touch of fatigue so I could stay home and watch. The wife knew what I was up to. Can't fool the ladies.

Burly Bear: (smiling and standing) Correct you are, sir; it's always good to remember that.

Colonel: (musing a bit beyond what you'd expect as he stares at the tabletop, apparently seeing his wife reflected in the glass) Saved my life, meeting her. Used to drink something fierce. She gave me a reason not to. Don't know what I'd do if... (He muses some more, then revives himself and climbs to his feet, smiling ruefully.) I'm afraid I wasn't overly helpful, Sergeant. Everything that's been said here tonight's been duly observed by the BPD.

Burly-Bear: (presenting his hand) To the contrary, sir.

Burly-Bear drives me back to Central Square in silence, both of us buzzing in our own heads about various moments of the evening. He speaks first as he pokes the nose of his car around the corner of my crooked little street.

Burly-Bear: Quite a fellow.

Me: I hope he did help, at least a little.

Burly-Bear: Have to admit, the idea of both lovers being male surfaced pretty early. Heck, you yourself brought it up at the guy's apartment, even before you seen the diary, way I recall it. Guess that makes you the sharpest tack in the box, huh? (I score a flash of teeth above that cute, bulging chin of his.) It's good, though, to have the same reading come from a real writer. Supports our theory with some authority, know what I'm sayin'? (Then, not waiting for an answer) What about you, though?

Me: What about me?

Burly-Bear: (pulling up by the hydrant in front of my place) You getting used to bein' on the minds of a bunch of homicide cops?

Me: (simply—always the best way to flirt outrageously) Not a bunch. Only one.

Burly-Bear: (Pauses to drink this in. His eyes are glittering, his neck and nostrils widening visibly as he gets out on his side. Soooooo, what's on his mind? He comes around and opens my door, clears his throat, and helps me out.) You do get that this ain't a game, don't you?

Me: (studying him as we stand on the sidewalk, inches apart.) Sergeant, I'm not afraid to speculate that Mr. Suicide's lover might have been female. It's not a risk because it's not me. (I take a chilly breath.) Get that through your head, won't you?

Burly-Bear: Look, did I say som'in'?

Me: (feeling myself flush and laughing weakly) No. No, you've been very supportive. A rock. But I don't want to walk away from this thing on the strength of how the diary "rings" to the ears of a pair of very chivalrous men.

Burly-Bear: Why not walk away any way it works out?

Me: Because then maybe you'll always wonder that you helped someone get away with murder.

Burly-Bear: (shrugging as if casual, but he's not) Maybe I don't mind wondering that.

Me: (icing up) I mind. (I go to walk up my front steps and he touches my arm.) I have to go. I have a call scheduled with my lawyer. (The words may read tough, but I say them softly, like I don't mean them. I don't tug my arm away from him, either.)

Burly-Bear: (turning me gently. I'm up a couple of steps from the sidewalk so we're basically eye to eye.) You got a lawyer, then? (He puffs the words into my face and I can't tell what's behind them—is he glad that I took his advice or thinking that only someone with something to hide would run for legal help? His breath is surprising—the musty stuff of cellars and caves. It clicks in my head that it's what home cooking smells like—meatloaf and potatoes. Does Burly-Bear live with his Ma, or does he just go "home" for meals? I am not into "family values.")

Me: (weakly) Yes, I got a lawyer. Actually, it's more that I had one foisted on me by our friend in Concord. (Suddenly I don't want to talk about the situation I'm in, don't want him in my apartment, don't want him on top of me in bed, kissing me, pawing my face and hair with his gentle, powerful hands, pushing his penis at me. I feel faint, just thinking about how long I'll have to wait for him to fall asleep so I can crawl out from under him to blog.) Look, I'm dog-tired. I want...(pointing vaguely over my shoulder) to be alone.

I go to turn away, but suddenly I get scared. He's the only guy on the inside who is on my side, the only one I can count on if things go very wrong, the only one who will guarantee that I will "walk away," as he puts it. I turn back quickly and let myself fall into his arms as I lift my face for his kiss. Being as it's real life and not RKO black-and-white, his mouth bangs against my face somewhere between forehead and ear. He pushes me away, not roughly—very subtly, in fact—but in that split second I experience fear, like a big, horrible crackle emanating all over my skull from its base, and for the first time in my life I get what they mean when they say that fear grips you by the spine. I cannot blow it with Burly-Bear. I turn my face up to his, brushing his chin with my lips, needing to get the kiss right, wanting it badly. He doesn't join me in the kiss—I'm momentarily devastated—but when I look up at him, he's staring over the top of my head, up at my building. I twist around, still pressing against him, refusing to fall out of his arms in spite of the fact that he's not holding me anymore.

I see what he sees. Through the glass of the front door's window and the glass of the vestibule door beyond that is the bottom of the stairs up, and beyond that is the door to my apartment. My apartment door is open and leaning against the doorjamb is my brother, looking rather scaggy, one yellow arm resting lazily across the top of his head, the other hand scratching around in his exposed armpit, and not all that carefully considering he's holding a lit cigarette. He's wearing nothing but a pair of once-white long john bottoms, riding low; his chest is bare except for the mantle of tattoos. He's in mid-yawn, and it turns out to be a real jawbreaker. He finishes up, sticks his cigarette between his lips, plugs one nostril with a thumb, and shoots a wad of snot at the wall. Then he turns, treating us to a view of his back tats before he lets my door fall shut.

Burly-Bear: Isn't that your place?

Me: (blinking innocently) Yes, it is. (I tilt my head and try to smile.) How'd you know that?

Burly-Bear: (throwing a glance back at my door) Friend of yours?

Me: Oh, he's just "a rootless creature, floating detachedly above the everyday world, with no point of contact." Except me, that is.

I try to deliver the Woolrich quote with the sarcastic lilt it needs, but maybe it comes off cagey. I see something enter Burly-Bear's expression—a hoggish bunching around his eyes. Guess he doesn't like the idea of me holding out on him, or maybe he's just disappointed that he's got no chance for nookie tonight now that something rather phallic has been spotted scratching itself against my doorpost.

Burly-Bear: Thank your writer friend for me. Tell him our conversation was invaluable.

I know that I should try for the kiss again, make it clear to him that the man inside isn't competition, but I'm afraid, so I just nod. He walks around the hood of the Mustang. I watch his taillights, realizing that I've effed something up big time.

GIVE IT TO ME STRAIGHT

i.went.to.harvard @ January 30 11:22 pm

> Burly-Bear said "invaluable?" Points for that. Would have thought that he'd think that it means "not valuable."

chinkigirl @ January 30 11:23 pm

> Maybe he does. Remember that he told fickel that he hadn't learned anything from the Colonel that the cops hadn't already considered.

roadrage @ January 30 11:27 pm

> Uh, since fickel is worried about Burly-Bear being frosted at her, and we're so convinced that he's on this blog, should we be getting all snarky about his vocab?

proudblacktrannie @ January 30 11:29 pm

excellent point, except that I, for one, no longer think he's on the blog.

webmaggot @ January 30 11:31 pm

Umm, hey, you with the man parts duct-taped between your buns? Aren't you the one who keeps warning us in all caps that the Burly-Bear's lurking here? Am I missing sum'n?

proudblacktrannie @ January 30 11:32 pm

U are, lovable dimwit: did you not catch the fact that the Burly-Bear has no idea who dickel is? If he had been on the blog, he'd have known that it's just fickel's brother. Oui?

chinkigirl @ January 30 11:33 pm

Brilliant deduction, proudblack! I for one am impressed.

roadrage @ January 30 11:34 pm

Yeah, but maybe Burly-Bear was faking it—*pretending* he didn't realize who the dickel was—maybe he was waiting for fickel to explain so he could "know" and then he got annoyed because fickel didn't rush to dispel the obvious erroneous conclusions he might have drawn.

webmaggot @ January 30 11:35 pm

Or maybe he was just pissed because he wasn't gunna get some funk no way no how, and he'd been majorly primed.

marleybones @ January 30 11:44 pm

You know, along the line of wondering whether Burly-Bear is aware of more than he pretends, how *did* he know that dickel was lounging in the doorway of *your* apartment, fickel? Is it clear from the layout of your building that your apartment is the one just past the bottom of the stairs?

hitman @ January 30 11:49 pm

How about it fickel? Burly-Bear onto us and pissed off or dumb to us and even more pissed off?

fickel @ January 30 11:55 pm

Jury's out. Way out. There are two apartments on the first floor, and I don't see how it could be apparent that mine's the one on the right. But the idea that Burly-Bear is...sigh...if the man is anything, he is inscrutable.

36-D @ January 31 12:12 am

I'm confused to the point where I've actually started taking notes on the side, and it's not helping. Would *someone* set me straight: is our theory that Mr. Suicide wrote the diary about some girl who was using him *OR* are we thinking Mr. Suicide wrote it about some freeloader gay scag who wouldn't push off but in the meantime was blowing everyone in the South End?

proudblacktrannie @ January 31 12:15 am

Reverse sexism!!!! Why is the straight female "some girl" while the gay male is a "scag"?

36-D @ January 31 12:16 am

Apologies. You *know* I'm a fag hag like anyone's maiden aunt.

proudblacktrannie @ January 31 12:18 am

Well (sniff, sniff).

chinkigirl @ January 31 12:22 am

I've been struggling with the conflicting views on E's gender, too. If we convince ourselves, as the Colonel would have it, that there's not a female within a mile of this thing, that works to fickel's advantage, and so I was sorely tempted to see it that way until fickel made her point that her strategy is to simply try to get to the *truth*.

marleybones @ January 31 12:25 am

Putting aside our *motive* for reading the thing one way and not the other, fickel's point that Mr. Suicide seemed to portray his early homosexual crush on a coach as an aberration seemed really strong to me, although it's based on a simple pair of quotation marks, which people use to signify so many things. So...E's female and Mr. Suicide is bi?

proudblacktrannie @ January 31 12:29 am

Giggle, giggle. Ain't that the twist? Me, I've been thinking that all Mr. Suicide's histrionics read awfully femmy. Do men—even bi men—get all hissy-fitty like that?

webmaggot @ January 31 12:30 am

Guy's a FAY-YUG foh shoh.

fickel @ January 31 12:32 am

But maybe that's why he writes it to himself and doesn't rant it right at her. He knows that if he lets loose with that kind of shyte at a woman, she's out-o-there. Any more votes?

i.went.to.harvard @ January 31 12:36 am

I have a thought: according to Mr. Suicide, the two lovers *discovered* themselves to be rutting creatures, i.e., they're outwardly polite, even uptight, upper-class, law-abiding citizens. Fits more the young woman + Mr. Suicide model than the young gay hustler + Mr. Suicide thing.

fickel @ January 31 12:39 am

So it's 2 votes for a female, 2 votes for a male. Any tiebreaker out there?

roadrage @ January 31 12:41 am

Here's something: he says that E always goes "Big Flipping Whatever" and rolls her eyes. I can only see a chick doing that. Either that or a reeeeeeeeally feminine guy...oh, wait a minute.

webmaggot @ January 31 12:45 am

Hey what about the "coquettishly exposed chest." Doesn't that make E a chick?

36-D @ January 31 12:53 am

Something tells me that you don't hang out with a lot of gays, maggot.

webmaggot @ January 31 12:55 am

Well, I used to mix more—you know how hip and secure I am—but it never worked out.

hitman @ January 31 12:59 am

You know what struck me, fickel: *you* could have been at the Berklee the day that Mr. Suicide and this he-or-she got introduced. I mean, you got a season ticket, don't you? And you like that weird modern junk—isn't that what Bartok is?

36-D @ January 31 01:02 am

O my lord you are scaring me—fickel do NOT answer if the answer is yes.

fickel @ January 31 01:15 am

Well, I'll say yes to my season subscription and yes to being into "that weird modern junk" and even yes to Bartók falling into that category. But I don't recall any program that put Bartók together with Beethoven, so I get to give that one a no.

hitman @ January 31 01:16 am

But the Colonel said that Beethoven thing in the diary was probably—what'd he call it—alliteration? Stop pussyfooting around: did you go to a Bartok concert last March?

fickel @ January 31 01:19 am

Could be, but I've heard Bartók on a couple of occasions.

hitman @ January 31 01:20 am

I'll take that as a yes. Did you see—what do we call them—the Peacock and Mr. Groin?

fickel @ January 31 01:24 am

Again I can't give you more than a maybe.

hitman @ January 31 01:25 am

Meaning what, the truth is suddenly getting hard to find?

fickel @ January 31 01:35 am

Meaning I may or may not have run into the Peacock during intermission at a concert last spring that featured Bartók. Believe me, it would not have been memorable. Her pattern is unerring: she'd greet me with indifference transparently gussied up as light warmth while at the same time she'd be assessing me from head to toe with her laser gaze as if just to assure herself that no style sensibility or silicone enhancement had been magically bestowed upon me. Once she'd satisfied herself that I hadn't grown a set of knockers since we last exchanged air kisses, she'd warble out something about what a saint I am to remain working with her irascible codger of a husband (which of course she *hates*), then she'd stop herself short as she laughingly "remembered" that I'm as much of a hopeless bookworm as he, and by this time she'd already be moving on toward wherever she'd been heading when she had the misfortune of bumping eyes with me. Got the picture?

As for Mr. Groin, like I said in an earlier post, until our formal introduction at the Colonel's Manor, I'd never laid eyes on him in a way that would distinguish him from every other self-satisfied swell using the mirror behind the bar to slick his hair back while fetching a blood orange martini for his feedbag. So I'll have to answer your question about whether I saw them at the Berklee last March with a solid "who the hell knows?" Helpful?

marleybones @ January 31 01:39 am

Wait—why would the Peacock hate that you're working with the Colonel?

fickel @ January 31 01:42 am

She's the jealous type. Not of me in particular, but of the fact that the Colonel is busy on a project that doesn't involve her in any way. You'd *think* she'd be grateful to me, as I'd definitely sided with her on the idea of having her portrait done (not that she hadn't been steering the Colonel toward that one for a long time before my "objective opinion" happened along, but sometimes you get credit for being the catalyst).

hitman @ January 31 01:45 am

You're glib, fickel, but I still don't get why you failed to mention that you were at that concert when the Colonel said his wife was there. Whether or not you remember running into her, it means that you and Mr. Suicide were there together. If you're after the truth the way you claim you are...

fickel @ January 31 01:51 am

Ah, what a detective. Your doggedness in pursuit of "the facts" is beginning to scream "dick" as loudly as a Brownie camera and bottom-drawer bourbon habit. Plus there's your tin ear for subtext—but let me explain something I consider rather obvious. This is a *blog*—it deals in *retrospect*—after-the-fact assessments of motivations and lessons learned. I don't walk around with these clear convictions about what I'm doing. I figure them out later, usually as I sit here blogging. So when the Colonel brought up the Bartók concert I still had it in my head that it had been some student recital, which is the only thing I could imagine that would included both Bartók and Beethoven pieces. Just because *he* said differently and happens to sport a moustache doesn't mean I went trotting down his line of reasoning like some lap pet. Also, to be frank, it wasn't until Burly-Bear questioned me about it that I got in touch with how scary it would be to just slip off the police radar with no answers—and also with no reason to think this whole nightmare might not resurface.

Look, I know that the above is going to come over as harsh, but you keep needling me so you did ask for it.

i.went.to.harvard @ January 31 01:57 am

Bravo, fickel (okay, brava). I'd like to add that even if fickel had announced to the world that she'd been at the Bartók concert, it wouldn't necessarily have been a "statement against interest." First of all, we've already established that fickel and Mr. Suicide both go (went, in his case) to the Berklee and dig that cerebral jaggy stuff—remember, both of them went to hear *Printemps* and then both rushed over to Newbury Street to buy their very own copy. Second, I'm liking the theory more and more that at some point Mr. Suicide noticed fickel across a crowded room and began homing in on her. Why shouldn't that have happened at the Berklee? So any innocent "coincidental" connections between fickel and Mr. S just help establish exactly what we've been claiming—*that Mr. Suicide might have known her, but that doesn't mean that she knew him.*

roadrage @ January 31 02:02 am

holy shizzle, beautiful mind, man! That is logical, now that you lay it on us. Something tells me that it's Harvard Law School you went to.

i.went.to.harvard @ January 31 02:03 am

Harvard Law dropout, actually. Jumped over to the Div School and finished that, instead.

webmaggot @ January 31 02:06 am

You're a minister? And me with my beautiful mouth.

i.went.to.harvard @ January 31 02:07 am

If you start censoring your comments I'll regret having revealed any of that.

webmaggot @ January 31 02:08 am

Far fuckin out, mon. The preacher rocks!

fickel @ January 31 02:14 am

Thank you for coming to my defense, i.went.to.harvard. It wouldn't suck to hear from hitman that he's taken my little lambast in stride?

fickel @ January 31 02:25 am

Ooooo-kay. And with that, I'm off to bed. Something called "work" keeps happening and I'm getting into a rut of staying up all night and being a Coke junkie all day (that's the diet soda, not the powder). First, of course, I have a bit of a bone to pick with li'l bro.

proudblacktrannie @ January 31 02:26 am

something tells me you'll need handcuffs and a strap-on to have an impact on dear dickel.

fickel @ January 31 02:27 am

Actually, I find that I catch more flies with honey, and you can sleep on that one, perverts.

18

LIFE IS PULP

Noir the Night Away With L.G. Fickel

January 31 @ 11:24 pm
>MYSTERIOUS HOTTIE ALERT<

> *"And you actually get the feeling that if you stepped out of line he'd kick your teeth down your throat."*
>
> *"My, ain't that wonderful!"*
>
> —trampy chick and old lush discussing Lawrence Tierney in *Born to Kill*

My life in three words: weird, weird, f-f-f-freaky weird.

Was sitting around the office today, crossing my legs a lot so that the new girl, Holly (whose manner of tromping about has got Noah calling her Holly-Go-Heavily) could admire my Taryn Rose Terry flats, when the Colonel's lawyer called—I suppose I should call him "my" lawyer—our own Mr. Groin. Apparently he'd been power-chatting with the Colonel and my name popped up. The Groin, btw, has this ballzy voice—deep, smooth, and oh-so-elegant—that I hadn't noticed at the Colonel's. I suppose I'd been too busy counting the many ways in which he came off as a supreme dick. Likewise, it didn't take too, too many seconds on the phone for his attudinal handicap to overwhelm his tonal virtuosity.

Mr. Groin: (brisk, clearly ticked) So are we sticking to game plan?

Me: Seems that way. I'm staying out of jail, and you're keeping your cell phone charged in case that circumstance changes.

Mr. Groin: And playing footsie with this cop who's been harassing you—is that part of staying out of jail, in your mind?

Me: Umm, no one's harassed me that I've noticed.

Mr. Groin: Thanks for helping me make my point. Heard you made a case for this mystery diary pointing a finger at *you* as the dead man's lover, after both the cop with the hots for you and our mutual writer friend agreed that the lover was some as-yet unidentified gay male.

Me: I'm not sure I'd agree that I did anything like that.

Mr. Groin: Don't care what you agree with. Someone's beginning to wonder if you're into the attention this situation is getting you. So, as my client, could I ask you to try seeing things in a manner favorable to yourself?

Me: What do you mean?

Mr. Groin: What I mean is that if some diary the cops have come up with indicates that this pathetic creature who killed himself was into pimple-assed boys, *let them think that*. Got it?

Me: (doubtfully) Is that all?

Mr. Groin: Unfortunately it isn't. I also mean that if the investigating cop's coming on to you, that's called harassment and you tell him that to his face, or at least straight-arm him and let me use the H-word—got it?

Me: Umm?

Mr. Groin: The strategy, in case you're not picking it up, is to get you uninvolved in this thing, and right now the horndog cop is the only logical reason I can see for them to be maintaining any level of interest in you. So blow him off and the bad dream blows away with him. Look, do I have to draw you a map?

Me: I'm getting it.

Mr. Groin: Good girl. Now try to remember it and we're golden. Capisce?

Me: So now that you've finished scolding me, can you tell me one thing? I want to know the dead man's name. (rushing ahead when he doesn't respond) Look, I know that you want me uninvolved and that this request seems to go against that, but it's really eating at me that the cops won't tell me his name, and I think that if I know it next time I talk to one of them and then reveal that it came from my lawyer, they'll stop seeing me as so vulnerable. That sounds like a good strategy, doesn't it?

I wait for his answer, and it takes me a moment to figure out that he's already hung up. What a *total* gland this guy is.

So I, too, hang up, and then I busy myself sending telepathic death rays (just tiny ones) at the Colonel for tattling to Mr. Groin that I'd had the temerity to be honest in conversing with Burly-Bear about the possibility of the "mystery lover" being female. Next, I bang onto the web and google around heedlessly for some clue as to the identity of "Mistah Pale."

What a little honest rage will do to focus a girl! Less than 15 minutes later I'm jotting down the directions to The Blue Pearl—a fine Boston jewelry establishment owned by one **Mr. Stephen Pearle**. Fortunately, most of the office is clearing out early for some little mixer we've set up at the top of the Parker for our newest author (we're publishing her first novel—about eight people who come out of one or another closet, from, like, a writer who publishes under a pseudonym to a pair of incestuous siblings—weirdly enough, it's utterly delightful. Unfortunately, the author has become more and more of a prima donna through the editing process until I *swear* I lip-read my boss mouthing the C-word as she got off the phone with her the other day—*god*, how I *live* for these little moments in life!). Anyway, my plan is to rush in late and claim that I'd gotten *so* engrossed in proofing the prima donna's fifty-third rewrite of her about-the-author blurb that the time had simply gotten away from me. Weak tea, true, but it gives me time to race over to the Jewelers Building before retail hours are over.

If you've spent any time in Boston, you've seen the Jewelers Building even if you don't know it. It's one of those old-style office buildings that sits incognito in the hurly-burly of Downtown Crossing—so dated that you practically expect to see the ghosts of men in fedoras and women in fox stoles and white gloves emerging from the place. Street people gaggle around out front with no real awareness of the mineral goodies stacked eight stories up inside (and at what discounts!). So I make my way over there, hop into the old-fashioned elevator, and emerge on the fifth floor with all sorts of anticipation about the kind of establishment our friend Mr. Suicide had run.

The Blue Pearl—picture art-deco-style scripted lettering on a semiopaque glass door, way-hay-hay down the end of a long marble hallway. The

Blue Pearl favors its headline color—the blueness inside the place is so pervasive and powerful that it actually bursts forth through the shop's very seams to shimmer off the hallway walls and floor tiles. When you enter, it's like you've grown gills and can breathe underwater. Swimmy shimmers of blue light bathe the walls. Blue-white rays radiate like Ice Age sunlight from light sources hidden inside ceiling fans, which rotate lazily, catching glimmers against their deep platinum blades to create a subtle wave effect. The display cases are halogen white, cold and pure, and the diamonds and pearls, which greatly outnumber the other pieces on display, glitter and wink like Christmas.

I hesitate, just inside, intimidated by all the watery bling. Down at the other end of the shop, a man stands at the counter with his back to me, writing something. He's slender to a fault, with those lovely slim buns that only black men have, and when he turns I see that he's so black as to be almost midnight blue in the lighting. He touches at his beautiful silver tie, checking the elegant dimple just under the knot. He doesn't smile but doesn't look hostile, as if he's one of those people who greet newcomers by simply drinking them in. I can tell, from some combination of his looks and manner, that when he does speak it will be with a Latin accent and, undoubtedly, a lisp.

I walk forward, wondering exactly what I'll say when I reach him. I'm not too, too worried about the small talk; any woman who can't dream up some reason to be poking around a jewelry shop needs to get her priorities in line. I take my time, glancing here and there (anyone interested in seeing me in a pair of chocolate-and-white diamond teardrop earrings with turquoise trim who has half a grand burning a hole in his pocket should get his tush over to The Blue Pearl, pronto), but when I look up at Mr. Slenderbuns all thoughts of making a purchase leave my head.

This is because, over his shoulder, I see a large photo on the back wall of the shop. It shows a necklace arranged on some swirls of velvet: an array of white-blue stones, six or seven of them quite sizable, strung together by an intricate netted arrangement of white gold chain. I stare at it, walking forward.

Slenderbuns notices my interest and half turns to view the photo with me. When he speaks it's with the liquid femininity that his every movement exudes.

Slenderbuns: One of Mr. Pearle's fabulous creations. Sixteen blue diamonds, some pear-shaped, some cushion cut, with the larger stones all a dark greyish blue with violet components. (He slides his onyx eyes from the photo to me.) Makes me feel like Nefertiti just imagining what that would be like to have around one's neck.

Me: (still not quite making the obvious connections) Mr. Pearle made that?

Slenderbuns: (touching my arm) He didn't make it, honey. He designed it. He had craftsmen who worked on commission. One of them did the assembly. But it's an original Stephen Pearle.

Me: And it's one of a kind?

Slenderbuns: (with a small gasp) No woman is going to tolerate there being two of something like that in the world. (He gestures, drawing a little dollar sign in the air with a pinky.) It's one of a kind with this sort of piece.

Me: Do you know who owns that particular piece? (Then, realizing that that's going to get me exactly nowhere, I hasten to go on.) I ask only because it reminds me very much of one I've seen lately, and I'm just wondering whether it was made at some point more than, say, eight months ago, for someone local.

Slenderbuns: (straightening the picture of the necklace) I couldn't say. Privacy and all that. (He makes a motion like he's turning a key in his mouth, then shrugs.) But what can I do for *you*? (He lets his eyes jump from my ears to my neckline to my hands, assessing, then tickles his fingers down his own long throat.) What I would do if I had a neck like yours. Nothing like *this*. (He shrugs a shoulder dismissively at the photo of the necklace behind him.) You need something sweet, but maybe elegant, too, just to give you something to grow into? (He taps a glossy nail on the glass and I glance down at a platinum bezel-set diamond scalloped necklace with floral detail. Damn if he ain't dead fugging on. Now I *need* a platinum bezel-set diamond scalloped necklace with floral detail. Retailing at $2,450.95. Thanx, homey.)

Me: (deciding to go with an honest approach) I'm not here to shop. I just found out...(The news that I've just discovered that Mr. Pearle is the guy who took himself out in front of me sticks in my throat.)

Slenderbuns: (smiling foggily, but only for a moment before his eyes widen, at which he draws his head back and whispers) *Oh my Lord, of course—you're the girl!* (He raises his fingers quickly to his lips—I can't tell if it's because he wishes he could take his words back or because he wants me to keep quiet. When he speaks it's in a louder voice, as if to drown out his prior words.) You knew Mr. Pearle? So sorry, honey, I didn't realize. (He comes around the counter again, graceful as a cat burglar, and takes my hands in his.) We all miss him so much. I haven't stopped crying for a minute. (His eyes, full of curiosity, are quite dry.) Today's the first day we're back, and it's really more in his honor than to sell anything. You know what I mean, hon?

Me: Umm, I can imagine.

Just as Slenderbuns turns me and starts easing me toward the door, this weird thing happens. I get this glimpse of a mirror, one of those big oval countertop jobbies that they have in jewelry stores, and something about the angle and tilt gives me a momentary shot of the space beyond the blue satin curtain that blocks the customers' view of the back rooms. In that moment I see a woman reflected. She's African American, or American Indian, or Asian, or, hell, maybe a concoction of all three—with hooded eyes, a flat-bridged nose, and that perfect brown skin with dark freckles that you sometimes get with people of mixed race. She's maybe fifty-something with a sagging, tired mouth and her hair oiled into a white lady hairdo. Her clothes are the type that big-shouldered women wear—there's some sort of scarf contraption around the neck of her paisley dress that's pinned in place with a glittering flower or something. She's sitting at a desk, a pair of cat-eye glasses in her hand like she's just taken them off as she goes through a stack of accounts. Next to her arm is a wet-looking sandwich, untouched, and her thick fingernails are painted a dark purple. I see all this, sure, but the main thing that catches my eye is that she's grieving—her face has that unmistakable air of ravage. She stares at nothing, which I realize in that flash of seeing her is because she's been listening. I also realize in that flash that she is the reason that Slenderbuns is leading me toward the front of the shop.

Me: (looking intimately into Slenderbuns' shiny black eyes as we walk) Maybe I shouldn't have come by. It's so hard to know how to react.

Slenderbuns: Of course it is. I'm so sorry, but we have to close now. You know how it is, honey, right?

I let him lead me into the corridor, then smile weakly as he kisses the air in my direction before ducking behind the door. I hear the lock turn before I have a chance to turn away.

> *Okay, pulp fans, in case you're thinking that that whole scene was a tad wack, THIS is when the poop starts snowing down really weird...*

I'm wandering toward the Parker House, planning on doing some heavy-duty mulling with my chin firmly planted in a glass of pinot noir whilst drifting among the cognoscenti, when I spot HIM. Yes, *HIM*! *The Mysterious Hottie*, sitting in the Starbucks on Tremont, his back against the window. He looks a little different—his jacket is more of a blazer than I remember it, and more fawn than brown, although it's still corduroy and scrumptiously beat, and his hair looks longer than it could have grown in a couple of days—but somehow I know that it is, in fact, the Mysterious Hottie, and my recognition is confirmed when he lifts the coffee and I see his ridged knuckles and that grimy thumb.

I stop quite suddenly, much to the annoyance of the commuter crowd that stomps around me. This all happens while I'm in one of those pedestrian walkways under some construction scaffolding, and I have to backtrack to find a place where I can slip through the supports and get into the Starbucks. By the time I do, I've had my feet stepped on too many times to remain cool, and I nudge my way clumsily through the tables to where the Mysterious Hottie sits with his knee up. A pad rests against his raised leg and he's sketching. His face is certainly handsome enough with its blond-brown downy chin-scruff and broad, broken nose, but it's only when he raises his eyes that you get that weak-kneed feeling.

I have no idea what I'm going to say to him—should I accuse him of following me, which I can no longer doubt he's been doing? Should I play it dumb, tell him I can't place him and see if he fesses up? Fortunately, I don't have to pick a tactic. I get to where I'm standing by the chair where his boot rests and I see in the window behind him a reflection of what he's sketching. It's a woman. Dark hair in an art-house bob. Prominent bones, judgmental eyebrows. Let's get to the point, sports fans: it's *me*.

He looks up. I feel my lips tighten and my nostrils flare as we meet eyes. He does not look surprised to see me. But then why the hell should he, having *anticipated* that I'd be walking down that street at that moment? Because there's no doubt in my mind that the man was waiting for me.

Then we talk:

Mysterious Hottie: Sit? (He raises himself a notch higher on his spine and lowers his foot from the chair. His voice is scruffy and *very* spare. You can tell that he never shouts, but, still, there's a power in his tone. This guy could whisper "fire" in a crowded theater and cause the proverbial stampede.)

Me: (not sitting, and doing a fair-to-middling job at meeting his gaze steadily) Would it be easier to sketch me at eye level?

Mysterious Hottie: (glances from me to his sketch pad. The tiniest smile slowly traces his lips. He turns the pad so that I can see. It is me, all right, or maybe I should say it is and it isn't. It's a penciled portrait of a woman's head, straight on like a mug shot. She has all my features, but now that I see the actual sketch the execution strikes me as primitive, like he's been sketching a mannequin version of me. Still, there's something about his use of line—he's either an artist or an art student, and probably talented.)

Me: Am I supposed to be flattered that some stranger is drawing me?

Mysterious Hottie: Wasn't counting on it.

Me: (dryly) Like hell. Come up with a new pickup routine. And stop following me. (I turn and knee my way through the chairs, hoping I can get out of there with the last word. I reach the door and pause, holding it open as a knot of students comes in. They are gaggling about and I'm forced to stand there, doorman style, while they bump and giggle-snort their way into the place. Not wanting to come across as frightened by the Mysterious Hottie and his otherworldly prescience, I turn my head and give him a look that I hope goes over as hard. Since I've discovered that I have a tendency to look pretty bloody hard when not attempting it, I figure I can pull off a glare.)

He's sitting there, one leg up, old jeans and crusty boots just so. He's sipping coffee and perusing his sketchbook, and he must get some inkling that I'm looking at him because he lifts his head and meets my eye. He says something, or maybe just mouths it—not in a stagey way but I'm meant to read his lips—and then he nods. His facial expression is not unfriendly or ominous—in fact, it might even be sympathetic, but then he's a guy and so doesn't show much of anything with his eyes. Bastard.

It takes me until I'm stepping through the revolving door and into the

Parker House, imitating his lip movements with my own, to figure out what he'd mouthed to me. It was "*I saw.*"

GIVE IT TO ME STRAIGHT

36-D @ February 1 12:15 am

Hon, your life is getting spooky. I hate to break it to you but that lawyer creep is right: you should be focusing on Getting Out of this case, not on getting in deeper. Screw the whole search for the truth about Mr. Suicide. GET AWAY FROM EVERYTHING TO DO WITH HIM.

proudblacktrannie @ February 1 12:16 am

Pepper spray? I know where you can get some easy. TTYOL?

fickel @ February 1 12:17 am

All good advice, but, putting aside the Mysterious Hottie for a moment, don't you see what is going on here? That is *the Peacock's* necklace photographed on Stephen Pearle's shop wall. What is the connection?

marleybones @ February 1 12:19 am

Maybe it doesn't connect. IMHO we have been building mysteries out of some very *unamazing* coincidences. Leave it alone, fickel. Unless you ARE Mr. Suicide's unknown lover and DID push him into the path of a train and therefore you need to stay close to the case so as to cover for yourself—all of which we know is NOT true—leave it behind.

proudblacktrannie @ February 1 12:21 am

And also blow off the Burly-Bear until he comes to you and *assures* you that the BPD are out of your life and he is off-off-off duty. That's the first moment you owe him any *hint* of an explanation about the tat guy living in your place. Do you hear me, girl?

hitman @ February 1 12:22 am

Blow off Burly-Bear? With this mind-reading doodler stalking her, mouthing vague threats across crowded coffee shops? fickel, B-Bear represents the closest thing to safety in your life right now. Here's some real advice: tell your brother to blow. Then call Burly-Bear and explain who your brother is, plain and simple. Then tell about this Mysterious Hottie, including the bullshit threat. Tell the cop everything and he will help you.

chinkigirl @ February 1 12:25 am

What about the weird necklace connection? Should fickel reveal that to Burly-Bear as well?

proudblacktrannie @ February 1 12:26 am

Not fickel's problem. Keep that to yourself.

chinkigirl @ February 1 12:27 am

I don't know. I have to say I was liking the sound of hitman's advice, now that this "Mysterious Hottie" figure has moved into focus. But if fickel is going to ally herself with Burly-Bear, doesn't it have to be all the way?

36-D @ February 1 12:30 am

Mysterious Hottie might be a cop, remember? He's also hot, so they've made his job to either seduce fickel and get her into some pillow talk or send her scampering into Burly-Bear's arms. The only one you can trust is Mr. Groin. You know where he comes from and he doesn't have any mixed motives.

proudblacktrannie @ February 1 12:31 am

wait, so she's blowing off BOTH hot cops?

webmaggot @ February 1 12:35 am

What are you on, ladies? Anyone who still has a "cop conspiracy" theory in his head needs to swear off TV for a couple of weeks and *adjust* to real life again. Cops don't go "undercover" for this kind of junk. This guy—Mysterious Rottie—is a psycho, plain and simple, who has got fickel spooked and confused because (and, with all due respect, here's the way the distaff sex thinks) he happens to be good-looking. If you doubt me, think about this: *if he isn't psycho, why would he stalk her when he could just walk up and ask for a little vagina action like the polite young guy he looks to be?* Well, apparently that's not how the guy works, fick. He needs to do his own freaky thing regardless of what he looks like and how easy it would be for him to have the sex life that all the rest of us would love to have. Think Ted Bundy, 'kay? Just pretend it's an ugly guy doing what he's doing and suddenly you'll see it exactly the way I'm telling it.

i.went.to.harvard @ February 1 12:44 am

Hear, hear.

fickel @ February 1 12:46 am

I'll think that through.

marleybones @ February 1 12:48 am

Here's something else to think through. This may sound like a stretch, but when I reread the diary excerpt that Burly-Bear and the Colonel analyzed, the so-called pandering pussycat from Sleepy Hollow sounds a lot like the Peacock!!!

i.went.to.harvard @ February 1 12:51 am

Although Sleepy Hollow is in upstate New York, or at least that's what my sketchy memory of Ichabod Crane tells me.

marleybones @ February 1 12:52 am

Actually, there's a Sleepy Hollow Cemetery in Concord, Mass. I just checked.

chinkigirl @ February 1 12:54 am

I'm finding this whole Peacock angle strangely ominous, but I'm not quite in touch with why. It's like I'm grasping about for a simple explanation that makes all of this go away, and instead it becomes increasingly complex.

proudblacktrannie @ February 1 12:55 am

Are we wondering if the Peacock could have been more than just a customer of Mr. Suicide's?

roadrage @ February 1 12:58 am

Wait—I thought she was supposed to be doing the dirty with the Groin Machine?

36-D @ February 1 01:01 am

No—all we got there is that he'd *like* to be doing it with her.

marleybones @ February 1 01:03 am

Look, guys, we needn't go so far as to put the Peacock in the middle of the action. But even if she weren't a personal friend of Mr. Suicide's, couldn't she have gotten to know him a little while he designed her necklace? After all, a commission like that makes people rather friendly.

i.went.to.harvard @ February 1 01:05 am

And couldn't she have, I don't know, fixed him up with some young sex toy she happened to know—the pool boy, the landscape guy?

fickel @ February 1 01:17 am

Or the girl who edits her husband's book. Isn't that what you're all thinking?

i.went.to.harvard @ February 1 01:29 am

It wasn't what I was thinking. Not at all. Anyone else?

fickel @ February 1 01:44 am

I see. Well, no Purple Hearts going out tonight. 'Til tomorrow, comrades.

19

FULL FRONTAL

EXISTENTIALISM ENGORGED

02.01 @ 2:43 AM:
KILLER CHICK 'N' SLACKER DUDE SITTING IN A TREE!

Dropped by Killer Chick's place t'othah night jes foh wu–up. The answer being nuttin', I go round back, just for giggles, like. Behind her place is nice and dark, with the butt ends of four-story walk-ups kind of crowded together, their wooden porches forming a crooked ring around some sort of shared blacktop parking area where six, seven cars are jammin like pigs round a troff. No laundry hanging out but it's that kind of yard, if you follow. No lights, either, except what cracks through winder shades. And no dogs. Dogs suck, so I'm real happy to not hear them (or step in their gooey piles of doo). Lot of TV angst floating round in the dope-tinged air. Warm night for winter, so a couple people r out on one of the porches, way high up, silhouetted against the night, smoking. Sigh—the sights you see when you ain't got a night-vision bolt action sniper rifle—hey wait I do but unfortunately not on me. All in all a homey hood, even "safe," in that easy-to-break-&-enter-but-nuttin'-to-steal sort of way.

So I swing me up and land light and sweet on the porch behind Killer Chick's place. She got no window looking on the porch, more the shame, but I ease my bum up onto the soggy railing and lean out a little to check out some rattan shades and, oh yeah there's my fav-o-rite girl hunched over some laptop. There's a ceiling bulb throwing some low-end wattage, but the place is generally doused in deep brown gloom, except for the bright white screen of the Vaio beaming up into her tweetie lil face.

Killer Chick is wearing a clingy pink t-shirt made of something ribbed and stretchy so I can count the bumps of her spine, and maybe some yellow-n-white striped boxers below—guy's boxers with the rim rolled over a couple times so they'll fit her nice. She's sitting in profile, so I can see one of her eyes in spite of the nerd-girl specs on her face that reflect the computer light—it occurs to me that these are different specs than the ones I've seen her wearing, and I wonder whether she broke her real glasses and so had to resort to an old pair (with an old scrip?—*not a good idea, KC*!)

She peers into that screen like a girl staring into one of those self-lit makeup mirrors you see in the pharmacy, hunting for beauty in that reflecting pool, but Killer Chick is looking at words, and her fingers don't play among little jars of makeup, no, they trickle over the alphabet keys that allow her to express herself—giving her the blush and bravura she seeks as much as other girls seek rouge and lipstick. Is it Killer Chick's *blog*, pray? And is this perchance an opportunity to take our relationship to the next level?

Shhhhhhhh. How I imagine us together, our date with destiny, approaching one another on an empty street in the deserted shopping district, the moonlight silver off the wet pavement, you in silhouette, your coat cinched tight at the waist, your hair an unruly thicket. You stop, seem to study me as I emerge from the shadow of an awning, and as I walk toward you, flicking open my straight-edge, you suddenly toss your cigarette off to the side, your gesture efficient yet loose and graceful. For a moment it seems as if you will run right to me, as you drift a step in my direction, but then you swing round and skitter down the steps of the T station with a little cry—whether excitement or fear, I cannot discern. I give chase, a smile involuntarily breaking across my face.

As I settle in to watch, Killer Chick is just swirling some booze around in a square-bottom glass while she reads her screen, then leans her head back and takes a throaty sip before she resumes her typing. I admire her for drinking the hard stuff. These girls hanging out in Cambridge with their sauvignon blanc de blanc bousheet I can stuff in a deserted Charles River drainage pipe (and have done, in fact, on one excellent evening some couple months back!) Occasionally she types; her keyboard style is like a journalist's—hard and spurty.

While I'm watching, who should come strollin' out from some unseen back hallway but the Slacker Dude, smokin a fat j and carrying a towel. First I think he's wearing some sort of t-shirt decorated like a comic book but while he stops to take in Killer Chick I notice he's playing with his belly button and so I catch that he's shirtless—much of his torso's just covered in multicolored tattoos. The reds especially seem brighter than most skin dyes you see. Dude's got some of them nipple rings going on as well, making me wonder if he's about to drop dead from blood poisoning—could happen, but it's not, like, the type of thing you would want to rely on.

Anyway, he wanders over to snag a look over her shoulder at what she's typing and I finally get the full picture: the boy'z bare-ass naked. He's got the towel bunched over his pubes and draped down the fronts of his legs, which is why I didn't notice his serious lack of pants before. But now I see the water dripping down his yellow tush. Just out of the shower, and not a speck of modesty on the dude.

Killer Chick doesn't turn from the computer; maybe she don't notice or just doesn't care that he's walking around nude as a doggie. She does care, however, about keeping what she's doing from his prying eyes. She tilts the screen down so he can't catch it, then makes a casual "bug off" finger flutter over her shoulder. He answers equally carelessly, parks his joint between her fingers and raises the towel to flip it over his head so he can dry his skull and then his back. Guy's got a hard little physique going on sho noh and is obviously proud as hell of his manhood, but she's not bothering to turn around so the show's just for me. Thanks, peckerhead.

Anyway, the Slacker Dude wises to the fact that his posing ain't catching much attention so he throws the towel aside and walks over to retrieve his doobie. He drags on it and then reaches around from behind her and places it between her lips. If she gave a shit about anything but what she's doing online maybe his come-on might be almost working, but she doesn't look interested even as she puckers up and takes herself a long, lush drag from between his fingers. Looks like these lovers are kind of used to it—bit odd, too, because he, at least, seems young to be in a fuck-rut. But, hell, you got a lot of ignorant folks doing each other at fifteen years of age, married just as soon as it's legal, middle-aged with six turd-crusted offspring at twenty-five, dead to one another long time before that. Some parts of the country it's quite common, I believe.

So anyway, the two of them start talking and it seems like he's making a case for her showing him more of what she's into on the Vaio and she's making a case for him a go fuck hisself, although neither one seems actually pissed off. She's pulled her feet up so she's resting her chin on her knees and she pushes a foot against the desk to kind of rotate the chair round so that, whether or not she caught on that he was starkers before, she sees it now. She hardly blinks, and seems to make a casual gesture over toward somewhere I can't see. Looks like there's some clothes she washed and folded for him but he turns back to her with some kind of complaint. So with a roll of her eyes the Killer Chick half stands up and shucks off the yellow striped boxers and chucks them over, all in one smooth motion. She pulls the bottom of her pretty pink t-shirt down over her bottom when she sits again to make a kind of dress out of it, not wut I'd call particularly quick or anything. Seems like she just wants something between her sweet little cheeks and the chair, and I only catch a sliver of her girlie-nest but I do in point o' fact *see* this and that's enough to know she's got nothing on under the boxers but the triangle of moss God supplied. The Slacker Dude flashes a smile—kind of brief and nasty like maybe he'd be up for some but has the idea that she's not in the mood. Maybe they just did it before his shower.

So kool as can be she crosses her legs and swings the chair back toward her Vaio, where she lifts her drink and tilts herself another trickle. Behind her, Slacker Dude stands there, his fist gripping the yellow striped boxers round his unseen member. After a couple of long seconds he gets over it. He pulls on the shorts, then the pants she's washed, and when he starts talking to her again I get the gist of what's about to happen. This is fortunate because I'm getting tired of sitting on that rail. I slither off my perch so I'm out front well before he emerges.

Sure enough, in a minute out pops Slacker Dude in his downy-fresh threads. I give him a follow until again I get the gist of whu-up and then I hustle while he stops to suck off the nub of his hay-bone before hitting the Avenue. So I'm way ahead of him and inside the internet café, even have time to buy two coffees and guzzle an inch of joe off one of them before he arrives. Even this late the place is jammed with a bunch of morons, almost all college and post-grad geeks by my eye—guess they got too much know-how to risk calling up their favorite fetish sites back at the dorm. I grab like eighteen sugars and dump them in the coffee I haven't tasted, then squeeze into the last available seat next to some fat chick doing it up in dyed orange hair, forehead zits and a knit cap. She is systematically chewing her fingernails whilst her eyeballs jizz all over some online garbage I don't even want to begin to imagine.

"Got a pen?"

Fat Red turns her head sharply and takes me in without missing a chomp on some thumb cuticle, one of her chubby cheeks squashed up almost into her eye what with the effort. For a moment her gaze is utterly blank, and then her eyes flood with yearning. She's asking herself if I might be some freak who's gonna chat her up and then rape her raw, like in the movies. She's not sure whether some stranger who asks her an innocuous question could turn out to be such a psycho? (*Just once, though, please, God, please?*)

"Like to write with." I mime writing in the air.

She studies me for another beat, then lets her eyeballs bounce back and forth between my two coffee cups. It takes her a second, and then she catches on to the implication of the second cup. She rolls her eyes and uses a tone like she's saying something sarcastic, which she isn't.

"Whutevurrrr."

She sticks a hand into her coat pocket, then pokes it, fingertips glistening with saliva and cuticle blood, in my direction. In her hand is a cheap ballpoint with no cap and the plastic nub chewed to pulp. Unfortunately, it's too disgusting to touch. My hand falters, all on its own accord.

"Yeah, that's okay," I say.

She stabs it into her pocket and turns furiously back to her screen. "Then wha'd you ask for?" she hisses, more to herself than to me.

"Hey, save my seat for a sec?" I say.

She hisses me a "*fat fuckin chance*," but while I'm snagging a pen from the Euro-barista I see her slap a hand down on my stool to prevent some hovering dweeb from claiming it. Chicks, huh? Each pathetic one bearing her own cross through life. Hard to imagine why they put the effort in.

I resume my seat and write on the cardboard cup I haven't drank from. Then I bang up Full Frontal, start typing, and sit tight, one ear listening for him. Sure enough, the door opens with the Slacker Dude's signature jam-jerk and I catch a glimpse of his hoodie-sleeveless jean jac combo reflected in the plate glass. He looks around and seems about to start fuming that there's no available stations, but I make sure that my tush is just leaving my stool when his eyes get around the room a second time and he homes in, intent on claiming my spot.

I turn, rubbing my eye like I've got nothing on my mind and then I "catch sight" of Slacker Dude and "realize" that he's waiting for a machine. I point at my spot like to ask "you want this?" and he pushes his way over, clearly eager to cut off whoever might have a more legitimate claim to the next available station. His eyes are bloodshot from the weed but he doesn't seem all that stoned. He's also not the type who is troubled by people's need for space; bumps me hard with his chest, then slides his whole torso against mine, half pushing me out of the way so he can take my spot. Sheesh.

"You're supposed to buy a coffee or something to score a computer, bud," I say kind of coolly, like I don't appreciate being climbed all over and so am giving him a little back.

He doesn't bother to answer, completely uninterested in me now that he's in my seat. But after a second or two the truth of what I've pointed out seeps in and he jerks his attention from the screen. His irises must be some light blue-grey color, because they come off as almost transparent with the computer's light shining into them, like two black pin dots with nothing around them. Fact is the guy's an ugly little rat when you actually get close up to him—a human scavenger, even down to the sharp little teeth. He's already typed in whatever search he's interested in and thus has closed down Full Frontal without a glance, but that doesn't trouble me. I've thought this through.

"You work here som'n?" he says. Talks like every other dropout dipstick you're going to want to meet. Pretty comical, when you think about it, that they all decide to adopt the same dumbass fake-o jive accent.

"Just telling you the way it is," I say.

He snaps his fingers and jerks a thumb over his shoulder. "Find it, fairy." Then he's back to the screen.

"Here," I say in a pleasant, patronizing tone. I put my untouched coffee on the counter next to him, placing the cup deliberately so he can read what I wrote on it. "My girlfriend didn't show, so it's yours."

He mumbles "blow me" and goes back to the screen, banging away with a couple of fingers and his thumbs. I know where he's going, too. He caught Killer Chick's url and he's been spying on her and her blog buds, and now he's hooked and can't wait to tune in to catch what they're gabbing about. Naughty little Slacker Dude!

I lean forward and push the coffee cup deliberately with my fingers, as if making sure it's away from the edge of the counter. A second later, I, too, have Killer Chick's url. Naughty me!

So I leave the internet café and, just for kicks because there's a handy bar diagonally across the street, I go in and order myself a Mountain Momma Rag, then lean against the window to watch. Sure enough, the Slacker Dude comes out of the internet café. Took him maybe fifteen minutes to find and get the gist of Full Frontal—not bad for a stoner. Out on the sidewalk, he looks around, slow and careful, then moves out from the doorway vaguely, not sure of which way to go. I know he wants to run back to Killer Chick's place, but maybe now he's considering whether he's being watched. He makes up his mind and turns deliberately away from home and starts walking quickly. Kind of stupid, but then he's that kind of fella. I don't follow.

Yeah, kid, so now you know. TELL KILLER CHICK SHE'S IN DANGER!!!

...or maybe you won't, scum pervert, after you read tonight's post...

---

tALK. NIHILISt DOGS

losmuertos @ 02.01 03:12 am

I'm luvin it, mon. What you write on the cup to get him to go for it?

fullfrontal @ 02.01 03:21 am

Wrote WATCH U SHOWER?—1 hr/$100

losmuertos @ 02.01 03:44 am

huh?

fullfrontal @ 02.01 03:45 am

So he sees that and figures out I left it for him.

bonitoestoria @ 02.01 03:47 am

So he go outside but you not there. So whazza point big boy?

fullfrontal @ 02.01 04:02 am

Figure it out, stupidos.

eddielizard @ 02.01 04:11 am

I think you sex-u-a-lee con-fuuzzzed, mon.

garbo @ 02.01 04:12 am

(Impatient eye roll.) The slacker kid reads the message on the cup and, whether or not he's interested in showering in front of a guy for a hundred bucks, he's certainly going to be curious enough to go to the history queue to see what the dude who left the message has been browsing. Annnnnnnd, just so's you don't need to ask, losmuertos, all the extraneous sugar in the cup is like in case the kid happens to actually sip the coffee, it'll be disgustingly sweet so that could also get him to focus on the cup, think back on the guy who gave it to him, and check the history queue. All of the above just increasing his chances of getting his nasty little eyeballs all over Full Frontal (the url, not our host). Ta-dah.

fullfrontal @ 02.01 04:15 am

Ah, a seer among the blind.

boytoucher @ 02.01 04:16 am

Still no get der big idere. Slackerdude find Full Frontal. So whad?

fullfrontal @ 02.01 04:19 am

And he reads it. Sheete youse sumfukass waysproduk.

bonitoestoria @ 02.01 04:20 am

o mon ju ess one clever fello. Still, I not getin for whut reasin dis slacker dude should get hissellf so work up 'bout tonite's postin. *You* be the pervert, man, wid you peeping. *He* got nothing to be embarrass about, where I'm from, to walk roun nikkid in front of his woman and to put her nice warm pannies up next to him. Wasso problemo????

fullfrontal @ 02.01 04:21 am

Trust me, it ain't sweet for that particular girl's pannies to be on that particular boy's stick.

garbo @ 02.01 04:32 am

(Shrug) People do a lotta things in private they couldn't possibly explain to the rest of us.

fullfrontal @ 02.01 04:33 am

Yeah well you got that right b'yitch.

garbo @ 02.01 04:34 am

Look, brain trust, I'm not much on rear window ethics, but if you don't like what you see when you peep, try not peeping.

fullfrontal @ 02.01 04:35 am

We're a race of peepers, honeyslot. Wuss dat we doin' right heah?

garbo @ 02.01 04:36 am

There are voyeurs and there are adventurers, comrade. But enough banter (exasperated flounce). When do *you and I* meet? You're one tryst away from true love after today's good deed, by my count.

fullfrontal @ 02.01 04:37 am

T.

garbo @ 02.01 04:38 am

You got trains on the brains, my friend. Is this a fetish?

fullfrontal @ 02.01 04:39 am

You got a label thing?

garbo @ 02.01 04:40 am

defensive about it, r we?

fullfrontal @ 02.01 04:41 am

chugga chugga choo choo, all a-bored the hunny egggg-spresss.

garbo @ 02.01 04:42 am

Tee hee!!!! OK, what line? What stop?

fullfrontal @ 02.01 04:43 am

Green Line. Hynes.

garbo @ 02.01 04:44 am

Why there?

fullfrontal @ 02.01 04:45 am

I luv old records. So how m'I gunna recah-nize you anywayz?

garbo @ 02.01 04:48 am

Oh I stand out in any crowd as you will see.

fullfrontal @ 02.01 04:49 am

Yeah this is zack-lee what I'm suspecting—lemme guess, you're the six footer with the wig and the scarf tied round your neck to hide yer man-lump?

garbo @ 02.01 04:50 am

No sweetie I'm regular height and it's a woman's neck, you can carve me a second smile yourself if I'm lying. But don't worry about finding me, I'll find you after I check you out and see if you're the pervert you pretend to be.

fullfrontal @ 02.01 04:51 am

Huh? Thought you was the one who was all hot for it?

garbo @ 02.01 04:52 am

Did you *read* your own post tonight? You're hot, lovah, but you're one weird wuff-wuff. I don't fancy myself next week's chick-in-the-dumpster.

fullfrontal @ 02.01 04:53 am

Pffffff. I make all the sheet on this site up. I'm just a sweet boy lives with his Ma. You ain't figured that out yet?

garbo @ 02.01 04:54 am

Mmmm, that's what all the psychos say. And it's probably true.

fullfrontal @ 02.01 04:55 am

Wutevah. Bring your mace, paranoid sistah. Time?

garbo @ 02.01 04:56 am

Uhhhhh, offsite. I don't need your circle of perverts showing up like dogs at a gang bang.

fullfrontal @ 02.01 04:57 am

yeh good point comma thinka it.

garbo @ 02.01 04:58 am

See that, swee-pea we're gettin along already.

20

LIFE IS PULP

Feed the Beast With L.G. Fickel

February 1 @ 3:24 pm
>SCENE OF ZEE CRIME<

I'm going to be scolded relentlessly by my favorite bevy of magpies but nevertheless I *have* to report that today I did something—quite spontaneously and without any conscious notion about it in advance—that's apparently been roosting in the recesses of my mind for days:

I went back to the place where Mr. Suicide did it.

The answer to "*egad, fickel you self-destructive ninny, why, why, why, why, why*?" is that, well, guess I needed to. "For the portent bade me understand... Some horror was at hand." Something like that.

Went as a lunch break from work, and—I swear, dolls 'n' dudes—I did not know where I was going at the time. In fact, my first clue that I was about to do something strange was that I took a lunch "break" at all. We junior eds pride ourselves on our prowess at the art of desktop dining. But today I rose from my computer with nary a glance at my cup-o-tomato basil powder or an eyelid flutter at the coffee bar, where Noah stood at the boiling water tap, busy reconstituting his favorite beef barley (the boy has *farty* taste in freeze-dried cuisine). I slipped into the back hall, claimed my coat from its cubby (yes, we have "cubbies," hardy-har-har) and was out the back door before you could say "whu-whu-whu-which way did she go?"

"Well, I am a sneaky one," I congratulated myself as I tripped on down the cobbled delivery drive.

And then I asked myself, "Self? Um, why, exactly, did I just sneak out like that?"

And that's when I first discovered, rather matter-of-factly, that it was "Because I am going to the Hynes T stop and I don't want company."

In the words of the immortal Garbo—"I vhun tuh be alun" (or "I vhun tuh be LEFT alun," as the great goddess always insisted the line actually went, although it sure as hell *sounds* like she skipped the word "left" and I don't actually get the big difference, anyway, myself).

So I let that little surprise sink in for a moment as I scurried down the sidewalk, energized by vain hopes that a quickened circulation might help me outrun the liquid chill in the air—yeah, right.

Then, when I'd let a bit of time elapse just for politeness's sake, I asked myself, "Uh, self? Why am I going to the Hynes T station?"

Self wasn't exasperated or offended in the least but at the same time didn't give what I could call an elucidating answer. "You know," self said. Didn't seem like self was in a mood to be toyed with. So I let the subject drop and simply went along.

Hey, guess what—the station looks the same as it always has. Here are its finest features, for those who live outside of Boston:

Eerie gusts from nowhere. Distant rumbles from the long black dirty tunnel holes you don't quite want to look directly into. People scuffing around like surly zoo animals. Human fixtures include the bearded guitarist with his open case at his feet, a couple of crumpled bucks scattered inside like so much litter. His voice is scratchy and high-pitched as he channels—Dylan? Neil Young? Joni Mitchell? Jump back, Jackson—is it *Chris Martin*? There's the ubiquitous sewer hag, too, prowling the edge of the platform down past the stairs where the humans don't go. The Hynes sewer hag is horrid to behold. Today she's wrapped in a down coat, red with black grime lining its seams, and appears to be muttering both sides of an imaginary argument.

For a moment I harbor a flight of fancy in which I stride into her lair and, in the space of a few deft questions, elicit from her that she'd witnessed the entire scene with Mr. Suicide—heck, she'd actually *seen* him attempt to take his fatal walk off the platform five or six times over the course of the hour *before* I'd happened along to witness the final effort. I stare at the old woman as I imagine this (*is* she even old? who can tell with that freezer-burn skin?), and then, as I notice her eyeballing me back, turn away abruptly. And that, friends, is when I see him. As in

HIM! HIM!! HIM!!!!

Who Him, you ask?

You need to *ask* that?!?!?!?!? I reply.

He's wearing his usual ratty corduroy jacket-coat and some dusky olive-green jeans, and as he walks toward me I get the sense that he's just risen from one of the benches, like—yup, you guessed it—*like he's been waiting for me.* This would be impossible, being as I only knew myself that I would be coming here moments before I arrived. My heart stops—it's one thing to speculate that some pretty-boy psychic sketch artist is haunting your life, following you to places that you didn't know you were going yourself, *and it's quite a-bloody-nother to have this fantasy verified.*

I feel myself going solid steel as he approaches—that's what I do when I'm scared shitless. Fortunately, I'm also angry. Definitely angry, this time.

He stops in front of me and rubs a thumb around his prickly jawline, studying me. Or giving me a chance to study him, perhaps. Probably this works with most women. Works pretty danged good on me—I can't *help* wanting there to be some explanation other than that he's a cop or a pervert. So, you know, we stare a while, me and Mr. Angel Face. Then we speak.

Mysterious Hottie: You're here.

Me: (My eyebrow may flicker involuntarily, but that's all I'll give him.)

M.H.: Go ahead. Take a long look. (He gestures with his head in the direction of the tracks. He's got that same near-whisper-that-you-can-somehow-hear thing going as the other time we spoke. It makes everything he says come out laden with meaning.)

Me: (pure steel) I told you to stop following me, didn't I?

M.H.: (studies me for a moment, then nods to himself) It's your first time back. Sorry. (He saunters off to lean against a support, his hands in his pockets, like a guy waiting on a friend who's off to take a leak or make a private call or something.)

Me: (walking over) Let's keep it simple, can we? I'm here to catch a train. You're here because you're stalking me. And I'm calling a cop. (I pull out my cell.)

M.H.: I didn't mean to crowd you, but there's no use pretending.

Me: Do I look like I'm pretending? (I stab out 9-1-1, half-expecting him to grab the phone.)

M.H.: (he utters a soundless laugh) You don't think the cops know I've come here? They know it. I know they know it because one of them asked me and I didn't see any reason to hide it. My guess is they think you've been coming, too. But you're just here to take the train.

Me: (not pushing the call button for 911 yet but keeping the phone raised to my ear) Are you saying you were here...that night?

M.H.: I thought you knew that.

Me: How would I?

M.H.: I recognized you. Figured you recognized me.

Me: You're lying.

M.H.: (patient, like I'm a child)

Me: Where were you, if you were here? (I cast an eye past him, toward where I'd been standing when Mr. Suicide had pushed by me) Hiding behind a post?

M.H.: (He stares at me for a second as if my half-baked attempt at an insult has caught him by surprise—like he had, in fact, been hiding behind a post that night, like he'd pushed Mr. Suicide from behind me, right past me and into the tracks.) I was on the train.

Me: (my turn to be caught by surprise—somehow I'd never given much thought to the perspective of the people on the train. I'd been almost smug about being the only witness, the only person who'd had respect enough for Mr. Suicide's anguish to stick it out and give an accurate statement to the cops. Now I find myself wondering if I'd even been useful, or if Burly-Bear and his buds had gotten the same garbled story fifteen times over from the poor sods who'd ridden the blunt instrument right into its victim.) You saw what from the train?

Mysterious Hottie: I saw you.

Me: (feeling myself go very faint. I can hardly feel my lips when I speak again.) What does that mean? You saw me...doing what?

M.H.: Looking. Watching it happen.

Me: And afterwards you decided to start following me? Is this some sort of a...I don't know...you see a woman witness a suicide and something about it attracts you?

M.H.: Don't think so. Seems more like fate.

Me: Fate? Fate has brought us together through this pathetic soul's suicide? My, the human capacity for egotism never ceases to amaze.

M.H.: (nonapologetically) He didn't die so we'd meet. Nothing as simple as that. We're just wrapped up in the same fate sequence, for lack of a better term. I don't think it started with this, and I have no idea if any one of us is more central to it than anyone else. Maybe it's about us, but maybe it isn't. Maybe it's just about you.

Me: (imperiously) Meaning?

M.H.: Is there anything in your past that's reminiscent of...? (He tilts his head toward the tracks.)

Me: (chilled to the core. Only deep-rooted cynicism allows me to lie convincingly.) Not a thing.

M.H. (continues to study me. He thinks I'm lying, but he doesn't know.)

Me: (feeling in control in the face of his ignorance) Guess it's back to the Ouija board, huh?

I turn away to head for the stairs to the street. Our entire exchange, although tense, had been delivered in modulated tones, and I doubt that anyone standing around us has even perceived it as a confrontation. To my surprise, however, Sewer Hag has wandered out of her little leper colony of one and is hovering a few fetid feet from me. Close up, she's even more frightening to behold—her face looks scarred by windburn, the lines around her mouth deep as knife wounds; her hair is like a matted mass under a moth-nibbled scarf she's fashioned into a head shawl. The quilted down coat mercifully covers what looks to be multiple layers of greasy black clothing—stuff you don't want to think about ever having been some woman's fashion choice before it was discarded and picked up by this unfortunate life. I stop short and accidentally look into her eyes—they're disquietingly prescient—before averting mine.

Sewer Hag: Mördare! Mördare!

She kind of croaks the word—my English translation online dictionary ID'ed it as Swedish for "murderer," but who knows. To my even greater amazement, she goes to spit at me, but Mysterious Hottie pushes me and her spit sprays him instead. He ignores her and continues to push me, his hand against my back, until we're hurrying up the stairs together. By now Sewer Hag is shouting that same word after us—the stairs go on forever—it's like we've fallen into some Ingmar Bergman art flick.

Me: I'm going to fall and fuck up my stockings if you keep pushing me.

M.H.: Granny hit me with a loogey. I need a rabies shot, fast.

Me: (glancing down at where a bubbly mucoid glob drips down the fly of his pants) Oh, God.

I hurry. By the time we hit a coffee shop, I'm fighting the need to giggle madly. M.H. drops me in a chair by the door and peels off for the restroom to de-expectorate. I could walk out right now, of course, but instead I climb to my feet and line up for a very, very large chai spice. I can still feel the pressure of his fingers against my back as I order one for him, too.

M.H.: (settling across from me. He seems unsurprised that I've waited—the guy is confident, I'll give him that. Not cocky, though. More like, very eye-to-eye in his behavior toward me. Is it a unique appreciation for women as equal, or a mating tactic?) So what's it been like? Nightmares or sleeplessness? Scouring the papers for news, or have you actually called the cop in charge to try and get info about who the guy was and why he did it?

Me: (shaking my head as I eye him steadily). Sorry, but first we cover how it is you know who I am and how you manage to be where I'm going before I get there. Start with the diner on 128. I normally wouldn't even have stopped there. And don't go near the word "fate." Just don't.

M.H.: (taking a swallow of tea, then meeting my eye. The look in his says he doesn't have much hope of beating my skepticism.) All I can tell you is that I saw you on the platform that night the guy did himself and then the next night I saw you in the diner up on 128. Just happened to glance up and there you were, reflected in that mirrored wall behind the counter.

You do this thing with your neck (he makes a motion with his hand) when you're reacting to something—I saw it through the train window that night, and you did it again when you entered the diner. Caught my eye. I watched you. You had coffee, tried to get through it neatly but your hands were not steady. You were impacted by the suicide. I hadn't been able to brush it off, either. But it wasn't until I was back in the city that I got that I wanted to see you again. Man, what is this *shit*? (This last is aimed at his cup.)

Me: It's called tea. You let it steep. And I'm not sure I believe in coincidence any more than I believe in fate.

M.H.: Hold the thought, will you? (He goes up and gets himself a coffee. Real men don't drink spiced tea, I suppose. I watch his back as he pays. Even in droopy pants, his lean loins make their presence felt. He comes back and drops a shortbread bar in front of me, half wrapped in tissue. He's got one for himself, too, between his teeth.)

Me: Thanks, but I don't eat processed sugar.

M.H.: (nodding agreeably, he picks up my shortbread and shoves it into his mouth next to his own, then flushes it all down with black coffee. Somehow it doesn't come across as piggish, but more like he's the type who doesn't bother eating until the opportunity presents itself, at which point he stokes up so as not to have to be bothered again for a long while. He cleans his teeth with his tongue and ducks his head to one side so as to belch discreetly behind a fist before he resumes talking. I have to say, I'm a bit charmed by his consideration, compared to the way most men eat.) So, anyway, the next night I was finishing up this job I'd been doing in Concord. It was raining like a motherfucker and I went back to the diner, not really expecting that you would be there, but, you know, it just seemed like a weird night and I wasn't so surprised to find that you were. Problem was, you were way into your laptop and didn't look like you were in the mood to be approached. So I laid back. I didn't even catch that you spotted me—if I had, I would have tried to sit down with you. Anyway, I haven't been back up that way since.

Me: (still skeptical) And yesterday?

M.H.: Oh. (He almost smiles, then sees my face and plays it totally straight.) That's less of a coincidence. I saw you in the jewelry shop. Pearle's place. I think I must have come up the elevator right behind you.

Guess we were after the same thing. I didn't go in because you and that gay guy looked like you were getting kind of intense. Just didn't seem like the right time.

Me: If you were there, why didn't I see you?

M.H.: You didn't look behind you. I was out in the hallway. Saw you through the shop windows and grabbed the elevator down before it closed.

Me: You're telling me that in the space of a few seconds, looking through a thick tinted-glass window, you could tell the clerk was gay?

M.H.: (shrugs as if to say "come on")

Me: (okay, he has a point.) Where did you learn that the dead guy was Stephen Pearle?

M.H.: Where did you?

Me: I'm not the stalker. I don't have to explain myself.

M.H.: I got Pearle's name from the cops, which is what I imagine you did.

Me: (skipping his last comment, although it's not lost on me that I'm not so sure that Burly-Bear or Escroto would actually have given me Pearle's name if I'd asked for it, those bacon-biters) And after, at the Tremont Street Starbucks? Just drawing me from memory, were you?

M.H.: (pausing to swallow coffee) Well, it's what I do.

Me: What do you do?

M.H.: Draw people from memory. Although it's usually from other people's memories.

Me: I don't know what you're talking about. Are you some sort of art therapist?

M.H.: I'm a police sketch artist. I draw bad guys after they stick up the local Store 24. Drive-by shooters. Whatever. People describe faces to me and I draw them. Sometimes they look like the assholes they're trying to look like. Sometimes not too much. Depends on how I click with the witness.

Me: (feeling myself color in spite of all efforts to resist) So you're a cop. Well, I have to say, that was my first guess. (I start to rise from my chair.)

M.H.: (laying a hand on mine to stop me, then lifting it quickly when he sees my facial reaction) Not a cop. Not on the force. I do the sketching freelance.

Me: (feeling myself relax a nick, but unable to resist stinging him) Cash while you wait for recognition as a real artist?

M.H.: Screw that. Working as a police sketch artist is not something anyone would do for reliable cash in this day and age. They've got computers now, pull together a bullshit composite of a robot, but in most cases that's all you get. You know how little the real artists are used?

Me: (not ready to trust him) Then why do you do it? Just in case you need a suicide witness's name and number?

M.H.: (He flashes a half smile, so I know that at least the idea of hitching up with me has at least crossed his mind.) I do it as a community service. Sometimes it works better for a witness or victim to work with a real artist than with some cop in front of a computer. Parent who sees a kid take a slug. Rape victim. They get something out of focusing on the sketch pad and my hands, drawing. Don't ask me what—I'm just the man with the pencil.

Me: How PC of you.

M.H.: Yes, but that's not my reason for doing it. (He pauses, then shrugs.) My brother was a cop. Got shot in the neck and killed when he pulled over some freak for speeding on 495. He'd gotten me into police sketch work when I really needed the cash, couple years back. So I keep myself available in his memory. Keeps me in touch with some of his friends in the department.

Me: (relenting a little but not resuming my seat) I'm sorry about your brother. And I get how you might have seen Mr. Sui—Pearle's death and how you might get a little obsessed with it and how that might include getting a little obsessed with me. But that ends now. I'm not some morbid fantasy. I don't want to see you and I don't want to "run into" you. If you keep this up, I'm going straight to the very cops who gave you information about me that they should never have given out. I'm going to tell them that you've been stalking me and that I've got a real bastard of a lawyer and...and do you get that?

M.H.: (mildly) For sure.

Me: Good. (I go to turn and leave, picking up my tea.)

M.H.: One thing, though.

Me: (of course the cool thing would have been to walk out, but I'm feeling pretty slick after having fumbling that speech out, particularly the tricky part about "morbid fantasy." So I turn to give him one last, shriveling look.)

M.H.: What if I've gotten further than you in figuring out who this Stephen Pearle was and why he committed suicide in front of you? Don't you want to know about it?

Me: (faltering in a major way, as all my pent-up fears and obsession and, yes, even curiosity tumble to the forefront of my mind. I mean, here is someone who could give me all the inside crap about the BPD and Burly-Bear that I want, and also share my desire to get to the bottom of the whole muddled load of crap I'd been wallowing in for days now. I mean, banding together with the Mysterious Hottie could actually *clear everything up.*) What do you call yourself? (I ask it without thinking, my voice thin and unfamiliar.)

M.H.: Ferguson.

Me: Does that come with a first name?

M.H.: Guy. (He reaches to shake, which I ignore.)

Me: Guy Ferguson. (then, childishly) You didn't borrow that off your favorite soap?

M.H.: (smiling) My mother was French, so growing up it was "Gee." Anyway, everyone just calls me Ferguson.

Me: Thank you. It's good to have a name, for if I need to file a complaint.

I leave, feeling a flicker of triumph at having been both sensible and morally right. By the time I get to my office, I'm not so sure. The fact is, as I blog this right now, I'm taking solace in the fact that, if I do decide I want to know what the Mysterious Hottie knows, I can pick it right up where we left off at the Starbucks.

Sigh. So what do I do?

GIVE IT TO ME STRAIGHT

wazzup! @ February 1 04:38 pm

> Brilliant scene as always! Got the quote in minutes: *Rendezvous in Black!* Kiddo, you are just sooooooooooooooo CW!!!

36-D @ February 1 04:42 pm

Okay, so this guy Guy—huh, he's right, we should just call him Ferguson—anyway, he is *nowhere* on the web. I have googled up and down for the past half hour. Plus it's true that some cop with the name Bill Ferguson was killed on 495 two years ago, and I got some stuff about him but nothing on a brother. But I did find out that Bill (Guillaume was his real name) was originally from Toronto. That means that Guy is probably Canadian as well.

marleybones @ February 1 04:44 pm

Having enough success as an artist to make ends meet does not bring you above the obscurity level. Think of all the actors who make a perfectly good living whom you'd swear never existed until they score an Oscar nomination at age sixty. Writers, too. And all these folks are TRYING to get noticed. Guy Ferguson could be doing hundred-and-fifty-foot murals for Madison Ave lobbies and keep himself fairly obscure, name-wise. Besides, if he's from Canada chances are he's still not a U.S. citizen, so that makes his identity even more difficult to just pick up.

proudblacktrannie @ February 1 04:46 pm

Oh my word, maybe he wants a green card. Could you just give him my number, I mean, since you're clearly rejecting him.

fickel @ February 1 05:52 pm

Am I?

21

LIFE IS PULP

The Noir Boudoir of L.G. Fickel

February 1 @ 7:44 pm
>BURLY-BEAR CAN SHOVE IT<

(AND I HOPE THE BASTARD IS LURKING SO HE **READS THIS**)

Okay if you thought I was self-destructive *before*, wait five. At around 6:30 this evening I leave work—if I may call my rendezvous with the Mysterious Hottie followed by several hours of blogging "work"—and who should be waiting outside in his M-tang but the Burlster. He's all businesslike about how it's his duty to check up on witnesses in a sudden death scenario but really he just wants to drive me home to make up for the little tiff that we didn't quite have over the guy shacking up in my place.

So I'm actually happy to see him, and even more chuffed when I realize that I'm wearing my E. Bompard cashmere V-neck that Noah has nicknamed my "tittie-nips" sweater for reasons rather evident to the beholder. So we have a decent ride up Mem Drive, and I'm *just* getting around to considering whether I'm going to open up about Mysterious Hottie and maybe even let him talk me into a little "cop on top" when he blows it. And I do mean utterly and in one fell swoop. My thick-necked Lothario gets all smirky and side-glancy and then he lets me know that he's taken care of my "roommate" problem.

I, in turn, go all blinky and reedy-voiced and "umm, not quite *getting* you?" He, sensing that this conversation is going sour before it even gets up and running, retreats into that torpid cop formality he's so good at and tells me that breaking parole can be a serious infraction and that some guys just don't learn when you give them a break, but he figured it was worth a little unofficial direct leaning to get my "houseguest" back where he ought to be. So I let a little silence go by and then ask what exactly "direct leaning" consists of, and he gives me some hogwash about delivering messages in the only language some guys can hear. Ah, cops. What would we do with our elementary school bullies without this professional avenue through which they may allow their natural tendencies to flourish "productively?"

At around this juncture I get a little more shrill than is probably warranted (in retrospect even I see this), and accuse him of using intimidation tactics to get my brother out of my life when he's the only true support system I have, the only *real* man I can trust. And then I hop along to the topic of what *business* it is of *his* to be checking up on my family just to try and figure out who the *guy* is who seems to be sleeping in my apartment.

Thusly, sad to note, I stab my sharp little tongue a tad too close to the testes of the matter. We all know that guys don't like it when they're revealed as, I don't know, *hoping* for anything out of a particular woman—that'd be just soo homo. (breathe, breathe, collect self, collect self—evidently I'm still a touch *verklempt* over the whole thing)

So, anyway, Burly points out that at least he guessed right when he figured there must be a family connection rather than figuring a tat-hound like dickel would be someone I'd be shacking up with voluntarily.

At that, I get rather *sputtery* at the idea that I associate with my brother on any basis other than a voluntary one.

This in turn prompts Burly-Bear to present a hammy fist out of which protrudes his fingers, seriatim, as he proceeds to *pronounce* some of my brother's litany of so-called "crimes," such as grand sleaziness auto, possession of a controlled body odor, operation of his sneakers under the influence, loitering with intent to scratch his balls, etc.

To be fair, the list might or might not be impressive, but all I know is I'll be *damned* if I'm going to hear it. As I've said, I have an understanding with my dizygotic other that I will *not* seek to know of his various activities that might tempt *others* who do not *know* him or *love* him to rush to condemn—so I proceed to block out Burly-Bear's big, bossy voice by slapping about heedlessly to drown out his preachy ass. This includes smacking the dashboard, glove compartment, seats, door, myself, and, when none of that works to shut him down, I find that screaming and aiming my blows at *him* works more effectively.

So he shuts up. We finish the ride rather quietly, actually.

By the time he drops me off I'm crying silently, my furious face aimed down at myself, my left hand supporting my forehead with its fingers spread, more or less to block Burly-Bear from my view, or maybe vice versa. I'm certain he'll tidy up his memory of the scene so that it's dominated by my "hysterics," but let me make clear to all that it was his *righteous*, *insistent*, and *stubborn sermon* that forced me to escalate, and let me make it equally clear that he knew *quite well* through every moment of it what effect he was having on me. He didn't want to convince me of anything. He didn't even want to justify his own actions. He just wanted to win the little bullshit skirmish we were having.

And so he did win. Goody for him.

To some people, winning is everything. I just feel lucky, whenever it occurs to me, that I am not one of those people.

I slam the car door and he drives off and I go in. dickel is cleared out as expected. No note, but that's not his style. As for how I'll fill my lonely hours without him, I suppose I'll be busy being harassed by Burly-Bear in a more official capacity soon. Rest assured he'll be less clumsy in the role of the hostile aggressor.

Somehow I can't get up the energy to call Mr. Groin. He is just *such* a prick.

GIVE IT TO ME STRAIGHT

i.went.to.harvard @ February 1 08:14 pm

Call the prick.

proudblacktrannie @ February 1 08:15 pm

Remember, luv, he's *your* prick.

hitman @ February 1 08:17 pm

Uh, not to come off all shruggy over something that was clearly a BFD for you, but I'm not sure your fight with the cop sounds all that apocalyptic. I mean, you went a little bloody rag on account of the cops strong-arming your brother. Duh fuck's wrong widdat? If Burlyclown ain't stupid, and by my read he is not, by now he's seeing that he walked his dick right into the old wood chipper back there, crowing about how he cleared your place out for him and you to have a little "space" without considering that maybe you actually *like* your own brother. Fact is, people get it, in the end, that you're going to side with family.

fickel @ February 1 08:24 pm

My left eyebrow rises up an otherwise still visage—why are *you* being nice, pray tell?

hitman @ February 1 08:25 pm

Up your vag.

fickel @ February 1 08:26 pm

What with, lust bucket?

roadrage @ February 1 08:27 pm

Well, I for one agree with lust bucket. Plus, a guy knows that when a chick's crying she's going to say like just about anything. Anyway, personally I would not write off some chick who showed me she knows how to dish me a little crappola when I've earned it.

chinkigirl @ February 1 08:32 pm

Wow. I have to say, five minutes ago I was devastated. But now that two mega-males have weighed in, it reminds me that men don't perceive these moments that absolutely horrify us women in the same light as we do. I actually think B-Bear will be back. I'm not advising you to *take* him back, fickel—I'm just advising you to be ready for him to have brushed off this thing as one of those "she's on the towel" moments.

proudblacktrannie @ February 1 08:35 pm

Besides, knowing you, you look good when you cry. You're the type who doesn't get all crinkly and spitty.

fickel @ February 1 08:36 pm

I crinkle. And I do not want him to come crawling around—trust me.

hitman @ February 1 08:37 pm

So what do you want, now that you're through fluffing the cop?

fickel @ February 1 08:38 pm

Look: Burly-Bear flirted with me and I responded. We got to know each other a little, and have discovered we are not compatible. End of story. And if this reads as snappish, it's doing its job.

hitman @ February 1 08:39 pm

Lucky timing. For you, I mean.

fickel @ February 1 08:41 pm

Care to explain *that*?

hitman @ February 1 08:42 pm

Explain the obvious? No (yawn) not tonight.

fickel @ February 1 08:44 pm

Then shove off.

hitman @ February 1 08:45 pm

Can do.

fickel @ February 1 08:46 pm

Care to demonstrate?

fickel @ February 1 08:59 pm

Good man.

fickel @ February 1 09:15 pm

I didn't mean to "shove off" forever, of course :)

leo tolstoy @ February 1 09:17 pm

Every time I tried to display my innermost desires—a wish to be morally good—I met with contempt and scorn, and as soon as I gave in to base desires I was praised and encouraged.

fickel @ February 1 09:20 pm

You I could lose for good, my friend. And no, I'm not being facetious. >:(

22

LIFE IS PULP

Feed the Beast With L.G. Fickel

February 1 @ 10:52 pm
>PRETTY LITTLE THING—THAT'S ME<

Well, it's been a "single night with the duration of centuries," and I have a long, strange tale to relate. Bear with me.

As my earlier post makes needless to say, I was feeling restless and uneasy in my place tonight. My fight with Burly-Bear didn't seem as valiant once I'd focused on the fact that dickel is, frankly, back where he belongs. Assuming he's gone home, that is. Still, in the space of five days I'd gotten used to having someone to talk to, late at night when it counts, and I needed to talk. You guys are so supportive, but every once in a while a girl needs to rest her head on someone's shoulder, and for that you need a shoulder in the room. After signing off the blog, I actually considered calling the Colonel for a dose of richie-rich reality, but I'm still wary after the way he tattled to Mr. Groin about how self-destructive I am. Also I am *so* sick of his wife pretending to think the worst about me. I'm almost beginning to think that her glarey little "smiles" when she slithers through the room (*always* hoisting a fresh drink) during one of my work sessions with the Colonel are supposed to be delivering a message to me that she's onto my "scheme" to "steal" him from her. Christ. I'd fit into her shoes about as well as I'd fit into those conehead brassieres of hers.

So, anyway, after being rather an a-hole to hitman (you're not going to write me off for one lame moment, are you?), I headed out to pick up some Kung Pao bean curd, but found myself gliding past my usual

Vietnamese pickup toward the Red Line. Forty minutes later found me on Mr. Suicide's street, the thin moonlight luminescent, the noise of my heels echoing off the buildings. It was very cold, down there by the wharfs; my breath left icy ghosts in the air. His window was dark but this didn't fool me. I studied it until I could discern the faint glow, the flicker of movement—a computer screen changing images.

Not considering the consequences, I heaved the heavy outer door. The air inside was as dank as a crypt, and for a moment I just stood, absorbing the silence. I knew I should turn and go. Instead, I pressed the buzzer, hard, for a half minute, maybe longer. No name next to it, of course—no "Stephen Pearle, Superior Jeweler"—and for a moment I shivered with paranoia, wondering once again whether the cops had removed a nameplate to keep me ignorant on that first day they brought me over.

The return buzz chilled me more than it startled me. I shoved through the inner door and faced the metal stairs, spare as scaffolding, twisting up into the dark. I heard nothing and, peering up, I saw no light. Mr. Suicide's place was on the fifth floor, and I caught my first whiff of cigarette smoke on the landing just below. The scent was a little strange—familiar, but I couldn't place it. I could see that Mr. Suicide's sliding slab of a front door was partly open, the space behind it a greyer tone of black. Some obscure X, tallish with heavy shoulders, was standing there in silhouette.

Me: Hello? (girlish—a naif in the woods—where's my basket of marmite for Granny?)

X: Oh. (long pause) I see. (The voice is rough, unaffected. Androgynous but not young. Another long pause goes by, then the voice resumes.) Well, come in, then.

I enter Mr. Suicide's place. X has moved off. The computer screen provides the only light, which glints off the windowpanes in eerie repetition. I sense disorder, books in stacks, vinyl albums half sorted on the pond of glass that serves as the desk, a picture leaning against a chair. A fluorescent desk light flutters to life and a core area of the space, larger than I'd remembered it—or maybe that's what night shadows do—is suddenly lit in a diagonal shaft of searing white light that renders the darkness around it all the blacker. Chiaroscuro, anyone?

X sits with a heavy, leathery squeak in an armchair, just outside the light. I hear more than see a glassy clink—some objet d'art making itself useful as an ashtray. X is female, I can see, mostly in silhouette. Still, I get the impression of an almost aggressively unfeminine woman wearing what looks like it might be a pair of utility jeans and a velour sweatshirt in maybe a plum brown. Her hair is held off her face with some sort of tightly wound scarf so that it frizzes out in a frantic puff behind her skull, and her jawline and body frame are decidedly square, although age has softened her edges. Her only real concession to femininity is some sort of loosely knit shawl, a colorlessness froth around her shoulders. I finally place her as the woman who'd been in the back of the shop at The Blue Pearl—as my eyes adjust to the illusory light I can just discern the coffee-toned skin with its dark spatter of freckles and the strands of silver wired through her hair. I walk forward and perch tentatively on one end of the sofa across from where she sits, taking comfort in the feel of my coat tightening around me as I lower myself. Somehow this reminds me of how easy it will be to leave—to run, if I have to.

X: I'm gonna guess you don't smoke. Stephen wouldn't have liked having a smoker around, once he quit hisself. Maybe you lit up on occasion when he wasn't around, though? (She picks up a pack of something and seems prepared to toss it across to me if I signal.)

Me: No. I don't smoke.

X: Huh. Someone who hung around here sure did. I found a half a pack of Gauloises Blondes buried in a dresser drawer. Having one now, matter fact. Now this here's some serious smoking for you. Haven't seen one of these things since, hell, I'm gonna say since the first couple years I was with Stephen, when he was smoking them hisself.

Me: I should make it clear: I didn't know him. Stephen, I mean. I didn't know anything about him until after he died. I'm just a witness.

X: (mulls this over as she lights up) Well, I can see how he may have put hisself over as deep and mysterious to someone of your age. Myself, I knew him about as well as a soul could. Damned sight better than he knew his own self, that's for certain. Thirteen years of marriage will do that, though. (She's boasting. But why shouldn't she?)

Me: That's a long time to be married. (Then, so as not to come off as patronizing) It must make it all the more difficult to come to terms with his death.

X: (smokes, then speaks as if taking my comment at face value) Suppose you could say that I've come to terms with a lot of things, these past few years. Death, well, that's one of them. You hit a certain milestone, whether it be turning fifty years of age, or maybe your own mother and father pass. Or maybe you just catch your face in a mirror when you're out somewhere and not expecting it, at a restaurant or the mall, and after that event, whatever it may be, death is always *there*, you might say, like a fly behind the curtains, buzzing, but quietly. A man hits fifty and he gets pretty certain he's gonna die, one way or another, even when he hits it as soft as Stephen did. I mean most people figured him for early forties, tops.

Me: (quoting one of the greats without thinking) "Death brushes you in a crowd sometimes."

X: Amen to that. (brief pause) That's what you're about. You and his other pretty little things.

Me: (stirring) I ought to clarify something. I wasn't one of Stephen's pretty little things. I was just there; I just happened to be there that night.

X: (moving the ember of her cigarette to the ashtray) No need to take offense. It was just a term we used between us, me and Stephen. Stephen's first company was called Pretty Little Things; did he ever mention that to you? It had a double meaning—see, your fine jewelry is generally going to be a smaller piece, and jewelry is something that a man gives to his pretty little thing, his wife or girlfriend. I came up with that, matter of fact. Stephen worried that it was sexist or whatnot, but we did just fine with it. Yes indeed, we did just fine on that name.

Me: (It's dawned on me that she's stoned—her tone is light, her cadence a touch draggy, and there's definitely something about the way the hand with the cigarette lolls about. I know they'll give you anything to cope with a death, and I get the sense—not without a prickle of guilt—that she'll ramble if I push gently.) So that was your first store? Pretty Little Things?

X: (pause to shake her head) Wasn't a store. We was strictly mail-order back in Nevada. He did all his own designs and made the pieces hisself. These here pendants I'm wearing? (She pauses to touch at her earrings, which I can't see much of in the dark, although I can tell they dangle and have a delicate angly thing going on. When she resumes, she recites, like a child saying the pledge.) Each a cluster of briolette-cut diamond drops against pavé-set diamond supports, suspended from a baguette-cut diamond mounted on platinum, total weight 16 carats. (She pauses to smoke.) They're one of his earliest pieces. Stephen's work is durable; we were both real proud of that fact. He never did believe in prongs.

Me: You met in Nevada?

X: (eyeing me for a moment like she finds it hard to believe I don't already know all this, then speaking as if she's decided that she'd just as soon take me at my word) Yes indeed we did. Fact is, I was the jewelry maker at the time. Polished stones. Brass wire. Wooden beads. You know the stuff. Used to sell it at the various tourist stops. The Burro Post. Mountain Pass Inn. Did okay. I could see myself...returning to it.

Me: How did you meet? I mean, if it's not too...(I let the sentence die.)

X: Happened pretty quick, all told. Stephen was new in town. (She pauses to smile in the dark.) "Town," as it were; we're talking fifty structures kind of wedged between a highway on your one side and a mountain on th'other. They used to have live music, weekly, long as I can remember, at the Hotel Apache. Everyone went except a couple of the church mothers. So I was there one Saturday night, spotted Stephen ordering himself a beer while I was on the way to the john. He had a Lite, I still remember, and I caught a glimpse of him pouring it kind of carefully into a glass—Stephen was always on the elegant side. Naturally refined in his mannerisms. Anyway, I said in my head, clear as a bell: "That's mine." And I went to the john and I put on some lipstick I'd picked up that very afternoon—coral pink, it were—and when I got back to the bar I stepped right up to him. I said, "What do you do, sir?" He half looked over and I could tell that he was not in the mood for a conversation, but he was always polite, Stephen was, and he said he did a variety of things and was just passing through. I think it was meant to brush me off kind of gently, but somehow it had the opposite effect. I said, "I ask because you look like you might be an artist to me. I myself make jewelry, and I'm always looking for an artistic eye to give me some pointers." He looked over at me then. Yeah, he did, and I knew I'd done scored. He moved into my trailer that very evening, although we both claimed it was a "one night" arrangement at the time. Just never left until we left together. Left forever.

Me: That's very romantic.

X: (considering) Maybe so.

Me: So then Stephen started making jewelry?

X: (nodding, still in slo-mo) I taught him a couple of basics, but he had the skill. Soon he was the artist and I took to managing the business. Been that way ever since. Fact is, when we came to Boston and he opened the shop downtown it was me who insisted that we change the company name. I mean—you got the name Pearle and you make fine jewelry—this is what you call a no-brainer. Am I right?

Me: (I clear my throat.) Yes, of course.

X: Stevie called it kitsch—that was one of his words. But I went ahead; I knew my way, somehow. I put some money to work—full page spreads in the *Globe*, that sort of thing. That was too commercial for Stephen, likewise. Too cool by half, that man was. He didn't like when we got successful and started hiring other artists to make the pieces he designed, either. And why not? Because, like I'm telling you: it was all tangled up in aging for him. Of course, if he hadn't had the success, he would have been down about life passing him by. (She sighs heavily.) He was a child at heart.

Me: He was innocent?

X: (She laughs, one quiet grunt.) Children aren't innocent.

Me: (Somehow stung.) They are until the world screws them up.

X: (She smokes contemplatively. When she speaks it comes across as if we've agreed on something.) See, that's the thing: for better or worse, you can't get away from the world.

Me: (feeling my ears prick up) You don't think that Stephen would have done what he did over depression that he was aging and couldn't, I don't know, come to terms with it?

X: Oh, I do think that. I most certainly do. I think he got to that fiftieth birthday and he looked in the mirror and I think he said to himself that the next couple years was his last chance to get back to what you might call "experimenting" in life.

Me: Experimenting?

X: Yes, experimenting. Like you're doing.

Me: I'm experimenting?

X: (she shrugs) No need to take it that way. I'm just talking about that life everyone leads through their twenties—the life that got a white boy like Stephen hitched up with some brown-skin lady to begin with. I think he wanted a taste of that again, before he died. Started with that pretty little thing he worked with. (She smokes for a long moment.) The opposite of me, in many ways, although when I pointed that out, Stephen said no, that weren't it. I think he didn't want to make it "about me." I think he thought it would hurt less that way.

Me: And did it? Hurt less?

X: It may have. (She goes to take a last drag, then changes her mind and drops the cigarette into her dish, where it smokes like incense.) At first I pretended it didn't, but when we got friendly again, Stephen and me, well, I think that was when I realized that I truly didn't see this stage Stephen was going through as being about "me" or "us" or what have you. I don't know much, but if a man gets into wanting to try out something I don't got to offer, well, some folk may say he needs to resist that urge until his dying day, but I think different, myself. I think that maybe he ought to just go get it out his system. Only got the one life God gave you; might as well use it up. Anyway, that's where I ended up.

(Here she seems to contemplate me.) I guess I didn't know him quite as well as I told myself. (She moves in her seat and the back of her head grazes the picture that's leaning against the back of her chair.) Oh. This yours? Poster of that actress lady, the crazy one said: "Gimme a whiskey." (She chuckles humorlessly at her Anna Christie.) You can take if you like.

Me: You need to understand, Mrs. Pearle. I was never in this apartment until after Stephen's death, when the police brought me. I'm only here now because it's been hard for me to get the whole thing out of my head. I'm upset about your husband's death because of how it happened. I know it's nothing compared to what you must be going through right now, and I'm not asking for your pity or even your concern, but I think it's only right, I mean for your own sake, that you understand that I wasn't in his life.

X: (Instead of answering, she looks around the dark space, and when she speaks it's like I never said a thing.) I basically been cleaning out. Sorting. I haven't decided what I want to do with the place itself, though.

I admit, at first I kind of felt angry towards it, like you might expect me to feel about a part of his life that I wasn't invited into. Funny thing is I'm beginning to be comfortable here. I may rent it out, or I may just keep it empty for awhile, if I can afford to. (She lowers her eyes to me and they seem wet, but when she speaks it's in the same unemotional tone as earlier.) It's a financial question.

Me: (It clicks in my head that I should give up on explaining my presence and instead get whatever I can out of her. I'm not sure I consider this an honest thing to do, but even as I feel my way through that thought I find myself nodding like I agree with her about the tricky matter of juggling real estate and tax issues.) The police are letting you clean it out, then?

X: (She pauses to light a fresh cigarette.) I suppose that's how it is, now you put it to me that way. The police are "letting me" into my husband's place. I must say, it took them more time to come to terms with the fact that Stephen's widow is from the reservation (she uses the term with jocular disdain) than it took them to accept the rest of it.

Me: (I should pursue the issue of whether the police have concluded that Stephen committed suicide and not let me in on it, but I can't help allowing the other reason I'm there—the need to know Stephen and why he did what he did in front of me—take over.) What's "the rest of it?"

X: (smoking) I suppose "the rest of it" is the fact that Stephen and I would stay together, stay married, continuing to work as business partners, and, yes, I'm going to say remain friends, too, while he was doing his thing. (She pauses and I catch her humorless chuckle.) But I guess a lot of cops have gone through a "midlife awakening," as the men seem to like to call them. Seein' some big-ass black lady from Nowhere, Nevada, hooked up with a well-to-do white fella for nigh on fifteen years—now there's something they don't have to wrap their brains around every day. Yes, indeedy, I dare say that was a new one for most of your Boston police folk.

Me: Do you think Stephen's death had something to do with his midlife crisis?

X: (her tone a tad sharp) I don't recall saying Stephen was having a crisis. I just think that the young man got used to Stephen—the lifestyle, this place, all if it—and didn't want to allow that it was temporary. Imagine not realizing that Stephen would eventually get back with his wife, though? That's the part I can't understand. (She tilts her head as if contemplating me.) But now I see a lot better why things might get nasty, if Stephen wasn't quite ready to return to his real life, but instead started up with another...pretty little thing.

Me: (I stand, cross to her, and crouch in front of her. When I talk my voice has an insistent tone.) You must understand, Mrs. Pearle. Stephen was a total stranger to me until the moment he died in the train station. I never saw him before he threw himself over the edge.

She sits, her toffee-colored eyes on mine, her hand frozen between her mouth and the ashtray, and for a moment I believe that she's finally getting that I was no one to Stephen. First I think it might give her some relief to realize that her husband was in fact not moving from some sort of gay experiment into an affair with a white woman about a quarter century her junior. That hopeful thought lasts a nanosecond because even in the dim light I see her face set. It occurs to me that she's about to kick my ass out of there for the rubbernecker that I am. But when she answers I realize I've hit a different note entirely.

X: Are you—are you trying to imply that Stephen killed hisself? (I recognize the mix of indignation and assertiveness in her voice—it's a tone I hear in my own voice when I'm trying to contain myself while still making clear that I am prepared to let go both barrels on further provocation. She hitches forward in her chair and I find myself only just catching the edge of the coffee table to keep from toppling backward.)

Me: I'm so sorry. What do you think—(I stop, then get my head straight enough to say) How did he end up dead, Mrs. Pearle, if it wasn't suicide?

X: (The bullish quality to her jaw remains unblunted by my quailing.) Stephen was *pushed*. Someone *pushed* my husband in front of a train. Whether it was because of who he was or whether it was just because he was there—that I can't tell you. But my husband was *murdered*. And there ain't no two ways about it. Do you understand, or would you like I should repeat myself?

Me: (I'm nodding like crazy and realize that I'm about to get the boot regardless of what I say, so I go ahead.) But I was *there* on the platform. I saw him. (I falter, anticipating her anger.)

X: (Her tone is calm, almost singsong, as if she's been through this particular conversation before.) Tell me, child, where was you looking when Stephen went in front of that train?

Me: What do you mean?

X: (patient) Well, did you watch him as he fell down into those tracks, or did you turn around to see what was going on behind yourself at that moment?

Me: (I clear my throat.) I watched. Of course.

X: So if someone had pushed him, maybe someone standing behind the two of you?

Me: (confused) But no one...I mean, I would have...I mean, wouldn't I have...?

X: (She makes a "hmmm" noise that means she'll leave me to think about this. I make an apologetic gesture and go to leave. When I reach the door she speaks.) *Voulez-vous votre affiche de Greta Garbo?*

Me: (shaking my head) It's been several years since I've used French. Could you say that again?

X: My mistake. Make sure the door shuts all the way, will you?

I race down the five flights. I'm sure she can hear my frenzied escape. Hope she got a chuckle out of it. So I run a couple of blocks to get away from how spooked I am and there's this freezing drizzle coming down, so after I slip badly and almost do a gutter flop I look up there's this neon blue tubing: **ALL NIGHT**. The diner.

I get there and push my way in. The heat's steamy and the smell is grease. I don't glance around, but just take the stool closest to the door. The sizzle of hash and the filthy cat staring at me from the counter make it seem as if the place has sat untouched, a movie set waiting for another take, since I was there a week earlier.

I pull some napkins out of the dispenser and use them to blot my cheeks and forehead. The counterman taps two fingers heavily in front of me and I raise my face, blinking the wet out of my lashes. He is, of course, the same old geezer as last time, his gaze as unanimated through his half-glasses as it was then. I ask for coffee and he shakes his head. Not getting it, I ask if he's about to close.

Grill Geezer: I closed for you. All a time. You go somewhere else.

Me: (feeling myself color) I don't understand.

Grill Geezer: You get nothing here, no coffee. You understand now?

Me: (somewhat stunned at his *righteousness* toward me. I race through my memory of our last encounter and can only conclude that he's decided that it was a betrayal of some sort for him to have mentioned Stephen Pearle's name to me.) I don't understand, actually. (I'm pretty amazed at my own verve, but something about his audacity—something about *everyone's* audacity toward me lately—makes me want to give a little back.) Why don't you explain yourself?

Grill Geezer: (shrugs, unimpressed) This my place, I serves who I wants. Simple. You go. (He turns away to scuff around angrily at his hash.)

Me: Was it the police? Did a Sergeant Malloy come to see you, a tall red-haired detective, or another detective, a Latino? Did they object to my asking about Stephen Pearle? Did they...hint that I might have had something to do with his death? Is that what happened?

Grill Geezer raises his spatula in a shooing motion, his gesture making me aware that we're being observed. I sense movement down the counter, some man standing from his stool. Something familiar, even out of the corner of my eye...

Me: (raising my voice as I stand) This isn't a police state, regardless of what the Boston Police Department might have you believe. If they've intimidated you, that's your constitutional rights they're stepping on as much as mine.

The Grill Geezer pays no attention. I feel for the door handle behind me, angry and confused and not yet quite free of the weird scene with X. Then the man from down the counter walks right into me, sliding an arm round my shoulder. I look, surprised, and it's the Mysterious Hottie, which startles me almost beyond thinking. Fact is, I don't know whether to be relieved or terrified silly.

Me: What are you doing here?

M.H.: Waiting for you. Let's get. (He hustles me outside.)

Me: (stopping on the street, partly to breathe the cold air gratefully and partly to separate myself from M.H.) Look, if you think I'm going another step with you...

M.H. turns to meet my eye. He seems to consider whether to address me, his stance cool, hands loose in his coat pockets. Then he shrugs and walks off. I watch him receding down the rain-washed street, its puddles splashed with the moon's vague gleam. I wait until he's well down the block, then make my way to the T station. I can't begin to describe how foolish I feel, and how annoyed and, well, kind of *hurt* that he didn't even try to call my bluff. Am I going cuckoo?

I'm thinking this stuff as I stand in the Park Street station, waiting for my train. For anyone who has never been, Park Street is one of those multitrack, multilevel stations with all sorts of platform configurations. I'm standing on a middle island where trains go by on both sides, and I'm just leaning out to see whether the familiar thunder is coming from my track when he saunters out from behind a post. The Mysterious Hottie. He's across the track from me. The train that's coming in is his and not mine, and he's looking at it. Spontaneously, I call his name (no, not "Mysterious Hottie"—I manage "Ferguson") and he jerks his head in my direction. My hand raises itself without my asking it to. He doesn't react and his train rushes in and steams to a halt, then takes off, leaving an empty platform. I am relieved, I tell myself. I turn my back on the silence to see him coming down the stairs on my side. Very light on his feet. I feel another surge of relief, this one stronger. He walks up.

M.H.: (responding to my quick smile with one of his own. Then he stops a few feet off from me, a question on his face.)

Me: I still don't know what I think of you.

M.H.: Just looking to not get pepper sprayed.

Me: (nodding my "touché" and half turning to glance down the track. This time the distant rumble is, in fact, my train. It gives me confidence.) This afternoon you said that we were both after the same thing and maybe we should tell one another what we know.

M.H.: Maybe we should.

Me: Okay. Tell me why you were at that diner tonight.

M.H.: (seems about to comply, then stops) You first, this time.

Me: (fixing him with a look that doesn't seem to faze him in the least.) Tonight I went to see Stephen Pearle's widow. He had a loft near the diner. I met her there. After I left, I went to the diner because it was raining. Also, I'd had a conversation with the grill man the first time I went there, and hoped to find out more. I have no idea why he blew me off this time.

M.H.: (something passes over his face that he submerges behind a nod) Got it.

Me: So?

M.H.: After you and I met this afternoon, I was curious about what was going on in the investigation. I called up a friend in the department, my brother's old partner, and asked.

Me: Who is he—your brother's old partner? (I have this weird premonition that it will turn out to be Burly-Bear.)

M.H.: She. Name of Cheryl Archer. Detective first class.

Me: (relieved to have been wrong) Was she there on the night your brother died?

M.H.: (reluctantly) No, at that point she was a different kind of partner.

Me: Oh. What did she tell you?

M.H.: Said someone had mentioned in her presence a desire to talk to me again about what I'd seen that night in the T station, so I should be ready for a call. Anyone talk to you?

Me: (working to keep from coloring) I've been in touch with one of the cops.

M.H.: (seems to be studying me but I can't tell for sure as I'm purposely looking down the tracks. My train's headlight glimmers like a ogre's eye. The silence means it's hovering at Boylston.) One of the guys you mentioned back at the diner? Malloy?

Me: So how did this conversation with Cheryl the screwable cop get you to the All Night in time to see me tossed?

M.H.: (I'm not sure he likes my characterization of his brother's old bedmate, but he lets it go.) She asked me if I'd been over to the South Station area lately. When I said that I hadn't, it seemed like that was the answer she wanted to hear.

Me: So you decided to head over immediately?

M.H.: More or less. And there's nothing going on around the wharf except a couple of gay bars and the All Night. So I figured what the hell and went for a cup of coffee.

Me: (admitting to myself that this rings true) With what in mind?

M.H.: Nothing. Well, actually, I showed the guy this. (He pulls a piece of paper out of his pocket and unfolds it. It's the sketch he did of me.)

Me: Ah. So what did you tell him that got him all worked up about me?

M.H.: I just said I was a police sketch artist and asked if he'd seen you. He was impatient, said he'd already talked to the cops about you.

Me: (a little too amazed to be annoyed) Did you get anything else? The name of the cops or the reason they gave the man to make him hostile toward me?

M.H.: No one would have to give this guy a reason. Someone comes in and says he's a cop and not to talk to some girl? The cops can make trouble; the girl can't. Best to blow her off.

Me: But who would have known I'd been there? Who would care?

M.H.: Don't know. (Then he draws his head back.) You're worried about this.

Me: I just don't like being treated like a pariah.

M.H: No, not about the old boy at the diner. You're worried about the cops, what they're thinking.

Me: (defensively) Well, so is Stephen Pearle's widow, if you must know.

M.H.: (willing to be deflected) So what's her angle?

Me: She thinks...(I purse my lips, knowing that I shouldn't tell, but at the same time sensing that he's my only hope.) She insists her husband was pushed.

M.H.: (I watch his face go from mild surprise to puzzlement. Then the penny drops and he focuses on me.) She thinks you shoved him?

Me: She's not completely deranged. She thinks someone did it from behind me and that I didn't look back at the pusher because I was looking at her husband go over the edge.

M.H.: Well, could it have been possible that someone shoved the guy past you and you didn't pick up on it?

Me: (The sound of the train fills the station. It rushes in behind me in all its Sturm und Drang. I feel my hair rise like Gorgon snakes. I mouth the words "no idea." The train doors spew their steam, then roll back indifferently.)

M.H. glances past me into the train car and gets that faraway look in his eye that guys get when they're thinking about getting laid. I glance behind me. There are just a few people on the train—a black kid in a bunch of layered coats and earbuds, an obese white guy dressed for kitchen work, sleeping with his eyes rolled back in his head, a grizzled wreck in the corner, nursing a brown bag. No women or girls.

M.H.: It's late. I'll ride the train with you, see you home. I feel like we have a lot more to talk about. I think you feel like that too.

Me: No. (I say it decisively, but not as a synonym for *never*.) But give me your email.

M.H.: Don't do email.

Me: (I blink unbelievingly.)

M.H.: I'm an artist, I need to be left alone.

Me: I'm going over to The Blue Pearl at around 4:45 tomorrow. Can you meet me? (I've stepped back into the train by now, and the doors close.)

M.H.: (smiles and raises his chin as goodbye. I have no idea whether he even heard me.)

GIVE IT TO ME STRAIGHT

36-D @ February 2 12:13 am

> You are, like, totally totally screwed up. STOP pursuing this. You are MAKING them think that you were INVOLVED with Mr. Suicide. Don't you SEE THAT?

marleybones @ February 2 12:18 am

> Wait. Before we berate fickel, I'd like to congratulate her, because I believe that she's uncovered a big lie told to her by that supposedly lovable teddy bear of a cop. Burly-Bear told fickel that some unidentified "witness" claimed that Mr. Suicide was arguing with a woman on the platform just before he fell.

roadrage @ February 2 12:23 am

Uh, grasping fruitlessly at why that makes him a liar?

marleybones @ February 2 12:25 am

I'd prefer to let someone else finish the thought. That way I know I'm not alone in my suspicions.

i.went.to.harvard @ February 2 12:32 am

Okay, I'll bite. If there was such a witness, why haven't we heard more about that person now that fickel's had contact with another witness (the Mysterious Hottie)?

webmaggot @ February 2 12:35 am

Do you one better: If there really was such a witness, wouldn't X have gotten wind of that fact as she urged the cops to investigate her husband's death as a murder rather than a suicide?

36-D @ February 2 12:36 am

But how do we know that X didn't know about the witness?

webmaggot @ February 2 12:37 am

marleybones?

marleybones @ February 2 12:38 am

Go for it, maggot.

webmaggot @ February 2 12:40 am

X couldn't know about some witness having seen her husband fighting with a girl before getting pushed into the track because if she'd known about it *she would have thought fickel was that girl*!

chinkigirl @ February 2 12:43 am

I'm very impressed. You should show your deductive side more often.

marleybones @ February 2 12:46 am

Absolutely. And unless the cops actually suspect X herself of being the pusher, I can't imagine why they'd keep that information from her.

i.went.to.harvard @ February 2 12:50 am

Sooooooo, Burly-Bear lied about the witness?

marleybones @ February 2 12:51 am

...which I find interesting.

i.went.to.harvard @ February 2 01:03 am

Another interesting tidbit that may implicate Burly-Bear, of course, is to wonder who warned Grill Geezer not to talk to fickel? I mean, what is that all about?

proudblacktrannie @ February 2 01:05 am

Just on—breathless air kisses all around. Three words, fickel: Call Mr. Groin (or get a different lawyer if you must).

36-D @ February 2 01:08 am

My offer is open: the Rottweiler will be at your side, growling deep in his throat and waiting for the sic command, the moment you say the word.

fickel @ February 2 01:10 am

I appreciate everyone's concerns. I'm just not ready to play hardball yet.

marleybones @ February 2 01:13 am

Also, I think you anticipate that any lawyer you call on is going to clamp down—shove you into "helpless female" mode and refuse to allow you to investigate Mr. Suicide's death yourself.

fickel @ February 2 01:14 am

Well, isn't that what you'd anticipate the Rottweiler would do?

36-D @ February 2 01:16 am

He'd shut your investigation down but he would never keep you in the dark. Trust me.

i.went.to.harvard @ February 2 01:22 am

Another moment of silence. I think that we must ask ourselves whether fickel is enjoying this whole nightmare, on some level. Perhaps "enjoying" isn't quite the word?

marleybones @ February 2 01:23 am

A woman tries to take control of her situation, and instantly she's "getting off" on being abused.

i.went.to.harvard @ February 2 01:24 am

Ouch. Stepped in that one, I admit.

hitman @ February 2 01:25 am

And another wuss apologizes for stating the obvious. Hey, femi-nazi: if women want to be treated like equals they can do like men and walk around topless at the beach. Until then, zip it.

marleybones @ February 2 01:27 am

What's your point?

hitman @ February 2 01:28 am

My point is that there's a lot more going on here than some poor female trying to get out from under, and if you haven't caught on to that you can take your famous "female intuition" you dykes are so proud of and stuff it somewhere.

marleybones @ February 2 01:30 am

Chuckle, chuckle. These misogynistic posts of yours reveal more about you than you realize.

hitman @ February 2 01:31 am

Make me LOL, lady. Why would I give a thought about what you "intuit" about me?

chinkigirl @ February 2 01:33 am

I'm not up on the literature, but I don't think feminists buy into the female intuition mystique.

proudblacktrannie @ February 2 01:34 am

Oh I have some intuition at work right now telling me some interesting things about hitman. And by the way, before you lay some crap on me, let me point out that I don't give a *damn* whether you *care* about what I think.

webmaggot @ February 2 01:35 am

Wait, so now gays have female intuition? Does this mean it's not linked to, like, how much testosterone you have, but more to whether you crave dick?

proudblacktrannie @ February 2 01:36 am

We call it gaydar, sweetie, and you don't even want to know what mine's picked up about you.

fickel @ February 2 01:39 am

Okay, guys. If you need some confirmation about where my head is at, well, I'm seeing this through. And if I'm frightened of anything it's the idea of having to lie back while someone else takes up my problems. I'm not sure I would call my mindset "enjoyment" OR "self-empowerment," but I can guarantee that it isn't rooted in feminism or romanticism or the desire to live out a pulp fantasy. There's a measure of stubbornness involved—that I'll confess. Anyway, I hope you all can understand.

marleybones @ February 2 01:40 am

I hear you loud and clear. Just watch yourself.

i.went.to.harvard @ February 2 01:41 am

Amen.

chinkigirl @ February 2 01:42 am

I'm almost afraid to ask, but what is your plan, fickel? You asked Mysterious Hottie to meet you at the Jewelers Building. What do you think the two of you can learn there?

fickel @ February 2 01:44 am

Slenderbuns. What he meant when he said that I was "the girl." It seems like *everyone* I encounter *assumes* that I had some kind of relationship with Mr. Suicide. I've got to break through that somehow. That means either finding the actual E or coming up with something that definitively separates my identity from hers.

proudblacktrannie @ February 2 01:45 am

And having the Hottie along? Is this a way to get closer?

roadrage @ February 2 01:46 am

Having him along sounds better than having him "pop up" as usual. (No, that is not a sex joke.)

fickel @ February 2 01:50 am

Actually, neither of those reasons occurred to me, although I'm not anywhere near comfortable with who he is in all of this. I mean, could he really be this suicide witness looking to lend a shoulder to the girl most likely to have been squirted with Mr. Suicide's eyeball juice? Well, it's less hard to swallow than it might come across.

But my real motive is that he seems good with strangers. I'm less good at getting them to listen to me and answer my questions. So, he wants to help and I want him to.

36-D @ February 2 01:56 am

He's like bait. Beefcake for Slenderbuns.

fickel @ February 2 01:59 am

Weeeeeeell, okay, maybe that also, just a wee little bit.

proudblacktrannie @ February 2 02:00 am

BEE-YITCH! I'm proud of you!

chinkigirl @ February 2 02:03 am

By the way, where is hitman? Shouldn't he be swooping in to point out that everything fickel's done and plans to do comes down to her being a slut or a whore?

36-D @ February 2 02:05 am

Did us girlies hurt our favorite sexist's feelings?

webmaggot @ February 2 02:06 am

I thought I was your favorite sexist?

roadrage @ February 2 02:07 am

Dewd. Next to hitman, you and me are chicks.

fickel @ February 2 02:08 am

Huh. Well, guess we'll just have to forge ahead without.

leo tolstoy @ February 2 02:09 am

He must escape from this power. And the means of escape every man had in his own hands...death.

fickel @ February 2 02:11 am

I don't want to bum you out, leo t., but you're beginning to sound kind of Russian? Shouldn't you be off writing something long and broody just before your spectacular suicide?

roadrage @ February 2 02:12 am

I got it in my head somehow that Rasputin had an eighteen-incher.

fickel @ February 2 02:13 am

Now *there's* something to hang yourself with.

23

FULL FRONTAL

EXISTENTIALISM ENGORGED

02.02 @ 2:37 AM:
WUH-UP, SLACKER DUDE?

Had an interesting yesterday, just returned to B-Town. Check it out:

I dug up sum wheels and am doing a drive-by, just to see if m'fave babe Killer Chick is around. Out comes Slacker Dude, carrying his rucksack. Kid's kind of boppin along like he's got distance on his not-giant brain and so I slides along to see wu-up. Dude's got his hoodie up so not looking out to notice some ought-o dragging ass to keep pace with him. Other words I'm kool but diss can't last.

Couple blocks down my boy is hip-hoppin along toward an intersection other side there stands a "No Entry" sign so dang it awl fo-sho my fun is ovah unless I go f'it. I shoves a little gas on up the engine and give a pop on the horn, then a "Hey, brooooo-dah! Little help, y'mind?"

He don't mind, which is aftah-awl NAWT a s'prize. Turns on the ball of his foot at a ninety degree and walks to my vee-hicle like he's been waitin for me to show.

"Pike, bro? I been driving around this fukin neighborhood for a fukin half hour and there's nothing but one fukin ways and no fukin entries. I gots to get to the Pike, man," I sez.

Slack rests his hand on the ruff of my vee-hicle, takes a sniff around the inn-terior, then a gander down my clothes, even chekin owt my hands up-on the wheel. Does he recognize me from the internet café? Seems like a "no," goin by his buh-lank faze, but you nevah knowz with a twist such as he. Any event, I seems to be wut he lookin faw and he tightens his grip on his rucksack.

"How faw y'goin'?"

I gives him the once-over like he did t'me now that it's "occurred to me" to give the dewd a lift.

I say "Alb'ny" and de boy bops round and gets on in nex-a me. Keeps the rucksack at his feet rather than slinging it in the back. Guess he's not big on leg room.

"Got anything fer gas?" I ask, offhanded-like.

"Y'right. Smoke?" He's already pulling a Camel out the pack with his teeth. Funny little twink.

So we travel I'm thinkin two hours out the Pike. Got some snow goin on, starts to hail and my wipers get to thrubbin and squeakin. Slacker Dude sho likes his tobaccee, plus poking at his bollocks through his oversized fatigues. Got radio ADD azzwell. I tell him to cool it with changing the stations and he raises his hands. "You d'man."

So I'm looking round for where this li'l old adventure is goin' when the motel appears down the highway. Big tall pole. REST, it says up top. I allus like a direct approach, so I slides on down the ramp. Road's slick and I fishtail.

"Use a drink? I'm buyin."

He's rooting around in his jean jac for another cigarette. "Sho' wudevah." Close your eyes, dis kid's a gen-u-wine black man.

I pull into the motel lot, cross to the packie for a bottle of bourbon, then hit the motel office. Wait until I'm climbing the stairs to the upper rooms before I jerk my head in the direction of my car. Tell you, I more'n half expect the little roach to have disappeared on me, but he pushes the car door, slaps it closed, and wanders my way. So he tricks after all; I kinnah wundahd.

I'm splashing us a couple when he ambles on in, slings his rucksack over by one of the beds. I walk over and offer him a glass and he kind of assumes the position, raising his arms and bringing his jac up like for a frisk. I snort-laugh and shove the door closed. Fuckah must be mighty well confused.

When I turn around he's seated on one of the beds, feet splayed. He rolls back onto one elbow, posin so's I can check him out. I notice he's keepin' one e-ball on the rucksack thru-out.

So I rubs my crotch, licks my chops like a hubby just home from the office looking for some cunny after a hard day, then I walk at the dude to make him make his move. His plan, u'course, is to roll me—guy's a fagg troll and he's thinkin to ovah-powah me while I'm groping him. He starts to get at it so's I grab his wrist, hard.

"Easy," I say. "Caught your act back in Central Square d'other night. Found out some freak's tailing your sistah but you don't warn her or nothing 'cause then she'll read in the freak's blog about what a perv you are. You are in fact a scag in need of some learning."

I give him a mo to catch up, and then another to react. As I figure, he's got nothing but bull to offer. "What's your fuckin...?" he starts, so I snaps his pinky finger back. I let go of him and lean back on my legs while he's still figuring where the pain's coming from, then just as he gets what's down I offer him a quick one-two-three to his face. Kid slaps down flat on his back and flips backwards over the bed. True I hit him hard enough, even cut my knuckle on his damned tooth, and the dude's lightweight but he ain't THAT light. I go round to see what's going on down there and sho nough the dude's in the rucksack. Blood on his teeth but I see that cause he's smiling and I get it: Slacker Dude's aiming to fleece my ass at *gunpoint.*

Cute. I'm on him before he can grab his piece. He does what comes to him, springing straight up from his ass to skull-ram my gut, fists flailing. Decent little fight style but he's no match and I proceed to beat the crap out of him. I let him feel some pain, backing him against the wall, slugging—he will learn to care for those who care for him, one way or another.

Anyhow, the kid sags his way up from the floor on all fours, trembling and swaying on his knee; don't know how the little fuk can see or even breathe, but then, you know, the human body is a remarkable instrument. He brings his pulpy face up, all bloody and squishy like a fistful of raw meat, and tries to say something. Some sort of plea, I would imagine. Like he wouldn't have blowed me an extra eyeball socket at point blank range, had he the chance. Like he didn't leave poor Killer Chick all vulnerable to the likes of me, back in Boston. I walk at him, lend him a gentle hand under his shaking armpit to raise him up a little, and then I lay an uppercut to his under-jaw, practically from carpet level. There's a sweet crunch, the whispery crackle of bone or teeth or maybe both, as his body arcs up and back and lands in a clutter, half on the floor, half against the wall. Still, it's all nice and quiet. Don't want to disturb the fat fornicators slurping up one another's juicies next door, y'know.

After I wash up, I turn on the tub tap. I go out into the room and over to Slacker Dude. He's lying with his head under the radiator where he hid it after I left off pulping him. Seems way out of it, but as I approach I see that his pants begin to go dark around the crotch. Guy pissing himself in his condition is a pretty sight—he's coherent, see? I lean in and check out his hands, his fingers spasming as they clutch the back of his neck. Protect the spine—now there's instinct for you. Remarkable. On the other hand, he's lying with his face pressed down in a pool of his own vomit. Stinks—what was Killer Chick servin' this punk? I mean besides herself.

I pick him up by his clothes and half carry, half drag him into the bathroom and dump him in the tub—just a lot of clatterin' joints against the rusty porcelain. I pop the shower tap. Living ought to feel good for him this day. Unless of course he never gets it together and ends up drowning in a couple a inches of water at the bottom of the tub. Poor little sleaze; what a way to go.

Before leaving I rustle around in the rucksack for the heater but turns out—no piece! Silly Dood lost his firearm. Why he didn't check while he was in my car waiting for me? I got no answer for that except maybe he had no suspicion whatsoever that it might not be where he'd stashed it.

Who to suspect of lifting it—Killer Chick? She is one *slippery* kitty. To be friendly, like, I break a glass in the sink, then take the time to carve her a message in the boy she likes best. What message? The one he should have left her himself, but didn't.

I'm feeling generous, and so take the couple pounds of tight-packed dope from his rucksack. Wouldn't want the cops finding that. Crap hayseed—bright Saint Patrick's farkin green.

---

tALK. NIHILIST DOGS

boytoucher @ 02.02 03:04 am

S'up wichu mon? U goin Sy-Ko?

eddielizard @ 02.02 03:06 am

Wantin dick does it, mon.

boytoucher @ 02.02 03:10 am

I donno. Seems more like this is about the chick?

fullfrontal @ 02.02 03:11 am

Like exactly, mon frere.

garbo @ 02.02 03:15 am

You are hot for this chick so you beat up her boyfriend? Are you back in junior high or at that point was it reform school?

fullfrontal @ 02.02 03:19 am

Dood tried to pull a robbery at gunpoint and got his ass wiped. Boo hoo.

garbo @ 02.02 03:23 am

What gun? The one in your imagination? Maybe he was looking for a tissue to clean the blood out of his nose from when you punched him out.

fullfrontal @ 02.02 03:25 am

Maybe he was looking to blow me and it didn't work out for him.

garbo @ 02.02 03:26 am

Maybe you acted exactly like that's what you were after as payment for the ride you gave him. Maybe it WAS what you were after, but you can't HANDLE it.

boytoucher @ 02.02 03:29 am

Sheeet you are such a raggin bitch. Wut you doin here?

garbo @ 02.02 03:30 am

Fuking with your heads, low-lifes. Had enough?

fullfrontal @ 02.02 03:31 am

Not frum you, honey. Never enough from my girl.

garbo @ 02.02 03:32 am

I'm just relieved I never met up with you. Now I know why you didn't show.

fullfrontal @ 02.02 03:33 am

Why would that be, pray tell?

garbo @ 02.02 03:35 am

I don't know—you got this tongue-in-cheek psycho thing going on here and maybe you don't want someone announcing that *it's for real.*

fullfrontal @ 02.02 03:37 am

And how would our meeting result in my revealing on this blog that I'm a genuine psycho, gash?

garbo @ 02.02 03:38 am

Maybe you're afraid I would post it.

fullfrontal @ 02.02 03:39 am

Maybe if I were psycho you wouldn't have fingers to post with.

garbo @ 02.02 03:41 am

Maybe I can type with my nose.

fullfrontal @ 02.02 03:42 am

You think you'd leave our date with a nose?

garbo @ 02.02 03:43 am

Creepier by the minute.

fullfrontal @ 02.02 03:44 am

I live to serve.

garbo @ 02.02 03:45 am

Serve? Serve who?

fullfrontal @ 02.02 03:47 am

My god: L.T.

garbo @ 02.02 03:48 am

And who's that supposed to be? Lawrence Tierney, that psycho from the movies?

fullfrontal @ 02.02 03:50 am

Try Lev Nikolayevich Tolstoy, b'yitch.

garbo @ 02.02 04:00 am

When do we dance, o prophet?

fullfrontal @ 02.02 04:09 am

I'll let you know.

24

LIFE IS PULP

Noir the Night Away With L.G. Fickel

February 3 @ 1:24 am
>I SEE A MURDER...LATER, I GET LAID<

I know you're all going to give me *ess-loads* of grief for what I am about to relate, but, as you know, it was bugging me how Slenderbuns called me "the girl" before closing down like a clam shack during red tide (and no, that's *not* a sexual innuendo). I wanted to talk to him, and decided to make my own chance to do just that. As you will see, however, sometimes those bold steps in life can blow up big-time. My fingers shake, to be truthful, as I write this.

My plan was to try to get Slenderbuns at closing, and so I called The Blue Pearl from my office to find out that this was eight o'clock—Friday being an "open-late" night. So I worked until then (Lord knows I've been overdue for some catch-up time) and hurried over, making sure to arrive around 7:58 p.m. Why such precision? The last thing I wanted was another face-to-face with X—I can't say I *feared* the woman after our shadow spar, but I wasn't sure how philosophical she'd be, away from the surreal atmosphere of his loft and her meds. I figured her for a late worker, and Slenderbuns for the type who punched out on the button, and I wanted to catch him sashaying out the door.

Of course, I realized (as you have) that this totally blew my idea of having Mysterious Hottie along, but this is what comes of a bloke playing hard to get with his email address. In addition, I cannot say that I didn't note the poetic justice of blowing him off—he shows up, Cheshire Cat-style, whenever he feels like it, causing me a jolt of discomfort, so now it was my turn to NOT show up unexpectedly. Touché, Mr. Lovely Face!

Alas and alack, none of my careful plans went my way. I arrived at the Jewelers Building at the designated hour, took the elevator up, did the both-right-then-both-left dance with a tall Jamaican lady wearing a pretty but out-of-season poppy-red chiffon dress, a shortie jacket in faux sealskin and matching hat (yeah, you heard right—a sealskin hat), and way, way too much floral perfume as she got on the elevator and I got off, then hurried down the marble tiles only to find that The Blue Pearl was locked up for the night. I could see a slice of light coming from the back room, and was toying with the idea of knocking for a followup interview with X on what it's really like to spend Thirteen Years Married to a Philandering White Bisexual, when the truth struck me like a belated knock on the back door of my skull:

THERE WAS SOMETHING WRONG WITH THAT JAMAICAN LADY AT THE ELEVATORS!

And what was that? The answer came immediately:

HER ASS WAS WAY TOO THIN FOR ANY SELF RESPECTING JAMAICAN LADY!

Yes, mes amis, because that she-Jamaican was a he-Jamaican—Slenderbuns in strappy ho shoes. The little vixen changes—metamorphosizes?—right at work. Why hadn't that occurred to me?

So I go racing back down and luck is on my side—my elevator drops like a bucket while Slenderbuns must have been on the vertical milk run. I spot the tail of his tomato-colored hem as he exits the building. That's when I decide—don't ask me why but life's been getting like this—to tail him.

I wrap my coat around me and button up—somehow that seems like the way to tail someone—and head after him. It's not hard, what with the glossy sealskin hat bobbing in the air amid the drab wool caps. He (she?) walks very distinctly—going for the subway, without a doubt, which is a relief because you can't tail someone on a bus. I'm just foraging around in my mitten for a token when I get my second suprise of the evening. Get this, crime fans—I spot the Mysterious Hottie, *also* tailing Slenderbuns!!!

How does this tricky bastard *always* outmaneuver me? My only solace is that I do not believe M.H. has spotted me—i.e., he thinks I made the

4:45 rendezvous and wandered off to sink my chin in latte foam and sulk. I watch him watching Slenderbuns as the three of us pick our way through the commuters milling around Downtown Crossing, and by the time we hit Park Street I'm confident Mysterious Hottie is not aware of my presence. This makes me feel all warm and smug inside.

Sigh. I'm SOOOO easy.

Slenderbuns, who gets his share of broad comedy double-takes as he catches men's eyes and then they pick up on what he's peddling, leads us on a short ride to where we switch lines at Copley (a sun-ov-o-bitch to pull off undetected), followed by a long ride on the Orange Line—Mysterious Hottie takes the train car one up from Slenderbuns and I scurry onto the car one down from our quarry just in time. I stand where I can spy Slenderbuns' bobbing foot—the fellow's ability to cross and then recross his legs just so is like nothing I've seen this side of *Scarlet Street*—so I am well prepared when he finally alights (believe me, "alights" is the only word for it) in a decidely iffy South End/Roxbury neighborhood.

I don't see the Mysterious Hottie getting off the train, a fact I find curious but don't have time to ponder because I'm busy preparing for my inevitable mugging/murder as I hurry up the subway stairs and into the seedy night. Darkness is falling fast, which is actually a comfort in this neighborhood where I stand out like a sore thumb—a very gangbangable sore thumb.

I follow Slenderbuns down a few garbage-strewn streets—he walks with the same deliberate sway that he'd affected in Downtown Crossing—and then he minces down some steep stairs and enters a sort of club or something. There's no signage, but I watch a couple of men—with good pecs and highlights—hustle down and enter, and I can hear bar bustle when the door opens, so I figure it's just a gay bar. I need to think about what I'll say to Slenderbuns when I "come across" him in said gay club, but I conjure up no opening line so I decide to just go for it. I hurry down the steps, groping in my purse for the undoubtedly outrageous cover.

I was under the impression that I'd been to gay clubs, but those were just theme clubs where girlie-girls like myself sip chocolate martinis with their boy pals from work. This is a *serious* gay bar. Lots of midnight purple—walls, seats, bartender's outfit, stage curtains. In spite of prevalent stereotyping, gay does *not* guarantee fastidiousness, and I have the sensation of microscopic DNA in the air, waiting to be breathed in.

Anyway, unlike the atmosphere when I've been out with Noah, which is one of a bunch of guys just giddy with excitement at the rare opportunity to go ahead and *get silly* in public, here there are all types of men, most of them not fey or pretty at all. The mood is about as sexual as, say, a health club that caters to suburban dads—these fellas are willing to be social, sure, but there's a sense of purpose in the air that's not frivolous in the least. I'm the only woman present, a fact that I would not have thought would be so obvious because I'd have figured there'd be a handful of transvestites fluttering around in taffeta, but there are no she-he's present—even Slenderbuns has disappeared.

In spite of my feeling of having infiltrated a slice of life where I utterly don't belong, everyone's abundantly nice enough to me—the door guy with his shaven head, the grizzle-cheeked bartender, the bar hound who scarfs peanuts on the stool next to mine, etc., etc.—it's like they are going out of their way to demonstrate that they're not out for trouble (and, no, they don't dress in macho-man leather—nary a silver chain, tattoo, or lip stud in the place). I'm tempted to order a whiskey with ginger ale on the side ("and don't be stingy, baby!") but instead I order a cosmo for God knows what reason—perhaps to wave the rainbow flag a little—and try to come off like I'm waiting for someone as I sip. Fifteen minutes go by and I am considering bailing when Slenderbuns himself comes to my rescue. He flickers out from behind a sparkly curtain that half blocks a back hallway, slips under the bar's flap, and pours himself a glass of something from the speed rack. When he raises his head to flash the bartender a smile in acknowledgment of his naughtiness, he spots me. He's left his dress somewhere and is wearing a circa-1930 negligee—like the silver-screen ladies wear during scenes when us real-life slobs would be schlumping around in sweats. His is an iridescent pink and, I have to admit, a good choice for his skin tone. His wig is gone. In its place is a multicolored kerchief tied in that complicated way all the black girls are doing. He cocks his head, smiles big, and hurries round the bar, clutching his vodka with two hands.

Slenderbuns: Oh my stars, it's you (running some fingers down my coat sleeve like I might be an apparition). Are you meeting someone? (His eyes flash to my near-empty drink, then to my eyes, as he gauges how long I've been sitting there and how blotto that makes me.)

Me: (considering what to say and coming to the realization that I am in fact a little drunk) Yes. I mean, I came to see you.

Slenderbuns: You came here to see me? (tilting head) Did you hear about...? (He flickers his fingernails in the direction of the shoddy little stage.)

Me: What? Oh, no, although I'd love to see it. (I try to collect myself—man, they are gracious with their cosmopolitans in this place.) To tell the truth, I followed you tonight.

Slenderbuns: (gasp—hand to heart) The girl at the lift? I *thought* that was you. I would have sworn you didn't make me. Devil you! It's my ass, isn't it? So ironic—every woman in the world is trying to carve hers down to what I've got, and for me it's a curse. (He looks ruefully over his shoulder.) But you followed me—I'm dying to know: why, honey?

Me: I...(I dip my head and smile as a pale-haired businessman I swear I made small talk with at a book fair a month ago stops to exchange a greeting with Slenderbuns. When I get Slenderbuns back I point at the curtained hallway.) Any possibility we could...?

Slenderbuns: Sure, honey. (He laughs, lifting the hem of his negligee.) A private moment in my dressing room! You make me feel like an absolute starrrrrrrrrr!

We go down into a narrow bare-brick hallway lined with naked bulbs, then turn into one of those windowless backstage rooms—long and narrow and vaguely crescent shaped because it wraps around the little rounded stage out front. There's a ton of costume-related junk—boas and bras and falsies and hats and wigs—all over the place, and a long Formica counter on which has been vomited an endless tangle of makeup, soda cans with cigarette butts stubbed into their rims, and glassy jewelry. Well down the room from where we enter, a man—white, hairy, and about as lithe as a manatee—is standing, one foot propped against the counter as he smokes a cigarette with one hand and runs a razor up his haunch with the other. He's either totally naked or wearing some sort of nylon thingy—I have no intention of getting a clear view of which—and the momentary glance we give to one another through the quarter mile of clutter sends the message that he's as interested in seeing mine as I am in seeing his. Slenderbuns drops gracefully onto a metal folding chair, then sweeps something drapey off a comparable chair. He cups his drink in both hands and hunches his shoulders, Monroe style.

Slenderbuns: Sit. Talk. This is about Stephen?

Me: Yes. Or I guess I don't know, actually. When we met in The Blue Pearl, you said something about me being "the girl." What did you mean by that?

Slenderbuns: But, honey, why didn't you just ask?

Me: Well, when I got a glimpse of Mrs. Pearle and you started steering me toward the door, I thought it wasn't the right time.

Slenderbuns: Mrs. Who? Oh, you mean Edie! (He drinks as if to smother a giggle.)

Me: Why is that funny?

Slenderbuns: (through the glass) It's not funny, sweetie. Not a bit, you're so right.

Me: Was that woman in the back of the store not Mrs. Pearle?

Slenderbuns: (slowly licking his lips) I didn't say that, honey.

Me: But I met her at Stephen's loft. She told me they'd been married for thirteen years. Didn't she tell you about her talk with me?

Slenderbuns: She doesn't tell me a thing, the meanie. But you tell me. What was it like?

Me: (caught by this additional fallacy in my thinking) You've never been to Stephen's loft?

Slenderbuns: (feeling at the head scarf as he makes big eyes) Me? Why would I go there?

Me: But I thought you were his...

Slenderbuns: (wide-open eyes for once looking genuine) Me? Stephen's lover? Honey, where did you get that? Did Stephen think of me in that way?

Me: No. I mean, I have no idea how he thought of you. I just thought, from my conversation with Mrs. Pearle, that you were the one he'd had his affair with.

Slenderbuns: (more wide-eyed staring)

A couple of boys enter. They crowd past Slenderbuns, tapping his headscarf affectionately. Both are skeletal and total screamers, essentially white versions of Slenderbuns, and they begin doing up their faces as they share a cigarette and complain about some "uberbitch" named Gerri—maybe Jerry, come to think of it. Neither of them gives me more than a glance, but it's clear my time there is limited.

Me: Look, forget about the you-and-Stephen idea. What I'm wondering is what you meant when you said that I must be "the girl." What girl?

Slenderbuns: (reaches for a pair of brown-toned pantyhose, and spreads his hand inside, checking for runs.) Well, I think of you as "the girl" in Stephen's life. As opposed to "the boy" in his life—who was most definitely not yours truly. (He's satisfied with the pantyhose and starts rolling one foot up over his toes, lifting his leg high in the air to do so. I have to say, the guy is so natural about it that it doesn't strike me as odd in the least, even when his negligee falls back. I can't help noticing that he waxes, and find myself wondering, fleetingly, what size pantyhose he takes. He's thin, but God gave this filly a pair of long, muscular calves—and quite a quandary, judging from the shape of his thong.)

Me: Did you and Edie ever talk about Stephen's private life? She seemed very open when I met her. Is that where you get this boy-then-girl idea?

Slenderbuns: Oh, no, no, no. Edie's a talker, but not to me. I got what I knew about Stephen from Stephen himself.

Me: (feeling like I've hit the mother lode) He confided in you about his love life?

Slenderbuns: Good lord, no, you silly goose. (He's finished smoothing on the pantyhose and drops back to his seat, crossing his fantastic legs.) I'm a listener and a watcher. Never at keyholes—nothing crude—but I like to keep my ears open as I go about my own little business. And, well, y'know.

Me: Y'know what?

Slenderbuns: (sigh, as if it's tiresome to have to spell everything out) Stephen did a lot of phoning during the day. Hushed conversations into his celly. Bicker-bicker here. Lovey-dovey there. You can tell when someone's changing horses, let's just say, particularly when it's from a stallion to a filly. (He giggles, then retrieves his drink and drains it.)

Me: And this gave you the idea that he was with a man, then started up with a woman?

Slenderbuns: (nodding at me while studying his face in the mirror, apparently planning his makeup campaign) That's pretty much it, doll.

Me: Just out of curiosity, what were the signs? I mean, I get the changing horses clues, but from a man to a woman? Come on—you can't tell me that shows.

Slenderbuns: Oh, but, honey, it shows, like, most of all. Stephen's whole tone changed at a certain point. With Blondy he was all boyish. Gay was a whole new thing, see? He was the newbie taking lessons from a stud, and he was grooving at being the stuttering ingenue. When he started up with you, he got, I don't know, more himself, back to the way he'd learned it, see? And you were younger. Anyone could tell. *You* were the ingenue. (Here he makes a little hand gesture that is meant to present me as the proof of all his theorizing.)

Me: (ignoring that for the moment) I think I follow. So did you know the guy—Blondy?

Slenderbuns: No, honey, contrary to popular belief, us faggots don't all know one another.

Me: Then how did you know that he was blond?

Slenderbuns: (puffing air through his makeup brush) Blond hairs on Stephen's jacket or sweater. Stephen wore a lot of black, remember?

Me: (watching him through the mirror as he brushes rouge on his cheeks) So you didn't know anything about the male lover except he was blond.

Slenderbuns: (rubbing some stuff over his eyes that makes the skin shine) You're totally off, hon. I know exactly who the male lover was.

Me: But you just said you only knew him because of the hairs.

Slenderbuns: (rolling his eyes) That's how I homed in. I *saw* him several times, however.

Me: (gesturing) In a place like this?

Slenderbuns: Oh, no, hon. Not Stephen's speed. Fact, that's probably why Blondy got tired of him. You decide to go gay, best to *go gay*. None of this hiding in the mainstream nonsense. No, I saw the two of them together in a business capacity.

Me: (wonderingly, although it instantly clicks in my head that this jibes with what X had said about the "boy from work") Stephen started up with someone he did business with?

Slenderbuns: We can be discreet, you know. I didn't catch on that they were lovers at that time; I didn't even spot the man as gay, and I have superb gaydar, if I do say so. I just thought Stephen was incredibly solicitous of him, like maybe he represented some fabulous commission or was some rich client's son. Then, when I figured out that Stephen was "dabbling" and caught on that his partner was blond, it all fell into place.

Me: But what about the girl? You can't say you ever saw me with Stephen—that I know.

Slenderbuns: (his eyes glazing a little) I'm seeing you now, aren't I? So that makes me the lucky winner of the Sighting Stephen Pearle's Lovers contest. Ding, ding, ding, where's my prize? (I go to respond but he cuts me off.) Look, I don't want to rush you off, honey-bunch, but I have a face to put on, right?

Me: But...(not seeing the point of straightening him out on who I was and was not, particularly if I'm about to get the heave). Okay, let me ask you this. What made you think I was Stephen's lover when you met me in the shop? I mean, that took some deducting on your part.

Slenderbuns: (without hesitating) You're the type.

Me: His wife's a black woman. His first lover's a blond male. This is a guy who had a type?

Slenderbuns: No, no, sugar: the type he started designing for these past months. Modest. Uptight. Classy.

Me: I'm classy? And here I've just reconciled myself to "boring but slutty."

Slenderbuns: (big sigh like I'm fishing for compliments) Tennis bracelets. Princess necklaces. Pearl drop earrings. Moonstones and platinum. (He flicks a hand in my direction.) Lovely, and easy to sell, but a tad boring, dare I say, without hurting your feelings too, too terribly?

Me: And that was it? You saw me and it reminded you of the jewelry Stephen was designing?

Slenderbuns: Ain't that enough, honey? Shall I suddenly remember a tattoo of your initials that I noticed on his left cheek at the racquet club?

Me: For how long?

Slenderbuns: Come again? (He's working with a pair of tarantula-sized false eyelashes now, and it's easy to see how this could get distracting.)

Me: For how long was Stephen designing jewelry for someone like me?

Slenderbuns: (holding one of the eyelashes with one of those metal presses that resemble a miniaturized instrument of torture) For *you*, hon, not for someone *like* you. Going to guess six months, minus maybe the past eight weeks, when he was trying to revive his Oriental thing from years and years ago. (He makes a face to let me know what he thinks of that move.)

Me: And prior to six months ago, when he was with Blondy? What was he designing then?

Slenderbuns: (small sigh) Pure art.

Me: Oh? Like what?

Slenderbuns: Wild and heavy. Outrageously expensive. (He presses the second set of false eyelashes into place. I get it—I see the Peacock's blue ice necklace before my mind's eye—all those fat, pearl-toned stones and the spatter of diamonds pooled around them—*like a quarter-million dollar cum shot*—and I realize that Slenderbuns is onto something.)

Me: (pretending to be playful) Could you tell that Blondy was all that "inspiring," just from seeing him once or twice?

Slenderbuns: (snorting a giggle as he rummages in a bin of plastic disks of lip gloss) Guys like him realize what they've got and, well, it just naturally shows in their way of carrying themselves.

Me: So what was he like? I mean Blondy. Good-looking?

Slenderbuns: (taking a moment from applying a plummy shade of gloss to his lips so he can smirk at me through the mirror) You just want to know who you stole him from.

Me: I'm just curious. I picture him as good looking with maybe tattoos?

Slenderbuns: (swiveling around to face me. I'm amazed at the lack of transformation of his face. Essentially, he looks like a man with makeup on. From the way he looked sans goop, I'd have thought he'd feminize up pretty good.) Blondy wasn't your type, sugar.

Me: (thinking "here we go again" as I feign interest) Oh? What's my type, then?

Slenderbuns: Educated, artsy-fartsy, (he looks me up and down) with a Sancerre fetish. Maybe wears an ascot, occasionally, making everyone look at you with pity smirks.

Me: (coloring) And how can you know that? You think that everything's right on the surface?

Slenderbuns: (reaches out to lift a wig off a styrofoam head and drop on his own. It's a white-girl wig, the ultra-synthetic hair, chestnut and long with heavy bangs. The transformation from passable drag queen to runway model is so instantaneous that I blink in amazement. I think Slenderbuns must see my appreciation in my face—I can sense him tucking away something snide he'd had on the tip of his tongue. Instead, he snaps open a bright paper fan and flutters it.) Well, that *was* Stephen, honey-pot, was it not?

Me: (a little sharply) I'm afraid I wouldn't...

Slenderbuns: (He snaps the fan closed and raises it in a warning gesture.) Honey, all this denial is beginning to wear on me. I know who you are and I know what you were to Stephen, and I have no intention of actually talking to that silly detective or of otherwise doing you any harm, so if you don't like hearing that I know, don't come here and talk to me and go back to your little fantasy that you and Stephen were a deep dark secret. If it's his suicide that's troubling you, well, then let me assure you, it wasn't *you* who caused it even if you *were* a total cunt when he dumped you. Stephen was *seeking*, honey; he was seeking and he wasn't finding. He got to the bottom of his Pandora's box and, well, I guess that left it empty. And that's sad. Sad enough to make you want to die. (He gives me a look.) You were just *one* of the little horribles that came out of that box, and the fact that you happened to pop out *last* doesn't give you any more credit for his death than any of the others.

Me: (kind of amazed at this outburst) How would you know so much about any of this?

Slenderbuns cuts me off with an answer of sorts. He raises his hands so that the insides of his wrists are displayed in my face. I see his cherry-painted fingernails, their half moons left naked in a classic French manicure, and then, below them, the two vertical scars, running from the base of his palms, down his wrist veins and maybe ten inches up each arm toward his elbows, the tissue thick and beige against his dark skin. The scars look old and well healed. Still, whenever it was that Slenderbuns had decided to check out, he'd meant business.

I go to apologize, but he shoos me rather curtly and turns away, an actress shaking off one emotion so as to envelope herself in another. I leave.

Thrown by the end of our conversation and still woozed-out by the cocktail, I stop at the bar for some water. The place has filled up and the clientele is more eclectic—more overtly gay, to my eye, which could be due to the fact that I'm still the only woman and no one's looking around as if something's missing. I feel invisible, not a completely unpleasant sensation. Some music starts up—a slushy Asian sound—and someone hits the stage with a hand-held spot. People half turn toward the entertainment with an air of polite amusement while others ignore it—they're not here for this stuff, but they're happy to view it before going back to the business of living a secret life of "normalcy" in a world defined by homophobia. Slenderbuns and his bony backup duo come walk-dancing out on the stage in time to the music, wearing silky costumery that shows a lot of leg. They fall into a languorous-limbed dance, complete with geisha fans, Slenderbuns in the middle. The effect is "drugged-out sex slave." Weirdly, I like it, and I move over to sit at one of the black-draped tables near the rear of the audience. Slenderbuns notices me at some point and aims an ironic smile in my direction, as if to say that if I watch carefully I might pick up some pointers on moving like a woman. I give a finger twiddle, then point at my table. He nods, then ignores me for the rest of his little taxi dancer routine.

After the smatter of applause fades, the two white-boy dancers stroll off the stage and into the audience, B-girl style. Slenderbuns seats himself on the edge of the stage and chats, seemingly having forgotten my existence. Nevertheless, he eventually says his goodbyes and heads my way, his pace languid, the fingers of one hand twiddling a lock of his wig.

I don't know if he's going to nail me to the floor or play it palsy now that we've had our little cat fight. All I want out of him is whatever I can get about this "detective" he sprang on me before giving my ass the boot. Burly-Bear? Escroto? Someone else?

I never get to ask. Slenderbuns is about eight feet from me and I'm leaning over to push out a chair for him when something explodes next to me so loud I instinctively throw myself across the little table, taking it to the floor. All I can think is that some sort of ceiling fixture has crashed down practically on me and so I scramble away from it, attempting to protect my head. People are hurrying over and a big bald man with a handlebar moustache—the bouncer, I realize later—helps me to my feet. Deaf from the explosion, I hold onto him, almost clawing him as he attempts to soothe me. I'm rather amazed that he isn't hustling everyone to safety, and I blink up into his face, then around at the room. The place is intact except for the table I toppled. I look at faces. Very few look back at me, fewer still at the place where I'd crashed to the floor.

Me: (up at the bouncer) What? What was it?

I follow the man's gaze and see Slenderbuns. His foot, anyway, with the high heel twisted half off in spite of the ankle strap. The bouncer is holding me protectively but I crane my neck and my eye travels up the prone body, up the stockings, up the splayed red satin robe and his smooth wet torso to the smallish falsies, the long neck, the painted face. The wig's fallen back and the illusion of femininity is somehow destroyed more by that than by the blunt fact of his male body parts. Finally my mind allows me to absorb what I'm seeing—the wet torso, the hole at about sternum level, the puddle spreading from below his back like a shadow. He's still smiling, still playing peek-a-boo through the synthetic hair strewn across his face, but there's no doubt about the fact that he's dead.

People are moving fast, some of them seem to be shouting instructions—911 has been called!—Don't touch the body!—obvious stuff. I alone seem to be on the brink of panic, although I hear some hysterical shrieking that seems to be from far off, and am vaguely comforted by the fact that some guys are freaking. I cower against the bouncer, knowing he'll understand. He seems to be asking me something and I look up at his carnival-strongman moustache and figure out that he's asking what I know, what I saw. I burble through uncooperative lips, vaguely, that Slenderbuns had been coming over to talk. He asks if we were friends and I nod my head, then shake it, then explain that we'd only met once before but I'd come to see the performance. The bouncer nods comfortingly, but he seems to want to extract himself—maybe he's got a lot to do, or maybe he thinks I should be able to pull myself together, being as I barely knew this person murdered directly in front of me. Then he asks me a weird question, which is whether anyone else, like a boyfriend of mine, knew that I was coming here tonight.

The next moments happen in stopgap motion. I turn to look at the table where I'd been sitting, maybe a yard in front of a swaying "wall" of gold chunks of glassy plastic, which sets off a kind of overflow area stocked with bare tables and a haphazard collection of chairs—I hadn't even registered that this area was there, earlier. I see myself in my mind's eye, anticipating Slenderbuns' arrival at my table, a little nervous that he might tell me off theatrically and, seeking to avoid that, leaning forward suddenly to push out a chair for him to signal that I want to be friends—and at that very moment hearing the explosion directly behind my head. I think about the gun, about where whoever it was must have been holding it at the time he shot it so as to hit Slenderbuns around mid-torso.

AND I GET IT.

The bouncer is wrapping me like a child with a chill. I feel the clamminess come over me from forehead to face to chest. I slump against him. What a pussy I am.

In my defense, I recover quickly after they gargle me whiskey. I'm at the bar now, not far from where I'd perched on first arriving. I push the glass away, not crazy about the image of myself sputtering booze down my chin, my clothes and hair a mess. Everyone is sympathetic—I thank the bouncer but shake my head at his offer of further assistance. There's a tragedy to attend to and it isn't me. I'm just some woman who doesn't belong there in the first place and can't keep it together enough to allow them to deal with what's happening. Somehow I get this across and they seem grateful. They move off, everyone talking, the bartender going back to someone on the phone. Some patrons appear to be sticking it out but others are escaping, walking quickly past me in that self-possessed way men have—that way of walking that just presumes that they've got somewhere to be and no one will stop them from getting there. And no one does; it seems understood that it's every man's choice whether he'll deal with the cops, who you can only presume will add a heavy dose of homophobia to the scene upon arrival. I'm reminded of the Hynes T station after Mr. Suicide jumped, how I sat where someone parked me while others raced for the exits. I remember how righteous I felt, even while in some mild form of shock, that I was doing the proper thing.

"Doing the right thing" sucks. I look around. No one is paying attention as I teeter on that barstool. Three men are passing by me, buttoning up their coats, faces ashen, eyes pinched, refusing to look at one another and acknowledge that they're fleeing the scene because of the crime they've committed in simply being who they are.

Well, I know how that feels. I slip off my stool and climb the stairs to the street. I hurry, like they do. We scatter down the sidewalk, hunching our shoulders secretively, like the countless private perversities blowing through the wee hours.

GIVE IT TO ME STRAIGHT

36-D @ February 3 08:18 am

I am, like, palpitating over my coffee. Are you SAFE right now?

webmaggot @ February 3 08:20 am

Chill, Lady D. I mean, she made it home, otherwise we wouldn't be reading this.

36-D @ February 3 08:21 am

Yeah I get *that*, but I've never been where someone gets *shot* right in front of me.

wazzup! @ February 3 08:25 am

Yes, I too offer high praise for this tale you are constructing! Please count me in as major fan of the site. THIS BLOG ROCKS TO THE ROOT, MAN! TO THE *ROOT*!!!!

proudblacktrannie @ February 3 09:02 am

yezz, well, rock on, lovelies. I just wanna comment like I know a thing or two that maybe I don't know, if it comes down to it: I'm seeing a LOT that's interesting in that poor dead sister's comment about Mr. S. I mean, first things first and rest in peace to a murdered sister and all, but also I went to respect some of her last words, and there was something TO that line about Mr. S looking and seeking and not finding and finally givin in. I mean, honey, I would *bet* on this poor deluded suckah having killed himself on this evidence alone, if it weren't for...

36-D @ February 3 09:05 am

IF IT WASN'T FOR WHAT?

roadrage @ February 3 09:07 am

Slenderbuns' murder, I'm thinking. It adds, like, a weird dimension.

We've either got a farkin lot of coincidences glomming together, or there's connections we aren't seeing.

chinkigirl @ February 3 09:10 am

I agree. So it seems to me that the thing to do is to pull it apart. fickel, I see a number of details in last night's post that I could comment on, but the most urgent, I think, is that you imply, if I'm reading you correctly, that *you* might have been the intended target of the bullet that killed Slenderbuns. Am I reading into it, or could someone have shot at you from behind that curtain of beads and only missed because you ducked forward?

fickel @ February 3 09:12 am

G'morning (sort of). And no, you're not over-reading what I wrote, chinkigirl. In fact, I'm sure that this was what the bouncer was thinking, which was what put it in my head. But, as usual, with some distance (i.e., 4 hours of sleep), I'm not certain anymore. I mean, if the bouncer thought I was the target, would he have just deposited me on a stool to hang out? And if it didn't occur to him but I only imagined it did, could it be that I imagined everything about this possibility—the angle of the shot, the closeness of the curtain to my head, the suddenness and degree at which I ducked down. And I can't help thinking that if someone was there to shoot me and had taken such a risk as to do it right out in the open like that, why not shoot again when he saw he'd missed?

marleybones @ February 3 09:18 am

Not to take this in an even more negative direction, but if the shooter was there for you, couldn't he have thought that he'd actually hit you? You were there, of course, but it could be that you started to move exactly as he went to shoot, and you went forward and over the table. No murderer, no matter how bold, is going to hang around, so maybe he thought he had succeeded.

proudblacktrannie @ February 3 09:20 am

I have *chills* just considering this. It means that if someone attempted to kill fickel, he could be out there, discovering his mistake and making plans to make a second attempt.

36-D @ February 3 09:23 am

One word, fickel: Rottweiler. *Please* give the go-ahead. I have his home number?

i.went.to.harvard @ February 3 09:25 am

Wouldn't this be more the time to call Burly-Bear? Physical protection seems like a priority, and he knows you've been nosing around so he'll understand where you're coming from.

fickel @ February 3 09:28 am

Unless, of course, I was totally wrong, and whoever shot Slenderbuns meant to shoot Slenderbuns. And, I have to say, this is the view that my gut tells me is correct, right now.

chinkigirl @ February 3 09:30 am

But not at the time. We humans have a strong tendency to deny that we are in danger, particularly where we perceive no way to avoid or control the danger. Could you be in denial right now? Wouldn't you be prudent to call Burly-Bear? He's police and it's true that the police have not been so straight with you, but nevertheless he comes across as a decent guy who is genuinely concerned about you.

fickel @ February 3 09:32 am

I'm definitely considering doing that, chinkigirl. I've actually started dialing twice. I wanted to hash things out here first, however. It's become my way of...I don't know, thinking. And I don't want to contact the police precipitously right now. I'm feeling vulnerable, and I don't take as much solace in the cops as others. I've seen, firsthand, how mistaken they can be, how eager to reach solutions, how prejudiced. For me, Burly-Bear is just some guy I've met recently who happens to be a cop, which is as much a red flag as it is a consolation. I don't even know if I trusted him as much as I did the Mysterious Hottie, based on gut reaction.

i.went.to.harvard @ February 3 09:35 am

Trust-*ed* the Mysterious Hottie? Is there more going on here than I've been picking up? Last I remember, the Mysterious Hottie never got off the train. How would your feelings have changed between then and now?

fickel @ February 3 09:42 am

He did get off, it turned out.

36-D @ February 3 10:05 am

Okay I am not liking this long silence crap one bit and am imagining all sorts of very scary stuff going on while we sit here staring at our computer screens. I'm ready to call the cops myself but what can I say—I need to talk to Sergeant Malloy about some girl I'm close with who I only know by the name of l. g. fickel?

marleybones @ February 3 10:08 am

This is a very long silence, fickel. Is something going on?

hitman @ February 3 10:12 am

She's giving us time to review last night's post, dum-dums. Read the title: she sees someone murdered and *gets laid*. You're in deep here, fickel, so let's get to it. The last thing you need to worry about is something like propriety.

36-D @ February 3 10:15 am

Weh-heh-hell, look who's over his huff.

fickel @ February 3 10:18 am

Sorry about the long silence, everyone—I needed a shower and my morning migraine tabs—so, no, hitman, it wasn't some suspense-building tactic. All that said, I have to admit that I've been guided by your "logic" over the past few days and am glad to have you back. So tell me, have you been lurking all along, or am I just lucky in having you pick now to play catch-up?

hitman @ February 3 10:19 am

You want this to be about me or you?

fickel @ February 3 10:25 am

Something tells me that that was supposed to be an easy question. Look, I'm afraid the shower didn't help. Maybe some more sleep will do it. I just had too much last night to think coherently.

hitman @ February 3 10:26 am

Full blown booze-up in the fickel flat after your "evening," huh?

fickel @ February 3 10:27 am

Well, I was thinking of Slenderbuns' death being the "too much," but now that you mention it, I've been steadying my nerves with my buddy J.W.B. while posting and, frankly, I think it's worked its magic. Got to refresh with zzzzzzzzzzzz's. 'Til later.

25

LIFE IS PULP

The Noir Boudoir of L.G. Fickel

February 3 @ 12:24 pm
>AH—THE PORN POST<

Okay. I wasn't quite ready to get into this last night, but I need to get it sorted out before I contact Burly-Bear—*if* I contact him, which I have not as of today. And, I am happy to report, I have had no contact from the BPD about Slenderbuns' murder. As observed by hitman earlier this morning in his inimitable "misogynist-cute" blog style, I wasn't fully forthcoming about last night, although the title of my post will attest to my original intention to bare all. In any event, I will proceed. Parental warning: strange scene ahead.

So, when I slip out of the gay club I hurry straight toward the T station. It's maybe four blocks but a straight shot, so in spite of the distance and the drizzle, I can see the big round T sign all the way, its white, flat surface glowing like a streetwalker's moon.

I have maybe a half a block to go when a police car comes swinging around a corner, blue and whites flashing but no sirens. Its tires shrill softly as it crosses two travel lanes and comes to a halt across the sidewalk, very close to the T entrance. Two cops, primarily in silhouette from my vantage point, emerge from the vehicle and start accosting people. I think that it's mostly the quiet that gives it its eerie quality, but I stop short. I'm not near to the cops, not within reach of the pulse of their vehicle's roof lights, but not far enough away to go unnoticed if I turn and walk in another direction. I can't help thinking that this police presence is about

Slenderbuns' death and I'm equally sure that they are there to find me, to grab me and hold me—that the bouncer has described me to the 911 operator and has sworn that I'd had something to do with the murder and fled the scene. With this rushing around in my head, I simply cannot go forward. I start backing off slowly, then quicker, and then I either see or imagine I see one of the cops swing my way and gesture at me.

I almost spin around—almost start running up the street like a grade-A idiot, but at that moment an arm grips mine and I find myself being walked down the sidewalk, straight at the cops. I look and it's the Mysterious Hottie, looking determinedly "curious" about the police presence. I manage to eke out, "Oh, so there you are," and at this point I faint.

MGM fans, you have counted correctly—twice in one evening, when the going gets tough, this rough-and-ready dame folds like a pup tent. But this one's not the momentary swoon I experienced back at the gay club, nor is it a full-fledged horror movie glam faint where the guy has to catch her and carry her as her skirt slips coyly up her thighs and her hair falls in a shimmery cascade. I kind of faint on my feet and slump against the Mysterious Hottie, then stumble along with my shoes seriously tangling. I'm also drooling (if it must be known)—all in all, not unlike a veteran alcoholic a-tumbled from the proverbial wagon.

M.H. handles it. He wraps my shoulders and half walks, half drags me directly past the cop car, where he whistles sharply—apparently he's one of those guys who can shrill one out without using his hand. He speaks with one of the cops—I have no idea what they say but it's not unfriendly and involves the words "six-month anniversary" and some low-register chuckling—and then I have a vague sensation of being piled into a cab. I remember rolling along some potholed streets, my head lolling against the duct-taped backrest, and I remember reaching out and feeling around me for my purse and finding myself groping the Mysterious Hottie's thigh—somehow I'd gotten the impression that he'd put me in and given the cabbie instructions, but I was wrong because here is his thigh right next to me. I decide that I can descend back into semicoherence based on the knowledge that this somewhat ominous stranger is watching over me, and I promptly do just that.

Then it's up a bunch of stairs, exterior and interior. I hear nothing—no cars honking, televisions playing, no piano tinkling in a distant apartment. I have not a clue as to what neighborhood we're in, or even if we're still in Boston. The Mysterious Hottie shifts my weight, still clutching me around the shoulders although I feel like I could stand if I wanted to, and I take some vague notice of the fact that he wears his keys on one of those chains he's hooked to his belt loop, which strikes me as sort of skinheady of him, but with my brother out there somewhere I'm not exactly judgmental on that score. We enter—there's street light filtering through some tall narrow windows but just barely—and the Mysterious Hottie turns and embraces me. It's like a victory hug—we're a couple of crooks in sanctuary for the moment—and I don't raise my arms to return the gesture but I do lean heavily against him, chest to chest, and try to feel our hearts beating through our coats.

"Where were you?" I whisper.

"Outside," he whispers back. "Waiting for you."

"Why didn't you come in?"

"Not gay."

Simple, but, I have to admit, logical from a male point of view.

"The boy we followed from The Blue Pearl was shot. He was standing right in front of me when it happened."

He absorbs this. "Dead?"

I nod, my face against his chest, rather than saying the word.

"One bullet?"

I nod again.

Then, as if to himself. "Good shot."

It's tough to catch tone in a whisper. I don't do anything for a moment, then pull my head away from his chest to observe his face. He's frowning into the dark, more like a crime scene guy analyzing a death than some homophobic sadist getting off on someone's slaughter.

"I might have to be sick," I say in my normal voice.

"Straight through."

I stutter-step through into a room that's inky black, where I grope at the wall until I slap a light switch. I find I'm in a low-ceiling kitchen, unused-looking and grimy. Ahead is a tiny windowless bathroom. I hurry in and shut the door, lean my back against it and breathe. Then I reach out with my foot and flush so he doesn't have to hear whether I'm heaving. The room is claustrophobic, the ceiling flaking, the sink skid-marked with red-green rust, the shower curtain studded with mold along its edges and pulled closed over a cast-iron tub. I don't even want to think about what might be behind there that prompts him to shut the curtain. Instead, I slap closed the toilet lid and sit on it, fumble in my handbag, then hitch up my skirt to prepare myself for what's coming. And no, pulp fans, I do not feel in the least like a whore. But thanks for wondering.

Back out in his living area, he's waiting in the semidark, exactly where we left off. With the kitchen light on behind me I can see the room better, which looks largish, unclean (even in the half-dark), and strangely vertical. I can see the door we came in, its various chains and locks dangling undone, and some kind of low couch next to it that may have a pile of blankets bundled on it and two or three dark beer bottles on the floor nearby. The Mysterious Hottie is leaning against the only important furnishing, a large, walnut-brown table, its top completely bare, its legs sturdy and festooned with a lot of muscular curlicues—a library table, made for working, not eating. Behind the table are a couple of windows, spear-shaped, cobweb-festooned—I'm about to fornicate in an old church that's been converted to apartments.

"You okay?" he asks huskily.

"I didn't get sick after all," I say, sort of hovering in front of him, not quite sure whether he wants me to return to where we were before I ran off. "I just needed some water on my face."

He reaches out and pulls me in. I'm about to assure him that I'm not thinking about Slenderbuns, not planning on obsessing about it, when I feel something against my thigh. So I guess he's taking for granted that I'm ready to move on to another topic. He kisses my forehead and undulates against me, almost as if he's not conscious of what he's doing, but there's no denying that he knows that I know what we're about to do if I don't back him off in the very near future.

So I don't. Back him off, that is.

After, he sits me down on the low couch. He walks away, his boots creaking on the floorboards, and I can hear him rustling around in the kitchen. I reach down and hitch my pantyhose back up to my waist and smooth down my skirt, adjust my coat around me, and touch at my hair.

I'm still humming—ah, if only girls were tuning forks, what a wonderful *wahh-wahh-wahhhhh* sound I'd be making—but I'm also exhausted. Frankly, I feel really, really nice.

I hear the sound of a teapot whistling—like everything else about the M.H., it is both comforting and vaguely alien. He comes back holding a mug, leans over me to snap on a lamp. As he fumbles with the switch, I inhale both the sweet, refined heat of the tea and the acid odor of his armpits—another mixed signal.

Me: (lifting the mug to my face so I can breathe the steam) I thought you didn't like tea.

M.H.: Got it for you.

He goes into the kitchen and I take in the parts of his space that I haven't yet seen. I get the sense of walls with major pockmarks. Across the room there's a bookcase built of cinder blocks and long bowed boards, three shelves crammed with books and bottles and smudgy boxes of various sizes. On the top shelf I make out a jar with something sticking out—dead flower stems?—no, it's paintbrushes, big, flat-edged ones. M.H. is a bohemian extraordinaire, oui? The lamp next to my head, a clumsy glazed ceramic number, sits on a plastic crate. It has a bandanna draped over its shade—yellow with some faux-Indian pattern—accounting for the weak, uneven glow. The other light he's snapped on is one of those metal accordion numbers, clamped to his work table. The bonnet shade is carelessly tilted away—in fact, the brightest point in the room is the reflection of its bulb off one of the spidery church windows. I see no canvases around, no easel, no rough compositions of charcoaled nudes tacked to the wall, nothing to support his claim that he's an artist except the paintbrushes...and the way he uses his hands. Through the entryway into the kitchen, I can see a rust-peppered refrigerator door with one of those beautiful hands resting on its upper rim—something tells me that he's staring in at some leftover lo mein and a lot of mold. Above the kitchen is a blotted-out space with a circular stairway in black metal leading up and a wood railing that someone's fashioned out of what looks like a ship's balustrade all round its edges. Like, does everyone but me live in a loft?

M.H.: (emerging with a cell) What are you in the mood for?

Me: (I hold the mug on my knees, cupped in both hands.) Not in the mood. For food, that is.

M.H.: (smiles briefly, apparently thinking I'm hinting at a second bout of him, which I'm not...or am I, come to think of it?) You're a vegan, right?

Me: (vaguely) Not that I'm aware of. (I take a moment before my next sentence, wanting it to come out right.) What do you think about the shooting tonight? I mean, do you have any ideas about whether this murder could be somehow related to Stephen Pearle's death?

He's looking at his cell, thumbing, and, I imagine, mulling over my question.

M.H.: (as if musing aloud) Freakin weird.

He clicks his cell off and heads right at me. For some reason I flinch like a puppy who's done a piddle, but of course all he's doing is reaching for his coat, which is hanging on a hook by the door. He sees the flinch and doesn't register a reaction, but after he takes his coat he leans over and kisses me. I look up and the kiss hits my lips dead on. It's a boy kiss, a lovely thing—those dry lips, unpuckered, pushing hard against mine for a rough moment. It's something he's giving me for my sake, some sort of assurance, like a pat on the head. It works.

He goes to the door and I don't bother following him with my eyes. I hear him pause and don't need to see that cute, snaggle-toothed smile to know what it looks like—and then he's gone. I hear his boots, light on the heel, tumbling gracefully down the stairs.

I put aside the tea, get up, and, without knowing what I'm about to do, start roving around the place, sampling the private areas. I run my fingers through the dark stain on his table where he'd lain on top of me earlier, and then, without thinking, I raise them to my nostrils. The odor is all mine, not his, not mingled. I wonder about how much DNA that table's absorbed while it's been in his possession, how many eager women he's had on that slab. I hope it's a lot. There's nothing as pathetic as a sex-starved male.

I run my eye over the shelves, the brushes and paint tubes, pliers and pincers. I stroke a finger through a bin of twisted metal and tickle the brittle sticks of charcoal jumbled in a black mesh box. His supplies are relatively tidy in a scruffy, fingerprinty way. I've never been in a real artist's space before, but it feels right. I meander into the kitchen. The light's a bare bulb. There's no counter or built-in cabinets—just the refrigerator, an oversized gas stove-oven that looks profoundly undisturbed, a metal table. The small, barred window seems to stare out at an air shaft. I duck back into the tight bathroom and pee, then gather up the stuff I left there earlier.

Emerging back into the kitchen, I spot the laptop on one of those little wheeled butcher blocks, up against the side of the refrigerator. It's an ancient Dell, its lid thick, keyboard massive. It's open. The screen is black.

Naturally, I'm drawn to it—me being me and all. I walk across and tap the mouse, one little jab with my third finger, just to see. To my surprise—I swear I expected nothing—the screen blinks awake and a bare-bones website appears. Amazingly, it's a blog. It's called *Full Frontal*, which I immediately like, but I can't tell if it's the Mysterious Hottie's blog or just one he'd happened upon and was reading. The page I'm on describes a robbery at a midnight greasy spoon, presented in the style of a sensationalist newspaper report. It goes something like:

> End of an Era as Wee-Hours Coffee Shop Owner Brutally Disfigured, Face Pressed to White-Hot Grill During Late-Night Attack—Female Customer Sought for Questioning...

I stop reading and turn away—gore has always turned me off, and I don't want to know what kind of crap M.H. might be into. It occurs to me that his laptop should be back in hibernation well before he gets back, but that if he's quick I'll just walk into the kitchen with him and flick the mouse "inadvertently" so it looks like the thing wakes up just then. Duplicitous of me, but a guy leaves a chick alone with his stuff all hanging out...I mean, we've all read *Bluebeard's Closet* at some point, yes?

Leaving the kitchen, I tiptoe up the circular stairs, listening intently for any clue that he's returning. I expect a loft bedroom; instead I find an easel and elaborately rigged lighting setup. I have to move carefully, as canvases lean in stacks against the railing and walls, but I manage to work my way around the place without putting a foot through any works of art. When I get there, I click the switch at the base of one of those bulbs-on-a-pole floor lamps, then stand up slowly to view the canvas currently resting on the easel. It's an unfinished oil, barely more than roughed in and rather startling in the raw promise of its wet, uninhibited brush strokes. It depicts a woman with a haughty bearing. She sits very stiff on what might be a throne, staring—staring down the viewer, you might say.

The colors are going to be bright, I think, mostly reds and black, or at least that's the way he's patched it out in what must be an undercoating. It's semiabstract, by which I mean the perspective has that art deco quality—purposely flat, although in spite of this the woman herself manages to stand out, her chin thrust forward, her eyes unpainted, unseeing. Behind her he's painted the word "MASSA," maybe to signify her imperialness.

I glance around at the rest of the studio space. The other paintings, leaning against the walls and railing, are a murky lot. Most don't catch my attention, but one's a sketchy outline done in thin, deft lines of black paint depicting a naked man, relatively well built, stern-faced, youngish, cut off by the bottom of the canvas along his upper thighs—obviously the M.H. is mocking the viewer for the way our eyes jump greedily to that spot. This might be a self-portrait, but I'm not sure, never having seen the M.H. fully naked.

There's an old dresser against the wall, paint-spattered with the gypsy air of having been dragged off the curb some midnight years ago. Its sculpted top drawer is crookedly open. I peek inside, past the clutter of paint tubes. I can smell the linseed oil coming off a paint-smeared rag that half drapes the drawer opening. Beyond it, there's a piece of paper, semifolded, wrinkled. For some reason I pull it out, extracting it gently, just two fingers. I open it. It's a sketch of a necklace. In pencil, the lines sharp, the detailing exquisite: an arrangement of larger and smaller stones, laced together by a netting of thin chain. Artfully penciled words like "bridge," "seam," and "twisted cable" surround the sketch, connected to it by tiny darting arrow.

Before I can even form a coherent thought about what I've discovered, an idea rises into my conscious mind with frightening, unanticipated clarity. I turn my head sharply to study the male figure in the nude study. This time the man doesn't look young to me—his arms and chest are buffed up but there's a hint of sag around his middle and a scrawny quality to the shoulders and neck—this is a middle-aged man who's working to buck the tide of aging. It's a study in vanity—cynical, maybe cruel—the artist has chopped it off at genital level to spare us an eyeful of fifty-year-old scrotum.

As if in a daze, I raise my eyes to the unfinished oil on his easel. Up near the top, the letters MASSA fall off the edge of the canvas—it's not a statement, but the beginning of a word...the word *Massachusetts*...as in Massachusetts Avenue, an exit at the Hynes T Station. The illusions of majesty tumble away. It's just a woman sitting on a bench, refraining from leaning against anything. Behind her is the tiled wall of a subway station. And she's not stiff with regality, her eyes bold—she's rigid as she represses her emotions, clutches everything in.

She's me, waiting for the cops, the image of Mr. Suicide's skinned face beating before my eyes.

I hear a noise from far away—someone yelling, a bottle breaking, nothing about it marking the M.H.'s return, but it jars me to action. I click off the light, this time managing to kick over a tall can of brushes in water that sits under the easel. I clatter down the stairs, grab my coat and purse, and go for the door. Thrusting myself through, I find myself in a public hallway, unlit except for what light seeps through a mottled, stained-glass stairway window. The hallway is narrow with tall ceilings, like his apartment, reinforcing my impression that this building was a church, or anyway something other than the artists' tenement it has become. I listen, peering down the exceedingly long straight stairway to what might or might not be the entry vestibule below. The runner is rubber and sandy with winter grit. I pitter-patter on down, softly as I can, only to find that this isn't the ground floor and I have to do it again, this time on a wide, elegant stairway with a curved banister. I'm about to take a flyer down these when I hear the outer door open below and a key rattling in the inner lock. I look around at the silent doors—for a place with few straight lines the public space is amazingly devoid of crannies. I retrace my steps as quickly and quietly as I can, only to find that M.H's door has locked behind me. Not wanting to be discovered in the hallway, I keep going and head up the next stairway. This set of stairs, I find, leads directly to a locked door—no landing—and I have no idea whether it's an apartment or just some sort of cupola. I crouch on the top step, listening to the M.H. ascend—those quick footfalls telling so much and yet so little. He thrusts his key, twists and shoves, like someone well used to his own door's peculiarities. I peer through the banister rails and catch a glimpse of him going in, his whisker-speckled jaw, a hand holding a plastic bag in which there are undoubtedly containers of pea pods and noodles and two pairs of chopsticks. He pauses, the door still open, apparently taking in the fact that I have run out on him. I hold my breath, but he doesn't come out to check the hallway. The door slaps to behind him and I immediately tiptoe past it and on down to my freedom.

Outside I have no idea where I am—Dorchester, Roxbury, J.P., some area of South Boston I've never been to in my life???—all have neighborhoods like this—tall brick walkups crowded together, narrow streets with old trees twisting through the sidewalks, chain link fences side by side with once-elegant iron gates, patches of wasted "gardens." I skitter along, sensing more than seeing or hearing a commercial district somewhere ahead. I emerge rather suddenly into a wide open street. There are very few people puffing the cold air, all of them at some distance from me and all looking very predatory. I try not to hesitate and start walking rapidly along the sidewalk, pretending that I know where I'm going and that it's not far. A car seems to slow and pull up near me. Its honk startles me and I steadfastly ignore it and stride along, my face ducked. The driver guns it and shoves ahead of me where he stops again and I glance up and see that it's a taxi. Amazing. The driver has his window open and is talking out at me, some sort of advice about being out at this hour alone not being safe. I glance over—he's an older man, Hispanic, concerned-looking, driving a cab. I get in and yank the door and he coasts away, lecturing me gently. I give him my address and close my eyes, wondering whether I'll have the money to pay him when we get there. Unbelievably, I fall asleep, and the driver has to talk me awake when we reach my place. I go for my wallet and that's when I realize that I'm holding the pencil sketch of the necklace—the one I'd found at Mysterious Hottie's place.

I come inside and bolt the door. I pour a drink and, bringing the bottle, sit down here without changing or showering. I write about Slenderbuns. I run dry, as you know, before I can sort out my scene with the Mysterious Hottie.

And since then? Well, he did not call today, but to tell you the truth, I don't know if he knows who I am well enough to even have called if he wanted to. I'm the chick at the train station who was freaked by the suicide and inspired a painting out of him. He knows my first name—not my last. And why should he call me, anyway? I ran out on him, so shouldn't it be me who calls? Haven't I made it clear—haven't I demanded—that I'm the one in control of whatever it is we're doing?

Sigh. Why do guys listen only when you're not sure you want them to?

I'm going to post this, then go out to forage for coffee. When I return, I'm sure I will find that one of you bloggies will have posted some brilliant insights. We will begin the task of figuring this out.

GIVE IT TO ME STRAIGHT

36-D @ February 3 01:12 pm

This is getting way, way freaky.

chinkigirl @ February 3 01:14 pm

I, too, am getting sweaty palms here. Could it be *possible* that the Mysterious Hottie doesn't present a threat? If so, I'd like to hear how.

roadrage @ February 3 01:15 pm

Well, the man isn't gay...so what's his connection with Slenderbuns?

proudblacktrannie @ February 3 01:24 pm

Lord, lord, lord, the pressure! Somehow I feel like this is my turf, like I should be the one to get at this from the inside—I mean, I do work at a gay club and I have even dabbled in exotic dancing. But I have nothing to offer except the obvious—gay folk can inspire hate crimes. We live with this danger. And, frankly, when the bouncer asked fickel if she had a boyfriend who might have known she was heading off to fraternize with the gay folk, I think he was wondering whether she'd unwittingly sparked a hate killing. We know better, of course, but unless some drug angle emerges in Slenderbuns' life, that's how this will go down.

i.went.to.harvard @ February 3 01:28 pm

Do we know better? This Mysterious Hottie has given us some indication, if fickel is portraying him accurately, that he's homophobic.

marleybones @ February 3 01:42 pm

No offense, but I've had occasion to think that about everyone on this site.

chinkigirl @ February 3 01:43 pm

Yes, but noir itself is riddled with homophobia. We're all aware of the true meaning of the word *gunsel*, yes? And obviously that doesn't bother any of us unduly or we wouldn't be here. So let's admit we're *all* comfortable, to some degree, with homophobia—including you, marleybones—and let i.went.to.harvard state his case.

i.went.to.harvard @ February 3 01:45 pm

Thanx. And, agreed, I'm not trying to lynch the guy for liking his sex straight. But, still, there's been a killing and he was there, so it's his homophobia that we need to analyze—fair enough?

marleybones @ February 3 01:46 pm

I am cool with all of the above. Write on, Freud.

i.went.to.harvard @ February 3 01:47 pm

Okay, first we have the fact that the M.H. won't go in the club even though he's tailed a fellow all the way there. Second, and far more condemning, he responds to the news of the boy's murder with the comment "good shot." Ambiguously as fickel presents it, that seems awful to me (and fickel, I've noticed, has an incredibly high tolerance for ignorance, including those of us with less than enlightened views about women and nonmainstream lifestyles). Third, he's also been in the vicinity of both deaths—Mr. Suicide and now Slenderbuns. I don't know what any of that means, frankly, but I am picking up other coincidental connections between the M.H. and the Mr. S situation. For example, he's a blond artist who apparently sketched a necklace, and Mr. Suicide appears to have been involved with a blond male artist at some point in the last year or so, during which Mr. S created the very necklace that M.H. sketched. He also has a painting in his loft that could be Mr. Suicide himself. Finally, and possibly most damning, he repeatedly turns up in places where he could anticipate fickel might show up *if* he already knows a great deal about Mr. Suicide and that fickel is trying to investigate the man.

I know that all of this may add up to very little, but my point is simply to question whether the man is safe for fickel to be around.

chinkigirl @ February 3 01:55 pm

Of course, when Mr. Suicide died, Mysterious Hottie was *on* the train. Close by, but not in any sort of position to have caused the death.

marleybones @ February 3 01:58 pm

Ah, but we don't know that. We just know he said it. We *think* that he was at the train station that night, because it appears that he must have observed fickel in order to have her image in his head for the painting he's doing. But there, again, he could have imagined it, if fickel or his cop friend described what happened. I mean, this *is* a guy who draws out of his head.

webmaggot @ February 3 02:02 pm

Well, the world wide web has bent me over again. I have been up, down, and around the internet, looking for a weblog called Full Frontal. It is unfindable. Must be one of those sumazzbichinsites that made itself invisible to search engines.

wazzup! @ February 3 02:04 pm

Hey favorite of all Americans! Just made excellent hidden clue connection and am bursting to share: the Mystery Hot Date has the chipped tooth—"snaggle tooth," fickel says, yes? EXACTLY LIKE "E" FROM THE STRANGE AND CRYPTIC DIARY! M.H. = E!!!

chinkigirl @ February 3 02:07 pm

Not to steal your signature line, proudblacktrannie, but oh my land and stars!

36-D @ February 3 02:09 pm

Plus she's noticed his manly chin a couple of times, too. Manly chin = chin with nail-hole dimple, in my cute guy scrapbook.

chinkigirl @ February 3 02:18 pm

You know, once you go back and reread, the clues begin to pop out at you—in his diary, Mr. Suicide says he first saw E on the street near the All Night, strolling around with some guy. Well, the M.H. certainly seemed to know that neighborhood.

roadrage @ February 3 02:24 pm

There's also that line in Mr. Suicide's diary about E being the artist and Mr. S the clay—Mysterious Hottie is an artist, and Mr. Suicide may have posed for that nude study fickel saw.

marleybones @ February 3 02:27 pm

Careful, now. This is a lot of word association play we're getting into.

i.went.to.harvard @ February 3 02:30 pm

Well, let's put it to fickel. fickel, could it be that the Mysterious Hottie is E?

roadrage @ February 3 02:32 pm

Hey. Something else? I used to live with someone who made jewelry. Those pincers and bits of wire and shit in the M.H.'s apartment are, like, tools of the trade. This guy makes jewelry.

36-D @ February 3 02:39 pm

OMFG—take it a couple of steps out from all this and X becomes a lot less delusional about what killed her husband. I mean, think of it: M.H. is a psycho. He has his fling with Mr. Suicide and, like, refuses to accept the fact that some men ultimately need to be with a woman. He watches Mr. S moving in on fickel, maybe even *follows* Mr. S as Mr. S homes in on fickel. Hell, gang, he could have been there, watching as Mr. S went to approach fickel in the vinyl shop that night, and then... gawd, I'm afraid to even write it.

i.went.to.harvard @ February 3 02:41 pm

Let me write it, then: if Mysterious Hottie shoved Mr. Suicide in front of a train, who is to say that he didn't shoot Slenderbuns in cold blood—the only person fickel's discovered who actually laid eyes on the M.H. and Mr. S together and identified them as lovers.

marleybones @ February 3 02:44 pm

Except for the fat pussycat.

i.went.to.harvard @ February 3 02:45 pm

Come again?

marleybones @ February 3 02:46 pm

The fat pussycat at the Berklee concert. Remember the diary? She set up E and Mr. Suicide—jeweler and jewelry designer—so she must have known both of them. Puzzle complete, or at least a lot more complete than it was for me ten minutes ago.

hitman @ February 3 02:49 pm

Hail to the nerdiacs. The dyke from the heartland scores in overtime.

marleybones @ February 3 02:50 pm

What makes you think I'm from—actually, yeah, I'm in Minnesota (where my partner is at the moment in the kitchen burning peanut brittle—what a stench).

hitman @ February 3 02:52 pm

Hey, don't feel like a walking stereotype. I'm just sensitive to nuance.

webmaggot @ February 3 02:55 pm

You're a walking dildo, actually. See, I'm sensitive to nuance too.

36-D @ February 3 02:59 pm

Look, all you dildos, I'm not sure where we're at?

hitman @ February 3 03:02 pm

Don't be dumb, Mrs. Cleavage. Guy Ferguson's an artist. It's already been speculated here or thereabouts that the fat pussycat in the diary bears a resemblance to the Peacock. And at their place is a recently painted portrait of the Peacock with some fancy necklace draped around her neck—the same necklace that's proudly displayed in a photo at Mr. Suicide's shop AND shows up in a sketch in the Mysterious Psycho's loft. Put it together, IQ.

fickel @ February 3 03:05 pm

Well, I'm back, toting a super grande deluxe triple espresso with extra skim froth, and I believe I get your drift, gang. So let me try to feel it out.

I guess we start with the Mysterious Hottie meeting the Peacock through one source or another. Lord knows he's talented enough to get himself recommended for a portrait. So the Peacock likes him—strike that—she loves him—strike that—she is *in heat* over him and so of course she agrees to sit for him. Hell, if only he'd insisted on painting her nude—hell, maybe *she* insists on some nude poses. Eventually, some sketches for the portrait develop, and—how are we conjuring this up?—the M.H. lays in some way-out-there necklace across her throat, just to goose up the composition a notch. Acquisitive creature that she is, the Peacock falls in love with *these* rocks even more than she has fallen for the artist's. She wants the portrait *and* she wants the necklace in it. So she gets her artist-cum-lover together with her regular jeweler (and yes, ladies like the Peacock have a "regular jeweler") to see what they can conjure up.

But self-adulation isn't *all* that's motivating the Peacock. The truth is she is increasingly nervous that her hubby is going to find out about her dalliance with the artist, which dalliance she's been justifying to herself by pretending to suspect her husband's "attentions" to a young freelance editor who's been assisting him in working up his memoir. In sober moments, of course, the Peacock knows that her suspicions are a lot of bunk. This is a good reason to break it off with the artist—HOWEVER, the Peacock has also sobered to the realization that her boy toy might be a touch psychotic, and so she's concerned about recriminations.

Translation: *she gets a glimmer of something in his character that scares her shitless.*

Imagine her relief when she learns that her jeweler and her artist have become more than business partners. She eases her way out of her tryst, chewing up the scenery in her role as the spurned woman. She pays both men well for their services, heaves a massive sigh of relief, and hangs her new necklace around her neck and her new oil above the mantel where she and the Colonel can admire it, safely together, if a tad suspicious of one another. She's escaped unscalded...or so she thinks.

In the meantime, however, the jeweler has stepped right into the Peacock's shoes: now *he's* the sugar daddy to a psycho. And, like his predecessor, he's afraid to let the pretty lad know that he's ready to whisper adieu and move along to more...tepid pursuits. Adding to the operatic aspect of the entire mess, the jeweler isn't *quite* following the Peacock's example by desiring to resume his state of monogamy. No, for this intrepid fellow it's a new conquest—the Colonel's freelance editor, whom the jeweler spotted at a concert, air-kissing with the Peacock.

Wild coincidence? Well, not *so* wild, when you consider that the Peacock started this whole charade with her head full of half-blown suspicions about her husband and this girl, which would give the older lady plenty of motive for talking up the younger one to any eligible males she might know who might be lured into taking the temptress of the blue pencil away from the Peacock's old man.

So the jeweler starts thinking more and more about the girl—maybe he spots her at another concert and speaks a word or two with her, maybe he learns about her blog and gets into her internet voice, or maybe she simply represents a return to relative normalcy from the man-to-man thing he'd thought was so daring a few months back. But he's got a problem: the blond artist's half moved in on him, and, like the Peacock (and how many others?) before him, our jeweler has come to realize that his snuggle buddy is psychotic. He's afraid to kick the lad out, and, to make everything that much more audacious, the artist doesn't seem to feel any compunction about *his* remaining monogamous with the jeweler. Indeed, our jeweler trails the artist sometimes, and learns that the guy is seeing other guys (cue the street scene outside the All Night). Jeweler-man lives in this limbo for some time, scribbling his self-loathing into his journal. Finally, however, he finds himself some courage and kicks the effer out for good.

Then what? Maybe he waits, fearing repercussions. When none occur, he begins his gentle dance, moving in slowly, as nice guys do, on his new conquest (me, for those who have lost their way). Maybe it takes weeks—or months, if he's extra shy. At last he sees an opportunity—they've been at the same concert, and then make their way to the same retro music store, and then to the same T station. It's all too, too meet-cute to pass up, and he makes his move. But just as he steps forward to speak to her at the Hynes T station, the psycho hops out from behind a post and shoves him right past the girl and into the tracks, where he meets his fate face first.

Psycho is a touch freaked at what he's done. He runs—that's his initial instinct—then maybe he returns, needing to know if he was spotted. He finds the girl sitting on a bench. He observes. The cops question her, let her go. He follows her out, trails her so he knows where she lives, and then peels off and T's it on back to the city, where he wipes all signs of his presence from the jeweler's loft.

He doesn't quite know it, but his fun is just beginning. The cops have some reason to suspect that the death was a murder, but no one seems to know a thing about *him*. The dead man's wife (X) has never seen him—all she knows is he's a he. The Peacock knows more than is good for her, but no one knows to come asking her questions and she has no incentive to go to the police and air her soiled delicates. The clerk from the jewelry shop (Slenderbuns)—now, he's actually *seen* the two erstwhile lovers together (Pearle and M.H.), but only as collaborators on a commission. Still, like the Peacock, the clerk could become dangerous to our psycho's peace of mind if the cops get lucky and start putting two and two and two together.

And how to keep in touch with what is going on? Well, there's the girl (me), a little fool of a thing whom the cops are sniffing around. So he follows her, moving in slowly when she turns out to have a sharp eye and a good memory for himbos. And so to the present...

webmaggot @ February 3 03:53 pm

That's a lot to swallow in one sitting.

chinkigirl @ February 3 04:02 pm

I'm likewise kind of boggled right now.

i.went.to.harvard @ February 3 04:05 pm

It's really a smaller tale than it reads—jealous hothead kills his ex-lover, then scrambles to protect himself against discovery.

wazzup! @ February 3 04:10 pm

BRILLIANT NEO-NOIR!!!! LOVE IT!!!! NEXT LET'S MAKE M.H. KILL THE PEACOCK, RIGHT? THEN HE GOES FOR THE GIRL AND THE COP JUMPS IN TO SAVE HER AND COP AND PSYCHO KILL *EACH OTHER*, LEAVING HER ALIVE BUT ALONE, SO SAD AND ALONE!!! PERFECT NOIR ENDING, YES? WRAP AND PRINT!!!

36-D @ February 3 04:13 pm

Umm, wazzup, hon? I don't think you're quite on our wavelength. This is real, not fic.

webmaggot @ February 3 04:14 pm

Give him a break—guy wears poplar shoes.

roadrage @ February 3 04:15 pm

I think I need to reanalyze everything, get the timing down, before I can swear I'm in.

marleybones @ February 3 04:16 pm

Ditto. Also, I sense some sort of puppet-master here, someone as yet unidentified whose presence will explain away any seeming coincidences.

hitman @ February 3 04:18 pm

So, okay, some fat-chewing going on, but basically it's unanimous. Your bloggies are with you. What do you do now, fick? Take the tale to Burly-Bear?

fickel @ February 3 04:20 pm

Sigh. How can I do that when, in spite of all of your support, *I don't believe the story myself*?

proudblacktrannie @ February 3 04:23 pm

Lawdy—she's ready to defend the man she's scared of.

fickel @ February 3 04:28 pm

I am, actually. I mean, sure, we don't know the secret demons that lurk inside the strangers we meet, but something just feels wrong about the idea of the M.H. as a full-blown psycho.

Look, let's put it this way: this whole buildup started from someone observing that the M.H. may suffer from a mild case of homophobia. If that makes a man a psycho, well which of you men isn't one of those?

proudblacktrannie @ February 3 04:30 pm

I'm assuming I'm an honorary woman for present purposes, hmm?

i.went.to.harvard @ February 3 04:32 pm

Well, I'm not homophobic, but it could be that they beat the "compassion for all" thing into you in div school.

webmaggot @ February 3 04:35 pm

I'm not homophobic either, but maybe that's because I shared a room with a gay brother for fifteen years and never once woke up with a sore butthole.

36-D @ February 3 04:40 pm

Look, not to come off like a broken record, but my Rottweiler works with some PI's who could check this M.H. guy out quick and quiet. I'm not talking about you learning anything personal—I'm just talking about peace of mind.

fickel @ February 3 04:42 pm

Yeah. Hire a detective to investigate a guy I'm just starting to...I don't know.

hitman @ February 3 04:43 pm

You *like* this guy? Geez-US. I mean, you can sit there pattering out a tight, logical tale in which the guy's a killer whose current vic list may include you, and at the same time you can *like* him?

fickel @ February 3 04:45 pm

...a little.

proudblacktrannie @ February 3 04:46 pm

The female of the species is romantic to the end. It's our fatal flaw, and often the death of us.

marleybones @ February 3 04:48 pm

Yes, well, putting aside the legendary failings of "the female," I think that what fickel's trying to say is that the tale she just wove about the M.H. isn't hers—it's ours, the one we were driving at, and just because she has the presence of mind to articulate it doesn't mean she buys it.

chinkigirl @ February 3 04:52 pm

Okay here's a question: why would Mr. Suicide refer to the M.H. as "E?" His initials (I mean, besides M.H.) are G.F.

fickel @ February 3 04:53 pm

Sigh. Could be a hundred nicknames, chinkigirl, although I appreciate the attempt to back up my skepticism. But the way things are, I *don't know* what I think, and I *don't* want to eff this thing up with the M.H. if I'm wrong.

proudblacktrannie @ February 3 04:55 pm

I am absolutely *tearing up*! It's so frighteningly romantic. And you cannot go to Burly-Bear with this, even though on one level you do feel endangered. How can you confide in one potential lover about another in a way that pits them against one another? It would be the ultimate betrayal.

hitman @ February 3 04:59 pm

Groin time. Time to bitch-slap your lawyer into doing something useful.

fickel @ February 3 05:02 pm

And how, pray tell, does a charity case bitch-slap her lawyer?

hitman @ February 3 05:03 pm

You lay a few facts out, chickenheart. Let me get you started: (1) He's your lawyer, and free or not, that means he's got professional responsibilities, so it's about time he started meeting a couple of them. (2) He has to keep your confidence, and you got issues, so maybe it's his turn to shut up and listen. (3) He's trained in logic and might be able to fill in or show you flaws to this whole story about the Peacock, and if he doesn't want you going to the cops with everything you know and think, he'd better start doing so. (4) He took you on as a client to please the Colonel, who obviously shovels him enough dough to make it worth it.

fickel @ February 3 05:06 pm

Wow. Y'know, you're actually making a little sense, there, pardner.

hitman @ February 3 05:07 pm

It's a plan. Beats doing it on a table with the prime suspect.

fickel @ February 3 05:08 pm

Not sure about *that*, but...

leo tolstoy @ February 3 05:10 pm

Without knowing what I am and why I am here, life's impossible; and that I can't know, and so I can't live.

fickel @ February 3 05:11 pm

So, uh, leo t? Don't you have another blog to lurk around on, tossing out the occasional brutally morbid and condescending quote? Please? :)

26

FULL FRONTAL

EXISTENTIALISM ENGORGED

02.03 @ 6:00 PM:
I MAKE HEADLINES—ABOUT ARFING TIME, TOO!!!

The partially decomposed corpse of a hideous old scag will be discovered two weeks or, hell, maybe two months from today, tucked into a small hollow about fifty yards up the tunnel of the Hynes T station, her face half chewed off by rats, her stinking clothes ravaged and blackened from having been burnt. The old bitch used to frequent the station, where she would haunt the edge of the platform and occasionally emerge to shriek foreign obscenities at one or another John Q. Public. Commuters interviewed after her rotted corpse turned up had this to say: "The old scag? Sure I remember her. Followed a buddy of mine, screaming shyte in Swedish for like two city blocks. Good to know she's dead—for once, some positive news." Another commuter: "Oh wow, yeah, the homeless witch from the T. Beaten and burnt to death? Wow. Oh well, that's my train—will I be on the 6:00 news?" Police might have concluded that the skanky old sack of disease had died from trying to warm her bones by lighting something with kerosene that somehow sparked the greasy rags she called clothing, except that her head was turned completely around the wrong way. Could she have been effed up enough to do that to herself? The BPD spokesman had this to say: "Yeah, when their head's turned around backwards, that's a pretty good indication that they either fell down a pack of stairs or got murdered." Alert readers will note that there is a long pack of stairs in the Hynes T station that could easily do in some raving lunatic homeless drunk, but then how would she have gotten her brittle, broken bones fifty yards up the tunnel? Guess Boston will never know.

You don't exist, you filthy swine, until you make it onto Boston—dot—com.

---

tALK. NIHILISt DOGS

boytoucher @ 02.03 08:12 pm

You a dead bag lady, full frontal, or am I missing som'n?

fullfrontal @ 02.03 08:18 pm

You are missing som'n. Like a brain, wizard.

losmuertos @ 02.03 08:29 pm

Dude. You sayin you did this? Zup wi dat?

fullfrontal @ 02.03 08:30 pm

Ain sayin shit, captain.

garbo @ 02.03 09:11 pm

Are you on a rampage? First you take out that punk, now this homeless woman. Who's next?

fullfrontal @ 02.03 09:14 pm

Got a couple in mind.

garbo @ 02.03 09:15 pm

As in a couple of additional victims or as in some married people you'd like to kill?

fullfrontal @ 02.03 09:16 pm

Whazzit t'u? Too deths iz too deths.

garbo @ 02.03 09:17 pm

I'm just puzzling over the idea that a degenerate like you would have dealings at all with a married couple.

fullfrontal @ 02.03 09:18 pm

Such a slice you are. Where does it end?

garbo @ 02.03 09:19 pm

You don't...get it yet?

fullfrontal @ 02.03 09:28 pm

Wid U and Me, til death do us depart.

garbo @ 02.03 09:30 pm

oh loooooooord you are so hopelessly romantic. I am all aflush.

fullfrontal @ 02.03 09:31 pm

Rip your larynx out, hunny, and don't think I'm lyin.

garbo @ 02.03 09:32 pm

Hey look at that: you can spell "larynx" but you usually can't spell to save your life. Such an enigmatic guy. Will you puzzle me foh-evah, luvah? (bats eyelashes coyly)

eddielizard @ 02.03 09:45 pm

Mahn this b'yotch NEEDS to die with huh fingahs cut off and a severed dick in her mouth.

garbo @ 02.03 09:51 pm

A severed dick? Are you volunteering or should we look for one the cops will actually notice?

boytoucher @ 02.03 09:53 pm

G'damn, is all b'yitches like this?

bonitoestoria @ 02.03 09:54 pm

for showah.

garbo @ 02.03 09:55 pm

(indulgent laugh) Ah, but your little "friends" are so useless, double f. Can't we be alone?

fullfrontal @ 02.03 09:57 pm

You vahn tuh be alun?

garbo @ 02.03 09:58 pm

Save the sweet talk for the big event.

fullfrontal @ 02.03 09:59 pm

Whut big event wud that be, she-dog?

garbo @ 02.03 10:00 pm

My "rape," your "death." You rid me of my pesky virginity, I rid you of your pesky life.

fullfrontal @ 02.03 10:01 pm

You're underage after all, eh, sparky?

garbo @ 02.03 10:02 pm

No more than you are, Mr. Evah-so-Worldly. (Petulant flounce) Look, I haven't been wasting my time here, have I?

garbo @ 02.03 10:31 pm

oh, loooooooooooo-verrrrrrrrrrrrrrrr?

garbo @ 02.03 10:35 pm

did I scare you off?

garbo @ 02.03 10:44 pm

(whispering) *chugga-chugga-choo-choo?*

fullfrontal @ 02.03 10:45 pm

Now THASS sum sounds I LIKES.

27

LIFE IS PULP

Feed the Beast With L.G. Fickel

February 3 @ 11:03 pm
>NIGHT OFF<

I'm checking in because I don't want anyone to worry. Frankly, I don't have it in me to write tonight. If you're in Boston, turn on the local news. It's the story about the couple in Concord.

I should have gone to Burly-Bear. I screwed up. I will fill you in as soon as I'm up to it.

GIVE IT TO ME STRAIGHT

webmaggot @ February 3 11:32 pm

> Okay, there's this story running about a couple in Sudbury (Sudbury's like "the other Concord," to Bostonians) who had something happen that might be murder. They keep looping the same snippet about carbon monoxide poisoning. This other local station that's more sensational (you should see the *tewl* behind the anchor desk) but it's reporting a possible suicide/homicide in Sudbury and showing the street view of a mansion—the kind with those rounded red-striped awnings hooding the windows and ivy all over everything. They didn't say the owners' name because relatives haven't been notified. That's all I got. Yeah, I suck as a detective.

36-D @ February 3 11:38 pm

Nothing on Providence TV. Guess the thing to do is to wait for fickel to report out.

webmaggot @ February 3 11:45 pm

Anyone got the feeling that we are sitting around with our dicks tucked between our haunches while some badass shit is raining down that we might have been able to do something about?

chinkigirl @ February 3 11:52 pm

Sort of.

webmaggot @ February 3 11:55 pm

Okay that's cool just thought I'd ask. Think I'll go j.o. to Instagram.

marleybones @ February 3 11:56 pm

Goodnight, quixotic world.

28

LIFE IS PULP

Noir the Night Away With L.G. Fickel

February 4 @ 6:23 pm
>COLD DAY IN PARADISE<

Thanks for understanding my need to black out last night. In spite of that, it's gotten so I can barely think without my fingers moving, so I actually need to be here. I will fill you in.

So yesterday, acting on hitman's advice (hmm, a phrase I've written before), I did the prudent thing and set up a meet with Mr. Groin. Well, to be more precise, I called the Colonel and let *him* set up a thing with Mr. Groin for last night at the Colonel's. And, yes, that's because I am a chicken and vaguely afraid of Mr. Groin.

My excuse for including the Colonel? Well, it occurred to me that if my little "tale" about the M.H. *were* true—and it did seem ***less and less plausible*** as the minutes ticked by—but IF it were true, then someone who had the Peacock's interests at heart had a right to know about it. It also occurred to me that the tale as told to the Concord crowd need not include any of our—okay, *my*—tawdrier speculations of the relationship between Mysterious Hottie and the Peacock. I thought that this simpler version might go down a tad smoother:

Point A—Artist paints lady with imagined necklace;
Point B—Lady sets up artist with jeweler to construct said necklace;
Point C—Artist and jeweler become lovers;
Point D—Things go sour and artist kills jeweler;

Point E—Folks who know about connection between artist and jeweler start dying.

Tight, tidy, logical, yes? And not a finger pointed *near* the Peacock's virtue. BTW, the Colonel did not ask me *why* I needed to see him and his lawyer. I found that telling. More so now.

So, after signing off yesterday, I set out to keep my appointment with the Colonel and Mr. Groin. I had the sketch of the Peacock's necklace that I'd snitched from the M.H's loft and, basically, nothing else to support anything I had to say. This was fine with me, and I was undecided about whether I'd even present the sketch. I wanted it crystal clear that what I brought to the table was a theory. I wanted them to poke holes in it a mile wide. For once in my life, I *wanted* a couple of alpha males to be *very* patronizing toward me. To withhold what I'd conjured up would be unfair to them. To have them buy it would be disloyal to the M.H. See my dilemma?

It's with that profound sense of ambiguity that I roll along the windy roads toward the Colonel's villa, enjoying the way the setting sun occasionally blinds me to everything—trees and road and pretty rock walls and all the secret mansions tucked inside this scenery. The Colonel's place is along a relatively flat stretch, its lawn wide and open, making the villa itself visible from the road, although the facade is buried to the second story in hillocks of fleshy black rhododendrons. I round a bend and see the vehicles first—a colorful local police cruiser half blocking the road, and six or seven neighborhood cars—mostly Mercedes and Beemers with the occasional antique Volvo among them—pulled over for decency's sake, their owners standing along the shoulder, hands deep in coat pockets, peering up the Colonel's drive. I crawl past the chubby lad on street duty who waves me through with that overwrought patience cops acquire as a means of coping with the lady-folk out in your more exclusive suburbs. I pull over just past the shrub barrier and slip back along the road's edge, doing my best imitation of a rich housewife—eyes wary, face still, fingers clutching my coat lapels closed. I move among the other gawkers, feeling very incognito, and stop by a mauve-colored BMW. Over its roof I can see up the lawn to the villa.

This is not your normal-sized lawn, I ought to clarify. It's a football field that got lost on its way to some university, making the people up near the house the size of board game pieces. From that perspective, here is what I see:

There's an ambulance, rear doors open. There's an old lady in a shapeless grey dress propped against it, surrounded by a couple of stout cops. She's frail, with yellow skin that seems to glow with decay even in the fading light, and long tendrils of wispy white hair escaped from some sort of chignon to float round her head. She slaps around herself as if at imaginary gadflies, apparently hostile to the idea of some paramedic forty-five years her junior pushing an oxygen mask against her face. The black kid with the mask seems ready to cram it in place if only to shut her up. It takes a moment for me to recognize her as an old biddy I'd barely registered as existing on my various visits to the house, although I have a general impression of her peeking through a crack in the dining room door at the Colonel once or twice while I'd been visiting, as if seeking some signal before creaking off to roost. The nickname "Chalkie" or some other backstairs affectation comes to mind, but I have no recollection of ever having heard a meaningful exchange between her and the Colonel, so I could be conjuring that up on the basis of how bloodless she looks.

Next I see the front door of the Colonel's villa open, and out from its deep shadows emerge three or four men. In the middle is Burly-Bear, looking rather hunky with his almost-spiky hair and small black sunglasses, his Burberry flapping to reveal the signature rumpled suit. These detectives cluster on the lawn as if comparing notes, and then Burly-Bear approaches the old lady as she bitches away at the medics.

Whatever is going on, I am dying to know, but have no desire whatsoever to become part of the drama being played out up that powdered-rock drive. So I stand there, mesmerized, until suddenly I'm startled by a voice just below me, speaking in one of those querulous English accents—picture one of those silly gits Dame Agatha used to name "Badger" or "Archie."

Silly Git: I *say*, miss, are you quite all right?

Me: What?

I look down to see that there's suddenly a man sitting behind the wheel of the BMW. I mean, he must have been there all along, but now he's powered down the window and is blinking up at me through round gold-rimmed glasses. He has red hair—but not like Burly-Bear's; this guy's a true carrot top. Below this he has one of those long jackrabbit faces and a jaw that only a Brit could cultivate. He's wearing some sort of belted wool coat, tweedy, and a purple bow tie. I step back from his car.

Me: Sorry. Was I leaning?

Silly Git: What's that? Doesn't matter. I'm just wondering if you're...you look a bit unsteady, actually. Someone you know up there?

Me: No. I mean yes, actually. I know him, the owner, and his wife, of course. I'd forgotten they had a live-in.

Silly Git: Yes, well, one does forget the help sometimes. Tiresome, remembering absolutely everyone, I always think. But, I say, would you like to hop in, have a sit-down? You seem as if you could use one.

He gestures behind him, and I hear the *ka-chunk* as he unlocks the doors. In the back seat lies one of those strappy, worn briefcases that academics carry. It doesn't score him points insofar as my assessment of him—academics and lechery of the most perverted nature are a highly reliable match-up, in my experience.

Me: (checking him out afresh now that he seems to be taking a stab at picking me up, or at least kidnapping me for a quick rape before throttling me with his coat belt and dumping my corpse in a leafy patch of woods somewhere near the New Hampshire border. He's one of those wan, bony types who could be any age from thirty-five to fifty. I shudder at the idea of him holding me down with one hand pressed over my mouth as he pokes his pathetic erection against my locked thighs.) No, I'm good. Do you know what's going on?

Silly Git: I don't, actually. I got the impression from the chit-chat that there's been some sort of accident, gas fireplace on without a flame, carbon monoxide backup from the furnace exhaust, silent killer and all that, you know. Both master and missus got rushed off quite a little bit ago.

Me: Both of them in ambulances?

Silly Git: Well, yes, that does tend to be the vehicle of preference for these incidents, wot? (He smiles hopefully. His teeth are every bit as horrible as expected.)

I raise my eyes and take in the scene up the driveway. The maid has been hoisted onto the stretcher and has the oxygen mask over her face, but that doesn't mean she's settled down. She seems to be clawing at one of the stocky men's arms and gesticulating. Burly-Bear has walked off and is talking to another man, heads bent together. As if in slow motion, it dawns on me that the old lady is pointing down the winding drive toward the street. I move my eyes back to Burly-Bear to see his companion raise his head to gaze at the old lady, and then he peers down the drive. It's Escroto, and I realize—suddenly and clearly—that I do not want him to see me.

Me: (quickly) Maybe I will take that seat. (I duck myself into the back of the Silly Git's car. Still, I don't underestimate Escroto. Guy could spot bird turd on a rainbow.) Could you drive me to my car? It's up there.

Silly Git: (twisting around to view me. I get a whiff of sourballs, or his natural breath?) Looks like someone's coming down the drive at a trot. May as well see what that's about, eh?

Me: (not looking) I need you to drive me now, actually. I have to get somewhere. I'm very late.

Silly Git: (giving me a sympathetic pout and at the same time taking in my assets) Are you quite sure you're up to driving? You look like you could use a stiff one, if I may say so.

Me: (moving to get out) Look, you said you'd help me, but if you don't want to, I'll go.

Silly Git: (quickly) Right-o. Happy to help.

He eases off the soft cinders and rolls. I hold my breath, imagining the megaphoned order to stop. None of this happens, and Silly Git rides me around the bend and past my own car. I let him take me beyond some faux mansion with white pillars, then order him to pull over. He seems puzzled afresh, being as we're not near any parked car, but he does as I ask and, I'm grateful to say, shoves off. I wait until he rounds a bend, then step among the gnarled branches of a little copse of yews that's spread out of control, backing my way through the soft, prickly needles until I'm about three feet in, then slowly squat down in my evergreen cave. Hands in my pockets, I wait. In less then a half minute a sedan cruises by, silently picking up speed—it's grey and unwashed and there are two men inside but I do not lean forward to see more. I wait until it is out of sight around the bend, then emerge from my yew hideout and walk, slowly as I dare, back past the hundred windows of the faux mansion to collect my car.

Then I'm in my car, hands shaking as I fumble the key into the ignition. Then I'm driving, slowly, silently, smoothly away from the scene of the crime. I don't start breathing regularly until I'm sitting in six miles of bumper-to-bumper traffic on Mem Drive. Finally I'm home. I blog about the fact that I'm not able to blog. Still, I'm with you guys. I'm safe.

GIVE IT TO ME STRAIGHT

chinkigirl @ February 4 06:51 pm

> fickel I am starting to worry a great deal. If it wasn't clear before I think it's clear now that something awful's going on—some situation that started with a case of reckless jealousy and is now a murder spree, and though you may believe your involvement to be collateral I'm not so sure. I'm really afraid for you.

i.went.to.harvard @ February 4 06:53 pm

> Why are you avoiding Burly-Bear? Don't you get that he'll help you?

fickel @ February 4 06:55 pm

> I'm afraid of him. Don't you get that?

i.went.to.harvard @ February 4 06:57 pm

> I don't, frankly. He's a cop who happened to notice that you're an attractive woman. He cleared your brother out for his own good—you admitted as much yourself. He's not the danger here, but someone else is. And it seems to be Mysterious Hottie.

webmaggot @ February 4 07:00 pm

> She can't see past his face. We all know that guys will let a pretty chick get away with murder—well, the opposite is true, too. If the M.H. is as hot as fickel's portrayed him, there's no way she can talk herself into mistrusting him.

marleybones @ February 4 07:02 pm

> Let's not get patronizing. fickel is in the situation and we are not. She's got as good a read on the people she's dealing with as anyone. And I've known a couple of real shits who wore badges. Let's lay off on second-guessing who's a black hat and who's a white hat.

chinkigirl @ February 4 07:05 pm

Okay, but another thing I'm starting to pick up that troubles me—it seems, fickel, as if you consider this blog some sort of sanctuary, as if you make the world the way you want it, just by writing it that way, and as if our concern for you affords you some sort of protection. That's truly understandable, but it's way, way off. You do need help. Live, flesh-and-blood protection. Pick whatever form you want. Do not mistake this chat group for the very real support you need right now. Is that totally harsh?

fickel @ February 4 07:11 pm

No, no it's not harsh, but I'm not the soul caved in on herself that you seem to think I am. I've already called Mr. Groin—from my car, truth be told. He didn't pick up but I left a message and, in fact, I'm seeing him tonight. I just...I've gotten really valuable advice on this blog, whether or not you want to credit yourselves for giving it. I need you guys as much as I need anyone right now. Don't shove me off.

i.went.to.harvard @ February 4 07:14 pm

No shoving from this quarter. And VERY interested in seeing you through this.

marleybones @ February 4 07:15 pm

Same here. I think all of us are just airing our concerns. It's anything but a shove-off.

hitman @ February 4 07:16 pm

So, lookit, not to cut off this sensitive moment, but speaking of providing "support" through our conversations—or whatever these are—I got to thinking about like how wazzup brought up the idea of the Mysterious Hottie being E, remember? So I went back and read the parts of the diary that fickel has posted, looking for clues as to whether E was the Mysterious Hottie or maybe not. I decided it was possible. I mean, everything that's said about E that could apply to a girl could also apply to a guy, and definitely to some self-absorbed bisexual artist. However, all while I'm doing this I'm wondering in the back of my head about how someone whose name is Guy Ferguson could have a nickname starting with E. But then I come across the comment where fickel describes the diary's handwriting as artistic. And then I have like this amazing brainstorm:

What if Guy Ferguson wrote the diary?
What if "E" is Stephen Pearle?

So I go back and re-reread the diary excerpts as if they were written *by* the Mysterious Hottie *about* Mr. Suicide—Mr. Suicide being "E," and it works. But don't take my word for it, folks. Read the thing. And, fickel, you can test this theory on parts we haven't seen.

wazzup! @ February 4 07:20 pm

BOY OH BOY this is like a major plot twist what I love to see!!! Mr. Hitman, YOU ROCK!!! IT'S PRACTICALLY LIKE YOU'RE FICKEL HERSELF!!!

webmaggot @ February 4 07:24 pm

Man, this whole thing is getting too sexually convoluted for my brain to take. Could *someone* just, like, do the deed in the normal way? It's really not so bad.

36-D @ February 4 07:25 pm

I thought the part where fickel had sex on the table was hot. What was abnormal about that?

webmaggot @ February 4 07:26 pm

Except the guy is a *psycho*. Otherwise very normal *and* hot.

chinkigirl @ February 4 07:30 pm

I am once again floored by hitman. You really are faking that Neanderthal thing, aren't you? I think this is a major step in our analysis. This is something you should take to Mr. G, fickel.

fickel @ February 4 07:33 pm

Look, I've skimmed some of the diary with this new perspective and I agree that it's worth a closer look. But you folks have to remember that I don't see the M.H. the way you do—I must be portraying him a bit off or something. He doesn't play as a hustler. The guy looks you right in the eye when he talks to you. He was easygoing when I accused him of something and was wrong. He's very comfortable with himself, very genuine. His clothes are not at all "sexy," except that he's the one who's wearing them. And he's a serious artist. Having seen his stuff I can't doubt that he makes a living doing what he does best—does that sound like a jealous guy? Most important, he just doesn't *smell* like a weird sex hustler gone psycho who's watching me for any reason, whether it's self-protection or sadism.

Oh, and I should say that this diary is not a key to anything. It's more of a series of letters. The last one, for those very into interpreting the thing, is a series of E's, pages of them, all in this style of writing that isn't like the rest of the handwriting. At the end it says "eats shit." Makes you think, huh?

roadrage @ February 4 07:34 pm

Absolutely. Like I think the writer went totally off the deep end at that point.

36-D @ February 4 07:37 pm

I know everyone is going to jump all over me for this, but I just want to say that I have dated a lot of guys and the ones who look you right in the eye and act totally comfortable when you accuse them of something (like screwing your roommate, as a fer-instance) turn out to be the biggest scumbags. Particularly if they have blue eyes—do not ask me why but I suspect it is because they know that chicks cannot stand up against blue eyes that look directly into theirs when the guy is saying something like all he thinks about 24/7 is how many ways he'd like to do her. Guy with steady blue eyes make that sound romantic. Anyone else says it, you mace him.

fickel @ February 4 07:39 pm

Sigh. Not jumping on anyone right now. I did enough of that earlier. I just...well, I've got to get dressed if I'm going to make my meeting with Mr. Groin. Wish me luck.

hitman @ February 4 07:40 pm

Luck? With you, baby, it's pure talent.

fickel @ February 4 07:44 pm

Why is that somehow vaguely insulting, coming from you? :)

29

LIFE IS PULP

Noir the Night Away With L.G. Fickel

February 4 @ 11:44 pm
>THE GROIN SHOOTS HIS WAD<

There's something about the dead silence of an office building at night. Not quite real. The traffic down below was something that didn't have anything to do with me...

—Dick Powell's opening monolog in *Murder, My Sweet*

This you had to be there to experience, so just suspend your propensity for disbelief, friends, and listen along. And, yes, I'm drinking. I don't know how to react to what I just found out, so a drink seemed appropriate. After that, another seemed like the way to go. Then I logged on.

First, just to set the tone: I hit the meeting with Mr. Groin, and the man was bawling. I kid ye not, this brass-to-the-ass, leads-with-his-left-hook, shiny-socked "turney's turney" was, like—well, let's toss the fellow some dignity and call it "heavy misting." But that hanky was WET, and not with snot. So I'm beginning to think that the suspicion I tossed off way back about the Groin and the Peacock was correct, but that maybe she wasn't quite as casual a squeeze as one might have surmised, or perhaps not quite as casual as she herself wanted to be.

From the top, you say? Well, plenty of Four Roses in the bottle. Warning, though: illegal activities ahead. Proceed prepared to be an accessory after the blog.

Sooo, while we were speculating earlier about the flip-flop of permutations that may be applied to Mr. Suicide's diary—an old queen (Mr. S) writing about a young hustler (M.H.) or the other way round—I was dressing for my meeting with Mr. Groin. Not that I was sure I'd find him in—I kind of pictured him clinging to the Peacock's hospital sheets, considering what it would be worth to prop a pen in her hand, stick a codicil underneath its business end, and move the document this way and that so that the unconscious woman actually "signs" all of her assets over to him—but some sixth sense told me he would make it, and that this would be a serious moment between us, thus warranting some serious apparel.

I slipped into my ruby-red crushed velvet knee-length gentle-over-the hips number with gold piping, high collar, and side slits, and scared up a pair of black semisheer denier glossies—and my peeptoe mesh-n-satin ankle strap heels. I gave my hair a spritz and crimped it beddy-heddy with my hands, smeared a shadow of soot-grey makeup around my eyes, and rolled some gloves inside my diamante clutch (with mother o' pearl clasp). I wanted to look young, jaded and not very happy—fact is, I wanted to look like **ME** tonight—and I achieved it. Then I slipped my box coat with the rolled lapels over my shoulders and headed for Boston's bizniz district where the tall buildings hang out like so many taut, silent erections against the star-peppered night sky.

Mr. Groin's office is in an old Boston "skyscraper," the kind built into the contours of the street they face, with a deep, narrow lobby lined with brass elevators and dark-skinned "security" guys in plum uniforms. I stroll in around eight, and, this being Sunday, it is like stepping into a tomb. I expect security to be a high hurdle but apparently 9/11 paranoia's gone out of fashion. I mention an appointment with Mr. Groin while touching at my hair in the building plaque's reflection and am ushered along without ceremony. The elevator shoots me up thirteen floors, and the doors fold back to reveal one of those grey-on-grey padded-cell style office corridors. I tread silently until I come across the tinted-glass doorway with the Groin Man's name painted in black with gold shadowing, along with those of other "name" partners. Inside everything immediately goes to imitation Stickley. There's no receptionist behind the pegged wood desk, and the glass-walled conference room is dark and becomingly untidy as befits a busy law establishment. Surprisingly (it being the Sabbath) I can hear voices from down one hall, barking in amiable combat, but something tells me that Mr. Groin will be found in the opposite direction, which seems the more exclusive end of the suite.

Sure enough, I find him sitting behind a nearly closed door in an office lit more by the twinkle of harbor lights behind him than by the emerald-shaded barrister's desk lamp, its glow reflecting off the glass-covered surface of his desk to create a sort of footlight effect for the comic opera we are about to play out.

I tap. He grunts. I slip round the door as he tips a splash of scotch for himself. Clearly, it's not his first of the evening, or his second—you realize that this is not a criticism, coming from me. He gestures with the bottle but I shake my head as I lower myself to the edge of one of his guest chairs and absorb the darkened room. Nothing appears askew about the place or Mr. Groin himself. He's wearing the very olive-toned suit that I met him in. Its padded shoulders are squared, his tie is straight, even his black hair is slicked back shiny. Only his face gives him away—his eyes bloodshot, his skin dead white—but whether that's from the harsh lighting or the shock of what he's heard I don't know. I take in the dampened state of the oversized silk hanky he's clutching in one of his hairy-knuckled hands and figure I should take the lead.

Me: I showed up out in Concord for our meeting yesterday, and—I'm sorry but I don't know what happened or how they are. What have you heard?

Mr. Groin: (staring at the surface of his desk before speaking) He's dead. She's brain dead. Hopefully her heart will stop pumping soon.

Me: (whispering) I'm so sorry.

Mr. Groin: Yeah. Me too. I'll enter his will tomorrow, and hers when she goes. (He drinks.) 'Course, she was to get everything he had. Which was really all she was after when she married him, so there's your happy ending, huh? (He drinks again, maybe a toast to irony.)

Me: How...?

Mr. Groin: (his voice sharp) How much is it worth?

Me: (blinking in noncomprehension, then shaking my head) How did it happen?

Mr. Groin: (stares at his desk for a long beat, then raises his dead eyes to stare across at me) You mean you didn't talk to your cop friend? He was there.

Me: I didn't talk to anyone. I saw an ambulance, the housekeeper, and a lot of cops. A neighbor told me there'd been an accident. I went home and called you.

Mr. Groin: You're telling me you just rubbernecked and then got the hell out of there? Why wouldn't you tell them you were there to see the old man? Didn't you care to know what happened? (Here he cuts off and clutches the hanky hard, staring ahead of himself.)

Me: A man outside said it was something like a gas leak and seemed to think everyone was going to be okay. The housekeeper was out on the lawn, and she certainly looked fit enough. Besides, last week you told me to avoid the police.

Mr. Groin: (snorting) Halle–fuckin–lujah. A client who listens for once.

Me: (a little stung) Well, if I was so thoughtless to drive away from Concord without thinking the worst, what about you? Shouldn't you be at the hospital, hoping for a miracle?

Mr. Groin: (looking off to the side for a moment) I had to take care of something, something she would have wanted me to do. (He shifts forward a little, swirls his drink and watches it go around for a moment before raising his eyes to mine.) Besides, I had you to deal with. I figured we ought to have a little talk, you and me.

Me: (blinking, then catching on) Oh. I understand that your services were only for so long as...You certainly didn't need to meet me here to tell me that. It could have waited.

Mr. Groin: (studying me for a long time before speaking) Good of you to understand our working arrangement so clearly. However, that's not all I wanted to talk about.

Me: (I wait, then give in) Well?

Mr. Groin: (still studying me) Why would that cop of yours be running out to Concord for something like this? Doesn't he have enough going on with his murder-suicide thing?

Me: Murder-suicide? What murder-suicide? Are you saying one of them turned the gas on purposely?

Mr. Groin: No. I'm not saying that. I'm asking you what you think your cop friend would be doing out in Concord.

Me: (I stand up, confused) I don't understand. What happened out in

Concord? You say he's dead and she's brain dead. But how? What happened to them, if it wasn't some sort of carbon monoxide or gas accident?

Mr. Groin: (looking up at me, and suddenly displaying his perfect teeth in an ugly, joyless smile) I don't know. Cops don't either, yet. I expect that we'll both find out real soon.

Me: (insistent) But how did he die? You know that, don't you?

Mr. Groin: (still smiling, eyes glassy from the booze, he slowly raises a finger to his temple and makes it like a gun, then mimes shooting himself in the head. I see a bead of sweat trickle down his temple, miming a trickle of blood.)

Me: (sinking back to my seat) How horrible.

Mr. Groin: She got it at the base of the skull. She wouldn't have felt anything.

Me: So he did it to her and then himself? Was there a note?

Mr. Groin: (He pauses to drain his drink.) No. (He looks at the empty glass a moment, then looks up at me, a glint of malice in his eye.) No gun, either.

Me: But there must have been.

Mr. Groin: Oh?

Me: Well, if...

Mr. Groin: If?

Me: If he did it, the gun would be there. Plus a note. People leave notes in these circumstances.

Mr. Groin: Do they? And you would know because...?

Me: Because everyone knows that suicides leave notes.

Mr. Groin: So I guess that means he wasn't one, eh, Sherlock?

Me: But you said it was a murder-suicide.

Mr. Groin: Did I?

Me: Stop talking in circles! Is this some sort of game for you?

Mr. Groin: Oh, no. Not for me. And I never said that there was a murder-suicide out in Concord tonight. I said that it was odd that your cop friend would show up out there, when he had his hands full with a murder-suicide here in Boston.

Me: But it's not odd. He went out there with me the other night, remember? Wait, though: what murder-suicide here in Boston?

Mr. Groin: (leaning back in his seat, then speaking quietly) Yours.

Me: (I stand up involuntarily) My murder-suicide?

Mr. Groin: Sure, sweetheart. Or, should I say, the murder you're passing off as a suicide.

Me: (I actually lose my breath, momentarily, as if he'd suddenly thrown the contents of his glass into my face.) How can you say something like that? Even drunk...

Mr. Groin: (he stands, too, and leans over the desk aggressively) I'm not that drunk, sweetheart. And I know. I looked into your background. I know all about you and your punk brother and the shit the two of you pulled in the past. I know about your mother getting away with murdering your freak pervert of a father for what he made you and your brother do with one another. But my suspicion is that it wasn't your mother at all, that she just took the fall for the two of you innocents.

To my amazement, at this moment I step forward, rear back a hand and slap him across the face. Being as I myself had no idea this was going to happen, he, too, is caught totally by surprise. The slap hits him loud, against the flat of his cheek, hard enough to throw his face to the side. He catches himself with his hand on his blotter. I can see a tiny glimmer of blood seep over the edge of his lip. I'm glad to see it, like I'm glad to feel my hand ringing from the contact with his face.

Me: (speaking more out of surprise than anything else, but sounding pretty damned incensed) How dare you repeat a pack of small-town lies...

And this, of course, is where he hits me back. Ah, yes—it figures that Mr. Groin wouldn't live by any kind of "code of chivalry," so I suppose I should have expected it. Maybe I was just too pissed off to be thinking defensively—imagine anyone repeating the *sewage* passing as gossip that stunk up my so-called "home town" after my father's death. Well, at least it taught me at a young age that the boredom born of unambitious lives can lead to evil. Anyway, Mr. G backhands me, his knuckles hitting my jaw in an upward sweep with a lot of shoulder behind it. He's drunk, of course, but he works out and I'm a girl, and so it's enough to send me to the floor. I manage to miss both guest chairs—what a mess *that* could have been—but I hit the carpet hard and am pretty dazed, momentarily.

Next thing I know I'm blinking at his elevated wingtips and feeling his hands gripping me. I figure he must be contrite about clocking me, but there I'd be wrong. This guy's even more of a prize than I thought. He pulls me to my feet, maintaining his tight grip on my shoulders, and absolutely spits his words in my face.

Mr. Groin: You may be one crazy bitch, but let me make something clear: if you think anyone's going to find that will you talked the old deluded soldier into writing, you're...

Me: (pulling back, if only to get away from his boozy saliva) Let go of me. Let go of me or I'll scream, do you understand?

Mr. Groin: (instead pulling me closer so that I can see the pink blood bubbles shimmering between his clenched teeth as he grinds out his words) I was *there*, bitch. For our meeting, remember? I'm the one who found the bodies. I'm the one who lied to the press about the gas leak. I found everything, baby, all of it. And if you think you're going to get a fucking cent...

Now, I would normally never even dream of my next maneuver, but I guess when a man is going really deranged on you, you get resourceful. I jam a knee upward, solid, into his crotch. I'm scared to death that I'll miss and he'll beat the crap out of me in retaliation, but luck's on my side and he quite suddenly starts gagging, his face going grey, and kind of half caves in on himself. I manage to pull myself free of him and stumble backward a few steps before catching myself. I'm out of breath from all the nutty stuff he's been spewing and half expect him to pull himself together and spring at me, but he doesn't.

He leans against his desk for a while, head hanging down, breathing, and then, to my relief, he limps his way back around and falls heavily into his seat. This is when he starts crying in earnest. He manages to find his handkerchief and goes as if to mop it across his forehead but ends up clutching the cloth to his face like a shroud as his shoulders shake.

Me: (All I can think of is that I have to calm him down, coax him out of his delusion that I had anything to do with these deaths. I find that my hands are trembling as I take a swipe at my hair and straighten my dress.) You're just deranged with grief. You loved her. That's it, right? You loved her and you found them dead and you need someone to lash out at. That's it, isn't it? That's all, right?

Mr. Groin: (He gathers up the handkerchief and lowers it, then sits blinking across the desk at me. The green glass shade of his barrister's lamp has gotten twisted around in our struggle, and now the harsh white light of the tube bulb beams full into his face. The deep creases that run down from his nose are wet. His slick hair is tousled and dangles down his forehead.) Fuck you. (His voice sounds defeated.) Fuck you, you pitiless cunt.

I back out of his office, leaving him sitting there, crying. When I get to the reception desk, I happen to notice that the office light from down the other hall, the one that had been on when I arrived, is now doused, the voices gone. Without thinking, I duck into the empty conference room, the one behind the glass wall, just off the reception area. I take a seat at the long, oak-veneer table and sit in the dark. I have no reason to be there, nothing in mind, but even as I tell myself this I realize that it isn't true. I'm waiting, I realize.

So I wait. Mr. Groin leaves about ten minutes later, passing ten feet from where I'm sitting in the dark, shrugging into his coat, his briefcase in his hand. If he'd turned his head he would have seen me and I would have explained that he'd upset me so much that I'd needed to sit it out. No doubt things would have gotten very ugly at that point. Fortunately, he doesn't see me. He steps behind the receptionist's desk, reaches his hand underneath it without needing to see what he's doing, then goes straight across to the glass door and through it. If I hadn't seen the man knock back half a pint in front of me, I'd have sworn he wasn't drunk at all.

I retrace my steps to his office. He's closed his door but it isn't locked, which doesn't surprise me—lawyers never lock their office doors because if they did the cleaners would skip their office, and they can't stand the idea of missing out on a menial service they're paying for.

Donning my brushed-leather dove-grey opera gloves, I do up the pearlescent wrist buttons as I cross the room to a thickset cabinet on the side wall, the one he'd glanced at when I'd asked him why he wasn't at the hospital with the Peacock. The cabinet is cherry wood, or something purporting to be, part of the Stickley collection that runs riot throughout the place. I try the "iron" latch but of course it's locked. I slide my soft-gloved fingers along the top of the cabinet and down its sides, although I know all the while that Mr. Groin will have the key on him or locked in some drawer whose key he carries. I try all the desk drawers anyway, then sit in his chair, swaying slowly back and forth, wondering how I will get into the cabinet. Because I will, of course. It's in the script, you could say.

The solution strikes me. I rise, leave his office, and duck my head into the office next door, then the one after that. There are about fifteen offices in all, and about ten of them are small, with built-in furniture, some without windows. Those are for the grunts-at-law. Five, including the Groin's, are larger. These are for the partners. And, as I'd hoped, one of the other partners has selected the same side cabinet as Mr. Groin. This partner has left the key parked in the lock of his side cabinet. Nothing to hide, I guess. I hook the key, glide back to the Groin's office, and slip it into the cabinet lock. It does not work immediately, but some minutes of patient wriggling and jiggling does the trick, and I'm in.

He hasn't taken any pains to tuck away what he's got—must think his bullshit lock really works. On the bottom shelf is a handgun, resting on top of a folded piece of paper. I hesitate at the idea of touching—even with opera gloves—what is undoubtedly police evidence connected with a murder investigation, but then I think about the outrageous things that Mr. Groin said about me and dickel and also my dear father (I still miss him with a pain that is palpable), and that steels me. I pick up the handgun and slip it into my purse. I pick up the paper on which it was resting and open it to read it, then quickly refold it and take that as well. I close the cabinet, lock it (another ordeal), then return the key to its rightful cabinet.

Out in the reception area, I duck down to explore the underside of the receptionist's desk, where I find a little box. I press the button, and a light begins to blink green. I have no idea whether this means I've disarmed the alarm system, but what choice do I have? I slip through the outer door holding my breath, and allow it to close and lock behind me. All is silent—but then there's nothing that says an alarm isn't screaming its bloody head off down in the lobby security office. I take the elevator down, scared silly that the doors are going to open to a squad of building drones, ready to riddle my body with rubber bullets. The lobby, however, appears deserted but for a couple of far-off security guys, scratching their asses and gabbing pleasantly. I make a beeline straight for the street exit, my heels clacking like it's 1942, and when the security guys call out that I need to sign out, I blow them a kiss, then hurry out to the street. When I peek sideways through the rotating revolving door to see how they've taken it, they're laughing. Guess I really do look like a high-price tart, in the right stockings. I half run all the way to the T.

Once home, I hide the gun (rather well, if I do say so myself), and read the document I'd grabbed from Mr. Groin's cabinet. It's just what it appeared to be: a handwritten will, in ink, looking rather shaky and recently written, and signed by the Colonel. I have no idea whether it's technically valid or even authentic. All I know is that in it, he leaves everything he owns to me.

GIVE IT TO ME STRAIGHT

marleybones @ February 5 12:19 am

Umm, kick my ass for being an inveterate old cynic, but can I ask a basic question: what are we doing here? I mean, all along this wazzup! fellow from the Netherlands keeps up this incessant series of compliments on our "fan fiction" efforts *and for the first moment it occurs to me that he may be correct.*

Please understand, fickel, I for one would be VERY happy if that turned out to be the case, because I like a good scary yarn and I don't like the idea of you being smacked around by some lawyer, but I'd kind of like to hear again that all of what we're going through with you is FACT at this point, because I've been sweating this out, long distance. So, is all of this for real, fickel, or are you playing us for a fictional thrill ride?

roadrage @ February 5 12:38 am

Well, if fickel's not going to answer, I can tell you that the couple out in Sudbury died. It's on the news, and they're being kind of ambiguous about how they died, although they keep pairing it with the story about the carbon monoxide bill. I'm not going to name their real names because that seems to be fickel's prerogative on this blog, but they're pretty much the way she's laid them out, I guess—him a retired old guy who looks kind of military, her kind of a pampered glam-ma'am, at least in the photo they're using. So these two deaths are for real, marleybones.

marleybones @ February 5 12:44 am

Okaaaay, but I'd sure like to hear all that from fickel herself.

36-D @ February 5 12:48 am

Look, I'm not too good with the long silences, so I'm going to confess something: I told everything to the Rottweiler. I was convinced that fickel wasn't protecting herself, and that she needed a lawyer looking into why the cops won't leave her alone about Mr. Suicide. So it all came pouring out yesterday (with tears), and he made some calls. I'm sooo, sooo sorry, fickel, and I know that you'll see this as a betrayal, but I swear to you it *just happened.*

Anyway, so this is what I now know: Some man did die in the T stop at Hynes, just like fickel said, but the cops won't say if they think he was pushed. They say that they have several witnesses they are "working with." Because the Rottweiler isn't representing any of them, at first he couldn't get any more from the cops, but he is the Rottweiler, like I keep saying, so I also know that the witness who claimed that some girl was screaming at the deceased just before the train came in is "unreliable." This is cop talk for a druggie or a felon or someone who has run off or, you know, all of the above. So, again, this backs up fickel.

I have to add that I am, like, sitting here typing this with tears *streaming* because I am scared to death that fickel is going to ban me for what I did. But I did it for the right reason and I actually feel some relief getting it off my chest, particularly now when I think that fickel needs as much support as we can give her. Okay, nuff said, that's it. I'm sorry.

marleybones @ February 5 12:51 am

Look, I'm happy to be wrong. It's just, well, this is all getting increasingly strange.

i.went.to.harvard @ February 5 01:05 am

So (awkward pause) if we're done with this bit of verification, which may come across as a betrayal of our faith in fickel but which I, for one, think had the effect of freshening our resolve, I'd like to talk about where fickel stands.

She's got no lawyer—Mr. Groin turned out to be as reliable as fickel depicted him from the start. She's also got in her possession important evidence related to a murder investigation. It's crucial that this be turned over to the police, and fickel must either do this herself or go the route 36-D has been urging all along and sit down with the Rottweiler. And the more time that goes by, the tougher it's going to be to turn over the gun and the will and walk away, protected by the truth.

roadrage @ February 5 01:07 am

In short, time to get back to where you started, fickel: Burly-Bear.

chinkigirl @ February 5 01:08 am

If these deaths are related—and they very well may not be, since independent (or maybe I should say slightly related) motives have been identified for all of them—but if they ARE related, then fickel could be in danger. She needs to get herself some kind of protection. Any kind. Now.

hitman @ February 5 01:15 am

Well, if everyone else is sitting there diddling themselves waiting for fickel to come around, I'll be happy to break the silence:

GET THE FUCK ON LINE AND STOP THE HEAD GAMES OR I'M GONNA PRINT THIS ENTIRE SITE AND SEND TO THE COPS MYSELF.

roadrage @ February 5 01:19 am

Dewd.

fickel @ February 5 01:22 am

Hi. Wow. Lots of confessions and accusations in my absence. I went to the roof of my building—it's one of those rare, unfreezing winter nights lately—to sit with a baggie of ice against my jaw while I think and smoke my once-a-year cigarette (four of my once-a-year cigarettes, actually), and, yes, to cry because I am very scared and angry and alone.

Some answers, which apparently are much warranted:

This is all deadly serious. I realize I've adopted a sort of cinematic tone at some points—somehow it seems to help me get stuff off my chest—but it's not intended to belittle the situation.

No, I don't mind that a couple of you have been checking my facts. I should have anticipated that, and if I'd thought about it, I would have realized it was going to happen, and, no, it wouldn't have stopped me from blogging, so no harm done, really. However, please leave me my autonomy and privacy. I want to make my own decisions about what to do next.

hitman, I don't play head games. If I'm offline for a while it's because I'm offline—silence does not equal silent treatment.

Next call is yours: you can believe me and stick around or flip me off and scram. But don't threaten me again. This is my blog and I'll go to the cops with it when I choose to. That's my say. No one is banned. I'm off to bed. And, yeah, guys, I've double-bolted the door.

hitman @ February 5 01:30 am

See you at the morgue.

wazzup! @ February 5 01:31 am

One of pulp immortal Ross Macdonald's most EXCELLENT neo-noir thrillers! A favorite of mine, aside from *this* read itself, OF COURSE!!!

fickel @ February 5 01:33 am

...sigh.

30

LIFE IS PULP

Feed the Beast With L.G. Fickel

February 5 @ 8:27 pm
>ONCE MORE INTO THE BREACH<

Today, probably as a means of avoiding figuring out what I am going to do about that pesky gun and its pesky mate, the Colonel's will, I once again left my office at lunch with a mission in mind. I swear that Noah is going to bust a blood vessel, he is so dying to know "who I'm seeing" and "why he roughed me up" (all the yawning and poor attention to my hair is giving me a very "beat in the sheets" kind of look, which the blue bruise to my jaw just accentuates). Anyway, I got to Downtown Crossing at around one, managed to slip through the crowds like a wraith, and found myself easing my way into the Jewelers Building in no time.

I enter The Blue Pearl and immediately experience a pang of remorse over Slenderbuns—I was whisked away from his body so quickly that his death hasn't seemed real to me until this moment, when my eye moves down those long swimmy counters and there is no undulating black merman touching his tie in greeting. Instead, X herself emerges from behind the curtain. She has on a dressy velvet blouse, blood brown with lots of silvery spangles, and has painted her lips a lugubrious purple. Up on top of her head, she's attached some sort of complicated headdress of braids that gives her this air—she is asserting an end to mourning or at least a beginning of a new phase in the process. I wonder if she was impacted by Slenderbuns' murder, or whether her husband's suicide consumes her too profoundly for the after-hours murder of a part-time employee to make a dent. She either doesn't recognize me or doesn't consider my presence to warrant a reaction. It doesn't matter—I'm not there to make friendly.

Me: (reaching the counter and getting out M.H.'s sketch of the Peacock's necklace) I'm sorry to barge in on you, but I'm wondering if you could take a look at something for me.

X: (seeming to "come to") I was expecting someone. (She seems to recognize me.) What is it? (She takes the paper up and studies the sketch of the necklace.) Yes, it's beautiful. But we aren't constructing jewelry currently.

Me: It's Mr. Pearle's design, isn't it? (I go to point to the photo of the Peacock's necklace, but it isn't there. In its place hangs a mirror that, to be honest, fits the spot like it's been there forever. I almost mention that the photo is missing, but stop. I mean, she'd know that, just as she must know that the sketch is of the same piece.)

X: (raising her eyes—she's on something but doesn't seem incoherent—*she knows she's lying to me.*) I wouldn't be able to tell you whether this is one of Stephen's designs without studying it. (She seems to have a new thought.) May I hold onto it?

Me: (It's dawned on me that maybe she has no idea who I am—after all, our prior conversation took place virtually in the dark. Maybe she thinks I'm someone who is gearing up to accuse her dead husband of having copied someone else's necklace. I debate whether to clue her in and finally figure that I'm not getting anywhere incognito, so I might as well go for it.) We met the other night. Do you remember?

X: Of course. (But it sounds like she's trying to place me and is being polite.)

Me: At Stephen's loft. That was me.

X: Yes. And how are you dealing with it? (Weirdly, something still rings false.)

Me: I don't know. I was wondering whether you knew who constructed this necklace? I understand that Stephen designed, but that he tended to commission others to do the actual work.

X: (She shakes her head, causing the skinny braids that top her hair tower to quiver along with a pair of oblong metal earrings.) I'm afraid I don't have that information handy, and I'm short-staffed. Perhaps if you called another time. (She's *so* lying. She couldn't possibly be ignorant about a piece like this, even if he'd created it while they were estranged. I mean, they'd remained business partners, hadn't they?)

Me: Well, what about us taking a look at Stephen's handwriting? We could compare it with those notations on the sketch. I have some familiarity with handwriting types. I could probably tell at a glance whether the writing on the sketch is or isn't Stephen's.

X: (raising her eyes. They're very dark, the type of eyes that could easily exude malice. I get nothing but a bland, patient desire for me to go away.) I wouldn't know where to find that. Maybe if you called back another time, I might have had a chance to look through some files.

Me: Mrs. Pearle, does the name Guy Ferguson mean anything to you? He's an artist who sometimes makes jewelry, and I think he painted a portrait in which the subject is wearing a necklace exactly like this one. It makes me wonder if he constructed the necklace for Stephen.

X: (shaking her head placidly) I'm afraid not. It's a pretty name, if I may say so. I hope it belongs to a pretty man. (She lowers her eyelids, then flutters a glance up at me.) A pretty little thing, like you.

Me: (realizing that she's not quite as out of it as she's acting.) Yes, well, thanks.

X: (eyes still on my face, she taps the glass in front of her with a spadelike nail) Will this do?

Me: (looking down to the blue velvet, where a bit of "parchment" nestles amid the trailing bracelets. On it is printed, in a dashing script, some drivel about craftsmanship, or should I say *materiam superabat opus*?) Stephen wrote that?

X: (reaching into the case and bringing out the piece of paper) Stephen did all the calligraphy for the shop. (She lays the paper flat so we both may admire it.)

Me: (trying to resist snatching the sketch back to compare the two) Can we?

X: (She lays the sketch down, keeping a secure grip on it between two of her thick-knuckled fingers. The handwritings are not alike. The script on the sketch is far more elegant, and Stephen's parchment effort is going for a similar effect. One is the handwriting of an artist—the other is not. X and I pretend to muse.) Well, it's hard to say...(she's lying, lying, lying) Perhaps I could hold onto the sketch and compare it to other examples of Stephen's handwriting. Plus I could figure out whether Stephen designed this beautiful necklace?

Me: (not happy about it, but more interested in something else, now that I have my answer) Well, I don't want to lose my sketch, but if you promise to take care of it.

I walk out, very aware of her eyes on my back. As I wait for the elevator, it occurs to me that I should have at least gone through the pretense of giving her my name and number so she could contact me when she'd done her "research." I walk back toward The Blue Pearl and stop short. The place is pitch dark inside. I try the door. Locked. Probably some service elevator back there. Sneaky bitch.

Of course, I have my sample of Stephen's handwriting to compare to the diary—the blurb about the tennis bracelets that I palmed while she was making her case for keeping the necklace sketch.

So maybe I'm the sneaky bitch, come to think of it. ;)

GIVE IT TO ME STRAIGHT

wazzup! @ February 5 09:09 pm

> Or maybe Mysterious Hottie a.k.a. Guy Ferguson is the sneaky BASTARD!!!! Ten to one as this excellent noir develops we will learn that HE WAS HIDING IN THE BACK of this jewelry shop, listening to every word. That lady would know she better end up with the sketch or she is one DEAD DUCK!!!! And probably the lady X is killed in spite of her effort to stay alive. No honor among thieves, and you know it!!!

webmaggot @ February 5 09:10 pm

> Whatever that dude's smoking in Amsterdam, I want some.

roadrage @ February 5 09:11 pm

> Best doobie in the world, those Nether-hounds. Trust me.

chinkigirl @ February 5 09:13 pm

> Hey, so I'll bite, wazzup!. I mean, we *are* noir fans. So why would the M.H. and X be in cahoots, and why would he kill her?

wazzup! @ February 5 09:15 pm

First, information for my favorite friends: I smoke Gitanes. Only the best.

Now, to answer chinkigirl: Here is my theory. Mr. Suicide never married X, see? Slenderbuns HINTS as much to our fickel, you remember? But X is terrific businesswoman—she makes a lot of CASH for Mr. S's business—maybe millions—but maybe all in HIS NAME and not hers, see? So when he starts to drift, she is maybe not so philosophical about it as she pretends. Maybe she's worried about her $$$!!! Maybe she does the digging and finds out something about this Mysterious Hottie that Mr. Suicide is shacking up with—something REAL NASTY BAD involving INCEST and MURDER. Then she plays a "wait and see" game. Maybe when Mr. S starts looking to move along from the NASTY BLOND MAN to the PRETTY YOUNG GIRL he spots at a concert, this is a danger signal for X, because it is now not looking so good for him to be ever coming back to X—1 fling is a LOT different than 2 flings, now am I right?

So X gets BUSY. She uses the "REAL NASTY BAD THING" to BLACKMAIL the Mysterious Hottie into KILLING Mr. Suicide. She promises him $$$—after all, she is Mr. Suicide's business partner—so she will own it ALL if he dies!!! Mysterious Hottie likes the idea, so he does as X tells him. Maybe he makes his move so fast that X can't change her mind! Shades of *Double Indemnity* and *Dial M for Murder* rolled up into one GIANT ball of NOIR FUN, eh?

36-D @ February 5 09:31 pm

So...go on.

wazzup! @ February 5 09:32 pm

Yes, you are right, my friend of the famous bosoms, as the best has yet to come.

Now X is stuck with what she has done—COMMISSIONED A MURDER, but also the Mysterious Hottie now has the "UPPER HAND" more than before. He's a class A lunatic—think Robert Walker in *Strangers on a Train*, eh?—and now SHE is scared to death. And Mr. Suicide's estate is one giant mess because X, remember, is NOT his wife. So there will be no money for a while, just the business, so she cannot offer Mysterious Hottie cash to make him blow away like a bad wind.

In the meantime, Mysterious Hottie KILLS Slenderbuns—*maybe* aiming his gun at the lovely fickel or *maybe* just not wanting Slenderbuns and fickel to talk anymore because Slenderbuns is one of the ONLY ONES who can put Mr. Suicide and Mysterious Hottie together. Either way, he don't need another person around, figuring out his CRIMES.

On a SPREE, Mysterious Hottie finishes off the last connection—the Peacock! He takes out the Colonel, too, as the Colonel KNOWS the artist as well. Now Mysterious Hottie is relatively SAFE...except that X could CRACK, particularly if she ups her dose of whatever drugs she's taking. So he engineers an overdose. Coming attractions, eh?!?

The last danger remains—fickel HERSELF. The only thing that keeps her alive is the blog that Mysterious Hottie knows about, on which he is DESCRIBED although the NAME he gave her is FAKE. If he kills her, the cops will be all over that blog, so he bides his time.

Good stuff or WHAT, my grand American cousins?

hitman @ February 5 09:40 pm

Yeah, it's good stuff. Any other time I'd call it real fine. However, could we knock off the black-and-white B-movie tales tonight?

marleybones @ February 5 09:44 pm

I have to agree. We've been screwing up enough lately with our lame attempts at humor and skepticism. Yes, and the list starts with me, so no need to shout me down, boys.

36-D @ February 5 09:45 pm

Wait, so we're not buying into any of that at all?

roadrage @ February 5 09:46 pm

Because I kinda was thinking that someone should tell a cop to take a run over to X's place and, you know, make sure she's not...

webmaggot @ February 5 09:48 pm

...rolling around choking on her own vomit with an empty bottle next to her.

hitman @ February 5 09:50 pm

Yeah, well, in the meantime, fickel, I'm assuming you've had time to compare the jewelry shop "calligraphy" and the handwriting in the diary. I mean, that was your goal in lifting the handwriting sample, was it not? Anything definitive?

fickel @ February 5 09:55 pm

Well, if I may dispense with the usual caveats about public vs. private handwriting and copies vs. originals, I think it's pretty conclusive that the writer of the diary is NOT, in fact, Mr. Suicide.

chinkigirl @ February 5 09:56 pm

Holy Smokes! The diary was written by the pretty little thing! That seems hugely significant to me.

fickel @ February 5 09:58 pm

Yes indeedy. You know, it struck me when Burly-Bear and I were together with the Colonel, the Colonel threw out some presumption that the police had verified Mr. Suicide's handwriting, and at that moment Burly-Bear had this *particularly* inscrutable facial expression going on.

roadrage @ February 5 10:03 pm

Pretty dumb of them not to check the handwriting against Mr. Suicide's.

i.went.to.harvard @ February 5 10:05 pm

Hard to believe, in fact.

marleybones @ February 5 10:06 pm

Mmm, my view is that the cops *did* compare the handwriting and were proceeding under the assumption that the diary was *not* written by Mr. Suicide. Hence Burly-Bear's slip, later that evening, that he hadn't gotten anything all that terrific out of the Colonel.

36-D @ February 5 10:07 pm

Well, what could he expect, when he set the old man up by never making it clear to him who'd written the thing. Like why would he do that anyway—O-M-EFFIN-G!!!!

fickel @ February 5 10:08 pm

My sentiments exactly. Burly-Bear wanted to see if something would come out that would allow the cops to identify the writer as ME. Just like bringing me to Mr. Suicide's loft to see if I'd know something about his place that I shouldn't. We have a new contender for the sneaky bitch prize.

webmaggot @ February 5 10:10 pm

The cops are, and have all along, been after fickel. You want to verify, lurking cop?

i.went.to.harvard @ February 5 10:13 pm

So think back, fickel. Did Burly-Bear ever elicit from you a copy of your handwriting?

chinkigirl @ February 5 10:14 pm

And—must say, I dread asking this one—does your handwriting resemble that in the diary?

fickel @ February 5 10:18 pm

Burly-Bear didn't have to stretch his talents to get my handwriting. I signed a witness statement the day he came by my office. Of course, a person's signature is the least reliable indication of their everyday writing, since a signature is what we call self-conscious writing while a diary, especially one written upon waking up in the middle of the night, would be pretty much the opposite. My guess is he knows that. He also got my phone number (and had me write my name next to it) the night he came by to warn me about the "other witness." Man, he'd be one low form of humanity if that whole scene was just an opportunity to get my handwriting.

36-D @ February 5 10:23 pm

But now you're going to tell us that your handwriting is nothing like the diary, right?

fickel @ February 5 10:28 pm

Wish I could, but the truth is my handwriting and that of the mysterious diary writer are passably similar. Both reasonably attractive. Both independent, mixing traditional cursives with creative, unattached lettering. Both use a Greek "E," which is relatively rare.

marleybones @ February 5 10:32 pm

My very limited understanding is that there are a number of handwriting classes or types—scholastic, Greek, independent, lefty, etc.—and so there are often superficial similarities between the handwritings of very different people.

fickel @ February 5 10:35 pm

True. Who knows, however, what an expert would say? And on that note, to all a good night.

leo tolstoy @ February 6 02:03 am

The truth is that life is meaningless.

fickel @ February 6 07:14 am

Oh, great, our ray of sunshine is back. Haven't you found a stout rafter beam and a rope yet? You can find instructions for fashioning a noose online at www.suicidemadeeasy.net. All my morbidly depressed friends swear by it.

31

LIFE IS PULP

The Noir Boudoir of L.G. Fickel

February 6 @ 11:31 pm
>LONG DAY'S JOURNEY INTO HELL<

Long day. Some of it good. Most of it bad. Ahh, scratch that, I'm tired of being the optimist in the house. All of it sucked. But my brother's alive, so there's a blessing to hang onto.

Today I arrived at my office early, my head full of plans to speak with Burly-Bear and "come clean," as Fred MacMurray might have put it, hand over the gun and the will and everything I know. I know, now, that Burly-Bear is not a friend, but I assume he'll do the right thing as a cop when I come clean. I also planned to attend the Colonel's funeral today. I knew him and had affection for him—not in a way that should have made him leave his estate to me, of course, but I've come to think that the handwritten will was the product of some ugliness that had developed between the Colonel and the Peacock over her *actual* dalliances and his *imaginary* one with me. Isn't love a horror show? The Colonel said something to that effect, last time I saw him. Guess he knew whereof he spoke.

Of course I anticipated that running into Mr. Groin at the funeral could be a tad awkward, with him undoubtedly suspecting me of having stolen from his office the will and gun he'd stolen from Boddy Manor. Anyway, all my worrying in that regard went to naught. My day went differently—very differently—than planned.

I'm heading up the street to my building around 6:30 am, skirting the steaming pile of poop some dog walker must have only just finished pretending not to notice emerging from her airedale's round-backed rump, when I look up and see the passenger door of a gunmetal grey sedan swing open, all by itself. The car is the one that cruised past my yew bush hideout in Concord the other day. I approach, ignoring the car, even crossing the sidewalk diagonally to avoid the car, and all the while feeling the gun, heavy in my purse, that I'd planned to turn over to Burly-Bear as soon as he chose to come collect it. The moment is so quiet that the toot of his horn causes me to start. I'm half about to ignore that, too—I don't really do responding to car horns—when he calls out. It's Escroto. No surprise.

I go over and duck down. He's looking particularly flush today, or perhaps it's just the squeezed-behind-the-wheel effect. He's got one of those seat covers made of wooden beads. His arm rests along the back of the front seat and he moves his hand, like "what am I waiting for?'

I get in and smell all ten thousand cigarettes that have been smoked here over this car's life. It occurs to me that I've never seen Escroto smoke. He has a toothpick in his mouth. Maybe that's his oral substitute. Maybe I don't care.

Escroto: (moving the toothpick to the other corner of his mouth) You're quite the early bird.

Me: Makes us birds of a feather.

Escroto: You planning on shutting the car door, there?

Me: (surprised) No.

He snorts like I'm playing a game, then hoists himself out on his side and walks around to shut my door. I slide half over to the driver's seat, take his keys out of the ignition, and lean heavily on the horn. I'm childishly amused to see him start, halfway around the hood of his car. Chuckling feels good—it's been a long time. As the horn blares, Escroto spreads his hands like I'm crazy. I jerk my head back at my side door and he retraces his steps and opens it.

Escroto: What the hell is wit you?

Me: I want the door open while we talk.

Escroto: You want the door hanging open while we're sitting in the car?

Me: You're quicker than you look.

Escroto: (seems about to ask why, then apparently decides that he doesn't give a shit) Fine with me, lady. You mind keeping your hand off the horn while I cross around this time?

Me: I'll do my best, detective.

He crosses around, adjusting his belt below his tummy in that way men do when they're annoyed. I slide over and he squashes himself back in behind the wheel and slams his door.

Escroto: You want to hand me my keys?

Me: (I look at them. His key chain is decorated with a pair of miniature dice. They're silver, with garnet dots.) We're talking right here, understand? I'm not agreeing to go anywhere with you. You pull off from the curb you'd better be arresting me, because the other choice is kidnap.

Escroto: (gets a real mean look in his eye, then retreats, slyly, into clown mode) What—I'm gonna drive away with my car door open?

Me: You might, when this is what you're driving. (I toss him his keys anyway. He catches them and sticks them in the ignition but doesn't start the car.)

Escroto: Caught your disappearing act in Concord. You realize I could have gone straight to your place and busted you? You got your pal Malloy to thank for that not taking place.

Me: I think it's the law I have to thank, unless there's some new statute on the books that says any person the police feel like picking up after a crime can be forced to go with them.

Escroto: (grunts a half laugh) That statute ain't new.

Me: So you want to know about Concord? I was there for a meeting. My lawyer was supposed to be there, too, but apparently he arrived early, found the bodies, and called the police. You must have heard all that from him.

Escroto: We like to hear from everyone. We're that way.

Me: Well, now you have.

Escroto: A meeting about what?

Me: About the cops, how you're harassing me.

Escroto: (points at me) You want to play games, you can get out of the car and expect a couple of uniforms to pick you up later in front of your fruity friends up there.

Me: (sigh—although he's scored a good shot) I wanted to talk to the Colonel about his wife. I think she was involved in Stephen Pearle's life. Pearle was her jeweler, and I think she introduced him to a man with whom he had a fling before deciding that he wasn't into men. (ol' Escroto snorts—a fag's a fag is what this undoubtedly signifies. I forge ahead.) I think that at the Bartók concert where the Colonel's wife introduced Stephen to this other man, he also saw her talking to me, and that later he asked her whether I was attached. I think Stephen was biding his time, extracting himself from his relationship with this other man while he homed in on me. I think the other man figured this out, maybe by reading Stephen's diary, maybe in some other way. I think that maybe this other man is a psychopath who did not like being rejected.

Escroto: (without a pause, as if they've got all this) You got a name for this other man?

Me: No. (It's a kneejerk response—I have no idea at this point why I would want to protect the Mysterious Hottie—I mean, at best he should have figured out who I am and called. I gave him a great lay and am giving him a great painting...oh, *men*.)

Escroto: Oh well. Nice little story you had going, though.

Me: You asked what I was planning on talking about with the Colonel and his lawyer. That was it. I was hoping the Colonel's wife could provide a name.

Escroto: And you're thinking that this psycho gay lover beat you to it—murdered the Colonel and his wife only hours—jeez Louise, one hour—before you was set to crack this whole case for us? That where we're at, here?

Me: There's more, unfortunately.

Escroto: Do tell (but his hostility has dulled a bit).

Me: (looking through the windshield and down the long hilly street. The traffic, both vehicular and foot, has picked up. I reach out without thinking and pull the door closed. I think about how to proceed, and when I do I speak carefully) I think the Colonel's wife is...

Escroto: Was. Lady died at 3:56 this morning.

Me: Oh. I didn't meet her many times, but I developed a strong impression of her as...

Escroto: As?

Me: (I swallow before continuing) As a sort of woman who would suspect her husband of having a dalliance. (I find myself short of breath and hurry to finish.) I think that this might have been why she'd have been happy to fan the flame of Mr. Pearle's interest in me. She'd have wanted to encourage something other than what she might *imagine* was going on between me and the Colonel, what with the book we were working on.

Escroto: She saw you as after her old man's bundle—that it?

Me: I would imagine that she saw all women in that light. Projecting, I think they call it.

Escroto: Not to, like, speak ill of the dead or nothing, huh?

Me: Exactly.

Escroto: But him. What would he be thinking?

Me: The Colonel? To him, she was a goddess. A peacock. I was a child, a mouse, someone he'd be happy to have his wife set up with a man, but not a married man. Maybe a good-looking artist who painted his wife's portrait (I stop to brush impatiently at my tears). Maybe you should check to see whether a portrait of the Colonel's wife is missing from their house—your partner saw it when we were there; he remembers details like that. But I don't know. That's the important point. It's all speculation. I don't know anything.

Escroto: You think she was having an affair?

Me: I don't know.

Escroto: With who? That lawyer of theirs?

Me: I don't know a thing. I caught up with the lawyer the other night. He was very upset and said some unintelligible things. It's only natural.

Escroto: You think he's the toad?

Me: The what?

Escroto: The toad in the diary. The diary you and Malloy read with the old man. Mentions a horny toad escorting the fat pussy at that concert.

Me: (Suddenly I emit a short spurt of laughter). Well, toads are a symbol for male genitals in romantic literature, did you know that?

Escroto: What the hell you talkin' about?

Me: (swallowing my giddiness) Nothing. I'm confused.

Escroto: (leaning in a little and grasping the back of the car seat just by my shoulder) Do you think the lawyer was having a thing with the wife?

Me: So what if they were? The Colonel finds out? He kills his wife and then himself? Well, if that happened there would be evidence, signs of a struggle, gunpowder remnants on the Colonel's fingers, at the very least.

Escroto: (after a pause) How'd you know they was shot?

Me: I talked to the lawyer, remember? He said he found the bodies.

Escroto: Oh, yeah? Tell you about the housekeeper, too? Old lady swears you were there earlier in the afternoon. Says she heard you and the Colonel talking.

Me: (I'm oddly calm about this half-baked accusation. When I talk it's in a gentle, singsong voice.) And, tell me, detective: did she hear a couple of shots, then my steps across the foyer, then the door close, all while perched in the kitchen, polishing spoons?

Escroto: (I don't look, but I believe he actually chuckles.) It's a big house. Lady went down for a nap. Only woke up when the cops arrived.

Me: Another star witness bites the dust.

Escroto: Another?

Me: (turning my head to glance his way) You know, that witness in the train station. The one who swore I was struggling with Pearle and pushed him into the tracks.

Escroto: (his little black eyes on mine) What witness is this?

Me: (spontaneously) Male. Blond. Artistic type.

Escroto: (he's got an okay poker face, but there's no doubt that in his mind he's about to score) Wouldn't be describing your own brother, would you, hon?

Me: What about my brother? (I can't help it—my voice drips with condescension, that he should even mention dickel to me.)

Escroto: (picking right up on my slip and loving it) Excuse me, ma'am, that'd be the brother who's been arrested God knows how many times since age fifteen. The brother who, as an even younger kid, put an end to what your father used to make the two of you do—

Me: (I want to sit there, coolly taking whatever he might say, then let myself out of his car with a dry word about fishwives' tales and forked tongues. But my hand moves on its own accord, like a snake, so independently of the rest of me that I wouldn't have been surprised to discover myself crushing the fat cop's balls. Instead, I press hard on the steering wheel. The horn blares. Some gulls hopping around the pile of dog crap outside rattle off into the sky, cawing. Escroto doesn't jump this time. Instead, he smiles unpleasantly. I push my door open.) I'm going to work now. You can go badger the next poor soul unfortunate enough to have crossed your path, you emotional blackmailer.

He forces a chuckle as I close the car door. I like the way the noise of the snorts coming out of him are cut off all in a moment, as is my ability to see him, when the car door closes and the window suddenly reflects the bright sky. It's as if he's been deleted. Nice feeling.

Escroto isn't finished with me, however. Thinking back, I now understand that last sleazy chuckle was more a giggle in anticipation of coming attractions. Wish I had squeezed his balls when I'd had the chance. Onward, though.

My office is deserted, it being 7:00. Grateful for the silence, I wake my computer and began the plod through the hodgepodge of emails, most of them offers for discount fares to exotic places, usurious rates on real estate, and, for the fellas, knee-length penises. Eventually I come to a message from my boss, Judith, asking me to see her as soon as I'm in. It's worded curtly. She is a sharp-tongued woman (Dame Judith, Noah calls her, a nod to all the evil old spinsters played by screen legend Judith Anderson), so in all likelihood she'd word an email about my elevation to full editor like a reprimand, but something causes me to swing around in my swivel chair to look down the open space toward the narrow door with the Venetian blinds in its window, behind which Dame Judith nitpicks her way through her day, whenever she isn't fawning (still, not without her vinegary edge) over the authors and of course especially over Mr. Bohnan (or, in Noah's vernacular: "He Who Must Be Boned").

To my discomfort—always jarring to be totally alone only to discover the presence of someone spying on you—the narrow door is ajar. And by leaning my head precariously, I am able to spy a shiny gold sleeve—an elbow. That would be Dame Judith's Victoria's Secret fantasy blouse, a poorly constructed piece of rayon/polyester costumery that someone undoubtedly told her looks good with her skin tone, which is that kind of curdled-cream color that comes from too much reading and not enough sun over a period of many decades. Getting yourself fucked raw with your head hanging off the end of the bed might help liven up that skin tone; merely dressing like a hooker does not. With this particular blouse, Dame Judith will be wearing her "confidence" suit—cream-n-brown "jailbird striped" jacket and pants—which means that it's to be a Bitch-Behind-Bars day (yes, another Noah-ism).

Anyway, I check the time on her email and it had been sent at 11:17 the prior evening. This is not good news, as it conjures up images of crankiness combined with righteousness at having worked so very late only to confirm her suspicions that one of her minions of—shall we call me a minion of "less than maximum diffidence?"—had left some menial task not quite completed by her strictly imposed false deadline. The way her mind works, she'd figure that I would tiptoe in on the fingers of dawn, smug in my subterfuge, to finish said task. And, fueled by the pure adrenaline of pettiness, she has managed to beat me to the office to await her moment of triumph. What a life that woman leads.

Ah, well, might as well start my day with a double dose of screwed. Twenty minutes later I'm "on second warning," which appears to be some on-the-spot invented status at my publishing shop for "fireable at will." As someone who's rarely been reprimanded by an authority figure, I mind Dame Judith's tart dressdown less than I'd have thought. It does bug me a tetch that I've somehow ascended to "*second* warning" without ever having been apprised of my "*first* warning." Apparently those go unpublicized, which seems to undermine their utility. Wisely, I don't press this point with Dame Judith, as I recognize it as a cleverly laid trap, a little goad designed to allow me to trip her dragon cord, after which she will let loose the flood of exaggerated as well as wholly invented transgressions she's been amassing all night, all of which is meant to culminate in my resigning on the spot at just about the point when my fellow minions are popping in, hopeful smiles on their faces as they anticipate the office smut of this shiny new day, only to find one of their own in floods of tears, packing her desk. I should make clear that it's not that Dame Judith hates me. Nor is she a horrible boss. It's just that her instincts compel her to propel these nasty little dramas into our lives.

Anyway, this unpleasantness is just one small pimple on the acne-ravaged ass that is to be my day. I get a phone call at around 9:15 from my mother. *My mother*—to whom I haven't spoken in, oh, what's it been—some four years? How she even knows where I work, I couldn't guess. I don't bother asking, either. Bit weird, the way I recognize her voice immediately. I mean, she sounds like a holy wreck of her former holy wreck of a self. Still, she manages to bleat out her message without meandering through meaningless preliminaries about how I am or how she is or how a fucking tornado should have ripped our old house out by the roots and slammed it down in smithereens but somehow forgot.

It's my brother, dickel. He's in a hospital out in the western part of the state. His back is broken. His nose is broken. His foot's broken. He's hypothermic and has been unconscious for days. Anyway, if I'd like to see him, he has some time on his hands.

Noah drives, competently and calmly considering his phobia about driving into a snowstorm. We talk about him, his recent breakup with this waiter, his teenage attraction to some of the lobster boat guys in the nowhere town in Maine where he grew up and that being how he figured out both that he was hopelessly horny for man flesh and had better either locate the other underground gayboys up Downeast or get his freak ass out of town forever. Hence college, which is always good to have done, whatever the motivation. Then Boston, the little towner's big city. And next, oh, who knows? One thing about self-banishment; there's a ripe lot of freedom that comes with that hellish loneliness that clings like a numbing ether to your otherwise shredded sense of self-worth.

We talk about Dame Judith, who was icy but not unreasonable about my (and Noah's) needing to leave immediately after my mother's call. Must have been quite a job for her to contain the gloat trying to burst through her scotch-ravaged face about how she's actually turned out right for once in her pathetic career. I *wouldn't*, in fact, be able to finish my accountings of the week prior, so she *would*, in fact, need to step in and do them for me. It's kind of kicky when those little shopworn morality lectures actually come true. Tee-hee. To her credit, though, she choked it back, along with any *immediate* plans to slingshot my ass to the unemployment line. Guess that'll wait until after dickel's off the critical list.

We get to the hospital around midafternoon, lost twice but not in a big way. Not sure the place actually merits the word *hospital* rather than *clinic* or, I don't know, *flophouse with pharmaceuticals*—we're talking a very local doc shop up a side street in a very local town, a mill town looking for its mill, you might say. Smokestacks, fast food joints, rocky hills strewn with mangy-looking pines, massive women everywhere, lumbering along the sidewalks in front-zipped galoshes through the soot-blackened slush, dragging gaggles of bedraggled children behind them.

My mother's in the waiting area of the emergency room, which is undergoing renovation. The renovation looks like it ground to a tired halt just in time to leave everyone sitting in plastic chairs on cement floors and the receiving nurses—with their requisite fat rumps—moody as hell behind their schoolteacher desks with the phone lines duct-taped along the walls. Mother's had her colorless hair crimped into one of those tire-track perms and has managed to find herself the ugliest plastic-rimmed glasses and knockoff camel-hair coat this side of the northern border. How the woman has managed to develop age spots on both throat and hands at age fifty-something is just another of her beauty secrets. She's reading Stephen King's *Face-Eater*. From the number of dog-ears, I'd guess it's her third time through it.

Me: Mother. Why are you here? Don't they have a waiting area on whatever floor he's on?

Mom: (folding her book over her finger. She isn't surprised by my lack of greeting—she's not the gushy type, either. Still, I see her assessing my "look" as she folds her glasses. Her eyes jump to Noah, who is handsome and nicely dressed, as always; she sees him for what he is and ignores him, although not disdainfully. I'll give her that—the woman learned enough in life to never disdain another human being for what their sex drive might compel them to do. She talks in her usual flat French Canadian accent—gawd, you would have thought that over all these years she'd have lost those bloody nasal vowels.) This is Emergency. He's in Emergency.

Me: They're doing long-term care in the emergency ward now?

Mom: (her eye glints for a moment—she'd like to see me try to have it out with the staff—oh, yes, she'd like to see that) He's got a bed and an IV and he's not stuck along the corridor like some people who have no insurance. Anyway, he's not needing much privacy as of yet.

Me: I'll see for myself.

I go to one of the receiving nurses, who's on the phone. She takes me in and flops a paw over the receiver, a kneejerk reaction to the out-of-town type. Likewise the bulgy-armed orderly standing by her manages to run an eye over me and look reasonably attentive. When I ask to see dickel and they figure out who I am, all that changes. Nursey slips the orderly a superior look as she goes back to her call. He, playing it straight, steps out to lead me. God I hate small towns. Why my mother hangs out there, waiting for senility to happen along, why she doesn't escape back to Canada, is something I'd ask her...but whatever. The answer is too complicated, too dreadful for either one of us to articulate.

dickel is down in a little side alcove behind a half-drawn bed curtain. I turn my head and signal for Noah to follow me just before rounding the corner, mostly to save him from having to small-talk with my mother, but once I see my brother I'm glad to have a hand to squeeze.

dickel's head is in some circular brace that looks like it's screwed into each side of his forehead, directly into his skull—this seems impossible, in this day and age, but that's what I see—and then attached to his body below via some sort of shoulder harness. He's got a massy bandage over his nose and the tape holding that in place covers a lot of his face. They could have done it neater, but it's not too caked with blood where it touches his nostrils, so at least they're changing it from time to time. Both his eyes are black and swollen to the point where I doubt he could crack them if he were conscious. There's a tube up his nose and one latched into the corner of his mouth, both taped to his face. He's got on one of those meager hospital gowns, so most of his torso is covered, but his arms rest along his sides, young and muscular. His hands, although his nails are bluish and blood-rimmed and two fingers on his right hand are splinted together, manage to look strong, their veins bulging. He's got a folded sheet draped over him from waist to knee, and below that his bare legs and feet are also bluish and bruised, his one foot in a splint, the other splayed, its sole black.

At some point I'm offered a seat. I ignore it. At some point Noah retracts his hand and steps away. I ignore that, too. At some point a doctor steps in to do some cursory checks on dickel's IV levels and the machine attached to some tube that's coming out of his side that I see only when the doctor folds back the blanket.

Me: What's that tube?

Doc: (glancing over. He's youngish, thick-lipped, grumpy, from the look of him. But I'm young and my tits don't rest on my stomach, which seems to cheer him up a skosh.) It's not as bad as it looks. He's had organ damage. Draining it is the quickest way to help it heal.

Me: (gesturing up at the neck brace) He'll walk?

Doc: (carefully casual) Are you the wife?

Me: Sister. (I don't smile or offer a hand. I'm not there to mingle.)

Doc: (smiles briefly) Oh, yes, now I remember. The twin.

Me: (for a moment I'm utterly shocked that he would say that—I mean, in that tone, and under these circumstances...then I realize that he doesn't know jack and is just being pleasant. Still, I have nothing in me that would allow me to push forth even the smallest smile.) Will he walk?

Doc: He has every reasonable chance of recovering from his back injury. A small bone in his spine was fractured but these tend to self-fuse over time. (He gestures to dickel's feet.) To tell you the truth, his bigger problem is his feet.

Me: (reluctant to leave this broken spine detail alone, but alarmed enough to blow by it for the moment) What's wrong with his feet?

Doc: Your brother was discovered wandering half-dressed at 3 a.m. along the shoulder of—

Me: (my voice sterile) I didn't ask how it happened, doctor.

Doc: (obviously ticked at having been interrupted, like every prick who graduates med school) Well, I think it's useful to understand his condition in terms of—

Me: Not how. Not why. I just want to know what his condition is. Can you stick to that? It'll get you on to other patients more quickly.

Doc: (slowly, studying me. He has intelligent blue eyes with pretty eyelids, incongruous on a short, unattractive man given to pudginess.) Certainly. He's had severe frostbite to both soles. This foot (he points at the one with the splint) is highly likely to recover, meaning he'll have pain but he'll keep it. This foot (he points at the other) he may lose.

Me: (refusing to look down at the foot) So why does he still have it? Is it infected? Could it kill him to keep it? Are you waiting for someone to show up with a checkbook? Because my lawyer is, well, he's known as the Rottweiler in Boston.

Doc: (nodding patiently, only the sneer at the corner of his lips hinting that he finds the threat unpleasant) If he's a quick healer, which he shows every sign of being, it could save him his foot. It's not a great risk to hold out, and there are always risks involved in removing any limb. (He pauses, then decides to do a little self promoting.) Once we take a patient and begin treatment, you know, the checkbook issues are no longer in play.

Me: (a little surprised at that speech, which I assume is patently untrue. I check his hand, like proudblacktrannie taught me to. No ring. Hmmm. Looks like dickel's going to receive something in the way of care after all. I nod like I'm being calmed by what I'm hearing, and try to force a smile.) He could get by with one foot, you know. A man loses two feet, he's stuck in a chair. But one foot—that's just a cane. If you have to take the foot, do it. (In spite of my efforts, my tone gets sharp again.) Just chop it off if that's what it takes.

Doc: (blinks at me like I'm nuts, then seems about to speak)

Me: Look, spare me your countryfolk morality. It's important that he lives. I'm just trying to make that clear. (We both look down to see that one of my hands has reached out to hover above dickel's foot—the dangerous one with the black sole. My fingers are trembling. I quickly clench the hand into a fist and try to speak, but my voice comes out a harsh whisper.) Just be clear on that. Running around on two feet like every other useless lowlife is not essential to his happiness. Having him alive is essential to mine.

Doc: It's very clear. (There's something in his tone—I look up sharply but his face is as bland as before. I nod at him to say that he's spent enough time with me. Dismissed, he heads off.)

I look around, then close the curtain around dickel and myself, scrape the plastic chair closer to the bed, and sit with my arm resting across his waist. His hair is growing out from the shave job he gives it—such sweet white-blond hair, just as I remember it from when we were kids—I plan to tease him about how pretty he's getting while he's still convalescing and can't go skinhead yet. Later I push my fingers up under his hospital gown and gently tickle his stomach, running my nails over the tattoos, teasing the edges of his belly button. He's always been sensitive about his belly button—won't let anyone touch it. I swear, even unconscious he feels me teasing him and almost smiles. Later, a nurse comes by, shoving the curtain way back—why the hell do they feel compelled to expose every patient in every way possible?—and runs through the usual useless check of vitals. Don't want any corpses lying around sucking down those precious pain drugs any longer than necessary. She gives me a black look when she sees where my hand is, but she keeps her ugly mouth closed. What a laugh this town hands me.

Eventually I get to feeling guilty about Noah. I gather myself up, kiss dickel on the tummy—can't get near his face—and notice something odd; there are a series of scratches peeking out from under the sheet that lies folded across his middle area. The scratches look relatively fresh, their edges white and puckered. They sit a few inches below the tattoo line, which bottoms out with a depiction of a seminude woman lying languidly on the roof what looks like a circus train. I squint at the scrapes, which look random, but then again don't. Without thinking, I push the sheet out of the way. I see the hollows on either side of dickel's loins. The scratches grow and suddenly there's a horizontal slash, then another. They're letters. Chilled, I flip back the sheet. The scratches spell out "full_frontal/title/tt0166924" upside down, half in his sparse pubic hair and half slashed into the base of his tummy. I stare at the crude letters, then flip the sheet over them and walk away.

I'm a little past amazement at the moment, otherwise I cannot tell you how I'd react to seeing Burly-Bear, standing there opposite my mother, talking.

I walk forward, past the nurse-receptionist, and they both notice me at once. I have no idea how my mother's face looks—her bland, shrewd eyes never did give anything away anyway, so never were worth checking out to read a situation. Burly-Bear's face is the opposite: I see relief there, a spark of genuine happiness at seeing me, maybe something stronger, some surge of...affection. Mostly, though, there's guilt. Guilt's one of those emotions that stomps all the rest of them right out of your face, if you're the foolish type who suffers from it.

Me: (politely enough) What are you doing here?

Burly-Bear: I heard. How is he?

Me: You heard? You mean you called his parole officer to make sure he'd checked in, and he told you?

Burly-Bear: She. (I look at him sharply but it's clear that the correction was automatic and not a wink at my kneejerk sexism.) Yes, I did call her. Part of doing my job. He okay?

Me: (Looking past him at the glass doors. It's still snowing, but the flakes are leafy, floating lazily about. It's night, or evening at least.) Not yet, but he will be. Where's Noah. (I don't ask it, because I know.)

Burly-Bear: He left. I offered to drive you back.

Me: (Okay, so that's what he was guilty about—rearranging my ride in a way I might not like. I'm relieved.) Well, let's go. (I don't bother looking at my mother when I speak to her.) I'll call the hospital to see how he's doing. No need for you to be calling me.

She babbles something about her phone bill and her fixed income or some tripe, maybe to save face—in front of whom, I could ask with a laugh, but why be needlessly cruel?

Burly-Bear and I drive quietly most of the way. I'm grateful for the constant snow-splatter that swoops through the headlights and against the windshield, where it's wiped away for the next splatter. Something to get mesmerized by, like staring into a screensaver. At one point, early on, I spontaneously ask him whether he's hitman. He doesn't seem to understand what I mean, but I can't tell if he's acting. He tries to press me on it, get me talking, but I shrug him off.

It's only when he's about to exit the highway that he has the guts to clear his throat.

Burly-Bear: You know that I sent your brother back because I had to. Once we discover someone's broken parole, we can't ignore it.

Me: I also know that you discovered he was my brother by looking into my background.

Burly-Bear: (driving through the toll station without pausing) Also part of the job. You realize that, don't you?

Me: No. (I relent a little.) Maybe. I'm defensive about my family. Obviously you know why.

Burly-Bear: What's the line about all happy families? Some Russian writer?

Me: (eyeing him sharply) All happy families are actually unhappy, and each unhappy family is utterly fucked up in its own sick and perverted way. Leo Tolstoy.

He doesn't answer and we sit for a while. Then I change the subject.

Me: The other witness who says I shoved Stephen Pearle in front of the train.

Burly-Bear: (he's opened his window partway to see through the falling snow, and his breath comes out in puffs that drift toward me as he answers) Uh-huh?

Me: You know who I mean: the deranged homeless woman who lives in the Hynes station.

Burly-Bear: (pauses—my guess is it's strictly against protocol to reveal a witness's identity)

Me: So has her gibberish dissolved into something too hopeless to rely on, or is it something else? Could she be missing?

Burly-Bear: (glances at me, then returns his eyes to the road. I hadn't quite noticed how small Burly-Bear's eyes are until this moment—small, clear, intelligent, with a sort of animal quality to them. His neck, I notice, is more an extension of his head than a separate part of his anatomy. Most cops I've met have these weird, almost savage characteristics to their physique.) Do you know something I should know?

Me: Your partner came by looking to mess with my head this morning. Something about the conversation—I can't quite put my finger on what—gave me the idea that your original reason for sniffing round my life, flimsy as it might have been, is now gone completely. So you're swinging from vine to vine: from some pathetic drunk's ranting, to the letter "E" in a diary, and on from that to a tragic incident from my childhood that... bears some vague resemblance to this one. I mean, that's where we're at now, isn't it?

Burly-Bear: (wheeling the car into the side streets of my neighborhood) Your father's death helps explain why you had the reaction you did to Pearle's death.

Me: (I laugh, surprised) Seeing the man's face sliced off wasn't enough to explain my going into temporary shock? Come on, Sergeant—what are most people made of?

Burly-Bear: (pulling up in front of my place—thank God for that trusty hydrant) You confessed, in the subway station. You said that it was your fault. You kept saying it, in fact. Then you switched over to talking about how he pushed by you and jumped, and we couldn't get you to return to the subject of how the death was your fault.

Me: (almost amused) Don't con me. I didn't say anything of the sort.

Burly-Bear: (mildly) You did, though. Shock's a funny thing.

Me: You mean I confessed and you let me walk out of there? That would be the day.

Burly-Bear: New perspective on the BPD, huh? I wanted to take you to see a doctor, but you were adamant about leaving on your own. (He shrugs.) Much as we'd like to, we can't do much to help people if they don't want it.

Me: I'm afraid you misunderstand. I didn't mean that you were careless to let a witness who might be in shock leave on her own cognizance. I meant that you would not let some girl wander off after she half-confessed to murder, signs of shock or not. I just don't believe it.

Burly-Bear: Yeah, well, I agree that my partner sees the similarity between your father's death and Pearle's as highly suspicious. Add that to the fact that Pearle and you weren't quite the strangers you claimed you were, and to him we're in the proof stage. But to me, the whole thing read different. I was the one who talked to you most, remember, and it wasn't tough to recognize that you were blaming yourself for not having prevented the guy from jumping. It's a classic reaction to a suicide. And, yeah, I was surprised that you showed up in Pearle's internet history, but, again, a little digging into his situation made it clear that he was a guy on the make, and his finding you attractive wasn't a long shot. (He pauses to shrug, glancing over at me.) The information that we've picked up about your past, well, it just makes it clear why you were so seriously impacted by Pearle's decision to take himself out with a train.

Me: (I turn away and stare out my side window for a while before answering.) You're not as dumb as you pretend to be, Sergeant.

Burly-Bear: Thank you, I think. (He taps the steering wheel as if making a decision.) You didn't...see your father do it?

Me: (shaking my head without turning to meet his eye) No.

Burly-Bear: Report I read, just your mother was on the platform. That was her statement, any rate.

Me: (sensing a question somewhere in his remark) We—my brother and I—were inside. My mother bought us some cookies out of a machine in the waiting room—shortbread, I think, stale as hell—we were busy crumbing those all over ourselves. This should have been a clue that something was wrong. Dad was the one who gave us sweets. Mother wasn't someone who put herself out in those little ways to make sure her kids felt loved. Anyway, they were out on the platform together, talking. They were tense, but then they were always tense. They hated each other from as early as I can remember. Why they would ever have married...when I think back on how really fine he was...(I turn my head sharply, then shrug.) And no—no one ever accused *her* of pushing him. It was a freight train and the engineer was hanging off the side—he gave the evidence that my father did it to himself. She was nowhere near the edge. (Burly-Bear tries to interrupt but I know what he wants to know—how his cop mind works—and so I just go ahead and tell him.) And, yes, the engineer who gave evidence became involved with my mother and married her, but that was later, after the whole thing was over, after he got to know her and saw how needy she was, with her feral son. (I can't help pronouncing the words "needy" and "feral" with the disdain they deserve.)

Burly-Bear: But he knew her from way back. From when she was a girl and used to come over the Canadian border to Star-of-the-Woods for partying.

Me: (I snort a laugh) My mother, down from middle-of-nowhere, Canada, to party in edge-of-nowhere, Vermont. Imagine someone remembering her from her wild days. (I shrug.) But, yes. Apparently this rather amazing coincidence is how they got started up, Frank and Attalie. Unfortunately, the rest of their lives together couldn't quite live up to their rather tawdry fairy-tale beginning. But, well, you know how it is. First you dream, then you die. In between, you eat your peck of dirt.

Burly-Bear: You didn't like your stepfather?

Me: Frank? What wasn't to like? He made a ton of money, considering he was completely unskilled, virtually illiterate, and about as ambitious as the rest of the OTB crowd. And he footed the bills for me and my brother to go to private schools. Of course, he whipped my brother like an animal every time we got the boot for something or other. Ah, but there's parental care for you right there. Yep, whippin' spells lovin' in the hearts of many a fine stepdad.

Burly-Bear: (nodding slowly. He knows it's the right time to tell me I don't have to continue, but he doesn't want to shut me down. I mean, he's working, you know?) So, why would the both of you get the boot from school when your brother would be the one to get in trouble?

Me: (shrugging indifferently) Well, they're not going to have me in one and him in another, so what was the difference which one of us got the boot?

Burly-Bear: (carefully) Why not separate you? Why shunt you around from school to school just because your brother's flailing?

Me: (still speaking at my window) He wasn't flailing. He just didn't like being treated like a grunt in reform school when he was actually just a teenager whose parents didn't give a damn about him. And they didn't dare separate us. She knew not to do that. If she knew one bloody thing it was that.

Burly-Bear: (real lightly) Why?

Me: (I go to get out of the car and he moves to stop me but doesn't quite dare touch me. I pause, though.) Look, thanks for the lift and thanks for coming out there.

Burly-Bear: Did your father ever touch you?

Me: (I freeze. I don't even have a voice for a moment and just stare at him over my shoulder, my mouth open. Finally I half-croak an answer.) Well, I love a funny exit line as much as the next gal, but...?

Burly-Bear: (ignoring my attempt at banter) I mean your stepfather, Frank. Did he ever try anything? I ask because I sense there's something you're holding back something painful.

Me: (I settle back into the car. I breathe out calmly and meet his eye.) You're a great cop, and you're a great guy, and I'm beginning to realize that you're more than just a little intelligent. But you really need to stop trying to help so much. Honest. Could you do that?

Burly-Bear: (I spread my lips into a smile and, slowly, he smiles back.) I could try.

Me: Good man. (I manage a wink before I hop out. I don't look back, entering my place.)

GIVE IT TO ME STRAIGHT

marleybones @ February 7 12:23 am

I have to say, I'm somewhat floored by how open you've become over the past few days. And I'm beginning to think that I've been a little "off" about you. You don't need much protecting. You've been handling yourself for quite some time. But, still, you'd be amazed at how useful it can be to have someone to lean on when you choose to lean. And, the way you write it, at least, Burly-Bear is aiming to be that support.

fickel @ February 7 12:26 am

Well, I gave him what he wanted.

36-D @ February 7 12:30 am

I am, like, bawled over. My closest friend growing up was molested by her father. She had one of those repressed memory awakenings—I would never believe this if it didn't happen like right on my street—she was in total denial about it but she confronted him, hoping he'd just say it wasn't so and then they could search for why she had a false memory, but instead he left the room while she and her mother thought they were still discussing it, and next thing they hear is a shot and he's dead in the basement.

i.went.to.harvard @ February 7 12:34 am

I would like to step in quick and say, with all sorts of respect for 36-D, that I don't think this is the time for a discussion of molestation. Burly-Bear is using his training, and maybe his gut senses, too, but let's not all pile on to such a very delicate topic. I know I'm not in a position to police the rest of you, but I can't feel more strongly on this one.

webmaggot @ February 7 12:36 am

And it's bowled over, tits, not bawled over.

36-D @ February 7 12:39 am

What*evah*—I wasn't saying it was like fickel was in the exact shoes as my friend. I just...aw, shoot, you're right as always, Mr. I.am.perfect. because.I.went.to.harvard.

i.went.to.harvard @ February 7 12:40 am

Hey, I dropped out, remember? No hard feelings, now, please? You'd be surprised how easily I lose sleep over something I posted.

36-D @ February 7 12:41 am

So sleep. I'm totally fine. :)

roadrage @ February 7 12:43 am

Uhh, speaking of losing sleep, has anyone else found this Full Frontal url?

chinkigirl @ February 7 12:48 am

Holy TOLEDO!!! I have just skimmed his verbal sewage! Do you think this guy's for real?

marleybones @ February 7 12:52 am

You know, it's interesting that this is your reaction. Because when I read it I kept noticing how the tone changes, as if someone's trying out different personas, sometimes pretending that English isn't his first language, sometimes forgetting about that and writing in fairly perfect grammar. And I noticed a number of interesting facts, if anything about it is to be believed. For example, if this guy trailed fickel home from the train station the night Mr. Suicide (excuse me, Pearle) died, then there's no way she could have made it over to Pearle's loft to remove traces of her presence (not that any thinking person would have bought that outlandish idea in any event). So there's some silver lining, if any can be identified, IF the thing is for real.

roadrage @ February 7 12:58 am

I noticed a couple of details like that, too, but to me that's not the first thing to worry about. fickel, this dude—whether or not he's putting on an act—is off his marble. If you give this url to the cops they can track him down.

webmaggot @ February 7 01:04 am

You want to square things with Burly-Bear, do it in one fell swoop by handing him this, the gun and the will. Not only will he "solve the

Concord mystery," but nothing makes a guy feel like he's got brass ones than having a girl who's pissed at him turn to him for protection.

fickel @ February 7 01:07 am

Well, I might do that (and not so he can feel his future children go to brass). On the other hand, I'm sure you folks understand that it's fairly easy to make a blog untraceable. They've got all sorts of services these days to encrypt data beyond random matching, even. I ought to know—you think this blog is easy to trace?

chinkigirl @ February 7 01:09 am

Nevertheless, I think that proudblack's fears are well taken. I think the cops are with us.

fickel @ February 7 01:10 am

I don't see how they could be, unless they've been on a computer where I've logged on. What makes you think that, chinkigirl?

chinkigirl @ February 7 01:14 am

I don't know. Lately I just get the feeling we're being watched. Maybe it was reading *Full Frontal* and finding out that we've had at least one ominous lurker.

fickel @ February 7 01:16 am

Shudder. I have to think. TTYL.

32

FULL FRONTAL

EXISTENTIALISM ENGORGED

02.07 @ 3:03 AM
EVY GUSTAFSON SUX

Evelyn Gustafson Evelyn Gustafson

Evelyn Gustafson Evelyn Gustafson

FUX WIt CHoo

33

LIFE IS PULP

The Noir Boudoir of L.G. Fickel

February 8 @ 4:04 am
>HOW BOYZ SPELL LUV<

One way or another, we all work for our own vices.

–brainy little sleaze in *Asphalt Jungle*

Well, I had a full day today—more than full, making up for lost time on two manuscripts I'm supposed to be blue-penciling, which turned out to be incredibly doable once I put my mind to it (and talked my fellow peons into doing a "fat lunch" over at Faneuil Hall, which apparently included some lovely desserts of a highly alcoholic nature, thus giving me much of the afternoon to myself). No message from Dame Judith on my "status" at the bottom of the editorial totem pole. With luck I'll just bite the big one at pay raise time and live on. Oh, and I called Burly-Bear and left a message to phone me. Thinking twice, I called again and left news of the *Full Frontal* site. So that should give him some bedtime reading that'll crisp his nose hairs.

Anyway, I'm in the office late enough to take a nearly empty train home and walk a few deserted streets to get to my place. By the time I get here I'm feeling like the whole of Cambridge has checked out and forgotten to tell me about the organized mass exodus. I do what I can to ignore the stillness. I drop my keys loudly on the kitchen table, click on lights, change to sweats and my favorite stretchy T-shirt, boil some red lentils, and put on some old Pink Martini (God I *love* that guy on trombone). By the time I sit down to blog, I've managed to create a reasonable mental facsimile of what my life used to be. Ha ha ha, aziff.

At 10:45 or so the buzzer sounds. I don't startle easily, but I find I've got warm prickles swimming up my skull. I go to the door, taking solace in the fact that it's closed with the chain on. I press the squawk-box button.

Me: 'Lo?

Him: Yo.

Even with the static feedback, I recognize Burly-Doll's basso rumble and hit the buzzer. I wait until I hear him at my door. Man walks softly for a big boy. He knocks—just knuckles—precise, but again soft. I pause, eyes closed, breasts pressing gently against the door's molding as I breathe.

Danger...nudging at my door...

...then I flip off the lock and open it.

The Mysterious Hottie is there, leaning a hand against the doorjamb, studying his own shoes. He raises his head and smiles his sneaky smile, eying me through his lank blond hair. I'm amazed and alarmed that it isn't Burly-Bear and at the same moment I acknowledge to myself that I'd subconsciously recognized the M.H's voice, and his step, and the way he would rap on a door.

The next moment I am—quite honestly—scared, based on what I now know, or think I know, or don't know at all but could be talked into knowing, about him. Y'know, like how he sorta kinda coulda been Mr. Suicide's boyfriend. And how he sorta kinda coulda stepped out from behind a post in the Hynes station and shoved Mr. Suicide to his death. And how he sorta kinda coulda been the person who attacked dickel. And like how he sorta kinda coulda needed the Peacock and the Colonel and Slenderbuns out of the way because they could connect him with Mr. S. And like how he sorta kinda coulda figured out that I'd lifted the sketch of the necklace from his place and thus had put him together with all the crap raining down on my life for the past days since the fateful evening that some lonely and confused middle-aged man decided to approach me in a deserted Boston train station and strike up a conversation, just as the train was about to roar into the station...dot...dot...dot...shit.

Me: (looking, I'm sure, exactly as if all of the above is ping-ponging around in my head) I'm not sure I want you here. (Still, I back up, which makes room for him to enter.)

M.H.: You want should I clear out? (walking in)

Me: (my spine bumps against my desk chair—it's one of those old office chairs, the kind that rotates, and one of my favorite pieces, and I grip it behind my back, not unlike the way a girl would grip a lucky charm in a moment of unbalance.) I'm online. On the blog. You know my blog, I mean, don't you?

M.H.: (Letting the door fall shut behind him, he chuckles briefly.) I'll see your blog 'n' you'll see mine—is that how it goes these days?

Me: (I shake my head briefly. I need a second to pull myself together and, like, locate some bug spray to squirt in his eyes if he should start rummaging in my knife drawer.) Beer?

M.H.: Be great.

Me: (I nod toward the kitchen and he slings off his coat, letting it fall on my couch, then walks through to the kitchen area and helps himself. I stand there, clutching the chair and admiring his sweater, which, although loose, is drapey enough to make clear that it's just him underneath it—as opposed to, say, him and the bloodstained ball peen hammer he likes to carry tucked into his pants at the small of his back. He turns and screws off the beer's cap, takes a swig, and tips the bottle my way. I shake my head and he, reflecting my own pose, lets himself lean back against the refrigerator. I begin again, awkwardly.) You know my blog, I'm sure, so if you've been tuning in lately you also know that my brother's alive. He's going to be okay.

M.H.: (pausing as if to drink this in) Your brother? Good to hear.

Me: (forging ahead, no use for amateurish bull) And you know, my brother may not be the type to talk to cops, not with his life experience, but he'll talk to me. I'll know what happened to him as soon as he's able to communicate. You can count on it. And if I decide to go to the police, well, I've gotten rather close, very close, just lately, with one of the cops investigating Stephen Pearle's death.

M.H.: (considering my face more than the news) Not sure what you're telling me. You've started dating a cop and it's getting serious. Is that what we're talking about?

Me: No. That's not it. But there's a cop I'm friendly with. And I trust him.

M.H.: That's dangerous, trusting a cop.

Me: Trustworthy or not, they're over worrying that I might have pushed Stephen Pearle. They've got it straight now.

M.H.: (wonderfully innocent and "interested") Do they?

Me: Yes, they do. Someone stepped up behind him, someone who was tailing him; the man stepped out from behind a post and shoved Pearle just as Pearle was about to speak to me. Some psychopath pushed an innocent man in front of a train.

While I say this I'm studying him for any sort of reaction—to my references to my blog, the police, the theory that makes him Mr. Suicide's killer. He reacts to nothing in any way that indicates a personal interest. When I stop talking he pauses to drink, then smiles his sexy smile.

M.H.: That's good news, then, right? I mean, getting the cops off your case.

Me: Good for me. Not so good for the psycho.

M.H.: (chuckles) He'll handle it, if he's psycho enough.

Me: Possibly. He certainly handled Slenderbuns.

M.H.: (tilts his head inquisitively, still smiling. His eyes glitter as he studies me. There's no tricking an admission out of him, and I resolve to stop trying.)

Me: That boy from the jewelry shop, the one who got shot, point-blank, while walking toward me in the gay club.

M.H.: (nods thoughtfully) You tell it to your cop friend that way, you'll make him start to wonder all over again whether you did it yourself. You being in point-blank range and all.

Me: The Colonel and the Peacock (I use their real names, of course) were shot as well. The papers claimed carbon monoxide poisoning but it wasn't that way. Four deaths, so different from one another, so seemingly unconnected, except for being violent and desperate...

M.H.: (studying me thoughtfully, his brow beginning to crease) Except for being connected with you in some way or other. Is that what you're worrying about?

Me: Did you grab your painting off the wall when you were out in Concord last? The portrait you did of the Peacock?

M.H.: (for the first time, I see a flash of something other than curiosity in his eyes. He's finally ready to admit something.) I did take it, matter of fact. She didn't like the way I'd framed it. That's why she had me out there, the night I noticed you in that diner. I told you that, didn't I? She wanted me to see the room where she'd hung it, so I could rethink the frame.

Me: And the next night? The second time you "happened" to spot me in the diner?

M.H.: (smiles briefly) She wanted me to see it again.

Me: (raising my eyebrows at this admission) Oh?

M.H.: Ah-ah-ah, not like you're thinking. Matter of fact, the lady had run off somewhere by the time I got up to Concord, so I just picked up the frame samples I'd left. Housekeeper had them. (He shrugs.) Rich clients. You get used to it.

Me: (remembering the way the Peacock had flitted out that night. There was no way she'd miss out on a second "conversation" with the M.H., not after she'd set it up herself—unless, just as I'd speculated, she'd begun getting some vibe from him, unless she was afraid, even after she'd successfully pawned him off on another rich squib to stroke his psycho ego for him...) Did you hear about the old woman from the train station? The old scag who spit at us?

M.H.: (his forehead creases, then he smiles) Man, you're jumpin' all over the place tonight.

Me: I think she's dead. I really do. I think you think so, too.

M.H.: (deadpan, as if he's sick of playing the innocent boy pal and wants to joke along with me) Price you pay for spitting at my girl.

Me: (fear piercing my chest at this "confession") Harsh price.

M.H.: Harsh world.

Me: Harsh for some.

M.H.: Like you?

Me: Yes, as a matter of fact, it's been a harsh world for me. Maybe it has for you, too.

M.H.: (puts his beer bottle down) I think you're telling me to go.

Me: (dropping an involuntary glance down his body, then up again) Am I?

M.H.: (smiling slowly, then gesturing with his chin) That's a'right, you can look. Look and see, because you're right if you're wondering if I'm hot for you. Right now, I'm a locomotive on steam.

Me: (I meet his eye for a while, holding myself steady but the tremble of my breathing is audible.) Full frontal. (I say it simply, my tone not quite accusatory.)

M.H.: (quietly) If you say so, ma'am.

He strips, right there where he stands, with no gimmick, no jazz, no ceremony—he strips like a man about to dive off a cliff. Then, naked, he walks toward me. I'm kind of in shock, seeing him like that, and I do nothing. And he walks right into me, fitting his body against mine, noses, lips, tongues, arms, legs, hips, top to bottom pressed together. He doesn't stop—just keeps walking, pushing against me, so that my rolling chair swings out of our way and I'm shoved back ungracefully against my laptop keyboard with him half on top of me.

I gasp for air, scramble to grip at him to keep from falling, surprised as he grabs the front of my sweatpants with a fist and yanks them out of his way—I hear something tear around back and the sweats fall to rest somewhere around my knees, then slide slowly down to the floor. My panties he just rips aside like paper—I'm soaking, I realize only when he strokes me, using two fingers to test my pliancy. Immediately after the touch of his fingers disappears he shoves himself in without pause. He's immensely engorged; I feel like he's mauling me—it's like a fist ramming me, and for the first time in my life I know what it means to "see stars"—yeah, stars...as in this vague spatter of jittery, blue-white electrical points leaving ghost tracks before my eyes. I open my mouth to scream, but I have no voice whatsoever, and just grip him round the neck the way you'd grip a man who was drowning you—half clutching, half caressing, somehow hoping against hope that the compassion expressed in simply holding another person close would somehow induce him to stop what he's doing. To stop drowning me.

He takes a while—I think it's a longish while, but I'm numb, so how do I know? I watch the ceiling light—two bare bulbs stuck into a clumsy plaster mold that looks vaguely like a fancy pair of lips—Man Ray lips, except white and with two yellow-bright gobs of spit hanging out from between them—the sight of it jerks before my eyes with his rhythm, along with my head, which lolls and then snaps forward, gently, again and again. Then I feel him tighten up, first groping with his hands at my shoulders and back, then finally gripping my buttocks hard, one cheek squashed in each of his hands, and he bucks against me, silently, for the however many seconds it takes. After that he lies against me for a little while, mouth open, breathing into my face, his tense body easing back, engine ticking down, little by little. I watch his closed eyelids, trembling against his eyeballs.

I am aware of being relieved that I can breathe again. When he's finally pulsed his way down to something approaching normal, he lifts himself off me, making a harsh gasping noise like when someone comes up from being underwater. The corner of my laptop is digging into the small of my back, but I don't move until he backs off a step, at which point I fall, my knees giving way so that I sit down hard, like an oversized doll, in my desk chair. He doesn't seem to notice and stands there close to me as he finishes breathing down, his face lifted to the ceiling, his throat jerking as he swallows. Then he lowers his face, glancing at me with an almost shy half smile, his hair plastered in streaks against his forehead. His eyes flick off mine and he strokes my cheek for a moment, then turns and walks off in his stealthy, casual, totally naked way. I hear the creak of my bathroom door, although he doesn't shut it.

I sit listening to the rattle and drum of the shower, realizing that I've rarely had the opportunity to hear it like this; usually it isn't running unless I'm in it. This reminds me of dickel, the last man who'd stayed in my place long enough to shower, and I find myself wondering, randomly, if dickel's ever raped a woman—he seems like the type who might not get it when a woman tells him to back off. Somehow I find something resembling comfort in this thought—not comfort itself, because I'm a little numb still even to be looking for that—but something vaguely like it.

I look down at myself, then pull my sweatpants off completely and let them drop to the floor. My T-shirt is long—it says *Algonkian Writers' Workshop* across the chest in cracked lettering, and I often wear it as a substitute for a nightie. I move around in my chair to check the computer. Nothing seems amiss—there's an ad campaign somewhere in there that's pure gold, but I'm just not up to figuring it out right now.

I blog. Not sure I should send this out, but I need to blog it.

Later: I go into the bedroom. He is lying on my bed, still naked, facing the other way. He sleeps like the dead, without snoring, without moving, without seeming to breathe—I know because I watch him for some time. I follow with my eye as the lights from a passing car trickle through the rattan shades to slither down the curve of his body, over his downy shoulders and his muscular back. His sinewy legs are surprisingly hairy, all the way up, like he's some sort of half-man, half-creature—a satyr.

I consider getting a knife from the kitchen and jamming it into his back, hard and deep, but the moment passes. I lie down next to him, stealing onto the bed like a naughty dog. He's damp from the shower and his skin smells wet. I position myself with my back toward his, curl up my legs. It could be that I doze for a while, but I can't say for sure.

Later, I hear him rise from the bed, all in one movement, very suddenly, as if he's heard some silent signal. I hear him rustle around, thrusting his legs into his pants, scratching his fingers through his hair—the sounds of a man preparing to leave. I pretend to sleep—or maybe I'm not pretending anything, maybe I just don't feel like moving or opening my eyes, maybe lying immobile is something I do a lot, so I can quietly adjust from the disorderly horror of my dreams to the very different but equally surreal landscape of my life. I feel the gentle depression as he leans a fist on the bed, then the feel of his fingers, moving my hair aside. Then comes the brush of his lips—he comes in from behind and catches only the edge of my lips. My face flinches involuntarily, and I push it into my pillow as if disturbed in my sleep. I don't hear him after that.

Once he's gone, I creep around, looking for a sign of his presence. The chain is off the door, but that's something I could have left that way myself and so isn't satisfying. Finally, as I step out of the shower, I notice the wet towel hanging over the knob of the bathroom door. It's a dark blue towel, ratty with a clot of unraveled threads dragging on the floor. Although I recognize it, it occurs to me that I don't know where it came from—I don't have any towels that match it. I don't touch it except to run my fingers gently down one of its folds just before I leave the bathroom. It's very wet, still, the water in it so chilly that it occurs to me that he must take his showers in cold water only. How very strange.

I leave the towel where it is, over the knob.

GIVE IT TO ME STRAIGHT

fickel @ February 8 04:47 am

> It's hard, I know, to think of what to say. What to think. I need to sleep for a couple of minutes, anyway. Talk to you later.

34

LIFE IS PULP

Feed the Beast With L.G. Fickel

February 8 @ 11:52 pm
>BREAK<

This morning I'm early again, hollow-eyed, my hair and clothes not quite lying on me as they should. But bright and early, yes, that I am, scuffing up the street at 6:50 a.m. so as not to get my ass fired on top of everything else. This time it is not a metallic grey deathbox on wheels but a seafoam-green Mustang at the curb. Instead of swinging the passenger door open from inside, he gets out of the driver's side and watches me over the hood. Instead of ignoring him, I stop and turn, face his direction, there on the cold, silent sidewalk.

Me: Hi. (It's less a pleasantry than an acknowledgment. My voice is uncontrolled, almost shrill—an early morning voice that tells of a bad, bad night.)

Burly-Bear: Buy you a coffee? (His voice, too, is rough—it dawns on me that he's kind of a mess. I like that idea, I have to admit.)

Me: (moving forward and getting in the passenger side of his car) A coffee it is, Sancho.

He drives against the stuffed-in traffic, which sends me into an odd, dreamy space—my life, totally against the tide. Somewhere in the Fens, we pull over along a winding reedy urban parkland, a bit of a no-man's land in the city's landscape. Burly-Bear exits the car without a word and I watch him walk down a ways to one of those trucks, the kind made of quilted silver metal. I get out of the car and lean against it, holding my coat wrapped around me.

Burly-Bear points with his head and carries the two cups across the dead grass to a bench that faces the park. I join him, crunching across the frosty lawn without enthusiasm, and take one of the coffees. Its heat hurts my fingers, even through gloves, but I don't relieve them. We sit, staring across the thatchy reeds at the naked weeping willows. Quite honestly, I could sit all day there, freezing my ass blue. Burly-Bear, however, has other ideas. He extends a hand toward me. I glance down and see the old photo, creased, rather blurry, between two of his fingers.

Me: Where'd you get it?

Burly-Bear: Who is the guy?

Me: (I raise my eyes and study the side of Burly-Bear's face for a long time. He doesn't turn his face and so eventually I take the photo from between his fingers and hold it up. It's of a man, maybe late twenties, with dark hair and a trim beard. He's smiling and his teeth look terrific, although one of the front ones might have been chipped. He's wearing some sort of beat winter sweater and appears to be outside, maybe by a back door of a worn, shingled building. He gives off a sense of having been at some strenuous outdoors activity, like chopping wood. I snort a humorless laugh and fork the thing back over to Burly-Bear.) I have no idea.

Burly-Bear: (not taking the picture) Look again. Give it a minute.

Me: (I look again.) He looks dated. The hair is kind of feathered over the ears in that 1980s way. 1990s if he's out in the sticks and so hasn't caught up yet. The clothes, the background, all that could be, well, anywhere cold and drab. (Eventually I shake my head.) He's no one.

Burly-Bear: (still not taking the photo back) No one's no one.

Me: (tamping down a sudden impatience) He's no one *to me.*

Burly-Bear: Does the name Steven de Carreau mean anything?

Me: No. (I say it too quickly. Then I shrug.) I mean, my mother's maiden name was de Carreau. But so was every other canuck's between Whistler and Saint George. "Der Crow" was how we said it. Classy lot, weren't we?

Burly-Bear: (nodding at my funny but not smiling) Your mother had a brother who lived with you for a while when you was a kid, right?

Me: Did she? (I cock my head and frown.) Maybe, now that you mention it. I haven't thought about the old days in forever. He was a lot younger than she was, the way I remember it, but maybe that's just because she always seemed old. His name was...(I shake my head) I can't pull it up, but it wasn't Steven. It was, like, Jacques or Yves. My mother spoke more French than English around the house.

Burly-Bear: What's Stephen in French?

Me: (affecting a breezy French accent) *Stefon, n'est-ce pas? Avez-vous obtenu ceci d'elle?* (This last is in reference to the photo. I pass it to him, or I try to. He doesn't take it until it's clear that I'd just as soon let it flutter off into the underbrush as hold onto it.)

Burly-Bear: It's your mother's, but I'll return it if you'd rather I did it.

Me: Hmm, that means you went back to talk to her after you dropped me off last night.

Burly-Bear: I did that, yes.

Me: Drove right back out into that snowstorm.

Burly-Bear: It was snowing, yes.

Me: Well. There's ambition for you.

Burly-Bear: (playing it dead straight) I do what I can.

Me: (angry but doing a good job at not showing it) I guess you needed to try out your theory on someone else when it got nowhere with me.

Burly-Bear: My theory?

Me: Sure, you remember: the one in which Dad molested me and then took himself out with a passing Erie-Lackawanna after Mom confronted him with the fact on the platform one night.

Burly-Bear: (adjusting himself on the bench. I'm wearing a long coat, while he's got on some sort of winter jacket that's clipped at the waist. I hope his unprotected ass is good and cold.) How long did your uncle stay with you, would you say?

Me: (I sigh angrily.) I don't know. (When he doesn't answer, I sigh again, this time resignedly, and squeeze my eyes closed.) One month? Six months? You have to understand; I was a rather fanciful child living in a world that was a little too grubby to really focus on. If some relative of my parents slept on our couch for a period of time it wouldn't have meant much to me. Grownups weren't important to me. Time wasn't important. All I cared about was the escape I got through reading. I suppose that's why I work in books now.

Burly-Bear: And your brother.

Me: My brother wasn't a reader.

Burly-Bear: No? What was he, then? How did he cope?

Me: (I pause, lips pressed together angrily, waiting for my sudden anger to tick down. When it does, I speak.) When my brother was young he was diagnosed with an enlarged heart. When he learned about the risk this presented, he immediately went off and swam across a local canal. When he survived that, he grew...addicted to risk.

Burly-Bear: (lets my tale sink in) You cared about your twin, growing up.

Me: (easily) Well, you got that right. Look, Sergeant, I've been a good girl and answered a bunch of blind questions. Now let's get off this track before you circle right back where I know you're going and I don't want to revisit, all right?

Burly-Bear: Where's that, then?

Me: My father's suicide.

Burly-Bear: We're heading to that? How?

Me: Doesn't everything?

Burly-Bear: (He sips some coffee. I don't join him.) This guy in the picture is your mother's brother, Stephen, who lived with you for about a year, ending about six months prior to your father's death. Your father was very generous, according to your mother, to allow Stephen to move in on the four of you. Money was tight. Space was tight. Your mother says she thinks that your father thought that her brother Stephen might be a good influence on your brother, who was already tough to handle. Your father was a lot older than your mother, she says, but Stephen was young, and himself a bit of a street kid, or he had been back in...what town was that your mother was from?

Me: (not harshly) Look, I'm sorry to undermine all the good police work you've been doing, apparently round the clock, but I'm afraid my mother's version of the past—or anything else—isn't anything that I'd call reliable. So *please* shut up before you embarrass the both of us, would you? (I offer the last suggestion with a little laugh.)

Burly-Bear: She says your uncle never touched you.

Me: (I close my eyes and shake my head. When I speak, my voice is icy.) Points for Mom.

Burly-Bear: (dogged to the end) She says your father always blamed Stephen, and so blamed himself for allowing Stephen to stay in the house with the two of you. She says she tried to get it through your father's head that he was wrong about Stephen, but your father wouldn't hear of it. Your father wouldn't accept that it was just...your own idea.

Me: (speaking without feeling my lips) My idea?

Burly-Bear: (swallows more coffee, then speaks plainly) Yours and your brother's.

Me: (doing an amazing job at collecting myself, if I do say so) Well, as long as my mother and all our kin on her side were wonderfully good and innocent people, that's all that really counts, isn't it? And Dad *was* delusional, of course. So there we have it. Nice and tidy.

Burly-Bear: Was he?

Me: Was he?

Burly-Bear: Delusional?

Me: (standing up to go) Well, he killed himself, didn't he? You'd have to be pretty fucking delusional to come up with that as a way to cure whatever ailed you.

He waits, finishes his coffee, crushes the cup and twists it in on itself, rather contemplatively, it seems to me. Then he gets into what's really eating him.

Burly-Bear: So, tell me. Who is he? The guy.

Me: (feeling a pang of relief that one of us has scraped together the intestinal fortitude to start talking about it. I sink back down to the bench.) I don't really know. I just think of him as "Guy." (Yes, I'm teasing by telling the truth, but Burly-Bear doesn't know it.)

Burly-Bear: (incredulously) You don't know him? Guy's got no name?

Me: Not much of one, now that you mention it. (Get it? What a card I am.)

Burly-Bear: What are we talking about, love at first sight?

Me: (mildly surprised) Love? No. No, nothing like that.

I feel him glance at me and realize I've hit a nerve. First that puzzles me and then it dawns on me—Burly-Bear imagines that he's in love with me, and that makes my blowing him off for someone I don't even profess to love that much worse. Sure enough, he decides to go with a coarse jab. I've just hurt him, and now he's going to give some of that back.

Burly-Bear: Just a case of lust, then. Well, that happens, too. At least you're honest about it, which is more than I can say for most women.

Me: (studying the wintery reeds) Oh, I'm not so honest. Not really.

Burly-Bear: (playing it decent when he realizes that my cryptic remark wasn't a lead-up to some sort of confession) Okay, well, it's not like you owe me an explanation.

Me: No, I guess I don't. (I say it softly—basically talking to myself, although I realize now, much later, that he must have been imagining that I was carefully maneuvering him.)

Burly-Bear: (speaking heavily—his tone that of the guy's guy who's reached his tolerance limit on the head games that some chick's been putting him through) Then I guess there's nothing else to say. (He gets up, smacks his gloves against his thigh.) That time, huh, killer?

I don't look up at him, but instead get up and make for his car, my head ducked, my shoulders pulled together in a hunch. It sucks udders to feel guilty over a guy. Immeasurably better to be the victim. Believe me; I've tried both.

We drive back to my office in silence. It's pretty damned excruciating, sensing how much he hates every interminable red light and every dildo who decides to parallel park right in front of us. By the time we get back to the spot where he picked me up, my armpits are drenched. I squeeze my elbows to my sides, certain that as soon as I move he'll catch a whiff of me.

Burly-Bear: (looking my way and smiling ruefully. I have to hand it to him, he's got nads enough to admit that he's hot for someone who apparently doesn't return the compliment.) Well, I hope this guy is worth getting messed up over. That's all I'll say.

Me: (laughing sharply, suddenly resentful toward him) If that's the way you want to put it.

GIVE IT TO ME STRAIGHT

webmaggot @ February 9 12:28 am

Look, am I, like, reading into this, or is the idea that Uncle Stephen used to make fickel and her twin brother, umm, "play doctor" as kids? And then later, when Uncle Stephen had moved along to find other recreation and the twins kept at it, someone found out?

roadrage @ February 9 12:30 am

Well, that's where I'm at. So, want to go on?

webmaggot @ February 9 12:31 am

I'm busy heaving on my end. Anyone else?

36-D @ February 9 12:33 am

Eye roll—why do I always have to supply the *balls* around here? Okay—after the I-word finally gets uttered, this led to Mom and Pop disagreeing over which parent's side had supplied the "strange-love" gene, ending with Pop (dads are always *so* accommodating) concluding that either way, he was ultimately to blame for either supplying the DNA *or* allowing Unckie Steve to "infiltrate" the household.

roadrage @ February 9 12:36 am

Pop broods, Mom needles, Pop offs himself, and then?

i.went.to.harvard @ February 9 12:37 am

Mom ekes out a numb sort of existence married to a much different sort of man while Uncle Steve—perhaps totally unaware that he's precipitated this family crisis, or perhaps well aware of it—rattles off to Nowhere, Nevada. There he meets X, recreates himself as Mr. Pearle, and emerges relatively unscathed as a Boston jeweler.

chinkigirl @ February 9 12:41 am

And the twins?

wazzup! @ February 9 12:42 am

One word to add, my fellow B-flick fanatics: JIM THOMPSON. Wahooo, brilliant!!!

webmaggot @ February 9 12:43 am

Look, do you have numbers in the Netherlands? Jim = 1. Thompson = 2. TWO words, brainiac.

36-D @ February 9 12:46 am

Okay, I don't want to drop another bomb, but I have news that I don't think would be right to keep to myself. Like I told you, I started talking to the Rottweiler about this mess, right? So he gets curious and then he comes to me and says he checked where I was going on the internet during the day, which is, like, his prerogative as my boss and I can't say I resent it (or not that much), and so of course he finds *Life is Pulp*. So he visits here himself and he goes to check out these cops—Tyler Malloy and Escroto. He says there is no one there named Escroto, and also there's no Tyler Malloy. But there is a Ty*rell Reed*, and what with fickel's thing about not giving people's real names, that seems like a match to the Rottweiler (and me). But that's not the important point, which is that Tyrell Reed is married. Wife's name is Lindy. There's even a baby daughter.

roadrage @ February 9 12:47 am

I get how Tyler and Tyrell are practically the same name, but how does Reed become Malloy?

webmaggot @ Feburary 9 12:48 am

Woah, guess you're not into "classic" TV, mon. Reed and Malloy—the cops from *Adam-12*. Best cop show in the world, according to my dad (yeah, he's an alkie).

chinkigirl @ February 9 12:49 am

I *guess* I can buy that connection, if the Rottweiler can confirm that the guy looks like Burly-Bear. Did he actually meet this Ty Reed?

36-D @ February 9 12:50 am

Not as of yet. I'll keep everyone posted.

roadrage @ February 9 12:54 am

Wait a sec. Just to clarify, 36-D, Burly-Bear's partner isn't really named Escroto. That's just one of fickel's nicknames. Means scrotum in Spanish.

36-D @ February 9 12:55 am

Oh. Gross, by the way.

i.went.to.harvard @ February 9 12:57 am

You know, even if all this subterfuge is true, I'm not so sure that Burly-Bear presented himself as something other than what he is. First, he might not wear a wedding ring for any number of reasons. Second, he could present himself as a nice cop because he is one, and a shoulder to lean on for fickel because he sees that she needs a shoulder to lean on. Third, he could have sent dickel back to where he belongs because it's his job. Fourth, he could have shown up at the hospital where dickel's laid up because he genuinely cares about fickel, and also because he's still investigating Pearle's death.

I mean, has the man ever actually made a pass at fickel? Sure, maybe he's attracted to her, but why shouldn't he be? Anyway, that's my gut reaction.

proudblacktrannie @ February 9 01:15 am

Why are you people obsessing over this SOAP OPERA NONSENSE? Can I remind people that *a young black male was shot in cold blood the other night*? Mr. Suicide may have killed himself. The Colonel and the Peacock may or may not have been victims of a domestic homicide-suicide. But that boy got shot to death in PUBLIC. Am I to conclude that we have pushed that one aside because he was black, poor, and/or gay?

36-D @ February 9 01:16 am

Who pushed anything aside? My Rottweiler's been looking into it. I'll report in as soon as he tells me anything.

chinkigirl @ February 9 01:18 am

Where have you been, proudblacktrannie?

proudblacktrannie @ February 9 01:19 am

About *time* someone asked, or did anyone even notice the *token nigger's* absence?

chinkigirl @ February 9 01:20 am

We noticed, of course. But, speaking of bloggie blackouts, I would very much like to hear from fickel, with everything that's been going on. fickel? Are you with us?

proudblacktrannie @ February 9 01:22 am

oh fine with me I will bide my time absolutely

webmaggot @ February 9 01:26 am

What's eating her? Him? Which are we supposed to use, again?

roadrage @ February 9 01:27 am

Dewd.

35

FULL FRONTAL

EXISTENTIALISM ENGORGED

02.09 @ 1:52 AM:
I DECIDE TO ES&D

I'm over. Outta heahh. Done my share of sucking air...sucking face... (never sucked dick but I have to say I don't regret that)...I am, at heart, sick of the rest of you schmucks.

Fucking sick of...

...every last fetid stinking bit of...

THE HUMAN CONDITION

Don't mean to be a downer. It's just that lately I've begun to see altogether too clearly that my *faith*—by which I mean that impulse that gives life its definition—has been a belief that there is in fact a meaning to life *that has simply eluded me*. So I've sought it. Mostly with my nose between the legs of various females. And what a crock that adventure has turned out to be.

Fun fact, though? I've always known this was coming, that I'd run out of tolerance for life. The first time I read Tolstoy—no, way, way before that—like, as soon as I got old enough to *get it*—to start meeting enough people to really *get* that *this was it*—humanity, what it was like, I faced the fact that this world just about sucks. This may explain why I've spent the past decade or so ramming poon tang like there was a contest on. Sigh, I knew there'd be a catch.

Rien ne forme un jeune homme,
comme une liaison avec une femme comme il faut.

They teach you a lot of moral crap through childhood, all while undressing you with their eyes. Ever believe any of it? I didn't, yet I believed in *something*. However, I can't think back to analyze what that something might have been without horror, loathing, and a shit-dose of pain.

The fact of it is, life is doomed, a tragedy dolled up as a romance, and God is the standup comic that made us unable to get that fact. We'd have been better off one way or the other, Big Fellah—animals or gods—and not the freak hybrids you cooked up. And now you don't even possess the nads to destroy us, leaving *us* the job of recognizing our futility and KILLING OURSELVES OFF. Like, thanks, Hozzanahh—waydabe. Can you blame us for being who we are? Can you blame us for the sheer mendacity of humankind? I mean "sheesh," phukah, take *responsibility*.

So you see, I'm not being shoved off Planet Sukz by the ugly masses. I'm simply taking my leave. Not due to despair but *by design*.

But why NOW for the big plunge into eternal damnation? I do believe that *U* are the answer, m'sweet—I believe that I always anticipated your arrival in my life, and that you would serve the function of shifting me toward the realization of this all-important goal of mine. I believe that I anticipated you and the pain you would so negligently, so *contemptuously* yet *inadvertently* inflict. Thanx, bitch, for fulfilling my destiny.

Hey, and thanx for cummin, one and all. Please remember to leave your life as you exit the weblog.

---

tALK. NIHILISt DOGS

garbo @ 02.11 02:14 am

> Glad to have been of service, traveling man. Say hi to Cerberus for me, wouldja?

fullfrontal @ 02.11 04.04 am

> I'm already dead, you clit. Show a little respect.

36

LIFE IS PULP

Noir the Night Away With L.G. Fickel

February 18 @ 4:14 pm
>DEATH...A LONELY BUSINESS<

Well. The worst has happened. Inevitably, it seems, although I do not know why.

It's been days since I last posted, but those of you in Boston will have heard about Anthony Cunio's death and seen the television coverage of the funeral. Tyler Malloy, I'm truly sad to report, was the name I picked, more or less spontaneously, for Tony Cunio when I wrote about him in *Life is Pulp*. You know my thing about not using real names. I'm sorry that I confused you and the Rottweiler, 36-D, into thinking that someone named Tyrell Reed was Burly-Bear, but the fact is I've never met nor heard of Tyrell Reed. I'm sorry if that got the Rottweiler after the wrong scent. Sorry to have caused any and all of you such a load of consternation. Sorry, too, that I wasn't able to attend Tony's funeral. Sorry, most of all, to have been the troubled woman somehow at the bottom of this good man's murder.

I've been rail-riding, actually. Found a sleeper to Seattle, and then a return via...well, what difference do the cities make? Rail-riding is just a thing that I do when life is really cruel and I need to be in limbo. I've been in limbo—am in limbo still, as I post. Don't know when or where (or how, actually) I will land. That's the thing about limbo. That's its risk element.

One thing that's been eating away at me is how predictable it all was. Here's this guy, Burly-Bear, the one healthy, decent guy in my life, so of course he has to be brought down. Like dickel. His opposite in so many ways, but in my mind his match.

Incidentally, dickel's made a full recovery—apparently that boy heals like a paraplegic at a holy roller tent show. Of course, none of you will accept dickel as a "decent" guy (moral majority snots that you are), but I know him. Also, he wasn't always the one who got us kicked out of private school. I messed up a few times—there was an English teacher at one school. MacLean Jared, his name was (cute name, yeah?), and a sweeter young pencil-dick you'll never meet, frail and anemic, pumping his skinny arms as he motored his way along those rural roads on his daily marathon. I was just looking for some assurance, some sign that—how would you put it, marleybones?—that all men aren't total dicks. I suppose I got that assurance from Mr. J, but not quite in the way I imagined. Anyway, I'm sure that my stepfather would have shackled me to the basement wall and left me there to rot if he'd found out, but dickel took the blame for our ejection (and quite a lashing) for me. So, you see, he's really the most decent man I know. He's the Christ to my Mary Magdalene, the martyr to my reformed whore.

But Burly-Bear was a close second, I mean for sheer *decency*, and he wasn't even my own blood. That says a lot, when you've lived most of your life in a dark corner...*Dans un coin noir*. The original name for this blog. Would you have come to such a gloomy place?

You know, it's like i.went.to.harvard said. Burly-Bear didn't really *lie* about being interested in me—not out-and-out. Of course he lied about knowing about this blog—they all knew, all the cops, *because of course it was in Mr. Suicide's internet history*. How stupid of me not to think of that weeks ago. I mean, if Pearle was stalking me, more or less—how did none of us figure out that *of course* he'd learn about my blog? After all, I wasn't secretive about it—why would I be when the point is to attract a circle of commenters? The Colonel certainly knew. Therefore, the Peacock could have known, easily. So why wouldn't Stephen Pearle hear about it from her, if he was asking her about me after seeing us exchange wan greetings at the Berklee? Naturally she'd steer him to *Life is Pulp*; it's me at my best, and she wanted me out of her life.

Pretty dumb, my not figuring out that one. Dumb, dumb, dumb.

Burly-Bear wasn't the one on "lurk duty," apparently—at least that's the way he told it to me in our last conversation. Escroto was the lurker.

Interestingly, Burly-Bear categorically denied that the cops were behind hitman, the one newcomer—now disappeared—who actually did motivate me to reveal myself in a number of instances. I don't know what to think of that denial. I mean, Burly-Bear had no incentive to lie to me, not in the end. At first I concluded that hitman, and maybe leo tolstoy as well, must have been this fullfrontal creature, but now I don't know. So many mysteries. So many lies.

As for the Mysterious Hottie—Guy Ferguson—fullfrontal????—damn, I have *no* idea what he should be called here, because apparently there is no Guy Ferguson, at least not any brother of murdered cop Guillaume "Billy" Ferguson (who is—was—real). The cops—I think it's the feds, actually—are busy pacing their way through the other two million Fergusons on the planet to figure out if and where Guy Ferguson is. And when they make him, they'll shoot him. Unless, of course, he's already dead.

But for now I'm just traveling. Riding rail. Waiting to hit the coast. What's that line again...

> *"The train was headed for the ocean.*
> *I had this awful feeling it would plunge in."*

Ah, Mr. Bradbury, such poetry. How you capture my noiry, noiry perspective on life right now. But perhaps I need to take that *plunge* and get to the point, though, for those of you who are not in limbo just now.

Burly-Bear. His death. His murder, I suppose I'd better call it.

Apparently he heard from his partner, who'd heard from us right here on *Life is Pulp*, that the gig was up and I was aware that my "rock" was married with child. Escroto, of course, did not give the proverbial poop that this might throw me emotionally—his only concern was that the big murder confession that he was anticipating I'd eventually murmur at his rugged partner was now derailed with the station in view.

Burly-Bear, of course, saw it differently. That night while you guys were arguing about who in the BPD might be Burly-Bear, he showed up at my door. See, you bloggies hit on the wrong cop, but the right secret. Turns out Tony Cunio is—was—married with children. Toddlers, just walking, named Cody and Carly. Love the alliteration.

I'd gotten home from work late, still fruitlessly attempting to backpedal from my impending pink slip, and so I'd done nothing about making myself comfortable or getting dinner or turning on a light. In fact, I'd cut straight across my living room to blog and was sitting there in just the screen light, still wearing my coat, when Burly-Bear buzzed.

What with my last experience opening my door, I was wary. I buzzed him in and waited for his knock. He did, identifying himself, and of course there was no doubt he was who he claimed to be. Still, I needed to talk through the door until my heart steadied.

I asked him what he wanted (he said he thought he might have some information I wanted).

I asked him why it couldn't wait until the next day (he claimed he hadn't been fully forthcoming with me—yeah, the guy got less and less inarticulate every encounter).

So as to help him to get to the point, I asked him whether he shouldn't be home with his family.

There he paused, on the other side of my door, then delivered a pretty moving speech. His wife understood about the job, that it was a twenty-four-hour commitment, and that sometimes there were good people out there, victims who might need real care and understanding. He said that he was lucky that his wife came from a family of cops, because his view was that this prepared her for the way she'd have to share him, his time and energy and his compassion, with the people he came across who needed his support, sometimes desperately.

I felt pretty miserable hearing him say all that, realizing that it was true, everything he wasn't quite saying, that there was this essential divide between us—*him* normal, upright, his life real—*me* warped, fragile, full of delusions, a burden on the healthy people of the world. I almost got sick, right then and there, but instead managed to fumble the lock out of the way. Figured I might as well let the guy have his say and get his ass home where it belonged. I opened the door and chickened out on meeting his eye, immediately reeling away across the kitchen to the cabinet where I keep the scotch. Heck, why should I worry about him seeing me throw back a fast one?

He came around the door tentatively, as if fearful he might find me, I don't know, posing in a negligee? Bleeding from a couple of wrist gashes? No such luck, though. Just your everyday mess, hanging out in her rumpled work duds, a finger of warm JWB wavering in her hand. He was nice, truly nice—*man*, "nice" is such a bland syllable for such a precious trait.

He clicked on the overheads and didn't bat an eye at what a mess I was. He explained, earnestly and seriously, about how he's allergic to gold and so can't wear a wedding band, and how he'd just naturally presumed that I would have a lot of sophisticated book guys barking at my heels and so until, hell, until our ride home from seeing dickel, he had just figured I viewed him as a cop, and a damned pig-headed one at that.

Not that I believed him, quite. He knew farkin well that he'd charmed me and he knew farkin well that he'd meant to, even if his partner had been keeping my little girl-talk bloggings from him (which I doubt). A guy knows how he's doing with a girl. He just does.

But I let him off the hook. I posed against the refrigerator, mugging like a hussy, and threw him my favorite line from *Asphalt Jungle*: "Experience has taught me never to trust a cop. Just when you think one's all right, he turns legit." Burly-Bear didn't recognize the source, but he cracked a grin and looked relieved.

Anyway, then he got serious and explained some stuff—how there were no freelance police sketch artists working for the BPD (they're all either active or retired cops who happen to be artists), and how there's no cop named Cheryl Archer, and how he was confident that the so-called "Guy Ferguson" will surface in time, but that this was not his immediate concern.

I offered him a drink and he said, aw, one quick one, and then he announced that he was "officially off duty and it was about damned time as it has been one helluva day." He seemed so happy that I was taking everything so well, so relieved, that it actually made me rather buoyant, very pleased to not be a "burden."

It was when my back was turned, my arm reaching up to take a glass out of my kitchen cabinet, that everything went, well, very weird, I guess you could call it...

I hear this strange, ungodly snarl and a crash. I turn around, too startled to be frightened, and there's some sort of large feline creature attached to Burly-Bear's shoulders, a large, mottled leopard or puma, its back rippling with muscles, riding the cop so that together they fall across my kitchen table, taking that to the floor. Burly-Bear almost goes down flat but he doesn't, instead stumbling heavily across the dim living room, crashing into walls and furniture as he struggles to get the animal off him. It's only then that I catch on—this isn't an animal. It's a man. A naked man, spare and ribby, yet frighteningly powerful. Wild as he is, he should never be a match for Burly-Bear, except that he's caught him off-guard. The attack will change at any moment, logic dictates; the victim will wrestle his attacker to my floor, twist his arm behind his naked back, snap cuffs on his wrists...

The struggling men flail against the wall and roll across my couch, and now I see the attacker's face, bloated with effort and insanity, glancing over at me with a wicked kindle in his eye. Even as he rides the larger man down to the floor, his sweet blond hair fluttering incongruously around his blood-engorged face and neck. Such pretty hair, I remember thinking, such a vicious face.

Burly-Bear, as anticipated, is gaining control. He's gripping one of the crazed man's arms and seems to be positioning his feet. He'll flip him have him flat on his back in moments...But it doesn't happen. Instead, Burly-Bear's attacker rears ups and hits him. It's an oddly balletic sort of motion...seems almost inconsequential in the scheme of the battle taking place before my eyes, at the moment it happens. He swings his arm in a full, round pinwheel that arcs over Burly-Bear's shoulder and ends with a staccato pop to the middle of Burly-Bear's chest. I say inconsequential because it doesn't seem like much of a punch. The fact is, I barely notice it. But Burly-Bear emits a momentary shriek, a horrid little yelp like you hear in the dead of night when some urban animals come face to face behind a garbage bin—after which he stops struggling and, without so much as a sigh, sinks gently, his coat draping round him, as if he is deflating. It's a trick, I think...the *bear* is playing dead...but I'm wrong.

His naked killer hulks on top of him, arched like a bobcat, riding him down to his death like some gothic nightmare incarnate, his spine rounded and ridged, his flattened muscles taut, his face buried against Burly-Bear's neck as if to suck the life-breath out of him.

I stand there in the background, washed out and colorless, a scotch bottle clutched in one hand, the empty glass still extended in the other, as if waiting for them to finish whatever ritual it is they are performing so that Burly-Bear can stand up and I can ask him if he takes his Johnnie Walker neat or on the rocks.

Later I will find out that it is the blade of a scissors that did it, one of the pharmaceutical variety, relatively diminutive. Too small to kill a person, you'd think. It is the scissors from my own bathroom that I use to occasionally trim my hair. How can such a commonplace little item kill someone so robust as Burly-Bear, you may wonder, but if you study those little household gadgets, you will understand quite clearly how a cruel, slightly curled blade can slide between the protective bones and slice through fat and muscle, penetrating a man's heart and killing him in an instant, if punched skillfully enough against his chest. I never see the scissors during the attack, as I later tell the police a million times, but there can be no doubt that Burly-Bear's killer had the blade of the scissors nested in his palm, the eyelets laced over two of his fingers, when he first leapt out of my back hallway and onto his victim's broad shoulders.

It is not until Burly-Bear's killer rears himself off his victim and stands that I recognize him. He looks across the disheveled kitchen at me, his nostrils flaring wide as he sucks in lungful after lungful of air, and he nods at me and points down at Burly-Bear several times as if this is supposed to be a message I will understand, as if he is assuring me that all of this is my fault...the result of my...disloyalty? My...sluttishness? You know, one of those traits men instinctively blame all women for that's really a catchword for their ownership of us.

Then he walks at me, his chest heaving. He's limping, I notice, but I have no thoughts of escape, no real fear or desire to get out, no instinct telling me to protect myself—hell, wouldn't that have been a laugh. He flicks his hand forward and swats the empty glass out of my hand. I hear it shatter when it hits the wall. Then he takes the bottle from my other hand and has himself a long, loud swallow. Satisfied, he rams the bottle down onto the counter—I swear I'm so numb I don't jump even then. He kisses me hard—I'm sure I'd have tasted blood if I weren't totally shut down—and then he walks away into the black hallway leading to my bedroom.

Immediately upon his leaving my sight, I sort of "wake up," and of course my first lucid thought is of the *gun*, the one I'd taken from Mr. Groin's office. The one I should have used to save Burly-Bear's life. I turn and reached for the oatmeal canister where I'd stashed it, but my fingers are thick and I knock the thing over so that it glances off the counter and hits the floor. The cereal splays on the linoleum like so much sand. I look down at the gun lying there and somehow this causes my knees to give way so that I find myself sinking down to a sitting position against the cabinets—I'm not fully coherent, you have to understand, so everything is weird and distant. There are little black turds in the oatmeal, I can now see, although I can't think how mice could have infiltrated a sealed canister.

In any event, I know I will not be standing up real soon, except if someone grabs a handful of my hair and helps me along. Still, I can function, more or less, even as I sit there all telescoped down with my knees bumping my chin. I reach over and pick up the gun. It feels heavier than I remember, heavier than its size. I hope that the weightiness means that there are bullets in it, because I'm afraid to check for fear that I'll be unable to close it again. I knew from reading that you have to cock a gun before you can fire it, or get the safety off, if there's a difference. Anyway, it has to be made ready to fire—women characters always fuck that up, useless black comedy clowns that we are.

Yes, and I fuck it up. I'm examining the thing, gently blowing oat dust out from behind the trigger and trying to figure out whether there is some angle from which I can detect whether it is set to go, when somehow I fire it. Goddamn thing doesn't peep when I knock it from a five-foot shelf and here I am handling it incredibly gingerly and it goes off in my face. Loud, too. Almost makes an Evelyn Mulwray out of me—later I will find out that the bullet actually grazes my forehead and probably lodges in the ceiling although I never think to look up and check. When I say it grazes me I do mean barely—I'm completely unaware of the fact that I'm bleeding (and rather copiously) until I see a mirror in the emergency ward—but apparently that's the way it is with a flesh wound to the forehead. The assault on my eardrums is by far the worst of it.

Anyway, immediately after the gun goes off I become aware of some commotion from outside, some very urgent vibrating, and then the front door of my apartment slams open so hard that the lower panel splinters against my couch. Next thing I can understand, Escroto is pointing his own very substantial-looking service weapon everywhere, taking in Burly-Bear, huddling over him for a moment or two with a finger on the dead man's neck, and then homing in on me, reaching out a foot to shove aside the broken kitchen table and stick his gun at my face. He yells at me and I have no idea what he is talking about or even whether he's speaking English, but the gun I'm holding topples from my hand of its own accord and apparently that is what he's yelling about so fortunately he doesn't shoot me. Again, the gun doesn't go off on hitting the floor—which I suppose, in retrospect, is lucky for me, since it landed directly next to my left ass-cheek.

I look across the room, feeling something pushing down at my lashes, some foggy pressure that wants me to close my eyes and make it easy on both of us, me and Escroto. But then both of us hear the thin shriek of my bedroom window, the one overlooking the street. It's the metal storm sash, of course—damn thing always sticks. Escroto races through to the bedroom and then immediately retraces his steps, scrambling past me and disappearing out my front door—he runs like all fat men, his feet splayed, his knees bent, feet scrabbling like a dog's. Lard-ass couldn't catch an ice cream truck in August.

I can hear a car, its tires screaming, at least a block away, well before Escroto comes back into view, shoving a few neighbors from upstairs out of his way, barking into a cell phone as he puts his attention back to Burly-Bear. But he knows and I know that Burly-Bear is dead. I never see the blood coursing from his heart. I never see the scissors, pushed deeper into his chest by his own weight. My only horror is the abstract one—the fact of death, and of murder. I am awed by the monstrous simplicity of all of it.

From the moment Escroto reenters my place, whatever else he is doing and from wherever he goes in the room, he keeps his weapon pointed at me. He makes sure I know that the safety isn't on. I suppose blaming me is his way of confronting the horror that I look in the face.

So, yeah. Burly-Bear, murdered, my place. "In the line of duty," they keep repeating on the news.

What else to say? They keep me under guard at the hospital, where I'm pronounced physically fine, then they hold me for a long time. Overnight? Over two nights? Couldn't tell you. In a police station, I think. No exterior windows, walls tiled, air thick and hot. The cops are grim and interchangeable, if all of them are, in fact, cops. No one plays good cop—mostly they drill me with the same litany of questions, repeatedly, like one of those job interview nightmares where they keep harping on that gap in your résumé: "But *where* were you taking a rest? What *kind* of rest? Who can we *talk to* about it?"

I suck at being a murder witness. I'm not stoic or calm or much help. I babble incoherently. I flame at myself for just standing there. I pull my hair and scratch my face and beat my palms on the table and collapse on the floor, snot and spittle smeared across my cheeks. They don't like these antics that can potentially lead to my bruising myself—they keep jumping in and reattaching the foolish bandage that someone had taped to my forehead at the hospital. At some point it dawns on me that they are worried about brutality charges so I redouble my efforts to hurt myself because I blame them as much as I blame myself and so they deserve to be in this hell as much as I do. In short, I'm a freaking mess, and their collective disgust shows in their faces. Why shouldn't I be a mess, though? *I'm in mourning.* All these deaths over such a short space of days, all the suspicions on me, all the posturing and toughing it out I've taken in stride. Well, now it has ended as badly as it can possibly have ended, and I am in acute mourning. Burly-Bear deserves my abject humiliation. I am keening for him.

I don't put it together at the time, but I've since come to realize that they—some of them, anyway—are looking for me to say that I'd killed Burly-Bear and then tried to end my own life with the gun, but flinched at the last second. Laughable garbage, but they are plenty bent on having me agree with it.

At some point I guess they decide to face the fact that Escroto himself heard my bedroom window opening, and so they know someone else had been there. Really must have bent him over to have to own up to that. He certainly didn't condescend to admit it in front of me.

In the end there is nothing they can do. I lie on the floor, half passed out, my eye fixated on a electric socket as I wonder what kind of fun it might be to lick my finger and stick it in there, while outside they must be tallying up how many of my constitutional rights they can violate before they'll face charges. Finally someone pulls me to my feet and shoves me into a bathroom where I pee with a dour female cop watching me before they send me out into the streets to find my own transit to hell. The last of them warns me not to leave the Boston area. I stumble through a halfhearted rain, hoping for relief, but no one obliges my need to be mugged, accosted, randomly shot through the brain. Besides, I'm sure that some cop is following me, now that I think about it.

Eventually I am at my apartment. I go around behind the building and fold myself up, wet and filthy, in the back seat of my car. When I wake up it's either still night or the next night. The rain has stopped, although the chilly air is wet. My hands refuse to uncurl. I find that I am thinking about trains.

"I stare at the wall outside the window—dark, light, dark, light, dark, light..."

I get out of my cramped car and head for South Station, where I have the presence of mind to comb my hair in the ladies' room before approaching the ticket window.

GIVE IT TO ME STRAIGHT

36-D @ February 18 06:02 pm

fickel, I sent the Rottweiler down to check things out. Might have been the reason they let you go at all. He says they bamboozled him and must have purposely had you leave out a back exit so that he'd miss you, then lied about whether you'd been there at all. Cops lie, like, without any hesitation, according to the Rottweiler, but this is *not* how to operate with him. He is furious and fully prepared to represent you, but he says you have to get back to Boston pronto. We know you're not running but this is how cops (and judges, and a jury, god forbid) will interpret your need to ride the rails. Get back east—and call me.

i.went.to.harvard @ February 18 07:10 pm

fickel, I wish I could offer something besides mere words. You must find yourself both legal and emotional assistance and I can recommend spiritual assistance organizations as well. You know how to reach me offsite. Please do.

36-D @ February 18 07:12 pm

Where are you blogging from, anyway? Do you get off these trains you're riding and spend the night anywhere? God, a couple of days on Amtrak would kill me.

chinkigirl @ February 18 07:14 pm

Much as we'd all like to help, I'm not sure it's wise for fickel to be answering any specific questions. I think she should get herself home, contact 36-D, and sit down immediately with the Rottweiler. I really see that as the only priority. That and keeping an eye out for the M.H., although I can only presume that he is as far away from Boston as he could get himself.

marleybones @ February 18 07:18 pm

The M.H? Weirdly enough, I'm not 100% certain that it's the Mysterious Hottie who murdered Burly-Bear. From what fickel wrote I pictured dickel—fickel's brother. It just read that way to me, and when the police kept fickel for so long I was thinking this was because she wouldn't name her brother as Burly-Bear's attacker. Am I totally off, here?

roadrage @ February 19 10:29 pm

Well, it's been hours since your question, marleybones, and my guess is that fickel is offline. I just want to say that I've noticed a lot of similarities between the Mysterious Hottie and dickel...blond, built thin, hard to control.

chinkigirl @ February 19 10:35 pm

Plus, both of them came and went in a similarly irregular way. What are we thinking? Just coincidental?

marleybones @ February 19 10:42 pm

Speaking of coincidences, there's also a similarity between proudblacktrannie and Slenderbuns that's been tugging at me.

chinkigirl @ February 19 10:44 pm

Wait a minute—now some of *us* are populating fickel's world?

i.went.to.harvard @ February 19 10:48 pm

I'm inclined to hesitate before going down the path of seeing all gay black cross-dressing males as interchangeable.

webmaggot @ February 19 10:49 pm

Wow you're so incredibly PC. Can I blow you?

proudblacktrannie @ February 19 10:50 pm

GOD I have been WAITING for one of you to NOTICE. I recognized Slenderbuns as myself at around the time he got SHOT. Not that I got shot at work, of course, but a fine black boy from my community did, and some people are saying that it was a YOUNG WHITE WOMAN or a WHITE TATTOO PUNK who did the shooting. As in fickel and dickel? You tell me:

This was at the West Rox pinball arcade. A young man named Lamont

Travers. Go to Boston.com for the full story. Nothing about the girl or the skinhead, and nothing about Lamont being gay, but he was shot at close range, one bullet, and I have spoken to a person who has a friend who was an eyewitness, and she says that this white girl was talking to him and the shot went off and this white girl threw herself down on the floor, as did many people of course, and that she was so upset and did not apparently have a weapon on her and had been standing near the entrance to the place at the time so everyone had assumed that the shot had come from just behind her. I mean, apparently this white girl could have run easily but did not, you see? So everyone thought she was another witness, but she took off—*melted away* before the cops got there, and then some people from outside started talking about having seen some skinhead running fast. This boy Lamont was no trouble—no drugs, gangs, girls—no nothing, so now people who were there are convinced that this white girl had something to do with it.

Well so now you know: she is a killer and a cunt and WE know that she is fickel.

marleybones @ February 19 10:59 pm

Don't take this the wrong way, proudblacktrannie, but why are you only telling us this now?

proudblacktrannie @ February 19 11:04 pm

Look my luv I have been a *very* loyal fan to this site. I am in tears even as I write. But I think our fickel is a pathological liar covering for her psycho maniac twin. I don't think there's any fullfrontal. I think that's *fickel*. I think hitman is *fickel*. I think she's done it all to cover for her fucking brother and that we've been her dopes all along.

webmaggot @ February 19 11:07 pm

You mean "dupes."

roadrage @ February 19 11:08 pm

Dude, he's upset.

webmaggot @ February 19 11:09 pm

She's upset. I checked with my brother. Most trannies use "she."

roadrage @ February 19 11:10 pm

Okay, cool, but shut up anyway.

marleybones @ February 19 11:14 pm

Look, proudblack, this is as wild a theory as the events fickel's been giving us taken at face value. Is there anything else you've learned about this man who got shot at the arcade?

proudblacktrannie @ February 19 11:15 pm

I have learned *plenty*. He worked in a *Boston retail establishment*. And he was murdered in *cold blood*, I swear by fickel who made him out like he was ME on this blog. And WHAT DID I DO BUT OFFER LOVE AND SUPPORT TO THAT DEMENTED CREATURE?

i.went.to.harvard @ February 19 11:16 pm

proudblack, I hope you will not read this question as hostile to your viewpoint, but how could dickel have possibly been involved in this shooting? He'd been in the hospital for days by the time this took place.

proudblacktrannie @ February 19 11:17 pm

But do we KNOW that? We only have fickel's word. We only KNOW that dickel was in the hospital as of the 6th, days AFTER Lamont Travers's murder. You are just in denial, like I was until the TRUTH just flooded over me like ICE COLD DEATH ITSELF. fickel is EFFED UP. What, you think that just because you LIKE someone they can't be EFFED UP? Dream on, naive people. There is nothing that says that an effed-up bitch who is STRANGELY CLOSE with her ANIMAL of a BROTHER cannot be UTTERLY CHARMING.

chinkigirl @ February 19 11:18 pm

Okay, we definitely are hearing your theory. But what about more information? Do you know what the retail establishment is where Lamont Travers worked?

proudblacktrannie @ February 19 11:19 pm

Of course I *know*! It was The Blue Pearl. This is what I'm saying—fickel took my online persona and—how do I say this—she *grafted* it onto this jewelry store clerk that she needed to kill because *somehow Lamont Travers knew she was Stephen Pearle's lover*. Maybe he *saw* them together and when she went by The Blue Pearl he *recognized* her so she had to *kill* him before the cops got around to asking him the *right question*. Don't you *see*?

chinkigirl @ February 19 11:20 pm

You don't think the cops would have asked him about who Mr. Suicide's lovers were?

proudblacktrannie @ February 19 11:21 pm

A *black boy* who is clearly *gay*? How do you think a bunch of *cops* is going to react to *that*? I can tell you how but the *language* won't be *pretty*.

36-D @ February 19 11:23 pm

Uhh, okay, just assuming that all cops are so prejudiced that they can't even accept someone like that as a witness, I hate to bust your bubble but there is no place called The Blue Pearl in the Jewelers Building. I checked it out personally last time I was up in Boston.

proudblacktrannie @ February 19 11:24 pm

I have had enough of this *shit*. This whole horror story leaves me cold, and now I'm a liar and a cop-basher, I see. Consider me a *memory*. Good nite.

i.went.to.harvard @ February 19 11:29 pm

Anything reasonably like The Blue Pearl, 36-D?

36-D @ February 19 11:31 pm

There was some place called Blue Diamonds, and I went in there but the lighting's not particularly *blue* that I noticed. Also, the lady I met, who seemed like the owner, was not X. She was Indian, but not American Indian, the other kind, wearing one of those saris. Plus she did not have an androgynous thing going on like X. And she was *totally* snotty—how she sells a thing I cannot tell you but maybe that's why the place looked like it's closing. Oh, and there was no blown-up photo of any exotic necklaces on the wall, OR a mirror in the back. So, you know.

webmaggot @ February 19 11:40 pm

Can you spell BIMBO?

i.went.to.harvard @ February 19 11:41 pm

Lay off, webmaggot. 36-D, don't you see some distinct similarities between the jewelry store you just described and The Blue Pearl as described by fickel? I mean, if you accept that fickel was attempting to mask the place's exact identity for some reason?

marleybones @ February 19 11:43 pm

Put it this way: are you *actually* a size 36-D? If not, I have a feeling your assets are still pretty impressive.

36-D @ February 19 11:44 pm

But proudblacktrannie said that there WAS a place called The Blue Pearl. And if he's going to start calling fickel a liar and a killer he's got to get his story straight.

roadrage @ February 19 11:46 pm

But aren't *you* establishing she's a liar by ascertaining that there's no The Blue Pearl?

36-D @ February 19 11:47 pm

Oh. Maybe. Look I have no idea WHAT to conclude. Did The Blue Pearl already close by the time I made it up to Boston, or was I in the wrong building, or what? Alls I know is that none of this added up to fickel or her brother shooting some unfortunate kid in cold blood.

chinkigirl @ February 19 11:50 pm

I agree with 36-D: this is getting dangerously speculative and not doing fickel any good. I think we should lay off before we start going tooth and nail at one another. Anyway, talk to everyone soon—sorry if by posting this I start something really upsetting.

37

GIVE IT TO ME STRAIGHT

marleybones @ February 22 06:02 pm

Anyone out there?

roadrage @ February 22 06:15 pm

Sup my fave dyke hippie momma soulmate?

marleybones @ February 22 06:38 pm

Clue.

i.went.to.harvard @ February 22 07:22 pm

I'm on. But clue? As in "I haven't got a...?"

marleybones @ February 22 07:23 pm

As in Clue. That's all I'm offering. If no one else sees it, maybe it's in my head.

i.went.to.harvard @ February 22 08:00 pm

Okay, I might have it. I was always a major fan. Fact is, I own all the versions.

marleybones @ February 22 08:12 pm

Talk to me, but be subtle.

i.went.to.harvard @ February 22 08:14 pm

The Colonel, the Peacock, Mr. Groin. Then there's the housekeeper "Chalkie"...?

marleybones @ February 22 08:17 pm

Right on, man-o-God. Sit tight, now.

chinkigirl @ February 22 08:32 pm

Oh my. I think I get it, too. But coincidence, perhaps?

i.went.to.harvard @ February 22 08:33 pm

From the street, the people in front of the Colonel's house looked like figurines on a board game.

roadrage @ February 22 08:48 pm

SHEE-YATT, PHUKAHZ: The Silly Git. Academic. Red hair: *2002 retro-classical set*!!!!

chinkigirl @ February 22 08:53 pm

But I'm just seeing a lot of dull tweed. Well, there's the purple bow tie.

marleybones @ February 22 08:54 pm

Beemer.

roadrage @ February 22 08:58 pm

mauve = purple?

i.went.to.harvard @ February 22 08:59 pm

A professional decorator you are not, apparently, but you've guessed it.

chinkigirl @ February 22 09:01 pm

Umm...implication of this "discovery?"

i.went.to.harvard @ February 22 09:04 pm

That fickel is playful in the face of a tragedy? Fanciful, or maybe even untrustworthy, in her reporting? marleybones? You brought it to our attention...

marleybones @ February 22 09:06 pm

Lying flashbacks.

wazzup! @ February 22 09:07 pm

Crossfire!!!! The killer as narrator!!! I LUV this blog!!!

marleybones @ February 22 09:10 pm

Look, I'm not trying to read in a lot of connections...

chinkigirl @ February 22 09:13 pm

Although if we follow the analogy...

i.went.to.harvard @ February 22 09:15 pm

fickel = Scarlet

roadrage @ February 22 09:16 pm

Hey, catch the number she wore to her meeting with Mr. Groin? Clue 1972, Asian Miss Scarlet is wearing that very dress.

chinkigirl @ February 22 09:19 pm

Wait a second—so what I'm gathering is that in addition to fickel's not very subtle references to Colonel Mustard, Mrs. Peacock, and Mr. Green, we've also spotted more recent references to Mrs. White and Professor Plum, which is far more jarring because fickel seems to have squeezed them in at a point where you wouldn't think she'd be in the mood for playfulness. So are we saying that these references are more than playful, but rather serve as some sort of hint?

i.went.to.harvard @ February 22 09:21 pm

And, with the connection we're now making between fickel herself and Miss Scarlet, are we saying that on some level fickel *wanted* us to consider *her* a suspect in the deaths of the Colonel and the Peacock?

chinkigirl @ February 22 09:28 pm

I don't get what you're getting at.

36-D @ February 22 09:30 pm

Hi, everyone. God I am so worried. Rottweiler and I have heard NOTHING from fickel. And, since it's always my job to be the literal one—fickel doesn't wear much in the way of red.

i.went.to.harvard @ February 22 09:33 pm

I, too, am mystified. Are we wondering whether fickel is *admitting* guilt in this "playful" way?

webmaggot @ February 22 09:37 pm

Killers can't resist that—I mean, we noir-heads of all people know this shit. Makes them feel smart. Or sometimes they can't live with it bottled up. Chick killers, especially.

marleybones @ February 22 09:38 pm

Chick killers. Is that women who kill, or killers with female victims?

webmaggot @ February 22 09:39 pm

Umm, maybe both? Hey, are you one of those profs who always

throwing out these clever brain-twisty questions that make people look stupid in front of all their friends?

marleybones @ February 22 09:40 pm

Pretty much sums me up. Look, I don't know where we're going with all this, exactly. Personally, I'm just thinking my way along and am finally coming to think that there's far more than meets the eye throughout this entire blog.

wazzup! @ February 22 09:42 pm

Yes, absolutely there is much MUCH more! This is always a feature of a fine noir, as I know we all agree! fickel, or should I now say Miss Scarlet, absolutely RULES!!

chinkigirl @ February 22 09:43 pm

fickel? Please tell us we're crazy...?

38

GIVE IT TO ME STRAIGHT

roadrage @ February 24 10:48 pm

Hey, 'sup blog? Something tells me I'm talking to myself, but if anyone's out there, I have some interesting information to report.

'Loooooo? Am I talking to myself?

marleybones @ February 24 11:18 pm

Not at the moment.

chinkigirl @ February 24 11:32 pm

Actually, I'm here now, too. I check in about twice a day, just to see if fickel's back. I also check Boston.com every day and I'm in touch with an old friend from Brighton who knows a reporter at the *Globe*—but so far I've got very little to offer. I am hugely worried. Has anyone heard anything—anyone from Boston?

roadrage @ February 24 11:40 pm

Hey, ladies. I'm back on. In answer to your question, you tell me:

Couple days ago, I'm up on Newbury (Classic Comix—best oldies comic book store EVUR) and I realized I was near the Hynes T station where Mr. Suicide—well, Pearle—got killed. So I went to check it out. Nothing, of course—just looked like a train station—not even any old lady screaming at me in Swedish. But when I got back to the street level, I'm looking around and there's this bookstore across the street—mostly secondhand junk and a big poster about their sci-fi collection, but the name of the store is—get this—*Dark Corner*.

I never really paid much attention to it before, which is totally weird because I'm definitely a used book freak and of course the store's name is kinda noir, but anyway, I go in and it's just like you think, all crammed with moldy paperbacks and some dweeb (I say that with respect—as in, I recognized and warmly acknowledged a fellow dweeb) sitting on a stool behind this high wooden counter, sucking on ginger gummies and reading *The Room with Something Wrong.*

So I find all of this homey and inviting. I go up to the guy and point out that he's reading a favorite of mine. He doesn't give a crap and says he's not a big noir fan (like sup dah?), so I asked him how he happened to pick up one of the greats. This is when he gestures to this rack of books under various Polaroids—one of those "staff choices" displays.

Sure enough, there's one with a bunch of noirs—*A Swell-Looking Girl, Death in the Air*, *Subway*. Anything strike you about this list?

wazzup! @ February 24 11:57 pm

TRAINS!!!! So super stoked to be FIRST with this connections!!!

roadrage @ February 24 11:59 pm

Exactly, expostulating Dutch man: trains. The person who put these books together is pictured in a Polaroid, like all the rest of them, but—dead end—she's not fickel. She's this very stocky woman with her hair dyed bright red, and wearing a worn over-the-head woolie and a big earthy smile—you probably know the type. I mean she's in her twenties and female, but otherwise not at all fickel. And her name is "Evy G," according to what's printed on the pic.

So I say to the clerk, hey can I talk to this woman you got pictured here because I have very similar taste in books, and he wrinkles his brow like he can barely place her and then says something to the effect of, "Oh, Lyn? She doesn't work here anymore," which sounds like he's pretending indifference but is kind of glad that Evy—or Lyn—or whoever she is, is gone. I should say the guy is coming off real...I wanna say persnickety (is that a word?), which I know scores a big "so what," but my point is that his views on anyone wouldn't exactly rule my world.

So I'm thinking *name starts with E, nickname starts with L*...but a bunch of girls' names have that feature, I think someone mentioned before: Liz for Elizabeth, Lanie for Elaine, Lisa for Elisa, Lyn for Elinor or Evelyn, etc., etc., etc. Anyway, so I ask what this Lyn did when she used to work there and he says something snide like "mostly bit her nails" while he points to the counter, which I guess is to say that she did the same thing he does, worked as a salesclerk.

So I'm all "cool, brother, love the store," and I'm about to push off but then it occurs to me to ask him whether the people who run the place actually publish anything. The guy rolls his eyes at how annoying I am, but manages to tell me that they have this tiny company called Midnight Ink that publishes two small-circ literary rags. Those are called *Night Sky* and *Night Streets. Night Sky* is their main mag, focused on sci-fi, and *Night Streets*, the up-and-comer, is on mystery. Midnight Ink has also published a couple of paperback originals—they got them on a special display that Mr. Doesn't-Like-Noir jerks a thumb at. In fact, he tells me in a sort of gloaty way, he got the feeling that my "friend" Evy G. left in a huff when the boss lady wouldn't publish Evy's own novel, which was one of those inner-healing numbers, but with this incest hint that the folks upstairs wouldn't leave in and Evy G. wouldn't take out. Of course, now I'm totally interested and I ask whether he means that literally when he says the publications' offices are "upstairs" and he points at the ceiling and makes a crack like "offices?" I ask if I can go up there and take a gander and he says no because they're "in lay-out" and, anyway, he seems to be sick of me—starts looking like he's getting ready to manufacture himself something to go do.

I pretend not to notice (playing dumb is my forte), and I ask what the offices look like and he kind of impatiently says it's like some big open space with desks and computers and mice and couple of little closet offices in the back, like what the hell should it look like? I stick him with one more question which is whether Evy G. ever worked up there. He thinks about it, then says that sometimes people who work in the bookstore also do typing, envelope stuffing, submissions logging, grammar editing, etc., upstairs, so it's possible. And that's about when the guy steams off to change his rag.

One more "coincidence": after the guy left, I checked the display rack, and he himself was pictured (guy's a Dickens ho). His name is *Webster*. You remember fickel's work pal, Noah? Maybe the guy soured a little toward her after she took off, especially if he has no idea why she's completely out of touch.

I don't know if I found fickel or got squat. Not sure I want to pursue it either, so if someone wants to go back and ask for Dame Judith, be my guest. All in all, it was a weird experience and I thought you guys might want to hear it.

webmaggot @ February 25 12:18 am

Excellent post, dewdster. But what's the name Webster got to do with the name Noah?

marleybones @ February 25 12:22 am

The lexicographer.

webmaggot @ February 25 12:24 am

I like when you talk dirty, bones, but, come on, we're trying to be serious here.

chinkigirl @ February 25 12:28 am

Noah Webster, of Webster's Dictionary. Webster = Noah.

i.went.to.harvard @ February 25 12:37 am

So, to recap: Lamont Travers's death = Slenderbuns. Blue Diamonds = The Blue Pearl. Now fickel's workplace. Does this lead logically to Evelyn G = fickel?

webmaggot @ February 25 12:45 am

Just had a **FARKIN MOHMENT**: *The chick in the internet café. The fat one chewing her fingernails who saved the seat for FullFrontal.* That weird entry where he spies on fickel and dickel (getting all yick-el together), then feeds his url to dickel in the internet café.

i.went.to.harvard @ February 25 01:08 am

This suggests what?

webmaggot @ February 25 01:10 am

That fickel is a fat dog.

chinkigirl @ February 25 01:11 am

Wow. If true, this certainly puts a new angle on the Burly-Bear relationship.

marleybones @ February 25 01:18 am

Just back. Greetings, all. Not catching your point, chinkigirl.

chinkigirl @ February 25 01:21 am

Well, I'm not sure I feel that comfortable explaining what I blurted above. Anyone else?

webmaggot @ February 25 01:22 am

Oh, yeah, just let *me* have my yams mashed, right?

36-D @ February 25 01:26 am

Just on, and I have no PC inhibitions (or yams), so let *me* put it bluntly: If fickel is hot, the way we were reading her all along, then you can't help suspecting that Burly-Bear was allowing himself to be—how to put it?—steered by his rod? Like taking her side when the other cops suspect her, making up reasons to see her, not letting on that he's married, etc., etc., etc.

HOWEVAH, if fickel is that chick from the cafe, it's a pretty different tale. Suddenly you find yourself wondering if maybe she's just reading into everything Burly-Bear and getting all lovey-dovey. And when she finally catches on that he's most definitely NOT interested...

wazzup! @ February 25 01:29 am

...she is one *dangerous femme fatale*!!! This I have been wondering all along!!!

webmaggot @ February 25 01:31 am

Thank you, Ms Rack and Amsterdam's most famous premature ejaculator. But now take it a step further. Maybe she's been hallucinating all along that he's even on her side. MAYBE IN REAL LIFE HE'S JUST OUT TO NAB HER SAME AS ESCROTO.

roadrage @ February 25 01:34 am

And maybe she gets hit with that reality and stabs him with a pair of scissors, then tries to take herself out with some gun she's got her hands on?

chinkigirl @ February 25 01:36 am

Her brother's gun. Remember him groping in his knapsack in that motel room? What would he be looking for but a gun? And who would he never suspect of lifting it so that he didn't check to make sure it was there before entering the motel room?

i.went.to.harvard @ February 25 01:39 am

But WHO is fullfrontal under this fickel-is-psycho scenario? Wouldn't fullfrontal be fickel?

marleybones @ February 25 01:44 am

Back up—I'm not sure I *believe* what I'm reading. So if she's fat, she's totally nuts and also screwed up about men? She couldn't be nuts and screwed up about men if she's hot?

webmaggot @ February 25 01:47 am

She could be screwed up about men either way—I mean, she's female so we accept that. Kudos to marleybones for that frank observation. However, if fickel's an ugg-o, then maybe she's a fucked-up nut who comes to realize that she's been pretending to herself that Burly-Bear is into her. If she's hot, then she never has that moment of white-hot rage-inducing truth because, trust me, married or not, he's into her.

roadrage @ February 25 01:55 am

Oh, giant fat lady whom nobody loves

Why do you walk to the sea in white gloves?...

chinkigirl @ February 25 01:58 am

Oddly, I like that. Is there more to it?

marleybones @ February 25 02:02 am

I'm losing more respect for this blog with every post.

36-D @ February 25 02:15 am

Look, anyone, male or female, can be a psycho. But we happen to be looking at a situation where a woman may have killed a cop that she was imagining was into her when he was really investigating her. That woman projecting herself on a blog as hot but turning out to be a dog sure brings it all together. Don't you see that, marleybones?

marleybones @ February 25 02:17 am

No, I don't. Sounds like "all fat girls should be shunned" to me. I just don't buy it.

webmaggot @ February 25 02:19 am

Wait, so that's not true, now?

roadrage @ February 25 02:20 am

Dewd.

chinkigirl @ February 25 02:21 am

Moving along. So let me understand something: are we speculating that fickel wrote Full Frontal? And that in that persona, she sees herself as overwhelmingly unattractive and needy?

webmaggot @ February 25 02:22 am

This is where I'm at.

36-D @ February 25 02:25 am

I'm sorta there, too.

i.went.to.harvard @ February 25 02:27 am

If that's the case, is fickel just the girl in the internet café, or is she the strange "Poppy Z" girl on the train as well?

marleybones @ February 25 02:30 am

Hell, why not! fickel is ALL fat women! And all fat women are crazy!

webmaggot @ February 25 02:33 am

This is why I admire marleybones—ultimately she's got the balls to speak common sense.

marleybones @ February 25 02:34 am

Grrrrrrrrrrrrr.

roadrage @ February 25 02:37 am

Just to correct the record, I never said that Evy G. from the bookstore was fat. I said she looked stocky, and it could have been the sweater she had on.

webmaggot @ February 25 02:38 am

You described a porker, man.

36-D @ February 25 02:45 am

However we put it, it looks like fickel is not the goth sylph she put herself across as.

roadrage @ February 25 02:48 am

IF Evy G. is fickel at all.

chinkigirl @ February 25 02:50 am

Did fickel put herself across as a goth sylph? Wasn't that more fullfrontal?

36-D @ February 25 02:52 am

But fullfrontal is fickel. Didn't we decide that???

i.went.to.harvard @ February 25 02:53 am

I think that some of us think that. It beats the alternative, which is that fickel has a stalker.

chinkigirl @ February 25 02:55 am

He sure writes like a male, while she does not.

webmaggot @ February 25 02:56 am

Meaning he writes what he thinks and not what he hopes won't hurt people's feelings? Speaking of which, I've just been THINKING, and now realize that there's a problem with my "fickel is Evy" rationale. Here it is: if fickel is a porker, why would Mr. Suicide have gone for her?

i.went.to.harvard @ February 25 03:02 am

Well, he went for his wife. Don't the rest of you picture X as...heavyset?

marleybones @ February 25 03:03 am

Although now that we're questioning fickel's word on everything, we don't know that.

chinkigirl @ February 25 03:05 am

Oh, good, you're still with us, marleybones. I thought the silly "fat girl discussion" might have disgusted you enough to make you sign off for a while.

marleybones @ February 25 03:06 am

Ha. I went through junior high long, long ago, but the protective callus remains. Hot flash jokes, however, might rub me wrong. Be warned.

36-D @ February 25 03:07 am

If X was the Indian lady I saw in Blue Diamonds, let me just verify that Mr. Suicide was FOJLO.

chinkigirl @ February 25 03:08 am

I'm almost afraid to ask?

roadrage @ February 25 03:10 am

Someone who likes much booty.

chinkigirl @ February 25 03:13 am

Gotcha. But even if X has a big rump, have you ever noticed that when American men go for non-American women, they don't have the same standards as they do with American women? White men seem harder on their own race when they're judging women's sex appeal, now that I think of it. I wonder why that is?

marleybones @ February 25 03:15 am

Because American men are bigger assholes than men from the rest of the planet?

webmaggot @ February 25 03:17 am

Don't you suspect that foreign guys are just assholes with sexy accents that make you American women all fluttery?

36-D @ February 25 03:18 am

He has a point.

proudblacktrannie @ February 25 03:20 am

Good GOD, aren't you people GETTING IT?

chinkigirl @ February 25 03:22 am

proudblacktrannie! I'm so glad to see you on!

36-D @ February 25 03:23 am

GAWD, I thought we'd lost you, gurlfriend! It was my FOJLO comment that brought you out of lurking—admit it?

proudblacktrannie @ February 25 03:24 am

I have NOT been lurking, and, anyway, look around—there is no BACK to get to anymore. This site is OVER. I'm just on to satisfy my curiosity and cannot BELIEVE that the rest of you have yet to put TOO and TOO together.

webmaggot @ February 25 03:25 am

It's "two and two," dudette.

36-D @ February 25 03:37 am

Way to go. Now she's gone again.

proudblacktrannie @ February 25 03:38 am

God you are ALL so blind and pathetic. Why doesn't someone take the lot of you outside and shoot you to put you out of your misery, you STUPID STRAIGHT OXEN?

webmaggot @ February 25 03:39 am

I thought marleybones was a dyke?

marleybones @ February 25 03:41 am

Apparently I'm an exception—gay *and* stupid—because I'm honestly not getting it.

webmaggot @ February 25 03:42 am

Plus you have a sense of humor—could such a dyke exist? Are you... Escroto *masquerading* as a fifty-year-old totally cool with-it lesbian in Wisconsin?

marleybones @ February 25 03:44 am

Look, proudblacktrannie, we're struggling here, and in spite of all the banter, this is a serious matter. I, for one, am worried for fickel's safety. What if all this speculation is wrong and fullfrontal/Mysterious Hottie exists? Then there's the other angle: what if he doesn't and it's all a ruse by fickel? Either way, fickel is in a dangerous place. Remember, fullfrontal's site ends with him professing that he is about to commit suicide, and it's convincing. We may be the only lifeline she has right now. So if you think you can supply some insight, let's go.

proudblacktrannie @ February 25 03:50 am

HUFF. Okay, fine. But I'm doing this for your sakes and not for fickel's. She's in a scary place all right. But it is OTHERS who are in danger.

Let's start with a simple fact: Mr. Suicide did not SPOT fickel at a concert and start pursuing this ATTRACTIVE STRANGER. HE was the one who was SPOTTED and being STALKED. By HER.

marleybones @ February 25 03:52 am

And she moved in on him.

proudblacktrannie @ February 25 03:53 am

YES

marleybones @ February 25 03:54 am

And *she* wrote the bitter diary about *him*.

proudblacktrannie @ February 25 03:55 am

YES. STEPHEN PEARLE WAS "E," YOU FOOLS.

chinkigirl @ February 25 03:56 am

fickel wrote the strange, dreamy diary about spotting someone on the street?

roadrage @ February 25 04:27 am

Y'know, I jotted some notes leafing through the excerpts fickel fed us. Here they are:

The tone, of course, is collaborative, rather than informative: the writer writes stuff like "you know" and the whole thing assumes there's a rapport between writer and reader. The punctuation is also intimate, with a lot of dashes rather than commas or periods. That's female writing, according to Wikipedia.

i.went.to.harvard @ February 25 04:34 am

There's also the generally impeccable grammar, marred by the occasional conscious fragment, which I read as another earmark of intimacy. As we've all remarked, this is supposed to be a sign of female writing.

chinkigirl @ February 25 04:46 am

I'm struck mostly by the artistic turns—"scintillated trance" and "catching kisses that might drip from his lips." Male or female, it reminds me of fickel's voice once I put my mind to it.

roadrage @ February 25 04:49 am

There's also the line about the shorter person in the couple being "comfortable enough with who you were," after being jostled on the street. That makes sense if the two street-kissers are men.

marleybones @ February 25 06:00 am

All fine observations, but I for one don't buy the theory that all men write one way and all women another. Anyway, if fickel wrote the journal, what's going on? She was Mr. Suicide's lover?

proudblacktrannie @ February 25 06:03 am

Ah, a light breaketh in the east.

i.went.to.harvard @ February 25 06:07 am

And then he brought another guy into the mix and she...felt spurned?

proudblacktrannie @ February 25 06:09 am

NO, AGAIN you INSIST on casting her as a VICTIM. It was ALL HER. SHE suggested the other guy. Pearle was a VOYEUR, see? He liked to WATCH others having SEX.

webmaggot @ February 25 06:11 am

Gag me. I don't even like thinking about sloppy seconds cause it involves getting my bod too close to where some other guy has been.

proudblacktrannie @ February 25 06:12 am

SHUT UP, you HOMOPHOBIC CLOSET FAG. Pearle was a lot more kinky that just being a VOYEUR. And FICKEL was a lot more kinky than HE was.

chinkigirl @ February 25 06:13 am

More kinky than two guys at once? Does it *get* much kinkier than that?

proudblacktrannie @ February 25 06:15 am

It does if one of the guys is...?

i.went.to.harvard @ February 25 06:18 am

...the Mysterious Hottie?

proudblacktrannie @ February 25 06:19 am

YES. And WHY would that be so KINKY, my THICK-WITTED INNOCENTS?

chinkigirl @ February 25 06:21 am

Because he's rough. He makes a woman feel almost abused, almost like she's been taken.

36-D @ February 25 06:23 am

Or...(and I cringe to say this) because he reminds fickel of dickel?

proudblacktrannie @ February 25 06:24 am

FIGURE IT OUT YOU TWITS. REMEMBER HIS NAME IS "GUY."

chinkigirl @ February 25 06:25 am

As in anonymous male?

marleybones @ February 25 06:27 am

I need to sleep! We've pulled an all-nighter on this. All I can say is tgiSunday. Okay, the one Guy I can think of from "our" kind of lit is Guy Haines from Patricia Highsmith's *Strangers on a Train*. Favorite of mine. There is some heavy stuff going on there about identity and double lives. Does that have some bearing on where you're taking us, proudblacktrannie?

proudblacktrannie @ February 25 06:30 am

"My brain a tumble of rage..." **WHY?**

"You drank me in without conscious reaction...You half smiled...Were you apologizing?"

WHY, WHY, WHY???

i.went.to.harvard @ February 25 01:22 pm

Okay, proudblacktrannie, I *might* be with you. Frankly, I am not proud to say that I have already meandered down this rather dark path of reasoning. But this is where it gets all gummed up:

If fickel met Stephen Pearle through the Peacock and the Mysterious Hottie also met Stephen Pearle through the Peacock, then fickel got together with the Mysterious Hottie and somehow Stephen Pearle ended up "in the way" and dead, why would this necessitate the Peacock's death? What could she know about them being a pair, except if they were together from *before* and her bringing them both to Stephen Pearle is one major coincidence...I am totally gummed up.

chinkigirl @ February 25 06:07 pm

Hi, back and refreshed... Coincidences do happen and Boston *is* a very small city.

roadrage @ February 25 07:24 pm

You know what the pulp dicks say: where there's a whopper of a coincidence there probably is no coincidence at all.

proudblacktrannie @ February 25 07:31 pm

OH GAWWWWWWD, YOU NINNIES...**THE BITCH SET THE WHOLE THING UP**.

LOOK, SHE COMES ACROSS PEARLE IN THE CITY ONE NIGHT—SHE *RECOGNIZES* HIM AND BEGINS STALKING HIM. WITH PRECIOUS LITTLE TROUBLE, SHE FINDS OUT HE'S A JEWELER AND IT DON'T TAKE MUCH MORE EFFORT TO FIND OUT WHO SOME OF HIS CUSTOMERS ARE. THEN SHE DOES HERSELF A LITTLE WEB RESEARCH ON SOME OF THEM AND FINDS OUT THAT SOME JEWELER'S WET DREAM (THE PEACOCK) HAS A RICH OLD HUSBAND (THE COLONEL) WHO USED TO WRITE MYSTERIES. FICKEL WORKS AT A MYSTERY MAGAZINE. SO SHE'S NOW GOT SOMETHING TO WORK WITH!!!!!

SHE MAKES UP A WAY TO GET TO KNOW THE COLONEL (THE NOIR READINGS AT HARVARD), TALKS HIM INTO HAVING THE PEACOCK'S PORTRAIT DONE BY THE MYSTERIOUS HOTTIE, INSTRUCTS THE M.H. TO PAINT A FANCY NECKLACE ON THE BITCH, AND HONEY IT AIN'T MUCH WORK AT ALL FOR FICKEL TO SUGGEST TO THE PEACOCK THAT SHE HAVE HER JEWELER GET TOGETHER WITH HER PORTRAIT ARTIST TO DISCUSS HAVING THE THING MADE UP.

THAT LEAVES THE EASIEST STEP OF ALL: HAVING THE PEACOCK INTRODUCE FICKEL TO PEARLE AT A CONCERT. LITTLE TRAMP MOVES IN ON PEARLE, AND BEFORE LONG SHE SUGGESTS A THREE-WAY WITH "THE ARTIST GUY," WHO PEARLE HAS YET TO REALIZE SHE ALREADY KNOWS VERY, *VERY* WELL.

YES, IT'S ALL A MERRY REUNION, A GODDAM CHRISTMAS SPECIAL, UNTIL...

roadrage @ February 25 08:02 pm

Okay (cringe in anticipation of being called stupid in all caps) I'm *kind* of following, but I don't get the last bit. It's a "reunion?" Until what?

chinkigirl @ February 25 08:04 pm

I'm not quite getting it either. Please don't leave me to speculate, because you have no idea of the rather unsavory things I'm imagining.

proudblacktrannie @ February 25 08:05 pm

EXACTLY. IMAGINE AWAY.

marleybones @ February 25 08:10 pm

I think that I get it and want to make sure I'm not alone. It was all a merry reunion, as proudblacktrannie says, until Pearle finally recognized fickel, and maybe the Mysterious Hottie as well. Since she'd recognized Pearle all along, maybe she'd even been telling herself that they *all* knew what they were up to and that they were just not mentioning the unmentionable?

roadrage @ February 25 08:11 pm

Wait. So now the Mysterious Hottie is *also* a blast from the past?

proudblacktrannie @ February 25 08:13 pm

Well, FAT BOY, YOU are the one who pointed out that Hottie reminds you of...

webmaggot @ February 25 08:16 pm

REMINDS HIM OF WHAT?

proudblacktrannie @ February 25 08:45 pm

You all are THICK.

webmaggot @ February 25 08:46 pm

You know what? LICK ME GAY BIRD. SEE WE CAN ALL HIT THE CAPS LOCK AND SOUND LIKE TOTAL DICKS!

i.went.to.harvard @ February 25 09:07 pm

Look, who is Pearle? How could fickel recognize him and have him not recognize her?

proudblacktrannie @ February 25 09:10 pm

HE wouldn't have recognized HER the way SHE would have recognized him because SHE had been a little girl and HE had been already a grownup so SHE would have changed a lot and HE would not have changed.

marleybones @ February 25 09:11 pm

Let me put something out here that I've been researching fruitlessly: Carreau is French for diamond, in some contexts, like playing cards.

36-D @ February 25 09:15 pm

We know that fickel's mother's name was de Carreau, but...?

chinkigirl @ February 25 09:16 pm

And the jewelry shop that fickel dubbed The Blue Pearl actually turns out to have been called Blue Diamonds, but...?

i.went.to.harvard @ February 25 09:17 pm

But *how*, according to X, did she and Mr. Suicide come up with a name for the jewelry shop?

roadrage @ February 25 09:20 pm

They named it after Pearle, right? *Egad*—the ultimate doppelgänger.

36-D @ February 25 09:37 pm

OMGGGGGGGGG. Uncle Steven and the twins, back to playing doctor as grownups. For once I am like SO proud to be the last one to get it.

proudblacktrannie @ February 25 09:38 pm

AH THE DAWN LIGHT HAS BROKEN!!!

chinkigirl @ February 25 09:40 pm

But all of this is *pure* speculation. Please, let's remember that!

marleybones @ February 25 09:43 pm

Actually, it's not just speculation. I've had so many ugly thoughts these past days I can't sleep. Like proudblacktrannie has undoubtedly done, I've reread the E diary from the perspective of a young female writer complaining about Stephen Pearle—or should I say *Etienne de Carreau*. I've also done web research about a Canadian inkmaker named Gustafson living in western Mass who attempted suicide by dropping himself in front of a train while his wife looked on and his twin daughter and son sat on a bench in the station waiting room. There's stuff out there, although all of it sketchy, highly circumstantial, and in no way reliable. I don't know if I want to find any more of it.

So, now that we all think what we think and don't think what we don't think, want my advice? Let's none of us take this any further.

i.went.to.harvard @ February 25 09:55 pm

Whether or not we've hit on the truth, I consider myself fickel's friend and will offer her any aid she may ask of me. She knows how to contact me offsite. Until then, I will think of her riding rails, anonymous, physically safe, emotionally recuperating. Until then, my friends.

proudblacktrannie @ February 25 09:59 pm

...and a hush fell over the blog...

39

GIVE IT TO ME STRAIGHT

marleybones @ February 28 02:01 am

Hey, big void. Just woke from this vivid dream and realized that I wanted to get it down in writing and also that only you guys would appreciate it like I am doing right now. Don't know if any of you will check in (is this blog even functioning at this point?), but here it is:

I'm a detective in this dream—in fact, I'm highly aware of myself and of how odd it is to think of myself as a detective, but it's one of those dreams where you realize you're dreaming and just go with it—(do others have these or is it just me?)—and, anyway, I am trailing fickel and this is a big moment because I believe that I have located her.

I am on some tropical island, having just landed in one of those tiny prop planes, and I am walking around, squinting at the ocean through palm trees, etc., all the time feeling rather uncomfortable because I'm wearing wool pants and a stiff shirt and patent leather dress shoes, almost like a man (and, I know what you're thinking but all lesbians don't dress like men—in fact I am an old flower child and so this is a *very* peculiar outfit for me). I believe that I know where I am going but at the same time I am wondering if I am lost.

After not walking very far, I focus in on this man near the beach. He is built and wearing a barely-there bathing suit and he is lying on one of those striped lounge chairs with a big tropical drink in his hand. I can't make him out very well because the sun is causing a terrible glare, but I start walking through the sand toward him (awkward in my dress shoes), and I come to realize that my excitement is not over him, but over the girl I can hardly see at all who is lying on a matching lounge chair, just beyond him. I can see the girl's feet. She's on her stomach, but she turns over, and then I see her hand reach for the man's drink and she kind of half sits up so I get a tiny bit of her profile and hair.

First of all, she is topless, with smallish, pointy breasts. She has thick disheveled hair, very black as if it's dyed and cut in a sort of Raggedy-Ann style, which looks quite cool on her because she's thin and lithe with sharp, almost disdainful features. She has large sunglasses on that hide a lot but somehow I am filled with this sense of triumph because I *know* that I have found fickel.

I start churning through the sand toward them, and fickel lays herself down again, disappearing from view, but then the man notices me and sort of half sits up to get a look at who is coming and this is the really weird moment—he's not a man, turns out, but is instead a *middle-aged, big-shouldered African American woman.*

I am, at that moment, frozen in place at the sudden, rather massive revelation that *fickel and X were in it together, from the start.* And then it occurs to me—flashes before me, if thoughts can do that—that *they were in it to steal the Peacock's necklace.* Insert your own wazzup-esque exclamation points.

Anyway, in this dream I have these two revelations, and then, rather than continuing to hurry toward them, I start thinking about this discovery, what it means and what I can ask them to learn more. Understand that I don't consider myself a threat to them at all—for me, this detective work is totally fact-finding. Unfortunately, my thinking about why I'm there and how I should approach them makes me increasingly aware that I am dreaming, and I struggle like hell to remain in the dream, on the tropical island, approaching fickel and X to question them...cross-dressing private dick that I am. But it's no use. I'm awake, and I lie in my bed, fully conscious, hoping against hope that sleep will return and I will manage to do what I've never managed before in my entire life, which is to resume a dream at the point it left off.

I lie there in bed. My dog snores. My S.O. grinds her teeth—this is news to me and I start thinking about what it might signify. Eventually I realize I'm not getting back to that tropical island. Then I get scared that I'll forget some or all of what I dreamt. So here I sit. Well?

roadrage @ February 28 07:14 pm

Wicked cool dream, marleybones. Anyone think we'd better set up an alternative site where we can continue this in case fickel ever surfaces and shuts our shit down?

chinkigirl @ February 28 07:19 pm

Hi, guyz. I've thought of that, too. Part of me is scared to lose you guys, your voices, your humor, your views. But another part of me thinks that this is the only place where we'll work like this, and that the best way to go is to let it run its course and evaporate, as all great stages in friendship do.

On marleybones's dream, I really have no view about where that comes from and how it may pertain to what's gone down with fickel, but, well, I, too, have something I might as well report. I can't say it's any more "fact-based" than the idea that fickel's run off to a tropical island with X to live off the blue diamonds they dug out of a priceless necklace, but here goes:

I have a friend who works in admissions at Dartmouth, and she's in contact with college advisors from a bunch of prep schools. So during that period when we were all wildly "sleuthing away" and trying to figure out the truth about fickel, I contacted Connie and told her a little of what we were looking into: twins who would have been in and out of a number of private schools, and probably not the best of them, about ten years ago, one of whom might have had some trouble with a young teacher named MacLean Jared. Of course Connie had nothing for me, but months later she got back to me. She said she'd totally forgotten what I'd asked her until she found herself sitting down with this guy from one of the name prep schools, and he makes this little joke about his name being MacLean Jared and everyone sticking a comma between, as if his name were Jared MacLean, and how his students get confused and call him Mr. MacLean. The guy is about thirty-five, and Connie realizes that ten years back he'd have been a newbie who might have gotten hit on my some ballsy young teacher's pet wannabe.

So she asks him, point blank, if he ever had trouble with a female student when he first started teaching. I'm just going to paste in her email to me below:

> *I asked about "trouble with female students," as if making light of it, but instantly the guy went white as an Irishman's tush. Truthfully, Prissy, he looked so shaken I was afraid to let my glance drop for fear of spotting a stain growing down his chinos! I made every effort to assure him that I knew nothing except that*

a friend of mine knew a woman who regretted having made some sort of "trouble" a few years back for a boarding school teacher with his name.

I think my tone reassured him, but later in the interview he couldn't help getting back to it. My impression was that he was concerned that some deep dark secret had somehow surfaced. So thanks, my friend, for setting me up to get a poor nerd in touch with his inner-paranoia! :) And he was cute, too, in a kind of pre-balding way. Not my type, but Occom Pond is frozen and I wouldn't have said no to an evening of ice skating followed by a little warming up in front of the fire in his room at the Inn. They do a sweet in-room continental breakfast, too. ;)

Anyway, doc, he managed to stutter out a tale about how in his very first semester of teaching, a student had pulled a Lolita number by rather artfully arranging herself—naked and undulating—across his bed in his "dorm-master's studio" while he'd been showering before dinner, and that when he'd come out he'd gotten the distinct impression, somewhere in and among clamping his hands over his privates and running out his back door, that there had been another person hidden in the closet! It seems luck had been with young Mr. J, as he'd found his across-the-fire-stairwell neighbor, another single male teacher, at home and willing to lend him a towel before returning with him to the scene of the non-seduction, which they'd found vacant. I asked him what had given him the impression that there'd been a person hiding in his closet, and he said he'd lost his recollection of that detail but that the impression remained firm in his mind, and that it could have been something as simple as the fact that he'd left the closet door open and when he'd emerged to find the Klayne School Mata Hari writhing on his bed, the closet had only been cracked, as if to allow a peeper just enough of a view! You begin to see, as I did, why the incident haunts him to this day?

That's all I got, doc—MacLean claimed to have forgotten the girl's name (unlikely) and also said that she'd disappeared from the school after the incident. No one ever questioned him, and he decided (unwisely, in my view) against reporting it himself. It rather amazes me, actually, that men feel so vulnerable to false accusations of sexual wrongdoing!

So I don't know if that adds anything to our knowledge. It does seem to verify that fickel crawled through various boarding schools and "experimented" at the art of seduction. Of course, she herself admitted as much, so it's a point in favor of this blog's veracity. Plus, it's not the first time a teenage girl would have tried something with an "older man."

roadrage @ February 28 07:36 pm

Although someone hiding in the closet kicks the whole thing into its own kinky zone. Is that for, like, blackmail pictures or a three-way?

chinkigirl @ February 28 07:40 pm

The teacher might have imagined that. A naked female student gyrating on your bed must be very alarming for a single male teacher.

marleybones @ February 28 07:57 pm

I don't know. If he walks out of the bathroom in the altogether and sees this girl on his bed, his first instinct is to get some pants on. That means the closet, but when he turns in that direction the door is propped just so. Instinct—not conscious thought—tells him to get the hell out, which is how he finds himself outside in the altogether. Now *that* makes sense to me, while if it were only the girl herself he thought he had to deal with he would have backtracked into the bathroom.

36-D @ February 28 08:20 pm

Yeah, but what's more alarming is that what he "imagined" about the closet was ***weirdly similar to some crazy guy jumping out at Burly-Bear when he was supposedly alone with fickel.***

chinkigirl @ February 28 08:21 pm

Whoa!!!! That did NOT occur to me.

marleybones @ February 28 08:22 pm

While we're on the Burly-Bear issue, can we talk about this: could fickel have possibly stabbed Burly-Bear through the heart with a scissors? I can imagine a woman having the strength and the knowledge of where to place the blade's point, but wouldn't he have had to have been prone or at least lounging in a chair and then just allowed her to walk up, place the point of the scissors against his chest, and then jam it in?

wazzup! @ February 28 08:23 pm

Shades of *The Maltese Falcon*, my friends!!! Sam Spade's hound dog of a partner would only have allowed a WOMAN to walk right up to him and blow him away. WAHOO!

webmaggot @ February 28 08:25 pm

That was with a gun, though, Dutchy. marleybones's point is that killing someone with scissors would require a pretty high amount of passivity on the part of the victim.

chinkigirl @ February 28 08:31 pm

Well, I can confirm that a woman with some degree of arm strength and determination could strike the blow if she knew where to stick him and had a long, narrow, sharp blade. The breastplate is vulnerable in several spots just north of the sternum itself, and I've seen victims when I used to work emergency who were killed or nearly killed from a blow to the chest.

wazzup! @ February 28 08:40 pm

> *All I could say is that we felt contempt as we faced each other, and I still didn't know why she looked so avenging, even at the last moment when the blade leaped out with a sharp snap and glittered through the air, because now she had thrown it and a great hand had been played!*

Source, anyone?

roadrage @ February 28 08:42 pm

Man, wazzup!, I have to say that you have read every noir in print. *He Died with His Eyes Open*—by the way, anyone know of a movie version of that?

wazzup! @ February 28 08:43 pm

My best of friends, like you I consider Derek Raymond the key to our fickel. Surely you all remember the last line from poor dead Staniland's cassettes:

> ***What shall we be,***
> ***When we aren't what we are?***

The cassettes themselves, I can add for your contemplation, were a *diary*!!! And who is that speaking if not our beloved fickel? Perhaps our beloved fullfrontal?

roadrage @ February 28 08:45 pm

The difference there, however, is that in *He Died* the cop's guard was down. Barbara and the hairy guy were in bed together when he burst in on them. Barbara's stark naked and sleeping—who could guess she slept with a switchblade under the pillow, just in case she felt like killing someone. Also, she knew what she was doing and could throw the thing across the room. Here we got a girl talking to a cop in her kitchen. I don't know—you think fickel could have *thrown* cuticle scissors to land in the guy's chest?

chinkigirl @ February 28 08:48 pm

Impossible. She'd have to have been right up next to him, face to face.

36-D @ February 28 08:50 pm

You do *get*, you guys, that this is not fanfiction? You get that we're talking straight here?

marleybones @ February 28 08:55 pm

I'm starting to think that wazzup! "gets" a lot more than the rest of us "get." I think that a lot of what fickel fed us *is* fiction—and I don't mean fanfiction; I mean real noir, translated for her purposes. I'm not convinced that she and Burly-Bear were chatting when a naked man burst out of her back hall. Maybe she was flipping out, feigning hysterics (or actually having them), and so could throw herself at Burly-Bear, weeping, and in that way get herself close enough to his chest to stab him. His guard would be down if she was pathetic enough.

webmaggot @ February 28 08:59 pm

But his guard wasn't down. Escroto was outside waiting. Burly-Bear wasn't totally off duty the way he told fickel he was. Also, there's no way the cops would have let fickel walk if she'd been alone with Burly-Bear when he bit it. There was a guy there, and we know who it was.

chinkigirl @ February 28 09:03 pm

Jiminy Cricket, again I am caught not seeing the obvious! Burly-Bear was totally *on* duty and there to score a confession out of her, and she was—or she and dickel were—onto him?

36-D @ February 28 09:04 pm

But are we saying that they planned to kill him together, or that dickel just went and did it and left fickel holding the bag as usual? And did dickel do it because the cops were a threat to fickel, or just because Burly-Bear was nice to her and dickel couldn't stand anyone touching his sister (but, like, him)? I mean, what are we thinking, guys?

marleybones @ February 28 09:05 pm

Not sure we're thinking at all. We're spinning theories here.

i.went.to.harvard @ February 28 09:09 pm

In that spirit, and since we are all putting out our true confessions about our hunt for fickel, I will reveal my own:

A month ago, I returned to Cambridge for a reunion. Naturally, I visited spots I used to frequent, including a coffee shop in Central Square where my ex and I used to suck down espresso and listen to George Michaels. (Yes, roadrage, I'm old, but not quite Eric Clapton old.) Of course, I was dying to try to find fickel's apartment, which I never did. My last night, however, I was online in a Starbucks when this guy caught my eye. He was thin, blond (buzzed hair with the nubs dyed platinum) and wearing a lot of black. None of this would make him stand out in the least, except that he also had very colorful sleeve tattoos. Even this did not particularly catch my attention (where I live you get a lot of motorcyclists passing through) but as he was leaving a young woman joined him. She was on the chunky side, wearing clothes comparable to the young man, and her dead black hair was thick and coarse and cut choppy, like a wig. She handed him one of those ubiquitous laptop cases and he slung the strap over his head and let it hang at his hip like any kid. Thus, nothing really caught my full attention until, just as the pair of them let the door swing to behind them, she turned her head, spotted me looking after her, and gave me a stare. Her eyes were blue-grey, her expression unpleasant—and *exactly* like the young man's—*causing me to wonder if this couple was actually brother and sister.*

My next thought was "she sensed that I was watching her," in spite of the fact that I've never bought into the idea that people sense when they are being watched. In retrospect, I believe that she hadn't turned because she sensed *my* attention. She'd turned because she was suspicious that *someone* might be watching.

All this tripped my next thought, and I was *sure* that this was fickel. I gave up my place in line and practically tumbled out after them, only slowing when I got outside. I spotted them walking off through the other night prowlers. She was wearing some kind of thick footwear, like mini work boots, with black stockings and a skirt. She didn't look back, although I had a feeling that she was preventing herself from doing just that.

That's it. Means nothing, I know, but at the same time...

marleybones @ February 28 09:18 pm

Quite a patchwork of half-tales we've woven. I've lost hope that we'll hear from fickel again.

chinkigirl @ February 28 09:23 pm

God I worry sometimes.

36-D @ February 28 09:31 pm

You and me both. The Rottweiler has, like, banned me from anything resembling blogging at work. He did, however, let me know that he is keeping tabs on fickel's "situation" as far as the BPD is concerned. They got nothing, and with a dead cop, you can believe it that they are looking. Not sure how that cuts.

webmaggot @ February 28 09:33 pm

Well, it cuts in favor of fickel's innocence. If there were a case they could build against her, she'd be on the America's Most Wanted list for killing a cop without a doubt.

roadrage @ February 28 09:35 pm

Not to mention the couple in Sudbury/Concord.

proudblacktrannie @ February 28 09:36 pm

And the jewelry store clerk. Can we *please* not forget him?

chinkigirl @ February 28 09:37 pm

Forget him? Somehow he's the saddest victim of all.

i.went.to.harvard @ February 28 09:39 pm

And the—what was her name? The bag lady who supposedly witnessed Mr. Suicide's death.

webmaggot @ February 28 09:40 pm

Sewer Hag. Got to hand it to fickel, she really could spin a tale, whether true or one big farkin lie. But to me, her disappearance makes things look pretty effin grim.

marleybones @ February 28 09:53 pm

You mean you think that fickel's run off, as in my dream?

webmaggot @ February 28 09:55 pm

No, I mean like she's dead. As in part of the Mysterious Hottie's body count.

36-D @ February 28 09:59 pm

I can't think that. It's weird, but I actually prefer to think of her guilty and gotten away.

webmaggot @ February 28 10:01 pm

Okay, then answer this: if fickel were guilty, why would she write a blog full of clues about her guilt? Two blogs—and you think that with a little perseverance the cops won't have figured out whether or not she's fullfrontal?

roadrage @ February 28 10:03 pm

Dewd. "Perseverance" in a sentence. I like.

webmaggot @ February 28 10:04 pm

spellcheck got me some ballz. How about it though?

chinkigirl @ February 28 10:15 pm

I've thought about that. If fickel was guilty, I think she wrote about it because she couldn't help herself. She needed an outlet. In fact, the whole thing hangs together, psychologically, as a person with rather uncommon proclivities involving her twin brother who had those proclivities reinforced by an uncle who found them exciting. Things could have developed from that point in a number of ways, except for the unfortunate complication of her father discovering the little den of iniquity and eventually offing himself over having failed to protect his daughter from the most intimate of sins. The guilt she feels over her dad morphs into anger—she's determined to convince herself that her brotherly love thing is not repellent. She travels, brother in tow, and occasionally sets up a compromising position, but all backfire and, if they teach her anything, it's that she is indeed responsible for her dad's death.

How's that for the dime-store psych analysis?

wazzup! @ February 28 10:18 pm

I can do you one spookier, my dearest friends! Maybe fickel's mother was right, and the uncle was totally INNOCENT! Maybe he arrived at the family house in rural Mass long ago and fickel discovered the "sexual creature" inside her, but he, being normal, rejected her, so she turned to the next best thing and an apparently willing partner: her crazy TWIN BROTHER!!!

marleybones @ February 28 10:21 pm

Sigh. We can fill in that fickel finds escape in the darkest forms of literature—noir, pulp, old police procedurals—many of them tales where aberrant sexual behavior is key to the theme.

i.went.to.harvard @ February 28 10:24 pm

So she casts a blog into the web-o-sphere, and finds a group of seemingly normal folk who are into this dark stuff, but, even better, we *like* her. Heck, she becomes our spiritual leader! And then what? The coincidental sighting of her original enabler on the street one night, going through his "gay experimental phase?" Or did she find him and start planning the family reunion even before coming to Boston herself?

roadrage @ February 28 10:31 pm

And *then* what, though? The reunion goes sour because Uncle Steve figures out that fickel and the Mysterious Hottie are his little effed-up niece and nephew, grown up, and now even *he* rejects them? Could a guy really get that involved with a couple of relatives he used to live with and not get what's going on?

wazzup! @ February 28 10:33 pm

Hey Everyone!!! Think about THIS: maybe when fickel finds Uncle Stephen in Boston, he *does* recognize her and *lets* her move in on him, even *remembering* the schoolgirl crush she'd had on him a decade earlier, but thinking she's outgrown it now!!! Maybe it's when she made a *pass* at him that he finally kicked her INCESTUOUS ass *out* of his pad, and maybe that caused her to moon over him, following him about. Naturally, Uncle Steve does not see her as a *big threat*—she is his NIECE, for Pete's sake!!! But *dickel* the *vicious wolf-man* sees *Uncle Steve* as a threat—because he wants fickel for HIMSELF!!!!!

marleybones @ February 28 10:38 pm

So dickel shoves him. She's the one who is full of guilt and rage, but he's the trigger-happy one. He sees that Mr. S is a big problem for fickel. He knows that she's so consumed that she's tailing the man. So he eliminates that problem one night in a style that's familiar.

proudblacktrannie @ February 28 10:40 pm

Yes, and THAT'S why she stayed at the train station to await the police. Even if she didn't KNOW that dickel was following her and Mr. S, and even if she hadn't INSTRUCTED him to shove the man in front of a train, she'd certainly SUSPECT it the moment it happened. So she had to WAIT and see what OTHERS said so she could COVER for her brother if she had to.

36-D @ February 28 10:47 pm

My God, and so right away she creates fullfrontal, to have a handy stalker-pervert-killer around in case everything starts homing in on her and dickel.

i.went.to.harvard @ February 28 10:48 pm

And fullfrontal beating up dickel in the motel room is...?

marleybones @ February 28 10:59 pm

Discipline? fickel herself punishing him for creating the mess they're in? What a stretch...

chinkigirl @ February 28 11:10 pm

Stretch is right. dickel was almost killed. Would she—*could she*—do that to him?

marleybones @ February 28 11:12 pm

Maybe she exaggerated it on the blog.

webmaggot @ February 28 11:13 pm

Maybe she should have punished him *more* severely, if he was responsible for the Colonel and the Peacock murders. That guy's ONE MAD DOG!!!

36-D @ February 28 11:17 pm

God, who even wants to figure this out?

webmaggot @ February 28 11:21 pm

But no one's got at my original question. If this shyte is true then fickel took a huge risk in writing it all down. She had to know the cops were onto the blog.

chinkigirl @ February 28 11:25 pm

All I can offer is—a need for approbation that is so strong it's worth every risk?

roadrage @ February 28 11:26 pm

And, what? No approbation if she doesn't reveal the truth, in one form or another?

i.went.to.harvard @ February 28 11:30 pm

She's confronting the unavoidable suspicions on everyone's mind that she did it. Not such a risk as long as people accept that this is what the cops are looking to prove from the start.

wazzup! @ February 28 11:35 pm

> *I was only trying to cheat death...to surmount for a little while the darkness that all my life I surely knew was going to come rolling in on me some day and obliterate me...*

The great Cornell Woolrich!!!

chinkigirl @ February 28 11:37 pm

wazzup!...whoa. Lose the exclamation points and you are truly wise.

marleybones @ February 28 11:40 pm

He's been expostulating wise all along. Look, have we been bamboozled? I mean all along. Maybe there was some incident in the Hynes T station where a man died, but couldn't everything else—and I mean everything—have been the product of a dark imagination, aided by events that just happened to occur in the Boston area as the story developed, and also, more significantly, aided by the tale-spinner's vast knowledge of noir?

webmaggot @ February 28 11:42 pm

Uh-oh, marleybones is pissed. Now we all get called misogynists.

marleybones @ February 28 11:43 pm

Actually, I'm not sure I mind having been bamboozled. Fact is, the idea gives me solace.

i.went.to.harvard @ February 22 11:47 pm

There are several facts—verifiable, in my view—that just don't support this hoax theory.

marleybones @ February 22 11:48 pm

Look, be that as it may, I'm through. Let's all be through. Let's let fickel be. I ask this of the rest of you only because I don't trust myself. I know I'm going to come back here to see what's being posted. I just... hope I don't find anything.

40

LIFE IS PULP

Noir the Night Away With L.G. Fickel

March 9 @ 10:00 pm
>MICKEY SPILLANE'S BIRTHDAY<

So it's Mickey Spillane's birthday, and in spite of a general malaise that's been hanging all over me for the longest time, I couldn't resist posting a happy birthday to one of the greatest pulp writers of all time. Guys like Mickey live hard but they last. Most of you probably know that he died a few years ago—July 18, 2006—unrepentant as ever about his writing style, his views on justice, his treatment of women.

I, the Jury. Seems like a lot of us have been playing jury lately, here on this site.

Obviously, for 100 reasons I should not be writing this. I feel flattered that you have maintained a level of concern for me over the weeks. Flattered and at the same time betrayed, of course.

Me as serial murderess. And a cop killer, no less.

Me and dickel as S&M incest twins.

Me as Miss Scarlet, as a freak on a train, as my own imaginary predator.

Me as a fat sadsack bookstore clerk with dementia.

Me as a manipulative web-liar, spinning a tale just for the pleasure of jerking around a bunch of decent people (ah, if only...)

Me and X as what exactly? Lesbian jewel thieves on the lam for conspiring to kill her husband and my lover? (Oddly, that one's less insulting than the rest.)

Me as fullfrontal—the ultimate in metadiagetic masquerading as the simple diagetic.

Deep. Very, very deep. But such is the dark, wonderfully repellent wilderness of low art.

I'm afraid, however, that none of the above is accurate. I'm nothing so colorful, really. To be honest, part of me would like to leave the rest of you in the dark forever. But I need to write, just this once more. Like Cornell Woolrich, I need to cheat death, just a little. And I need closure.

Sorry. I've been AFK, so it's much later now than when I took my first stab at this post. I was distracted by the people upstairs, who keep walking around as if in time to some beat that I'm hearing in their footsteps and also independently. My guess is that this happens to a lot of people. It's weird, though.

I suppose I should apologize for having been away from—for having abandoned—the blog for so long. I'd like to say that Mysterious Hottie and I raced off to Reno for a quickie nuptial and are now screwing every night in freakoid bliss, but, alas, I have seen neither hide nor hair of the man since... Wise of him to disappear from the face of the earth, but, still, I can't help wishing he'd knock on the door, be there with that through-the-eyebrows leer of his and his weight thrown carelessly on one hip, only to vanish like smoke while I sleep.

No, I've had no contact from Guy—if that was his name, but of course that's as it should be, as I suppose the police are watching me still. I don't believe Guy was fullfrontal, or a murderer, or that he committed suicide. If you'd met him you'd be exactly where I am, but I can't worry about that anymore. I have enough on my hands, what with dickel being diagnosed with clinical depression. Like father, like son, they say, but I'd never really bought the idea of my father jumping in front of that freighter and then killing himself with his own meds a couple of months later. I was always sure that my mother and Frank pulled off those stunts together.

Sigh. Well, well, you live and learn. Somehow it doesn't leave me with any sort of need to apologize to my mother. After all, she condemned *me*, so why shouldn't I think the worst of her as well? Ah, but you all have mothers, so I'm sure you know how it is.

I've moved away from Boston. I needed to be where I could keep an eye on dickel. And of course I couldn't live in that apartment after Burly-Bear's murder.

Burly-Bear. Or should I say hitman? In spite of his assurances to the contrary, I finally put that together. Did anyone else? My breakthrough was "cya." I thought hitman was using "cover your ass" in a sort of "fresh" way. No, no: it's "correct you are." Review the archives. It works. And we know whose signature phrase *that* was. Sad, that Burly-Bear died with a lie on his lips. Sad that to the end he simply couldn't go off duty and just be straight with a girl. Fucking cop. It's a calling, I guess.

I am bothered but not startled to find that even I refer to Burly-Bear's death as a *murder*. Understandable, of course, since that's the label the police affixed to it—creed of loyalty and all that—but when someone comes to a woman's aid, surely that's not *murder*?

But Burly-Bear, you are saying with incredulity! Such a stand-up swell guy, you are insisting! Such an American idol! So public spirited! Such a beautiful wife and child!

You know what? Every red-blooded American folk hero had a libido. We've all got dark recesses, but the male of the species' darkest secret is poisoned with testosterone. He can't help himself. He can't just *think* dirty; he's got to *do* dirty.

Let me play the part of wazzup!, our prescient Netherlands cheerleader: Shades of *A Swell Kind of Guy*!!! I win, my companions in pulp admiration!!!

Yes, well, exactly. And Escroto knows about it, too. You die with your pants around your ankles and distinct bruises shaped like your hands on the inner thighs of the girl sitting on the floor across from you, well, it's not such a mystery what was going down when you got jumped. Ah, but why get all righteous...

> *The commandment that has never been written down...because every goddamn fool's supposed to know it—yea, verily...take not advantage of thy neighbor with his pants down...*

Anyone recognize that one? Of course I have no problem with the idea of Burly-Bear being fashioned a folk hero. Hell, he was every bit *my* hero, right up until he tried to stick his dick in me without so much as a "may I." A momentary lapse, right? I've got no incentive to destroy the myth of the masculine hero. It's my favorite fairy tale. But the truth is we're all antiheros. We're all struggling through our own inner noirs...

Hey, did you know that there are websites that make their entire theme suicide—people collect suicide stories from around the world and get off on savoring them, often with pictures...

...Indian woman commits suicide by fire...

...suicide skydiver cuts parachute line...

...father suicides over son's accidental death...

...16-year-old girl commits suicide after breaking up with boyfriend...

...self-electrocution of young man...

...classic black-and-white suicide pictures...

...principal hangs self after student's bizarre death...

...suicide by alarm clock...

...decomposed body of female suicide discovered in Romanian wood...

...body of male who hanged himself in tree discovered in park...

...7-month-old fetus stabbed to death...

...suicide by metro...

...remains of 18-year-old Palestinian suicide bomber...

...mother takes daughter with her in jump under train...

...Botswana man lies on train track...

...Israeli girl decapitated after jumping under train...

...Beheaded by train in Mexico...

...Morgue images inside!!!!!!!

Sigh. Anyway, I'm tired and I can hear dickel waking up. I've sworn off the blog, promised him that in return for his promise that he won't flush his pills and saw his wrists open with the rusty edge of the medicine cabinet again. A fair bargain, don'tcha think?

> *You may be wrong, and exist comfortably in a world of righteousness, but you may not be right and live in a world of error, the kind of world that we seem to live in.*

I'll check in again, though, when it's safe. After all, I am...ever so very... fickle.

GIVE IT TO ME STRAIGHT

chinkigirl @ March 10 07:10 am

I'm in shock. I don't know what to think.

proudblacktrannie @ March 10 011:21 am

SHE IS LYING. TRACE THIS BLOG ENTRY, MR. ESCROTO OR WHATEVER YOUR DAMN NAME IS WE ALL KNOW YOU'RE STILL ON THE BLOG.

i.went.to.harvard @ March 10 06:33 pm

I think we leave it alone.

roadrage @ March 10 07:04 pm

harsh, dewd. But I gotta agree. By the way, chinkigirl, I want to say before it's too late that I'm totally in love with you. Honestly. I'm glad we're never going to meet because that would suck, but your voice will be in my mind for the rest of my life. I love you. Please don't reply, okay?

36-D @ March 10 07:07 pm

Oh, god, I am in tears now. I mean I'm bawling like a kid, here. I don't even get why.

webmaggot @ March 10 07:09 pm

Uhh, you're an emo wuss?

36-D @ March 10 07:11 pm

Oh, shit, you *would*—now I am laughing and crying at the same time, and you have no idea how I *hate* getting all femmey and emotional.

marleybones @ March 10 07:17 pm

I think that's all we can do. Weep like ninnies, each in our own blog doghouse. People go mad every day. Life goes on around its victims.

fickel @ March 11 01:00 am

...and a hush fell over the blog...

41

www.lowart.org
Group Fiction
Author: Penelope Dreadful
Date: August 24
Genre: neo-noir

TRAIN WATCHING

Anyone could see they were in love. Why, there wasn't anything subtle about it—the way they held hands when walking down the rutted road, the way a smile would pool in her eyes as she watched him drinking a coffee in the train station café, the way he'd notice that smile and then pull her chair around so that they'd be crowded together, elbow to elbow at the tiny wrought-iron table. Love's a cinch to spot, and such a pleasure to observe, particularly when the boy and girl were as young and as commonplace as they were. Yes, somehow that doubled their charm.

On his own, you see, the boy might have been perceived as some trouble, as he gave off an air of being a tough lot, with that length of chain looped from his belt and the ropey beard that sprouted only from his chin. And didn't that t-shirt he favored bear a logo that almost resembled a swastika? Overall, in fact, his wolfish lean suggesting an almost feral belligerence that was impossible to overlook.

But when people saw the boy with the girl, how the two of them related to one another, well, it was almost as if all of the boy's antisocial affectations came across as puppyish, and he really could seem rather sweet, particularly to the womenfolk. For the girl was really special, fine and merry and with a bright, accepting look in her eye that made every new person she came across feel momentarily blessed, and what kind of no-good punk could have won over a girl like that? Sure, she had that black-dyed hair that looked like she might cut it herself, and no apparent interest in makeup or perfume. But when she first met you, and she quirked her head to one side, tilting her eyes a bit upward and smiling—all quite unwittingly—ah, what a flight of sunshine she cast! True, she might not have been as fine-boned as today's magazines would have you think a girl should be, but it was undeniable that she was all real, with a milky glow to her skin and a soft curve to her shoulders and hips—well, she certainly caught her share of glances from the men when she went about in her snug-fitting jeans, even if she did wear them with high-topped utility boots and one or another of the rather worn sweater sets she seemed to fancy.

The girl did everything for the two of them, it seemed. It was she who found them their rental unit over the garage out behind one of the fine chalet-style homes near the edge of town. It was she who steered the boy into a salaried job riding the freight line, and she who dealt with the tradesmen and neighbors and internet provider. It was she who sold several of the boy's oil paintings—fine, rough landscapes, they were—through one of the local shops. It was her presence that made their landlady—herself a reclusive woman—come to perceive the young couple as a fixture on the property, strolling up or down the long shale drive, together or alone. Yes, the girl soothed whatever small ripples there were that inevitably develop when new folk settle in an isolated burg with no discernible reason for having done so, no seeming outside connections or history.

Of course, the Canadian countryside had much to recommend it: there was the clear air and a relative lack of traffic, the windy fields just outside of town, and a sense of quietude about the entire region. But most young people seem to flee from such bucolic settings, while these two were doing just the opposite, and no matter how sensible that might seem from the vantage point of age and experience, it was undeniably different. And so it was the girl, through the countless little ways that her appreciation for the simple life broadcast itself: the tucking of a tiny spray of brilliants behind her ear, the easy declination of an offered ride when strolling home in a sudden snow squall, the willingness to stop a while with women far older than she to laugh at some gossip. It was in these ways that she caused the two of them to meld into the local scenery, become an uncomplicated, unheralded element of a tiny community, within months of their arrival.

In truth, no one knew for a fact that they were married. In this day and age, one can never tell, and it's considered awfully provincial to ask. He didn't wear a ring, but then he was a painter who worked on the trains and rings get in the way when you need to wash up a lot, and, anyway, lots of men find jewelry bothersome. On her part, she wore on her ring finger a blue-white stone, about the size of a robin's egg, that some folks might have guessed was an opal or even blue jade, mounted on a rose gold band, quite plain. Who could know what this treasure signified. She also used the boy's name, a meaningful gesture in a day when so many women retain their own last name upon saying their wedding vows. But whether or not these two were formally married, they were without a doubt newlyweds. Every night, at whatever time his freight rolled into town, she was there for him at the rail junction, waiting. Sometimes when he had an overnight or a three-day stint away from town, she'd go down to the junction anyway. Anyone who happened to see her would have to remark to themselves that she really did get a thrill out of watching trains...

COMMENTS

Penelope Dreadful @ August 24 06:32 pm

I'm HUGE into group fic. :) Sooooooooooooo...any takers?

Printed in the United States
by Baker & Taylor Publisher Services